Also by Tarah Benner

The Defectors
The Last Uprising

Enemy Inside

By
Tarah Benner

Copyright 2014 Tarah Benner

All rights reserved

Printed in the United States of America

First Edition

Cover design by Adrijus Guscia

This book is a work of fiction. Names, characters, places, and incidents either are the product of the author's imagination or are used fictitiously, and any resemblance to actual persons, living or dead, is entirely coincidental.

No part of this book may be reproduced, scanned, or distributed in any printed or electronic form without permission. Please do not participate in or encourage piracy of copyrighted materials in violation of the author's rights. Purchase only authorized editions.

ISBN 978-1500609146

www.tarahbenner.com

To Sam. For lovingly and patiently putting up with my writer craziness.

Chapter One

Cold fingers closed around my throat. I choked, feeling the burning pain as hands pressed down on my windpipe.

My body jerked awake, and my eyes snapped open. Eyes watering, lungs burning, I could just make out the dark outline of my attacker. His silhouette was superimposed against the canvas flap of my tent. I clawed at his hands, kicking and twisting to escape.

I tried to cry out, but nothing except a helpless mew escaped my constricted windpipe. I swung my fist against his ear — hard — and I heard a muted yell of pain.

There was a shimmer of gold in the weak light, a soft gasp, and the fingers relaxed.

Finally freeing my leg from the straightjacket of my sleeping bag, I aimed a forceful kick into the gut of my attacker. He flew backward, falling through the tent flap and into the morning light.

It wasn't a him; it was a her.

"Oh god," Logan breathed from the floor.

I gasped for air, trying to catch my breath as I pieced together what had happened.

"What . . . the . . . hell?" My voice was raspy from the dry air.

Enemy Inside

Logan was splayed on the ground, her golden curtain of hair fanning out around her. Her face was ashen.

Gingerly, I felt my throat where her hands had choked off my airways. It was on fire.

"I'm so sorry," she said. "I think I had another nightmare."

We both had. I looked down to see my own sleeping bag twisted around to the middle of the tent beside hers. I'd been thrashing in my sleep again, and I must have jerked right into her.

I couldn't remember my dreams, but if I had to guess, they involved the blood on my mother's pillow, the look in Amory's eyes as I fell through the air, and Max suspended in slow motion after the PMC filled his chest with bullets. These images had been on a constant loop in my head for the past few weeks, and I could only imagine how awful it was for Logan.

She had seen him die. We all had, but Logan was in love with Max. I knew from the way she woke up screaming or sobbing that she could not shake that horrible final image. This wasn't the first time I'd awoken with her hands wrapped around my throat either, but it was better than the alternative. I didn't want to sleep alone.

I tried to laugh, but it sounded hollow and forced. "Maybe I should bunk with Greyson," I said, watching her face carefully. "He's not much of a snuggler, but at least he doesn't know Krav Maga."

Logan's huge green eyes quivered, and I felt a pang of guilt. It was too soon for humor.

"I'm sorry," she whispered. "I don't know why I —" She broke off, putting a hand to her mouth to muffle a sob threatening to escape. Her eyes were swimming with tears.

"Shh. It's okay." I crawled over to where she lay and

pulled her into my arms. "I'm sorry."

"You're sorry?" she cried. "I almost strangled you."

"You didn't. I'm fine."

She let her head fall against my shoulder and started to sob. I squeezed her and rested my chin on top of her golden head, willing myself not to cry. It had been a horrible few weeks. I carried the weight of Max's death like a dead albatross around my neck. It was my fault he was there to begin with, and I didn't deserve to be the one who had survived.

Some days, the thought of rescuing Amory was the only thing that kept me going, and lately, even that seemed so far out of reach. Today would be just another day suffocating under the weight of that sick, helpless feeling that burned my throat and made my stomach ache. It never stopped.

When Logan's tears dried up, I pulled her to her feet without a word, and we shuffled out of the tent into the early morning sun. Neither of us would mention it again. It was easier to pretend we didn't feel how heavy a load we carried. Going through the motions was the only thing to do.

The rebel camp was situated at the top of a hill a few miles outside the border of Sector X. Dozens of tents stood in neat blocks among the fir trees, leading to the blazing fire at the center of camp where people gathered to thaw their fingers and warm their bones from the constant bite of cold. We crunched through the snow toward the mess tent, where several groups of people were already huddled over bowls of runny oatmeal, their shoulders hunched against the wind.

Winter was here in earnest — the earliest snow I could remember — and I caught daily whispered concerns that it would be impossible to make it through the season with no permanent shelter. Shivering in my ragged military-issue sleeping bag night after night, I could imagine everyone was beginning to feel mutinous, wondering when their mission would finally end.

The rebels gathered at breakfast were an odd, jumbled group of people. There were lots of runaway teenagers and edgy anti-establishment guys with long, matted dreadlocks and gauges in their ears, and now the camp was overflowing with the influx of prisoners from Chaddock and Waul.

The former inmates were tough to manage. Rowdy and skittish, a fight could break out over an extra dinner roll or the warmest spot by the fire. They trusted no one and fought their orders at every turn, but since they had been arrested in service to the cause, the rebels were reluctant to turn them away. Repeat offenders were brought to Rulon, who doled out his own brand of sick justice in the tent at the end of the block.

Standing in line waiting for the surly, tattooed cook to spoon out my breakfast, I skimmed the large chalkboard that denoted everyone's duties in a childlike scrawl. I rejoiced when I saw I was responsible for gathering firewood that day. If I worked quickly, it would be easy to slip away to train with Logan. Our secret lessons were the only thing I looked forward to most days.

Logan wasn't a great teacher, but training me was the only thing that seemed to bring her back to her former self. It was a good distraction for me, too. Doing nothing was killing me, but it wasn't my choice.

I slumped down onto the log next to Greyson, feeling the frustration and boredom wafting off him. Doing the rebels' laundry wasn't exactly how he'd imagined his role in the revolution.

"I can't do this anymore," I breathed.

"I know." He was spooning out his watery oatmeal, letting it slide back into the bowl twice before bringing it to his lips.

"Her nightmares are getting worse."

He sighed, and I could see the exhaustion in his eyes. "Saving Amory isn't going to bring Max back, Haven."

"But we have to try."

"We *have* tried."

I stiffened, thinking of our botched rescue attempt the day after the riots. I'd roused Greyson in the middle of the night to help me sneak back into Sector X, but we'd only gotten to the edge of camp before we were spotted by the rebel guards and hauled back to await Rulon's punishment.

I'd expected Rulon to torture or threaten us when we were caught. After all, I had disobeyed his orders twice, and breaking back into Sector X was more of an emotional decision than a rational one. But he hadn't punished us. He'd just brought us into the leaders' tent, where a map of Sector X lay spread across the table.

After so many rebels infiltrated the city, security measures had been tightened, he explained. Sector X was on lockdown. The PMC had called in all available reinforcements to round up any illegals who had been freed during the riots. Rebels were killed on sight. It was too dangerous to attempt an extraction until the dust had settled.

Rulon's explanation made sense to me, and that day he'd treated me with uncharacteristic kindness — even if his goons had hauled us back to camp like disobedient children.

I knew it would be nearly impossible to infiltrate Sector X without the rebels' help, so I'd resolved to be a good soldier. Rulon ran a tight ship with a strict hierarchy where soldiers waited for their orders. If I wanted them to take me into Sector X, I had to play by their rules and hope they would help once the PMC's operations had returned to normal.

Enemy Inside

"It's been three weeks," I said, feeling edgy. "I can't wait any longer. They're torturing him, and once they get the information they need..."

"So what's the plan?" he asked, rolling his eyes indulgently. "Come on. I know you've been formulating a plan for days."

I grinned. He knew me so well. "Time's running out. We have to find out how to get into Sector X and where they're keeping Amory."

"Rulon said it's on lockdown."

"The rebels have to be getting in somehow. I know they're stealing food from the PMC. How else could they be feeding this whole camp?"

Greyson nodded, looking down at his bowl of slop. "So we find out who's going inside and tag along."

"How are we going to get him out once we find him?" Logan asked, making me jump. I hadn't heard her coming up behind me. "Amory's bound to be locked up in some maximum-security prison." She swung a leg over the log and scooted in until her shoulder brushed against mine, as though she wanted to remind me she was still there.

"Somebody here has to know something. They go into the city all the time."

"When do they make supply runs?" Greyson asked.

"Early in the morning."

We sat in silence for several moments. Finally, Logan spoke again. "They've got someone on the inside."

I nodded, feeling impatient. "We already knew that."

"No. I mean *really* inside," she said, sneaking a furtive glance at the people eating nearby. "The rebels must have a mole who's at the top. Otherwise..." She broke off, deep in thought.

"What?"

"Otherwise they never would have gotten those CIDs we used to get past the rovers during the riots."

"They must have taken them from officers," I said. "Cut them out."

Logan shook her head. "That wouldn't work! I should have remembered before. If you remove a CID, in the system . . . you're dead."

"But —"

"They can still track you, but your other information dies with you. They do that so no one can cut open your arm to steal your identity. You can't remove your own CID unless you want your money, your social security number, and everything else wiped."

"So that means . . ."

She nodded. "Those were fake identities. Every one of those CIDs was uniquely created by someone working inside the PMC."

"Do you think the mole is someone here?"

"It would be really stupid if they were!" said Greyson. "Can you imagine what the PMC would do to them if they found out everything they'd done? They're probably the reason the rebels knew that big meeting was happening at the base. I guarantee the PMC didn't broadcast that."

"Well, whoever it is, he knows how we can get inside and find Amory." I stood up. "I need to talk to Rulon."

Logan and Greyson looked surprised but did not argue. Rulon didn't like us much, but he was the only person I knew for sure would be able to get us into the city if he wanted to.

Enemy Inside

The rest of the day passed in a blur. I restocked the firewood near the mess tent, the massive bonfire in the center of camp, and the supply tent. On my last trip, I doubled back into the woods to find Logan in the clearing where we sparred. It was far enough from the edge of camp that no one could hear my yells when we practiced throws, and most of the snow had been packed down to a deathtrap of ice and mud from our constant scuffling.

That afternoon, I was hitting the ground a lot more than I should have been. When Logan flipped me onto my back for what seemed like the hundredth time, she let out an exasperated cry, holding me to the ground with her forearm pressing down on my windpipe.

"What's your deal?"

"Sorry," I panted. "Just distracted."

"You're a mess."

I bit back the urge to remind her she was the one who tried to strangle me in my sleep.

"Just working out what I'm going to say to Rulon."

"I don't *care*," she growled. "Don't bring that in here. Your head needs to be in the fight." She shoved off me, looking annoyed, and I fought back a grin.

Logan was a stickler for focus when we sparred — a rule that was in place as much for her as for me. Here, she didn't have to be the sad girl who'd lost Max. She was in her element.

We went again, and this time she didn't hold back her fury. I blocked her first few hits but stumbled when she lurched, and she seized the opportunity to grab me and aim a knee jab into my gut at full force. I doubled over, fighting the urge to puke, and she sighed.

"We're done for the day. Come on."

Enemy Inside

She already had towels and a change of clothes for both of us, so I followed her down to the creek to wash up for dinner. It was a miserable ritual that involved breaking a thin layer of ice and splashing ourselves with the frigid water until most of the sweat and grime was gone. We changed, shivering, and I contemplated dunking my whole head in the water. It was guaranteed hypothermia, but my hair was filthy. I desperately needed a real shower.

I had purposely waited until dinnertime to broach the subject of breaking into Sector X with Rulon because the rebels were more relaxed when they had plenty of beans, bread, and whisky in their bellies. If Rulon's guards were inebriated, they'd be less likely to bother me. I wandered around the mess tent, pretending to look for a place to sit, scanning the crowd for Rulon.

I didn't have to look far. He was sitting close to the fire, wrapped in an enormous fur coat. The firelight was dancing in his cold eyes, and his dark skin was glowing with heat. He had an intricate dragon design shaved into his short hair that wound around the back of his head, making him look even more intimidating.

"What do you want, runaway?" he asked, taking a swig from the cup in his hand. The smell of whisky made my stomach turn.

"I need your help."

"You'll have to be more specific."

"I want to break into Sector X and rescue my friend Amory. He's been there for three weeks now."

He nodded. "Captain Elwood's boy. We've already had this conversation."

"Yes, but I know they're torturing him to find out what he knows. He's much more of a liability in their hands."

Rulon looked at me with those hard eyes. "That may be

true, but we cannot risk infiltrating the facility where he is being held. I know what he means to you, and I'm sorry. But I must lead in a way that is best for the group as a whole. One person does not outweigh the needs of many."

"We can't leave someone behind just because it's dangerous!"

"We can." Rulon's tone was short and clipped. "And we have. I was lenient with you and your friends after the riots, but I have not forgotten that you disobeyed my orders . . . twice."

"It won't happen again," I said. Even I could hear the desperation in my voice. "Please. I'll do it alone, and I'll do it on your terms. But I have to try to save him."

"It's a suicide mission," he said. "And it's not an option. I won't discuss this again with you."

"But I know you're breaking into Sector X!" I felt my voice wavering with anger despite my best efforts.

"You know nothing," snapped Rulon. "Do *not* make the mistake of believing I overestimate your capabilities the way your friends do. The others may mistake your recklessness for courage, but I don't."

His words felt like a sharp slap. Three weeks of cold helplessness and fear turned to molten hatred in my gut, and I felt my tongue sting with the toxic accusations I longed to hurl at him. My hands curled into fists.

"What would you know about courage?" I spat. "You get people to run this camp and do whatever you want, but that's only because everyone thinks you have a plan. They think this is part of something bigger — for the greater good — but people go off, and you won't tell anyone what's happening out there. The riots in the city killed hundreds of officers, and the PMC has already rebounded twice as strong. I came here because I thought we would actually be *doing*

Enemy Inside

something, but you all just *sit* here getting drunk every night in the PMC's backyard." I stood up. "This revolution is pathetic."

Several nearby rebels had turned to stare at me, but I didn't care. *Somebody* ought to call Rulon on his bullshit. Godfrey was watching me out of the corner of his eye, too. It was hard to tell in the dancing firelight, but I thought I caught the flash of a grin.

Rulon's face looked as though it was carved from stone. He betrayed no emotion, but I knew my words had touched a nerve. I wanted to knock the whisky out of his hand, but instead, I stormed off into the woods.

I heard two pairs of feet crunching over the frozen underbrush behind me and felt Greyson's worry hovering in the darkness before he even spoke. He and Logan had been sitting nearby, and I knew they had heard everything.

"What the hell was that?" Greyson hissed. "Are you trying to get us all killed?"

Feeling the anger ripple through me again, I refused to look in his direction. "I know you like these people, but the whole point of joining forces with them was to rescue Amory. They were *never* going to help us. It's time to try something else. I don't need Rulon or his men."

He stopped, grabbing my arm and spinning me around. "You think I *like* these people? I was in that closet when they were torturing you, remember?"

In the darkness, I could just make out the whites of his eyes. I swallowed. How could I forget? The three rectangular chemical burn marks on my arm were a constant reminder. They wouldn't heal like regular burns.

Miles, the rebel who tortured me, had been killed on the bridge by the PMC. The man who had stood by and watched had gone AWOL. Nobody at the camp ever talked about the rebels' interrogation methods, but I could never pretend it hadn't happened under Rulon's command.

"I'm sorry," I said. "But I just can't sit here doing nothing if there's even a chance of saving Amory."

Greyson's smile stood out in the darkness. "When do we leave?"

I sighed. No matter what had happened to him in prison, at least the important things about Greyson hadn't changed. He was still my most loyal friend. "Whenever we can find out how they're breaking into the city and where the PMC might be keeping Amory."

We stopped walking. Greyson fidgeted, chewing on his words. The silence hung between him and Logan, and I knew they were both dancing around something they did not want to say to me. That wasn't like Greyson.

He took a deep breath. "Haven . . . if they think he has information about the rebels, he's not going to be in good shape when we get him out." He swallowed, as if trying to keep his next words down. "If he's still alive."

My stomach clenched. Even though the horrible thoughts of what the PMC might be doing to Amory were on a constant loop in my head, hearing Greyson say it made it real.

"I know. But I won't leave him."

"I wouldn't expect you to."

I paused, mulling over Rulon's words. "Rulon said 'facility,' not prison."

"What?"

"I don't think they're holding Amory in prison."

Greyson snorted. "Well, the rebels destroyed all the prisons. They've just been killing all the illegals they find."

Enemy Inside

"Why would they hold on to Amory, then? The other rebels left in the city would have more information."

"His father doesn't want him killed."

"No. His father wouldn't want people thinking he was being soft on his son. How would that look? Amory defected. He's a traitor."

"What does Amory have that the other defectors don't?"

I thought back to something Amory had said in the rebel bunker — how his father used him as one of the first test subjects for the CID.

"There was something different about his CID," I said. "They tried to modify his behavior. It obviously didn't work very well, because they haven't tried that with anyone else."

"That we know of."

I shivered.

"I know where he is," said Logan, startling me. She looked pale in the anemic glow of the moonlight filtering through the bare trees, and the dead look in her eyes gave me a chill. "They've got him in Isador."

Greyson and I exchanged blank looks, and she continued.

"I never thought it was a real place, but they sometimes talked about it when I was in training."

"What is it?" I asked.

"No place you want to be. It's off the books, but it's where the PMC runs tests on people to develop new technology. At least that's what I've heard."

"How do we get there?"

"I don't know where it is. Just that it's somewhere in Sector X."

"Rulon knows," I said through gritted teeth, feeling the

Enemy Inside

hatred boiling in my veins. He had the information we needed to rescue Amory, and still he did nothing. He would let him die.

"We need those maps," I said, thinking of the ones Rulon had shown me in the leaders' tent. "They had all the safe routes marked."

"Tomorrow," said Greyson. "We'll wait until Rulon and his guards leave camp, and then we'll sneak in and steal them."

The thought of letting yet another night pass while Amory was in the hands of the PMC made me sick, but we couldn't go running into Sector X without a solid plan again. That was what got us into this mess.

We felt our way back through the trees, stumbling occasionally over exposed roots and underbrush hidden in the snow. I began to wonder how far we had walked into the woods. I could no longer hear the sounds of laughter and slurred conversations.

Finally, I saw the flickering light of the fire through the trees, but something was wrong. It was too quiet.

Someone shouted, and I heard the sounds of heavy footfalls crashing toward us. A hulking shape emerged in the darkness, and I took an automatic step backward, bumping into Greyson. An enormous hand closed over my arm, jerking me forward and almost yanking my arm from its socket.

"Found her!" the man shouted.

I twisted reflexively, bringing my elbow up to knock the man on the side of the face just as Logan had taught me, but he was too fast. A huge, muscular arm twisted around my throat, pressing down against my windpipe. I choked as I was lifted off my feet and dragged through the trees. I smelled sweat and alcohol on his breath, and I started to panic.

We emerged into the clearing where the fire was still burning, but no one was drinking or laughing. They were all staring at me with anger and distrust. Rulon stood alone in the middle, looking smug.

"We have a traitor among us," he said loudly to the watching crowd. "And traitors must be punished."

A hiss rippled through the crowd. Rulon took a step toward me, wearing an expression of cold disgust. "Take her in."

I tried to look for Logan and Greyson, but I couldn't move my head. My captor's arm was still wrapped around my throat too tightly, and he continued to drag me through the camp as all the rebels watched. Whatever was happening, no one was going to stop it.

We passed down the rows of tents, and I felt the dread burning in the pit of my stomach. We were heading to the large black tent at the end of the block. It stood apart from the others in shadow, as if no one wanted to be that close to it.

The man tossed me inside as if I were a bag of trash. Caught off guard, I fell forward, knocking my head against something hard as I hit the ground. The pain radiated through my skull, and I squinted through the darkness to the man who had grabbed me. I didn't know his name, but I recognized him as one of Rulon's closest guards. He followed him everywhere.

Light fell across the trees outside, throwing shadows over Rulon standing in the entrance to the tent, his face unreadable. Someone muttered behind him, but he didn't turn his head to the speaker.

I recognized that voice.

As Rulon and his companion crowded into the tent after

the guard, I felt the sharp smack of betrayal.

Godfrey met my eyes, and there was no remorse in his expression. Although I knew he was a rebel through and through, I'd always thought I could trust him. Godfrey was the only rebel who had seen what happened on the bridge. He watched Amory throw me into the water and sacrifice himself to the PMC. He knew why I had to go back.

Rulon hung the lantern on the ceiling and looked down at me with an expression of pure loathing.

"I'm sure you know why you are here."

Chapter Two

Rulon edged closer to me, and I could see the snow melting on his boots. "You've been busy, I hear."

I said nothing. If this was what happened to rebels who spoke out against Rulon, I would have a better chance of walking away unscathed if I did not argue. I took my time rising into a sitting position, trying to decide what I should say.

How had he heard me talking to Greyson and Logan? Did he have spies in the woods?

"Godfrey tells me you have been training others in combat without authorization, and now I hear you are trying to shift the tides against me in my own camp!"

I tried to arrange my face to hide my confusion. If Godfrey had really seen me and Logan practicing in the woods, he would know she was training *me*. Something was wrong, but I could not tell them about Logan. If they knew she was trained by the PMC, they would think she was a spy.

"We were just practicing," I said.

"Practicing?" He laughed once, cold and sharp. "For what?"

"To fight the PMC," I said. "We want to be of use to the cause."

"You? You and your friends from the farm?" He laughed again. "I have moles embedded in the PMC . . . former marines and snipers at my disposal. How could you possibly help our cause?"

I bit down on my tongue, the anger welling inside me. So it was true that the rebels had people on the inside.

"I don't know why you would be teaching our comrades to fight in secret, unless you were working against us."

"I'm not!"

He continued. "I have been naïve. I probably wouldn't have believed this treachery until I saw it for myself tonight. Your friend Amory is probably lounging in the PMC barracks as we speak. This was all an act to see what we knew — learn our operations. I have been right to play my cards close. I can see that now."

Rulon looked at the man who had dragged me here and flicked his eyes to the chair I had hit my head on.

In an instant, the strange man's hands were on me, pulling me up and shoving me into the chair by the front of my coat. I struggled, kicked, and tried to hit him, but he slapped me hard across the face. My skin stung with heat, and my eyes watered.

While I was subdued, the man stuffed something in my mouth: a piece of fabric. I gagged, but he just shoved it in farther, and Godfrey moved to help him. It tasted like sweat and diesel fuel.

I heard the loud rip of duct tape and felt the sticky adhesive close over my mouth. Someone wrapped it around my face, and it clung to my hair and pulled at my skin. I was too terrified to move.

The larger man held my wrists while Godfrey taped them together and bound me to the chair. I breathed hard against the tape, trying to find air, and I felt myself begin to hyperventilate. My chest seized, and I felt tears well up in my eyes. *Where were Logan and Greyson?* Perhaps the other rebels

Enemy Inside

had ganged up on them and they were in trouble, too. If they couldn't save me, no one else would.

I was so distracted by the sudden restraint that I hadn't noticed Rulon digging in a box on the floor. He retrieved something I recognized: a small white case no bigger than a man's wallet. He flipped it open, and I tried to scream through the fabric inside my mouth.

Rulon dragged another chair directly in front of mine and sat down, a smile twitching at the corners of his mouth. He grabbed my bound arms roughly and twisted my left arm to reveal the three perfect burns.

"Hmm. Last time you got fire." He licked his lips. "I'd like to try something new."

You bastard, I thought. So Rulon *had* been the one who instigated Miles's torture.

He pulled one of the tiny strips of film out of the case. This one was black. I tried to jerk my hands away, but his grip was too strong. I thrashed around, remembering the fire licking my skin, the smoke and suffocation, and my own charring flesh.

Rulon's guard had me in a headlock from behind, and for the first time, I saw Godfrey's eyes flick away.

The piece of film felt cold as it suctioned to the skin parallel with my red burns.

A flash of cold prickled up my arm, tickling my spine as I shivered. But it was not ice as I expected; it felt as though I was being doused in frigid water. The water moved up my body in splashes, freezing and jarring, but not excruciating as before. It lapped at my ankles. I was wading in a cold pool, the water rising quickly to my knees and thighs. Suddenly, it was at chest level, splashing against my neck and chin.

As it rose up my body, the water got colder and choppier. Before I was wading in calm waters. Now I was treading in the middle of the ocean.

Waves splashed against my face, filling my nose and mouth. I coughed and spluttered, but I could not clear my throat. The water was rushing in too fast.

I beat my arms and legs, trying desperately to keep my head above water, but I just sank farther.

Thrashing desperately, I tried to come up for air, but my legs and arms were too heavy. I could not swim. The weight of my body pulled me down into the dark water, as if I had sandbags strapped to my chest.

The water engulfed my head, beating down on me. Like a whirlpool, the water was churning — forcing itself into my airways. I choked, and my chest tightened as I fought for air. I moved my arms, trying to surface. It was no use.

More water rushed into my lungs. They were on fire. I couldn't breathe.

Black spots appeared at the edges of my vision.

I was drowning. I was going to die.

Then my body started to feel weak and heavy, as though it were made of lead.

I floated down, down, down, until I finally settled against the bottom of a pool of brackish water.

The rough concrete scraped my skin, but it felt nice resting there. My legs and torso were too heavy to stay buoyant. Everything was so heavy. It was easier down here.

I thought about Amory kissing me up on the cliff. It was strange — like watching someone who wasn't me being kissed. That seemed so long ago. Amory was so far away. I just wanted the agony to stop.

Something flickered in the back of my mind. I could not sleep at the bottom of the pool.

Enemy Inside

As my head went light and fuzzy, I felt an urgency stirring in my chest. Raising my head, I tried to remember which way was up. I squinted through the blackness to the bright light refracting off the water's surface. I pushed off toward the light, feeling the water flowing through my fingers. My head broke the surface, and I felt the cold sting of air against my face. I gasped.

Coming up was awful.

I choked, and the pain in my throat matched other pains I had not felt in the water. I retched, but no water came up. People were moving around me, talking in low voices. I ignored them.

Someone kicked me in the gut. I whimpered and withdrew into a ball but did not move. I just wanted to be left alone.

I couldn't remember why someone tried to drown me, and I found I did not care. I closed my eyes, willing them to go away. They did.

Then I felt something brush against my cheek like the wing of a bird.

Someone tugged on my ponytail gently. It was such a soft gesture that called back to another time: me, ten years old, being awoken in the middle of the night at summer camp. We were sneaking out to the lake to look for frogs. Only one other person could remember that.

Slowly, I opened my eyes. Greyson was staring down at me, looking horrified. I was lying on my side against the tarp on the ground, still taped to the chair with my right arm wedged painfully underneath me. I must have thrashed hard enough to knock myself over. Someone had removed the tape and fabric from my mouth, and my scalp prickled where bits of my hair had ripped out with it.

"Come on," he whispered. "We have to get you out of

here before they come back."

He withdrew his knife from a back pocket — the knife I had carried in my bag over a thousand miles for him — and cut the tape binding my wrists. He ripped it off quickly like a Band-Aid and began cutting me out of the chair. As I struggled to roll over into a sitting position, my limbs felt strangely weak, and my head was still spinning.

I looked down at my arm. There were four clear strips of film stuck to the skin there; the color had leeched into my bloodstream with the poison. I tried to peel them off, but my hands shook. Greyson saw me struggling and did it for me. There were new marks there now, these ones shiny and raised as if the flesh had bubbled as it burned. They looked like tally marks ticked off in a row.

Looking down expectantly, Greyson held out a hand to help me to my feet. My gut ached painfully where one of them had kicked me, and I felt other bruises beginning to form along my side where I had crashed to the ground. There was a tender skid mark on my cheek from falling over onto the tarp.

Greyson held on to me as he poked his head outside through the flap. Seeing no one, he pulled me out into the snow and around the side of the tent. We made our way along behind the row, careful to stay out of sight as we moved down the block to the tent I shared with Logan.

We entered through the back flap, and Logan jumped as she heard the rustle of canvas.

"Oh! It's you," she sighed. Even in the dark, I saw her expression change immediately when she saw me. "What the hell did they do to you?"

I shook my head, shivering as I sank onto my sleeping bag. My clothes were soaked with cold sweat.

"They tortured her," Greyson spat. He was shaking with

anger. "They used four this time!"

"You got through four?" Logan looked at me in disbelief. "I've never heard of that."

"What are those things?"

"HALLO tags," she said. "They were developed by the PMC to be a more 'humane' form of torture."

"*Humane?*" Greyson rounded on her. "There's nothing 'humane' about it! Did you learn how to use those?"

Logan glared at him. "I did what I had to do. I'm not proud of it. It's not like I enjoyed torturing people."

He looked taken aback.

"And anyway," said Logan. "They should never have used that many on you. They could have *killed* you." She sat down next to me. "Did they use the fire ones again?"

I shook my head. "It was like I was drowning."

"Waterboarding."

"Why did he do it? I don't understand."

"You challenged him openly," said Logan in a quiet voice. "He's weak. Everybody says so behind his back. It's just that no one's ever stood up to him."

"He tortured me because I *talked back* to him?"

"He has to keep order somehow."

I turned to look at her. "We can't stay here."

"One step ahead of you. Our bags are already packed."

I glanced over to the corner of the tent, where our rucksacks stood ready to go.

"I grabbed some extra clothes and stuff for you, too," she said to Greyson. "Plus everything from your tent."

I felt a pang of sorrow when I remembered what few

Enemy Inside

items Greyson had left in this world to call his own. Just the picture of his family and the knife I had brought with me from his apartment after his arrest.

"Where should we go?" I asked.

Logan threw a shifty glance over to her sleeping bag. Looking closer, I could see a map smoothed out over it.

"I stole those while Rulon was busy torturing you," she confessed. "It's the only way we're going to get into Sector X. All their routes are marked. I haven't quite figured it out yet, but it's better than nothing."

Amory. I let out a long breath I'd been holding since Rulon's tent. "Let's go."

Bundled up in all the warm clothes we had, the three of us slipped out the back of the tent. We hugged the line of trees and moved in the shadows to avoid attracting attention. After the commotion at dinner, the last stragglers were returning to their tents, talking in low whispers.

". . . *never thought she was PMC, but I guess it just goes to show . . .*"

"*You can't trust a defector. I know it sounds bad, but they're just not like us.*"

I felt my face grow hot with anger and embarrassment. I hated that Rulon had made such a scene.

"Hey!" Greyson hissed, swatting behind him. "Wha —"

Logan clapped a hand to his mouth, and I saw the glint of his knife in her hand. For a minute, I thought she had gone off the deep end, but then she crunched through the snow toward the weapons tent and slipped in through the back flap.

I exchanged a look with Greyson, who had gone bright red.

Enemy Inside

"What? She just frisked that off me!"

We waited in the shadows, my heart pounding in my throat. Any second now, Rulon could return to the tent to find me gone. It would be impossible to get out of here once the camp was on alert. I was just about to go after Logan when she emerged carrying a serious-looking gun. Two more were strapped to her shoulders, and she also had a bag full of ammunition dangling from her arm.

"They had HK416s *and* FN SCARs," she whispered. "I haven't seen one of these since my dad's." Logan ran her hand down the side. "He's ex-military."

Greyson eyed her warily. "You're a little scary, you know."

She rolled her eyes and shoved one of the rifles into his hands. "Just for that, you don't get the other SCAR."

I took the rifle she handed me with numb hands. I never really knew what to do with a firearm.

"We need to get out of here *now*," she said.

"So why did you take my knife?"

Logan looked guilty. "I may have used it to threaten the poor kid who was guarding the tent."

Greyson snorted. "A tent full of assault rifles, and you hold up a guy with a dull knife."

Making our way down the hill toward the edge of camp, Logan led us deeper into the trees. We still had to get past the lookout who was stationed at the foot of the hill. Peering through the trees, Greyson stopped and pointed.

If I hadn't been looking for him, he would have been impossible to see. The lookout was perched in a tree, dressed in dark camouflage. With no fire and no protection from the wind, he must have been freezing.

Enemy Inside

Suddenly, I heard the crunch of heavy boots through the snow and a low whistle. I squinted through the darkness back toward camp. There was a figure ambling down the hill with a gun slung over his shoulder. The scraggly beard and slight limp told me it was Godfrey.

"Hey, Kinsley," he called. "Go ahead and pack it in. I'll take over for the rest of the night."

The lookout in the tree mumbled something in acknowledgment. "I thought Sanders was on this shift."

Godfrey shrugged. "Bad chili. He'll have the shits for a week."

Kinsley gave a low whistle and began his descent from the tree. "Thanks. It's freezing up there."

Godfrey nodded and watched him go.

"What now?" I hissed. "He knows."

Greyson raised his rifle, training it on Godfrey, but I pushed it down and stepped in front of him, forcing him to make eye contact.

"What are you doing?"

"He's gotta go."

"No!" I couldn't believe Greyson was about to shoot someone. "You don't want to do this. This isn't you."

"He tortured you, Haven."

I shook my head. "It doesn't matter. We can't kill him anyway. We'd wake up the whole camp."

"She's right," said Logan.

"You can come out now." The voice made me jump out of my skin.

I wheeled around, and Godfrey was standing in the shadows under the tree just a few yards away.

Enemy Inside

Greyson and Logan snapped up their guns, aiming them at his chest.

"You let us tie you to a tree so we can escape, or I'll put a bullet in your brain," Logan growled in a low, deadly voice.

"Fine," said Godfrey. He raised his hands in surrender. "Just thought I might be of help."

I exchanged a glance with Greyson, but Logan wasn't having it.

"I'm done letting rebels torture my friends."

Even with two guns on him, Godfrey looked relaxed. "It had to be done," he said. "How else were you going to steal Rulon's maps?"

Logan blinked — something I'd never seen her do when she had her gun trained on a target.

"I had to throw the heat on her so you could get in there."

"He's telling the truth," I said. It all made sense now. "He lied to Rulon and told him I was training *you* in combat."

Godfrey frowned. "You really need to tone it down," he said to Logan.

She looked confused.

"You don't hide the PMC thing well. I saw you coming a mile away. It's dangerous."

Logan lowered her rifle.

"We need to get the hell out of here," he said. "They probably already know you're gone."

"You first," said Greyson.

Following Godfrey through the woods back in the direction of Sector X, Logan and I kept exchanging nervous looks. It was possible he was leading us into a trap, but we didn't really have another choice. We had the maps but no definitive plan for getting through the PMC checkpoint. And if Godfrey was lying, we couldn't leave him alive *or* kill him without bringing all the rebels down on us.

"So how do we get into Sector X?" I asked finally.

Godfrey smirked. "Are you telling me you three didn't have a plan? Not even a bad one?"

I felt a sting of irritation. "I was a little busy."

He shook his head. "I figured as much. Well, your friend is being kept at Isador as a PMC guinea pig. The only way you're getting in there is if you have someone who is real PMC. Those fake CIDs aren't going to cut it. You need security clearance."

"What are you saying?" snapped Logan.

Godfrey turned around, eyebrow raised, waiting for us to figure it out.

"You're the mole," I whispered. "You're helping the rebels get into Sector X to steal food and supplies."

"Among other things, but yes. That's the general idea."

"What other things?" pressed Logan.

"Weapons, ammunition, first aid supplies . . . toilet paper."

"Explosives?"

"That's my specialty."

"That's why you weren't in the riots at all that day," I said. "You stayed out of the city so you wouldn't blow your cover."

He nodded. "The fewer people on our side who know, the better."

"Did Mariah know?" I asked. I thought back to when

Godfrey had left us outside Sector X that day.

"Yes, she did. Everything Rulon knew, Mariah knew. In fact, toward the end, it was hard to tell who was really calling the shots." His tone was even, but I could detect the undercurrents of resentment in his voice.

"She's out there," I said.

"That is a big risk for us, but since she's infected, going to the PMC would be mutually assured destruction."

"What if she's caught?"

"She won't be. Mariah always had a knack for . . . self-preservation."

"I don't understand why you're helping us," said Greyson. His voice was still harsh, distrustful. "They're going to notice you're gone. Don't you think they will figure out you helped us escape?"

"I was ready to leave. Rulon's camp has outlived its usefulness to me, and, truth be told, I'm sick of their methods." His dark eyes flitted to me. "You want me to blow up a building full of PMC officials? Fine. But Rulon and Mariah always had this way of preying on the weak. The kids they can't scare into following them into the fire, well . . . you know."

"So what, you're a free agent now?" asked Logan.

"I suppose I am. I'll go where I can put my skills to use. Right now, that is not with Rulon's division. He's floundering, and when Haven told him off tonight, I knew it was time to move on."

"What will they do for food now that you're gone?"

"They have everything they need."

We walked in silence for a long while, and Greyson finally lowered his gun. We still had a couple miles before we would reach Sector X, but we were far enough away from camp that he seemed convinced we were not headed into an ambush.

Godfrey still had his gun slung over his shoulder, and he had not made a move to reach for it. He also carried a large rucksack, which made me think he had really packed up his belongings and left the camp for good. Like the three of us, all the rebels seemed to be able to carry everything they owned on their back.

He was dressed for the weather in a bulky black coat with what seemed like infinite pockets, a stocking cap, and enormous combat boots. With the snow sticking to his bushy black beard, he looked rugged and oddly more cheerful.

Logan, Greyson, and I had decent boots, but we were only dressed in layers under our thin jackets. We had been issued hats and gloves from the supply tent, but heavy winter coats were coveted items in the rebel camp.

Finally, after what seemed like hours, Godfrey stopped and turned to the three of us.

"You three need to prepare yourselves for what we're about to do and what we might find. People who go into Isador don't come out normal. Most people never come out at all. You need to accept right now that your friend Amory might not be himself anymore."

I nodded, but I felt sick. I couldn't stand thinking about what the PMC might have done to him.

"I need to know," he said. "How far are you willing to go for him? Are you willing to do what needs to be done?"

I shuddered, nodding once.

Greyson pulled his shoulders back and straightened beside me. "I am."

"Me too," said Logan. Of the three of us, she looked the most excited for what was about to come.

Godfrey shook his head. "You need to really consider this. If we get in there and he's too far gone, we have to leave him. We can put him down if it's the best thing for him, but we can't bring out someone who's a liability. Understand?"

Greyson and Logan were looking at me. I bit down on my lip to keep the tears from coming.

"Haven," said Greyson. "It's what he would want. It's what any of us would want."

I took a deep breath and nodded.

"All right." Godfrey clapped his hands and reached in his pack. Logan's hand twitched to her gun, but he pulled out something white and folded. "Put these on."

He tossed me the white bundle of fabric, and I caught it as he pulled out a few others.

I let the stiff folds of the material fall open in my fingers and gasped when I saw the insignia: the image of one all-seeing eye flanked by three stars inside an embroidered circle. *Order. Compliance. Progress.*

We were dressing as PMC.

Chapter Three

The PMC uniform was stiff and unfriendly. Even when I tucked the starched pant legs into my combat boots, they were still too big for me. The jacket was boxy and too light for the winter, meant to be worn under full riot gear and a bulletproof vest.

I gasped a little when we all turned to face each other after changing. Greyson looked imposing in a way I never would have believed possible. Clean-shaven with short hair, he would easily pass as a real officer, and his dark eyes were unforgiving,

Logan looked ordinary. Her usual radiance was muted by the stiff white polyester, and her bouncy golden waves were pulled back into a French twist. Only her bright green eyes stood out against the stark whiteness of the uniform, but they seemed less vibrant, too.

Seeing her hair pulled up, I struggled to twist mine into a bun. It was too short in the front and slipped through my fingers, but Logan appeared at my shoulder.

"Let me," she said. She worked quickly, and within a minute she had my hair wound into a tight knot at the back of my head.

Next she moved to Greyson, reaching up to fasten the last hook at the neck of his jacket. "We don't want to draw attention to ourselves with a uniform that's not regulation," she muttered.

Enemy Inside

"You'll be needing these," said Godfrey. He held up three plastic wristbands with the stolen CIDs. Out of everyone, Godfrey looked the least at home in his uniform. Maybe it was the bushy black beard or his ruddy complexion, but either way, he seemed to stick out like a sore thumb.

Logan cleared her throat. "What about your beard?" she asked.

He grunted. "I'm not active duty. It's fine."

I fastened the band around my wrist, examining the gold ridge around the edge of the white chip. The CID was so small and so benign looking, yet it controlled so much in our world.

Godfrey clapped his hands together. "All right. Let's get a move on."

Storming through the underbrush in his wake, I began to wonder if he planned to walk right into Sector X on foot. He was talking fast now. I knew we had to be getting close. "You three are Fuller, Hellmack, and Woeden. Remember your names. Always make eye contact, but don't speak unless spoken to. Your pins will be your home sectors: 573 and 314."

I examined the name etched into the plastic wristband: Rebecca Fuller.

"You're new recruits, so your fingerprints and retinal scans won't be in the system yet. We will have to do that when we get into the facility. Don't do anything stupid. These aren't burner CIDs like the last ones. You have no idea what I had to do to get security clearance for a bunch of interns. And for god's sake, don't let anyone see that scar on your arm," he said to me.

Through the trees, something white caught my eye. As we approached, I could see it was a light utility vehicle like the ones the PMC used. We got inside, and Logan sat in the back with Greyson. Of all of us, she posed the greatest risk of being recognized.

"Won't it look suspicious for us to enter the city in the middle of the night?" I asked.

"No. The beta unit rarely does its business in the daylight."

The engine roared to life, and we barreled forward through the underbrush. It was a rough ride, but I began to feel a slight twinge of hope that I might see Amory soon. I tried not to think about how they must be treating him or what shape he could be in; it only mattered that we got him out.

"Your CIDs are set to go live when we're half a mile out," said Godfrey. "They're staggered because it's a little suspicious if three people come online all at once, but all the tree cover makes signals pretty shitty out here."

We stopped, and Godfrey squinted through the trees. Seeing nothing, he barreled onto a dirt road. Behind us was a locked gate, but I couldn't see where the road went.

"PMC storage facility," he explained. "We're getting close. Put on that riot gear in the back. Every officer in the city is wearing a set these days."

Logan reached behind the back seat and pulled up a bulletproof vest and a helmet. She passed one to me, and I fastened it over my chest. It was stiff and heavy. I didn't know how officers were supposed to run when they were wearing one. The helmet was white like everything else, but it had a black strip running down the middle. I put it on, feeling ridiculous but slightly relieved that it would hide part of my face.

"Here we go," he said.

Glancing behind me, I saw that Greyson's mouth was set in a hard line, his eyes cold and empty. Logan looked nervous, but sitting there in her white uniform, I could see her inner fierceness beneath the surface that made her who she was.

We pulled onto the main highway, where several other white vehicles were visible up ahead. I had the immediate urge to shrink down in my seat to avoid being seen, but then I remembered I was dressed as an officer.

Following the flow of traffic off an exit ramp, we slowed to a crawl in a convoy of other utility vehicles just like ours. We followed the one in front of us onto another major road, and I saw the bridge up ahead. I heard Logan's involuntary intake of air, and I knew she was thinking about Max and Amory.

The bridge had seemed impossibly long when we were swimming across the frigid river below, and now that we were trying to cross back to the other side, it seemed just as long.

We came to a stop in a line of vehicles passing through the checkpoint, and an officer approached the truck in front of us, shining a flashlight.

"Is this normal?" asked Greyson, sounding alarmed.

"I guess it's their new nighttime protocol," said Godfrey. "Don't say anything unless you have to."

My heart started to pound a little faster, and I clenched and unclenched my hands to release some of the tension.

The beam of the flashlight flew over in our direction, shining through the windshield and making me squint.

I saw the bright white of the uniform outside Godfrey's window, and the officer motioned for him to roll it down.

"Good evening," said the officer. It was a woman with piercing blue eyes and a severe look to her face. *Maybe her bun is too tight,* I thought.

Enemy Inside

"Hello, officer."

"Hello. And . . . I'm sorry . . . I don't recognize these people."

"New recruits," muttered Godfrey.

"Woeden, ma'am," said Greyson.

"Hellmack."

"Fuller," I muttered.

The officer shined her flashlight beam in each one of our faces before returning her attention to Godfrey.

"What's your business in Sector X tonight, Lieutenant?" Her words were clipped and impersonal.

"Transport," Godfrey grunted.

"Pickup or delivery?"

"Pickup."

"And may I ask what you're picking up?"

"I'm afraid that's classified," said Godfrey. "Beta unit, you understand."

The woman smiled, but it was not friendly. "Of course. I just need to verify your identification."

My stomach lurched. Godfrey hadn't mentioned that.

He held out his arm, and she flashed him a condescending smile. "Lieutenant, we need to verify your paperwork and cross-reference it with your Citizen Identification. I'll need to see the order from your commanding officer."

Godfrey sighed. "Hmm, yeah. Well, as I said, our directives are classified. I can only share that information with the overseeing officer in Sector X."

"I'm sorry, Lieutenant. I cannot let you through without

verifying your paperwork."

Godfrey raised an eyebrow and leaned forward against the open window. "Do you know who the overseeing officer is, ma'am?"

Her fake smile twitched at the corner of her eyes.

"It's Captain Elwood. You can certainly call him up and ask for verification, but he has bigger things to worry about than the Sector X welcome committee. You understand."

The officer's smile faltered, and she looked angry. "Fine," she snapped. "But I'll be radioing ahead to let the exit officers know they will need to see some type of paperwork on your way out. Perhaps Captain Elwood can write you a note."

"Thank you very much."

The officer turned abruptly and walked away, and Godfrey rolled up the window. Logan breathed a loud sigh of relief in the back seat, and I sat back in silence, not trusting myself to speak.

We rolled on through the darkness, and I saw the mouth of the bridge with its dozen quivering ID rovers poised to lock in on our CIDs. Four rovers' lights blinked red, and I saw the tiny light on my CID do the same. I held my breath. If it stayed red, we were done. The officers on the bridge would know we were frauds, and they would arrest us.

After what seemed like several long minutes, the lights on the rovers turned green. We rolled under them, the four of us breathing a collective sigh of relief.

"Lucky bluff," I muttered to Godfrey.

"It wasn't a bluff," he said. "I know Elwood. He doesn't know we're about to break in to Isador and steal his son, but neither did she."

"You know Amory's father?" I whispered.

Enemy Inside

Godfrey nodded, narrowing his dark eyes on the road ahead. "Oh, I knew him — from the Marines. We were both deployed to Anbar during the Iraq war. He was an eager son of a bitch, even back then. The constant killings, no sleep — it got to you. But not Elwood. Rose through the ranks very quickly. I didn't see him again for a while after that, but when I heard he joined up with the PMC, well . . . I wasn't surprised. They probably recruited the hell out of him, and he was made captain immediately."

"And you?"

"I was recruited for . . . less honorable reasons. Less for my work ethic and more for my skill set."

"Explosives?"

He nodded.

"How did you get involved with the rebels?"

Godfrey sighed, and I knew he did not like talking about himself. "I was given an assignment to blow up a building. The PMC had the intel; it was definitely a threat level red. I thought it would be an old factory or a construction site lousy with carriers. Easy in, easy out.

"But I get there, and it's a shelter for undocumented kids — a bunch of teenagers and a few social workers all holed up off the highway. I couldn't believe it. Well, of course, Rulon was there making the rounds — recruiting for his little army. Didn't care much for him right off the bat, to be honest. But Mica was there, too. The place was really for minors whose parents had died or gone north, and they were wanting him to leave. That's when I fixed him up with Ida. Good kid, Mica."

He ended his story with a gruff sound, as if he were clearing his throat. Everyone else was silent.

We crossed under the overpass where Max had died, and I couldn't breathe. It felt as though I had a pile of bricks on

Enemy Inside

my chest.

The last time we were here, all the buildings not repurposed for PMC facilities stood empty. It was a ghost town, but signs of life were still visible. All that had changed.

Block after block after block was flattened to mounds of rubble. Buildings stood in heaps of wood and concrete and ash, great chunks of brick and broken glass scattered everywhere. The few cars parked along the street were covered in a layer of speckled black snow, and the slush in the gutter mixed with the soot raining down.

Logan gasped. "What happened?"

"The PMC is demolishing the city."

"But . . . why?"

"They're spinning their wheels," said Godfrey. "The riots last time happened right under their nose. They're flushing out any illegals hiding in the city. Rebuilding from scratch."

Looking up over the felled walls of destruction, I could see silver buildings on the horizon. They stood out like broken teeth against the landscape, looking strangely untouched.

"What are those buildings?"

"The start of a new city." Godfrey's expression was grim.

We passed Saint Drogo's, one of the only buildings I recognized still standing. One wing had been destroyed, but the rest of the building looked as menacing as ever. The steely "XX" mounted at the top of the tower still sent a chill down my spine.

Driving through the destroyed city in the darkness, I felt a sense of foreboding. We were in a war zone with nowhere left to hide, and we were the enemy.

"When did you join the PMC?" I asked Godfrey.

"About five years ago."

"Five years?"

"What? Did you think the PMC came out of nowhere right before the Collapse?" He laughed. "It's always been around, and when you're ex-military, well . . . I saw the way things were going."

"But why?" asked Greyson.

"It wasn't always like this, if that's what you're asking." Godfrey gestured at the destruction around us. Despite all the wreckage, the rovers were still operational. They scanned us at every intersection. "We've been using independent contractors in this country since the American Revolution. No one ever thought it would be what it is today."

"Where is Isador?" Logan asked.

"It's past the main PMC block. We never took it out during the riots, which was a mistake."

"What do they do there?" I asked, knowing I didn't really want the answer.

"It's mainly a testing facility. Research and development."

"So Amory's . . ." I trailed off. I couldn't say it.

Godfrey stared straight ahead. He acted as though he hadn't heard my question, but I knew he had.

"How are we going to get him out?" asked Logan.

Godfrey glanced over his shoulder at her. "By playing the game." He stared down the road, eyes darting out of the range of our headlights into the shadows. "Remember what I told you. If we go in there and he's too far gone . . . we can't take him with us. You understand?"

Everyone was looking at me. I swallowed. "I can do what needs to be done."

Enemy Inside

Even as I said it, I wasn't sure it was true.

We passed the wreckage from the base, and I felt sick when I remembered the horrible moment standing outside with Amory before the explosion, knowing it was too late to save those inside. Now the granite building was no more than rubble. The marble steps that led up to the front door now stopped at the mound of crumbled concrete, granite, shattered tile, and twisted metal. Stairs to nowhere.

Just past the destroyed base, the streetlights were much farther apart, and there was a fresh dusting of snow on the road. We were entering a part of the city where most of the old buildings still stood untouched by the PMC's demolition units. These buildings hadn't been occupied for years. Their foundations were sinking under crumbled brick, windows shattered. Even the graffiti was faded.

We turned down a dark street, and I began to feel a strange prickling on the back of my neck. There were hardly any streetlights, but I could still see the ID rovers winking at every corner.

For a moment, I wondered if Godfrey had led us into a trap; it didn't seem likely that the PMC would build a test facility out here. But then I saw it.

Sprawled out across a snow-covered courtyard the size of a city block stood a building that did not belong. It was not made of brick and steel and glass. Its smooth walls looked as impenetrable as stone but were constructed from a reflective material that caught the light from our car and illuminated the entire facade.

I half expected Godfrey to pull around back to a parking lot, but he drove right from the street to the wide courtyard. There was no bump of a curb. There were no mailboxes or street addresses or plants outside the building. There wasn't even a door.

From the perimeter, the building looked like a silvery box

Enemy Inside

sitting in the snow with no way in or out. But as we approached, the ground dipped sharply downhill, and I could see an opening in the lower level just wide enough for a vehicle to pass through. Squinting inside, I could make out the other end of the tunnel on the opposite side of the building, the exit the size of a postage stamp.

A glass door slid open, and we drove inside. It was brighter inside the tunnel than outside, but it was impossible to identify the source of the light. The walls, the ceiling, and the floor all seemed to glow with an eerie white light.

If it weren't for the exit opening on the other end of the tunnel growing larger in the distance, we might have been sitting motionless. The stark white walls bore no distinguishing features to show our movement.

I felt the seatbelt tighten around my chest, and I could tell we were driving downhill again. The opening in the tunnel grew smaller and then disappeared. The tunnel went dark. We were driving underground.

"There aren't any rovers," Logan whispered.

"Don't need them," said Godfrey. "Illegals who break into this place don't come out."

I glanced at Greyson, who looked uneasy. Small spaces used to give him panic attacks when he was a little kid, and I wondered if his time spent in solitary confinement in Chaddock had brought back his old fears.

Lights flickered on around us, and I saw we were in a parking structure. Godfrey killed the engine and turned back to Logan.

"Got those maps?"

She nodded, pulling the bundle out of her rucksack.

"We can't leave with Amory the way we came in. Not unless we want to shoot our way out."

He spread out one of the maps on the middle console, dragging his finger from the block we were on to one of the highlighted routes.

"This is a little bit of a gamble because no one has been in Sector X since the riots *except* through the main bridge, so we don't know for sure what security will be like. But —" He stopped, tapping his finger on the map. "One of you will take Amory and leave through this old tunnel. It's been out of service for years, but you might be able to get through."

"I'll go," I said quickly.

He nodded. "Memorize this route. The rest of us will go the way we came and say our pickup wasn't ready yet, but we left you to push the exit paperwork through. If you run into trouble, don't try anything stupid." He looked at me, and his eyes were serious. "You won't win in a shootout with the PMC. Just lay low until we can come back in and get you."

My hands tingled with nerves. The thought of being stuck in Sector X was terrifying.

Godfrey circled a block on the map and scribbled down an address. "Most of our old safe houses within the city have been destroyed, but this one's not far from here. You can stay there for a few days until we come for you." He looked up at me. "Memorize this. Can't risk taking the map in case you're captured."

I stared at our escape route and the four numbers of the safe-house address, burning them into my brain.

I could feel Greyson's eyes boring into the side of my head, but I didn't want to meet his gaze. I knew what he was thinking: There was a high likelihood Amory and I would get caught.

"You don't have to go alone, you know," he whispered.

His show of solidarity warmed my heart.

Enemy Inside

"Oh yes she does," Godfrey grumbled. "It's suspicious enough that I'm leaving with one fewer officer than I came in with. Now take off those helmets. You look ridiculous."

Before anyone could argue, Godfrey was out of the car, reloading his gun. Logan followed, looking pale.

She came around to my side of the car, and I saw that her eyes were glassy. "If anything happens —"

"Don't hug," said Godfrey, not looking up. "There are cameras everywhere."

Logan's lip trembled, and she looked very young. I decided the uniform did not suit her; it stole everything about her that was vibrant and unique, and it melted away her self-assurance.

"Nothing's going to happen," I said, sounding more confident than I felt. "This is Amory we're talking about. I went back for Greyson, and I would do the same thing for you. We're not the rebels," I added in a whisper. "We don't leave people behind."

She nodded once, and I saw the strength and determination in her eyes.

I grabbed my gun, and the three of us followed Godfrey to an entrance blocked by a glass door. There was no lock and no handle, but a rover above the doorway scanned each of us, and the glass slid back. I felt a prickle on the back of my neck. Someone somewhere was watching us on the cameras.

Crowding through the entryway, we emerged into a small, sterile-looking white room. It was empty except for a single station with a half-moon head scanner and a raised glass table. There was another rover and a security camera over interlocking elevator doors.

Godfrey stepped up to the station, put his head up to the scanner, and placed his palms flat on the glass surface. Three

Enemy Inside

low beeps followed by a single high tone illuminated a green light over the station, and the elevator doors slid open. Godfrey shuffled into a chamber just large enough for one person, nodded at me once, and disappeared.

I glanced at Greyson, not daring to say a word. The security camera jerked in my direction, and I took that as a signal to step up to the station. Discreetly wiping my sweaty palms on the stiff polyester pants, I placed them on the glass table and waited. A ripple of white light moved through the glass, scanning my fingerprints.

Reluctantly, I leaned forward and placed my forehead against the half-moon scanner. A light flashed, scanning my retinas, and a feminine tone sounded from tiny speakers near my temples.

Please state your full name.

"Rebecca Fuller," I said, parroting the fake name Godfrey had assigned me.

Please enter your Citizen Identification pin.

I looked down and saw a keypad illuminated in the glass. I punched in the code and heard the same sequence of beeps that had followed Godfrey's identification.

The metal doors swung open again, and I hurried inside. I looked wide-eyed at Logan before the doors snapped shut again and I was thrust into darkness.

Chapter Four

My stomach flew up to my throat as the elevator plummeted down. I had the wild fear that the PMC had identified me as an impostor and was dropping me to my death instead of taking me to Amory.

But when the doors of the elevator swung open, Godfrey was already waiting, standing against the wall in a long white hallway. With his bushy black beard, ruddy complexion, and wrinkled uniform, he definitely looked out of place.

He didn't say anything when I emerged, and I took his silence for a confirmation that there were still security cameras watching and listening to everything we said.

A moment later, Greyson appeared, closely followed by Logan. He looked unnerved by the process, and I hoped no one was monitoring the security footage that closely. Anyone would be able to spot his pale face and darting eyes.

Godfrey led us down the empty corridor in silence. There were steel doors spaced every few feet, but none of them had locks or handles. Four-digit numbers were punched into the metal, but Godfrey did not glance at them once. Reaching the end of the hallway, we rounded the corner. This passage had no doors, but up ahead, I could see another elevator — a larger version of the one we had just taken.

The rover over the doors jerked from side to side, reading each of our CIDs. The doors flew open, and we all piled inside. The panel next to the door had dozens of numbered buttons, but Godfrey selected the button near the bottom labeled "A."

The elevator doors closed, and we plummeted down again. As we descended, I felt weightless, unable to breathe or speak. Greyson looked pale green, as though he might be sick. Logan wore a grim expression. After a minute, the elevator slowed, finally stopping with a dull *ping*.

Atrium, said the robotic female voice. The doors swung open.

We stood in an enormous round room. The walls were white like everything else in the building, but the ceiling was velvety black. Looking closer, I could see it was a projection of the night sky with infinite silvery stars. It could have been beautiful, but there was an unnerving rhythmic, Christmas-light quality to the twinkling stars and a weird stillness to the dank basement air.

I glanced at Godfrey, but his expression had gone empty. Logan's wary eyes were darting around the atrium.

We passed a dark room that was empty except for a metal exam table. Leather restraints hung from the sides, and I shivered, imagining Amory bound to the table. *What were they doing to him?*

I could hear voices. And strange music.

Heart pounding, I moved forward — toward the source of the noise — but Greyson grabbed my arm. He shook his head once almost imperceptibly, but I jerked out of his grip. Across the open atrium, I could see another room off to the side. The door was open. Every once in a while, a bright light would flash. I heard a scream, and my heart seized in my chest before I realized it was the canned sound of a recording. Someone was watching a movie.

I walked through the open doorway into the dark room and instantly wished I hadn't.

Enemy Inside

On screen, a man had a woman by her hair. He was pummeling her skull with a hammer, spewing blood everywhere. Her piercing screams filled the room, and I realized it wasn't a movie; the film had a shaky amateur quality. The screaming woman disappeared. She was replaced by a man with a black canvas bag over his head. He was sitting in a dark room with his hands bound behind his back. The camera shook. Another man appeared to the side with a gun and shot three times, four times —

I tore my eyes away from the screen, willing my ears to shut out the sound of gunshots. Then a crisp voice began to narrate over the violent picture.

Such a dangerous world requires a new generation of soldiers . . . a force for good to keep ordinary citizens safe from evildoers . . . safe from the violence of rebellion and the abominations created by the modern age.

An artificially grainy image of a carrier appeared, doctored to look extra frightening and menacing.

The Private Military Company of the United States is always working to protect and serve . . . Order. Compliance. Progress. This is our credo. Go forth and do your duty, citizen. Your country needs you.

Without warning, the screen flickered to silver, and the same voice from the elevators rang out.

End of simulation.

Then the screen went black.

I looked around the room. There were ten rows of white chairs lined up facing the screen, but only one of them was occupied.

Sitting there staring up at the screen was Amory. I could only see half of his face, which looked blank — emotionless. He was wearing a white T-shirt and cotton pants that looked like scrubs. He sat up in his chair straighter than I remembered, but otherwise he looked exactly the same.

"I don't need an adjustment, so you can come back later," said Amory. His voice was clipped, cold.

I stood there frozen, unsure what to do.

Amory sighed, twisting in the chair. "Why don't you —" He stopped short, staring at me as if he had seen a ghost.

He stood up abruptly, and my body tensed, preparing to run or fight if he was so far gone that he did not remember who I was. But then he did something I had not expected.

Navigating around the chairs, Amory crossed the room and threw his arms around me.

"Haven," he whispered into my neck, crushing me against him.

Everything about Amory came crashing back: his wonderful woodsy smell, the feel of his warm muscles through his shirt. Somehow, he was exactly as he had been. I tightened my arms around him.

"Wait —" Amory pulled away slightly, a look of confusion knitting his brows together. "Why are you here?"

He seemed to be working to piece something together, as though it had been years — not weeks — since we'd last seen each other.

"I —"

"Break it up, you two," Godfrey grumbled behind me. "Could be cameras."

We broke apart, and I looked up into his face. His gray eyes looked tired, but that fierceness was still there. His chiseled cheekbones looked a little more gaunt, but it was nothing a few days of good food couldn't fix. He was alive.

Then his arm fell into my peripheral vision, and I stifled a gasp. All up his forearm, crossing over the jagged scar from his CID, were twenty HALLO tag burns lined up in a row

Enemy Inside

like tally marks. The tender raised flesh looked painful, irritated. He had to have been tortured at least five separate times.

"What have they been *doing* to you?" I whispered in disgust.

Darkness flickered in his eyes. "They didn't break me right away." He swallowed, a muscle in his jaw flexing. "I fought it. Haven, I tried, but —"

Godfrey's voice cut him off. "We need to get the hell out of here."

I turned around. Greyson was watching Amory with apprehension, but Logan's eyes were swimming with tears. She looked as though she wanted to throw her arms around him, but she restrained herself in case we were being watched.

Amory and I followed them out of the room into the main atrium. Looking up again at the artificial sky, I felt the hairs stand up on the back of my neck. Something about the perfect constellations was unnerving. Like everything else the PMC created, it was just an illusion.

What made me the most nervous was that no one was guarding Amory. There was a rover mounted above the entryway to the atrium, but there was no sign of PMC officers anywhere. In fact, there was no sign of any other test subjects, either. There were more dark rooms branching off the atrium, but I was too terrified to investigate further. Even if we found other people, it would be too risky to take anyone else out with us.

As we exited the atrium and started down the long corridor to the elevator, I turned around to ask Amory about the guards. He wasn't behind me.

Amory was standing just inside the atrium, looking out at us with mournful eyes.

Enemy Inside

"Come on," I hissed. "We have to go."

He shook his head slowly, looking confused again. "I don't think I can."

Logan rolled her eyes. "What do you mean? Of course you can."

"No," he said, shaking his head slowly. "I've tried to come through here before. It's like there's an electric fence."

I backtracked until we were only a few inches apart and placed a hand on his chest. "Just run through really fast. Don't focus on the pain. Focus on me." I locked my eyes on his. "We're getting you out of here."

He nodded and took several paces back. I stood and waited as he let out a long burst of air and gritted his teeth, bracing himself.

Amory lurched forward like a sprinter exploding off his blocks, running toward the threshold. His face instantly contorted in pain, and he staggered off to the side as though he'd run into an invisible wall. He looked wounded but undeterred.

Keeping his eyes on me, Amory took a step forward but pulled back instantly as if he had been burned. He tried again, this time more slowly, his face turning ashen as he tried to walk out.

He stopped, panting. "I don't know what's wrong with me. I can't explain it. Every time I try to —"

Again, he moved forward, face screwed up in pain. He stopped, clutching his head as though he were physically hurting.

Godfrey sighed. "They've implanted a new CID. That's why he's a test subject here. They're experimenting with controlling people's behavior. Whenever he's in range of a rover, his CID emits a signal to keep him in bounds. When he tries to leave, it causes him pain."

"What?" Greyson looked aghast. "But how can they —"

"The behavior modification with the old CIDs never worked, but for a long time I suspected the PMC was trying to get it right."

"How do we get him out?" I asked.

Godfrey sighed. "He has to walk out. Only way. If we try to remove him by force, he could turn on us. We don't know what they've conditioned him to do in response to pain."

Amory shook his head. "I can't."

My heart was starting to beat more frantically. "Amory, just turn it off. The pain is all in your head. They're just trying to control you."

He looked scared. "They do control me," he said in barely a whisper.

"Just try." I was trying to keep my voice calm, but I could feel the panic welling up inside.

"You don't understand. I physically *can't.*"

"Yes, you can," I said fiercely, fighting to keep my voice steady.

Logan shook her head but didn't speak.

"I'm sorry," said Godfrey in a low voice. "If he won't go, we can't take him with us."

It took several beats for his words to sink in. *They wanted to leave Amory behind.* He was healthy and beautiful and alive, but they wanted to walk away and leave him in this horrible place to be controlled by the PMC.

"No!" I snapped. "We can't . . . I won't leave him here."

Tears were streaming freely down Logan's face now. "Haven, we said —"

"I said I could do what needed to be done. We *need* to get him out of here!"

I stared at Amory, who looked utterly helpless. That familiar resolve was gone from his eyes. They looked dark and far away.

"Why is he like this?"

"They've been conditioning him," said Godfrey with distaste. "Pain, the simulations, probably drugs to distort reality. They've been breaking him down. He's been here a long time."

I turned away, trying to keep a hold on the runaway panic filling me up. "I'm getting him out of here. You three can leave, but I won't unless he's coming with us."

I could see Greyson watching me closely. Perhaps he was remembering what it was like to be the PMC's prisoner — to be on the inside not knowing what would become of you or if anyone was trying to get you out.

"I'll help you," Greyson said. I met his gaze, and I wanted to hug him. Greyson was back, and it was us against everything else once again.

"Haven." Amory was looking at me as though he was trying to break bad news. "I can't walk out. You need to leave."

But my determination had already taken over. "If you can't walk, I'll drag you myself."

"I don't know what I'll do. I could hurt you."

"You won't." I was already back in the atrium, and Greyson appeared on Amory's left side. Gripping Amory by the upper arms, we pulled him forward toward the threshold. He dug in his heels like an ox, but Greyson helped me heave him through the doorway.

Amory yelled out in pain, and I saw beads of sweat

glistening on his forehead. He was out of the atrium, but the pain had not stopped. If anything, it seemed to have gotten worse.

"Come on," I said, threading an arm under his shoulders and pulling him forward. He dragged his feet, and I pushed against him. His face was screwed up in agony, and his bright eyes had disappeared into the creases of his face.

He yelled again, but Greyson clapped a hand over his mouth. I heard a sound like knuckles cracking, and Greyson swore under his breath.

"He bit me!"

Thinking fast, I undid the cloth belt of my uniform and tied it around Amory's mouth.

"Sorry," I whispered, but he did not seem to hear me. He was clutching his head, his knuckles white as though he was trying to split his skull in two. He groaned into the fabric around his mouth, but Greyson continued yanking him forward.

Then Amory did something I had not expected. He swung out a fist, almost connecting with Greyson's jaw, but he was too slow. He wailed through the fabric, lashing out again, but I dug my fingernails into his arm to hold him back. He jerked out of my grip, lunging toward me instead, but the pain was making him weak. Greyson yanked him back, shoving him down the corridor.

Amory looked back over his shoulder, and the look in his eyes pierced my heart like a dull blade — the look of a cornered animal about to die. I averted my eyes and took his other arm, focusing instead on inching him forward. Greyson and I were getting him out of here.

It was slow progress down the passage leading away from the atrium. Godfrey's eyes were darting all around, searching for hidden cameras. It was against his better judgment that he stayed.

When we made it halfway down the hallway, Amory collapsed onto one knee, his face red and his shoulders shaking. Tears were streaming silently down Logan's face. She could not look at him writhing in agony, and for the first time since we'd met, I was angry with her — angry that she wanted to leave Amory. She was weak — too weak to do what had to be done. She would rather have let Amory rot down here as the PMC's guinea pig than watch him suffer like this.

But after a few horrible moments, I almost had to agree. As we rounded the corner, Amory's pain seemed to escalate. The fight went out of him, but it wasn't because the pain was subsiding. He was giving up. I saw tears in the corners of his eyes, and his yells through the cloth were desperate, pleading. We had broken him.

"It's not too much farther," I said. My voice hitched, but I would not let the tears come. If I gave up, there would be no one left to fight for him.

"We have to get him out of the building and hope that takes him out of range," said Godfrey.

Amory was doubled over now. Greyson and I were half dragging, half carrying him down the hallway. His whole body was shaking, and he yanked down the gag.

"Please," he whispered. "Please don't, Haven. Leave me, please."

He broke off, falling to his knees and retching on the floor. I bit back my tears.

"Just a little farther," I said, trying to pull him up. My voice hitched. "I'm sorry. We're almost there."

Greyson heaved Amory's arm over his shoulder and dragged him the few yards to the elevator. I saw the rover quivering, searching for CIDs.

Enemy Inside

"Get him out of the way," said Godfrey.

Reluctantly, Greyson pulled Amory back a step.

The rover settled on Godfrey, Logan, and Greyson, and the elevator doors swung open.

Godfrey raised his rifle and shot at the rover once. The black dome shattered. "Get in. Quick."

Greyson and I dragged Amory into the elevator, and Godfrey punched the button for the parking structure.

"I don't know if we are going to be able to get out," he said. "Any time a rover goes down, the officers all throughout the city are alerted. It's the middle of the night, so that buys us some time, but —"

I wasn't listening; I was too busy holding on to Amory. He was doubled over in pain, dry heaving, his face wet with tears. My heart tore in two, and I worried whether he would be all right. What if the pain was too much and it killed him? The farther we got from the room, the more it seemed to amplify.

As the elevator dinged, Amory yelled out. He crumbled onto the floor, and I lost my hold on him. He collapsed onto his hands and knees, gasping for air.

"We have to get him out," whimpered Logan.

The doors to the elevator flew open, and my stomach dropped. Four PMC officers stood blocking our exit, their helmets glinting in the artificial light.

"What is going on here?"

Logan and Godfrey fired. The officers looked surprised, and then two collapsed onto the ground. One officer shot at me, barely missing my left ear, but Godfrey landed a bullet in her chest. Greyson looked stunned. He was holding my rifle as well, and I realized at some point in the struggle with Amory I had handed mine off.

Enemy Inside

Logan dropped the last officer, and Godfrey stepped out of the elevator into the small room off the parking structure. The glass door slid open, and he jumped out to secure the dimly lit garage, rifle raised.

"Hurry. There will be more."

Amory was still writhing in pain, seemingly unaware of the four dying PMC officers outside the elevator.

I tried to pull him to his feet, but either he had finally succumbed to the pain, or it had intensified once again. I grasped him under the shoulders, trying to move him, but he was too heavy.

Greyson appeared at my elbow with both guns slung over his shoulder and yanked Amory to his feet. He was much stronger than I remembered.

As we pulled Amory toward the car, he let out another yell of pain. I wanted to curl up inside myself and die. His suffering was almost too much to bear.

"Get the stuff out of the truck," Godfrey barked at Logan. "We have to switch vehicles."

Godfrey grabbed his rucksack and turned to the PMC cruiser next to ours. It was unlocked.

Greyson helped me push Amory into the backseat, but as soon as he was inside, he began clawing at the door, trying to get out. I slid in behind him, pulling him against me, and Greyson followed.

Logan threw our bags into the cargo area and then climbed into the front seat, looking ashen.

Godfrey pressed the ignition button on the dashboard, and the engine hummed to life. One of the perks of top security clearance seemed to be an all-access pass in Sector X. He peeled out of the parking spot and flew toward the ramp.

"If they warned the others, we won't be able to get past the checkpoint," he said. "Haven, take him and go through the tunnel. If you can't, hide out at the safe house. If we're not back in three days . . . you'll have to figure it out."

My stomach lurched. I'd forgotten about this part. *What if Amory still wasn't himself when we left the building?* We couldn't get past the PMC with him like this. We wouldn't make it out of the city.

As we approached the exit, Amory began to shake uncontrollably in the backseat. He yelled, and it reverberated inside the small space. I wondered at what point the pain would become too much for him.

We entered the main exit ramp, and I grasped his sweaty hand. It was now or never. It had to stop.

Godfrey seemed to be thinking the same thing. He floored it. We'd only made it halfway to the exit when a horrible screeching alarm sounded. An urgent feminine voice echoed through the tunnel.

Intruder. Intruder. Intruder.

I could see the sliding glass door up ahead. Amory was flailing next to me on the seat. I looked at Greyson in horror.

At the speed we were approaching, the door should have opened by now. Godfrey wasn't slowing down.

As we crashed through the door, the shattering of glass drowned out the screech of the alarm, but it wasn't enough to cover Amory's horrible scream.

I looked down at him. He had gone limp against the door. He was unconscious.

For several seconds, all I could hear was the purr of the engine and the heavy breathing of Logan and Greyson. They sat bolt upright, frozen in shock.

"Well, they know we're here now," Godfrey mumbled.

I checked Amory again, confusion and fear welling up inside me. He wasn't moving.

"Is he —" Greyson asked, unable to finish.

I shook my head, tears clouding my vision. But truthfully, I did not know.

Terrified, I bent my head to his face, listening for the sound of his breathing.

Without warning, he gasped in sharply. His eyes flew open, and his hand went to his chest. My heart stuttered, and I held on to him as he took several labored breaths. He lay there for a moment, shell-shocked.

Logan let out a quiet sob, putting her hand over her mouth.

Godfrey sighed audibly.

Amory turned his head, eyes focusing on me.

"Are you okay?" I whispered.

He breathed out slowly. "I am now, I think."

I sighed, gripping his hand tightly. He managed a weak squeeze in return.

"Holy shit," said Greyson. "What the hell happened to you in there?"

I shot him a look. He hadn't seen what was on that screen. He didn't know what the PMC had been using to brainwash him.

But Amory's sharp eyes flickered, uncharacteristically uncertain. "I . . . I don't really remember," he faltered. "I remember . . . the simulations. Carriers . . ."

I exchanged a look with Greyson.

"How long was I there for?"

"Three weeks," I said.

"Oh, wow." He shook his head. "The bridge, my dad . . . They took me to another place. It was a hospital. That's the last thing I remember before . . . wherever I was."

"His CID," I said, grabbing his arm.

"Fucking hell," said Godfrey.

I turned Amory's arm over, searching for another incision near his old, jagged scar.

"They wouldn't insert it there again," said Godfrey. He was watching me in the rearview mirror. "Not after he cut out the last one. I don't know if we'll be able to extract the new one. They're much more . . . sophisticated."

"What about the rovers?" I asked.

"Doing my best to avoid them."

I looked around. Sure enough, we were driving down a dark side street. Before we reached the intersection, Godfrey made a sharp turn down an alley and pulled out onto another street.

"If any of those gets a reading on him, there's a chance they could activate whatever that was again."

"Is that new?" Greyson asked. "Or can all the CIDs do that?"

Godfrey shook his head. "I've known for a while that they were experimenting with behavior control, but if they're still testing it on Amory, that means they're working out the bugs. If they were near the final stages of development, there would be a hundred test subjects walking around with those things."

"They were controlling me?" Amory asked. His face had gone ashen.

I met his gaze, uncertain what to say. I didn't want to

Enemy Inside

voice aloud my concern that he had been brainwashed. But if he didn't remember anything, maybe none of the PMC's experiments worked.

"We don't know for sure," I said.

"How are we going to get his CID out?" Greyson asked. "He can't be walking around with that thing."

"Stay out of range until we get out of the city," said Godfrey. "We'll have to see if anyone on the outside knows how to remove those."

"Where are we going?" asked Logan.

Godfrey didn't answer. Looking up ahead, I could see why.

At the end of the road was a PMC blockade. Lights flashed all around, illuminating the ruined buildings and casting dark shadows over the wreckage.

"This is your stop, kid," said Godfrey.

"How are you going to get out?" I asked.

"Don't worry about us. You're going to have your work cut out for you. If you make it through the tunnel, rendezvous past the bridge where you came ashore after the riots. If not, go to the safe house."

I nodded.

Godfrey looked serious. "Don't forget: three days. If we're not back by then . . ."

I glanced at Logan, who was biting her lip.

He waved a dismissive hand. "We'll be back. Just keep him away from the rovers," he said, nodding at Amory.

I smiled. "Thanks, Godfrey."

I turned, and Greyson grabbed me roughly and pulled me into a hug. I let the warmth and comforting familiarity of him wash over me and tried not to think that it could be the last time I would see him.

"Don't get caught," I whispered into his jacket. "I just got you back."

He nodded, his chin bouncing on my shoulder. Pulling away, I exchanged a look with Logan: *Take care of him.*

Greyson rummaged in his rucksack and pulled out an extra jacket. He tossed it to Amory, who was still wearing his thin white scrubs.

"You'll need this," he said.

Amory took it and forced his arms clumsily into the sleeves. "Thanks."

Nodding at Godfrey, I grabbed my rifle and opened the car door. Amory emerged slowly, rubbing the back of his neck and still in a daze from his episode. Strapping the gun over my shoulder, I grabbed his arm and pulled him into the cascading pile of rubble between two demolished buildings. The truck pulled away toward the flashing lights, and I forced myself not to watch them go.

Chapter Five

"Where are we going?" asked Amory. He was still very pale, but it was encouraging that he was aware enough to inquire about our plan.

"We can't go through the main checkpoint with the others, so we're going to try to get through one of the old tunnels."

He shook his head in disapproval. "You should have gone with them. *You* could have gone through the checkpoint."

"I'm not going to leave you on your own."

I squeezed my eyes shut, visualizing the route we needed to take to the old tunnel. Squinting through the darkness, I could see a street sign still standing at the end of the collapsed block. I recognized the name. We were on the right track.

Grabbing Amory's hand, I pulled him along through the alleyway, picking my way between chunks of blasted concrete and ribbons of twisted steel. He gripped my hand tightly, and I felt a tingle of warmth spread from my fingertips up my arm. Nothing could change the way he made me feel.

As we reached the corner, I stepped out into the street and looked around to check for rovers. I didn't see any. If we stuck to side streets, it might be possible to avoid them altogether. We moved cautiously down the block, ears

Enemy Inside

piqued for any sound that we were being followed and scanning the shadowed street corners for hidden rovers.

"So, you really don't remember anything except the simulations?" I whispered.

Amory didn't answer right away.

His pained expression made me wish instantly I hadn't said anything.

When he spoke, his words came slowly. "I mean, I remember the adjustments," he said.

I didn't ask what "adjustments" were.

"They made me take a pill. I didn't like it. I remember trying to leave . . . the pain. It was awful because the way that . . . that *thing* made me feel, I would rather have stayed than fight it."

"I'm sorry."

"No. *I'm* sorry. I could have hurt you."

"You didn't."

"I would have if Greyson hadn't been there," he muttered. His voice was bitter, steeped in self-loathing.

We fell silent, and I began to feel slightly awkward. We weren't touching anymore, and I wondered if maybe things *had* changed between us. Something was off about the way he spoke. His voice was stiff and formal.

"You had to know I would come get you out," I said. "You had to know I would try."

He gave me an odd sideways look. "I kind of hoped you wouldn't. When they took me, I really hoped you would just . . . leave it alone."

"What?"

I grabbed his arm, jerking him around to face me. When

our eyes met, there was a look of frustration there. "You should have left me, Haven."

His words felt like a slap. After I had risked everything and persuaded Godfrey and Greyson and Logan to put their lives in danger, he would have preferred me to leave him with the PMC.

Things definitely *had* changed.

Out of the corner of my eye, I saw him watching me, but I avoided his gaze. He seemed confused. That was nothing compared to how I felt.

Hot tears stinging in my eyes, I wiped them away with the scratchy sleeve of my PMC uniform.

It didn't make sense. After everything on the farm and his kiss on the hill, I knew Amory had feelings for me. But that was before he was captured. Now he probably resented me for those weeks of imprisonment and torture. After all, it was my fault we were in Sector X that day to begin with. Or maybe he just wasn't capable of feeling that way after everything he'd been through.

I couldn't blame him.

I fixed my eyes on the street, blinking back tears and forcing myself to concentrate instead of forming a response that would make it hurt even more.

As we made our way along the street Godfrey had marked on the map, I knew we had to be getting close. We'd been walking for over an hour, cutting through crumbled alleyways, and I was starting to get cold. The adrenaline had worn off, and now I could feel the frigid wind biting through the fabric of the PMC uniform.

I knew Amory had to be cold, too — he was wearing thin cotton pants and Greyson's light jacket — but I wouldn't look at him. After the initial shock of his comment, I felt only sadness and humiliation. It was foolish, given our situation, to be worried about the way Amory felt about me, but it was more than that. Maybe his time in Isador had fundamentally changed him.

We passed more demolished streets lined with crushed cars, trash, and rubble. It was hard to believe what it had once looked like. The damage was so severe that it was impossible to tell where one building ended and the other began.

Finally, the destruction gave way to a small, crumbling road leading to the highway. There were no working streetlights, and the guardrails were warped and rusted from years of neglect. We were getting close. My limbs thrummed with the anticipation of freedom. Once we got out of Sector X, everything would be fine. At least that was what I told myself to keep my feet moving.

We followed the road to a derelict overpass covered in a washed-out rainbow of graffiti. This was the point on the map Godfrey had marked. I squinted, searching frantically for the tunnel.

Between the darkness and my fatigue, I thought my eyes were playing tricks on me. There was not a tunnel, but rather a solid wall half-hidden behind a thicket of overgrown tree branches. Upon closer inspection, I saw that the crumbling stone entrance to the tunnel was sealed with bricks.

My heart sank. We stood there, taking it all in, and I felt the prickle of tears in my throat once again.

How could Godfrey have sent us here? How could he have made such a huge mistake? The faded neon profanities told me the tunnel had been sealed long before the PMC evacuated Manhattan. It had been our only option for escape.

The Sector X Expressway was destroyed in the riots, and now the only way in or out of the city was through the main bridge. We were trapped here.

Enemy Inside

The scream of a siren broke through my misery. I looked up to see a PMC cruiser on the overpass. Whoever was inside had spotted us. They knew I had helped Amory escape.

"Run!" I yelled.

We tore back through the demolished alley the way we came, crisscrossing through the streets. I quickly lost track of where we were. All I could think was to make it as difficult as possible for them to find us.

I could still hear the siren, and I was reminded of running from the PMC with Greyson.

I forced my mind elsewhere. It couldn't be like that again. I was stronger now — smarter. I wouldn't let them take Amory.

Snow was beginning to fall, and it stuck to my face and eyelashes. I blinked away the heavy flakes, not feeling the cold anymore.

It was difficult to tell where the PMC cruiser was. I could still hear the wail of the siren, but the sound reverberated off the rubble and sounded strangely far away.

Stumbling across the street, I glanced over my shoulder for Amory, but he was frozen on the corner, staring upward. I followed his gaze to a burnt-out stoplight. Mounted on top, its beady black dome swiveling onto Amory, was an ID rover.

Amory fell to his knees in the snow, holding his head in his hands and trying to stifle his cries of pain. I ran over to him. Panic pounded through my veins, clouding my judgment.

His face was screwed up with pain again, but this time, the pain seemed to have progressed more quickly. Learning of his escape, the PMC had increased the intensity of the signal.

Enemy Inside

"Amory," I whimpered. "Get up. You have to move. If we get you out of range, the pain will stop."

Folding in on himself, Amory hid his face in his hands. I knew he didn't want me to see the tears there. He was rocking back and forth, shaking and struggling for air as if he were having an asthma attack.

Along the back of his neck, an angry red patch like a burn mark had appeared.

Summoning every ounce of strength I had, I grasped him beneath the shoulders and pulled him to his feet. His legs were shaky, so I wrapped an arm around his waist and dragged him. I tried pulling him across the street away from the rover, but he yelled and swung back at me, and I knew there must be another in range. I changed direction down the street. He was struggling in earnest now, but we couldn't go back.

I could hear the sirens approaching. They were definitely closer now. I felt trapped — unable to move in any direction without causing Amory more pain. He was fully doubled over, clutching his head between his hands.

There was only one way to go: through the range of the ID rover.

Praying there weren't any more rovers on the other side, I pulled Amory through the snow. He was resisting, dragging his heels as I yanked him toward the source of the frequency, and I had to summon all my strength to fight against him. My back screamed in agony, and my arms ached from holding him up, but I knew if I released him, he would collapse.

I stumbled, and his wet cheek brushed against mine.

No. They would not get us.

Amory made a choking sound as we crossed under the rover, and I kept my eyes straight forward. I couldn't look at

Enemy Inside

the pain on his face. He dry heaved again, and his muscles twitched. For a horrible moment, I thought he was having a seizure, but I did not stop.

The sirens were blaring now. There was no time.

I squinted desperately to the next intersection, but I couldn't tell if there was another rover. As I pulled Amory along, his cries of pain grew farther apart, but he was still shaking and unsteady as we plowed through the fresh dusting of snow. With the weight of Amory, the strap of my rifle cut into my shoulder painfully. It was useless now; I could not shoot and hold him.

Looking over my shoulder, I could see the lights from the PMC cruiser bouncing off the building behind us. They would turn the corner soon. We could not outrun them.

Amory's head went limp, and then his entire body collapsed. I staggered, bent double under the sudden dead weight.

He had passed out.

Legs shaking, I struggled to keep him upright, but I was fighting a losing battle. He was much too heavy.

Gasping for air, I stumbled into the shadows with him. There were no buildings for us to hide in — only great heaps of rubble and ash and splintered wood. It was our only option left, and I could not carry him anymore.

As gently as I could, I dropped Amory into the snow. He fell limp into a pile of crumbled brick and insulation. I looked around desperately for something — anything — to cover us. I spotted a ripped piece of cardboard. It was wet with snow, but it was big. I threw myself down on the ground and curled up around Amory, pulling the piece of cardboard over our heads and rolling us into the rubble.

The sirens were deafening now. They shattered the peace of the snow and the darkness as the cruiser came barreling down the street. I knew my boots were exposed, but the part of my pant leg that showed blended in with the snow. I held still, breathing loudly into Amory's chest.

The cruiser slowed to a crawl, and I could feel the officers' eyes scraping the shadows, looking for a flash of white — anything to betray our location. The tires crunched loudly through the snow, and I tried to quiet my labored breathing. Surely it was loud enough for every PMC officer in the vicinity to hear.

But the cruiser moved on, and the sound of the siren faded into the destroyed buildings. I lay still, not daring to move. There were probably others. Now that they knew whom Amory had escaped with, every PMC officer in the city would have my picture from the cameras at Isador.

My rifle was cutting into my back. I rolled over, and Amory gasped, his chest heaving against my cheek. He thrashed around under the sheet of cardboard, muscles tensed, but I pulled him tightly against me.

"Shhh."

"What's going on?" Amory's voice was panicked, and I felt a twinge of guilt that he had to wake up this way. After his time with the PMC, I knew it must be terrifying.

"Lie still," I whispered.

"Are they gone?"

"Yeah. But there could be others."

Amory's thin T-shirt was damp with cold sweat, his chest rising and falling rapidly, and I was suddenly very aware that every part of my body was pressed against his. I felt the heat rising up my face and was grateful he could not see.

After a while, I couldn't hear the sirens anymore. The night was completely still.

Cautiously, I lifted the cardboard off my head and peered

around. Nothing.

I sat up and pushed the bits of rubble off us. Amory pulled himself into a seated position. He was shivering.

"Come on," I said. "We have to get to the safe house."

I visualized Godfrey's map. I knew we were still several blocks away. I didn't want to cut across the main roads and risk another rover, so we made our way slowly around the perimeter of our route until I found the street we were supposed to take.

Amory was silent as we traipsed through the snow. I worried his last episode had taken a toll on him, but I didn't want to ask. Running from the PMC, it was easy to forget that he resented me for breaking him out and making him a fugitive again. But now that it was quiet, the distance between us seemed to grow.

Sneaking a glance in his direction, I could see he was shaking from the cold, and his lips were turning blue. He had his hands tucked inside Greyson's thin jacket.

"We're getting close," I muttered.

He nodded but did not look at me.

The trip back in the direction we came seemed twice as long as the journey to the tunnel. Then, I had felt relieved that Amory was all right and hopeful that we would escape Sector X. Now, we had no prospect of leaving, and it was becoming very clear that Amory was *not* all right.

I knew we were almost to the safe house when buildings began to rise from the rubble. I should have felt reassured to have more cover from the eyes of patrolling PMC officers, but instead, the rising apartments and offices made me feel boxed in and trapped like a wild animal. Any escaped carriers that had survived the riots could be hiding in the shadows. My hands were freezing where they gripped the cold metal of my rifle, but I was on high alert and ready to shoot

Enemy Inside

anyone or anything that posed a threat.

Walking the streets, it was easier to see the remnants of what had been Manhattan. We passed an abandoned newsstand, a market, a cleaners, and several restaurants. The buildings here were older, but the scars of a more recent evacuation were fresh. Parked cars stood collecting snow, trash bins overflowed, and boxes of belongings people couldn't take with them were piled in the alleyways.

Finally, we reached the block Godfrey had marked on the map. Remembering the address, I squinted up through the darkness for a building number. We counted down the block, and when we reached the building with the correct address, I knew instantly that we were in the right place. Stenciled onto the brick with black spray paint was a lion just like the one that marked Uprising Pub.

The building was boxy and nondescript, sandwiched between a police station and another abandoned apartment building. Fire escapes snaked up its flat face of brown brick, and all the windows were dark.

I tried the door, but it was locked.

"Did he give you a key?" Amory asked.

I shook my head.

"How are we supposed to get inside?"

I didn't know. I racked my brain, trying to remember if he had given me any special instructions. He probably expected me to figure it out, but I was cold and exhausted, and I felt as though I might collapse.

Amory's eyes drifted up toward the fire escape. "Do you think . . .?"

"It's worth a try."

The ladder hung over my head several feet out of reach.

Enemy Inside

"Here," said Amory. He crouched down in the snow, and it took me a moment to realize what he was suggesting.

I breathed out slowly and swung a leg over his shoulder. He held out a hand, and I took it for balance as I sat on his shoulders and swung my other leg over. Gripping my thighs, he stood up easily. I wobbled, clutching his upper arms for balance.

"Don't drop me."

"I won't."

My heart was thudding. It felt strange to be sitting on his shoulders like a child, but he managed it as if I weighed nothing. I didn't trust myself not to lose my balance, but Amory had a strong hold on me, and I trusted him. I reached up and grasped the ladder, the metal creaking in protest as I yanked it down.

I felt Amory move beneath me. He sank to one knee and held out his arm to help me off his shoulders. Without looking at his face, I clambered off him and climbed up the creaky ladder to the first landing. Amory followed. The fire escape shook slightly, and I noticed that the entire landing was covered in ice.

The window was grimy, but when I pulled up, it slid open easily. Peering through the darkness, a draft of musty air hit my nostrils.

"Don't go in yet," Amory murmured. I jumped. I hadn't realized he was standing so close behind me.

"Why? This is it."

"You don't know what's in there."

"Neither do you," I snapped.

He shrugged off the sting of irritation in my voice and gently pushed past me. Ducking his head under the windowpane, he swung a leg over and stepped inside. As I shivered out on the landing, I watched him move about the dark room.

"Hey!" I hissed. "Take this."

Amory turned, and I handed the rifle through the window. He took it and moved cautiously to the door on the other side of the room. He opened it and, seeing nothing, disappeared down the hallway.

Chapter Six

I felt exposed standing out on the fire escape in my stark white uniform.

Why had I let him go without me?

The seconds ticked by, and I began to panic.

When I couldn't stand it anymore, I ducked in through the window and closed it behind me to shut out the freezing air.

Even inside, I could see my breath, but at least I was out of the wind.

I was standing inside a tiny abandoned studio apartment. The smell of mildew clung to the walls, as if the apartment had been closed up for a long time. It was completely empty except for a bare mattress in the corner, and the peeling wallpaper looked faded and dirty. Across from the bed was a kitchenette with a rusted sink, and next to that was a tiny bathroom with grimy tile.

I knocked the snow off my boots and moved to the open door. The hallway was dark and smelled faintly of stale cigarette smoke.

The apartment we landed in could not be the safe house Godfrey had in mind. We needed food and water, and that unit looked as though nobody had lived there in years. Moving silently from one door to the next, my muscles thrummed with anticipation. I half expected the PMC to jump out at any moment, and I was beginning to wish I had my gun.

Through the darkness, a glimmer of silver caught my eye. I squinted through the dust and shadows, positive I was imagining the tiny bell hanging from the doorknob of one of the units. It blended in perfectly with the dusty bird wreath the previous tenant had left hanging on the door. I remembered the code the rebels used to mark their safe houses: across the street, three doors down.

Filled with a childlike sense of glee, I counted three doors down on the opposite side of the hallway. Sure enough, there was a tiny lion carved into the beat-up wooden door.

As I reached for the knob, the door swung open, nearly knocking me backward off my feet. My heart stuttered violently, and I aimed a hard kick at the door. The person on the other side grunted, stumbling back.

The door creaked to a stop, and I saw a flash of white scrubs. It was Amory.

"I'm sorry!" I whispered, stepping into the room and searching his face for any sign he was hurt.

"Haven?" he spluttered, rubbing the side of his arm where the door had slammed into him. "I told you to hang tight while I checked it out."

"I know! But you took such a long time . . . I was worried."

"So you kicked in a door on me?"

"I didn't know it was you. You surprised me."

He sighed. "Well . . . I think the place is clear. The other units on this floor are locked, but check it out."

Amory stepped back, flipping the light switch.

At first, nothing happened. Then I heard the quiet hum

Enemy Inside

of a generator, and the lights flickered on.

I looked around the room and felt a glimmer of hope. Godfrey had not let us down after all.

The two-bedroom apartment was cramped but luxurious compared to the studio. There was a small living room area with a squishy couch that had seen better days, a banged-up coffee table, and even a rickety bookshelf.

The kitchenette had pallets of canned food and bottled water stacked against one wall and a small wooden table against the other.

Amory and I went from room to room, taking in the comforts of home. The tiny bathroom had clean towels hanging by the shower and a fully stocked medicine cabinet with toothpaste, soap, and first aid supplies. Both bedrooms had stacks of extra blankets and a mishmash of black rebel clothing piled in the closets.

Most of the clothes looked like the sort of garments you might find in the lost and found, and almost all of them were twice as large as what I needed. It didn't matter. Now that we were safe, I couldn't stand to wear the stiff PMC uniform for another minute. I rummaged through the clothes, searching for something that might fit.

Amory wandered back into the kitchen, and I fished out a black T-shirt and a pair of pants that looked about my size. They fit perfectly, and I wondered if they had belonged to Mariah before she became infected and wasted away. The thought made me cringe.

When I emerged from the bedroom, Amory was already standing over the stove, heating a can of chicken soup. Deep in thought, he looked as though preparing the soup took every bit of his concentration, and I noticed for the second time the dark circles under his eyes and the sharpness of his cheekbones.

Enemy Inside

While he stirred the pot, I cracked open the pantry to see what else we could eat. I salvaged a packet of saltine crackers and grabbed two bottles of water from one of the pallets on the floor.

Amory ladled out a steaming bowl of soup for each of us, and we sat down in silence to eat. I brought a hot spoonful to my lips, savoring the warmth that spread from my throat to my fingertips.

I scarfed our feast down quickly and felt the nourishment begin to wear down some of the hard edges of my despair. I thought back to what my grandmother used to say: *Nothing seems as bad once you've had a hot meal.*

But after the initial relief of safety and food had worn off, I felt the awkwardness fall over us once again. Exploring the apartment, it had almost felt as though we were *us* again, but now I remembered that this Amory was not the same person as before.

I washed our dishes in silence, and an intense wave of fatigue hit me. My body ached all over, and I realized I had not slept at all.

"I'm going to lie down," I said.

Amory stood up suddenly, nearly knocking over his chair. "Haven, wait —"

His hand wrapped around my arm, holding me back. I turned. That familiar fire was burning in his eyes, a flickering reminder of the Amory I recognized.

Before I could say or do anything, he pulled me into his arms and kissed me. His lips were soft, tentative. I felt the dam break in my chest, and all the longing came flooding through. I wanted him to kiss me harder. I wanted him to be fine. I wanted everything to be as it was.

It was too painful.

Enemy Inside

As I pulled away, the look of hurt in his eyes was undeniable. Heart pounding, tears threatening to burst in my throat, I gently pulled out of his grasp, crossed to one of the empty bedrooms, and shut the door.

Collapsing on the bed, I let the tears come. They were tears of anger, fear, and grief. The PMC had stolen so much from us. They'd killed my parents, they'd killed Max, and they had broken Amory.

I tried to muffle my sobs in the pillow, but Amory must have heard me.

A moment later, the door creaked open.

He didn't say anything, but I heard him cross the room. The bed shifted as he sat down next to me, and I could hear him breathing.

I felt ridiculous. After everything he had been through — the torture, the behavior modification, and who knew what else — *I* was crying. It was selfish, too. I was crying for what *I* had lost.

His hand brushed my back, tracing small circles into my skin. It felt good, and it hurt. It hurt too much to have him right here when it wasn't the same. I didn't know what he had meant by the kiss, but it wasn't how he had kissed me on the hill that night. It was a thank-you kiss, a pity kiss.

I felt his hand move to my hair, smoothing out the waves, damp from melted snow. My tears had finally stopped, and I turned to look at him.

He was wearing rebel black now instead of the white scrubs.

"Did I do something wrong?"

I shook my head wordlessly, fighting back more tears that threatened to emerge. I hated myself for crying, but I had swallowed down my emotions for the last three weeks, and

Enemy Inside

now they were bubbling up uncontrollably.

"I'm sorry I'm . . . different," he said. "After everything with the PMC . . . I don't know what they did to me in there. And I don't know if I'll ever be right again."

He took a deep breath, his voice shaking a little. "Sorry I kissed you. I understand if you don't want to pick up where we left off. It was stupid for me to assume . . ."

My heart was breaking. *He* thought I didn't want to be with *him* anymore? I sat up.

"No," I whispered. "Of course I do."

"I just don't want you to think things have to be like they were before if you don't want that. I know things have changed. It's a lot to deal with."

"I thought *you* didn't want that anymore."

"Why would —"

"You said . . . you said you wished I wouldn't have come for you. I thought you wanted me to leave you alone."

His eyes widened in shock. "*That's* what you thought?"

I looked away, feeling the heat rise in my face.

"I just meant I didn't want you to put yourself in danger."

"I thought you didn't want *me* anymore . . . after what you'd been through."

"Not *want* you anymore? Haven, you're all I thought about in there." He grasped my hands. "The only thing that kept me going was thinking I had to just get through it all so I could see you again."

"After what they did —"

"That couldn't change the way I feel about you."

My heart wrenched, and the words that had been playing in my head for weeks came pouring out all at once. "I'm so sorry for getting you captured. It's all my fault. If I had just —"

He shook his head. "It's not your fault," he said firmly. "I was the reason the rebels turned on us in the first place. And I would do it all again."

"But Max . . ."

"Max got to be the hero for Logan," he said, and I could hear the lump in his throat as he said Max's name. "She was all he ever wanted, and he got her in the end."

He brushed away the tears suspended on my cheek with the pad of his thumb. His eyes were bright and fierce, even through the darkness, and I knew he was still the same Amory.

"All of us know the risks, Haven. People are going to die. It could be you, it could be me, but that doesn't mean we stop and hide to protect ourselves. That's the cost of fighting the PMC."

We sat there looking at each other for a long moment, unsure how to proceed.

I wanted to give him time to recover, but with our present safety, the two of us together, we both felt the urgency. Leaning forward, I brushed my lips against his to test the waters. With a sharp intake of breath, he returned my kiss with fervor.

It was more incredible than I remembered. So many feelings I had been suppressing came flooding to the surface. He was alive. He was all right. He was *here*.

The moment escalated quickly. We had lost time, and who knew how much we would have. His lips were hot and anxious on mine, his fingers ghosting down my cheek and neck. I shivered.

I ran a hand through his hair, and he groaned softly,

Enemy Inside

pulling me into him. He kissed a trail down my jawline, and my skin burned where he touched it. My breath came faster. Running a hand down his chest, I could feel all the perfect muscles there. My fingers itched to rip off his shirt, but I did not trust myself. With Amory, everything was more intense than I expected.

As if reading my mind and deciding to push the boundaries, Amory rocked me back against the bed. Holding his weight off me with his arms, I could still feel every part of him pressed against me. My skin tingled with longing and anticipation as my fingers sneaked under his shirt, exploring his lower back.

His hips pressed into mine, and I couldn't stand it anymore. I yanked the hem of his shirt up to his shoulders, and he stretched up to pull it over his head. The look of him straddling my hips startled me. His chest, shoulders, and abs were taut and sculpted to perfection. His smooth skin gleamed in the silvery light from the window and begged to be touched. I had only ever seen him this way for the necessity of bandaging his wounds, and my memories couldn't do him justice. The one thing that was different was the row of burns from his time in Isador. They formed a pattern over his arm with the jagged scar from his CID.

I drew in a sharp intake of breath. In this context, he was even more beautiful — and somehow more dangerous. Amory's brow furrowed, almost self-consciously.

He cleared his throat and looked at me sideways. "Do I look . . . different to you?"

I shook my head once, unable to tear my eyes away. "You're perfect."

That was all he needed: validation that the way I felt about him had not changed, that his time in Isador had not diminished him in body or in spirit. He fell against me, and all my senses were thrown into a frenzy.

Enemy Inside

I explored him methodically with my hands, memorizing every detail — his perfect back, broad protective shoulders. My fingers traced the soft skin at his sides, and he tensed. He was ticklish, apparently. I moved on to his chest, feeling my way down his abdomen.

His breathing was shallow against my mouth. His hands were in my hair, cradling my jaw, moving down my side and around the hem of my T-shirt. A ripple of excitement shot down my spine. We were both thinking the same thing: This was incredibly unfair.

I bit his bottom lip, and he tasted my impatience. Needing no further encouragement, his fingers brushed under my shirt and pulled it up to my ribs. Ignoring the ugly bruises from Rulon's men, he slid down against me, kissing his way from my hip bone to my abdomen. I breathed in sharply, shivering, but a fire was burning in my core. He paused.

"Is this okay?"

"Yes," I breathed impatiently.

"I just can't control myself with you."

"Then don't," I whispered.

Needing no further instruction, he pulled my shirt over my head and reached behind my back to undo my bra. Over the thud of my own heart and our heavy breathing, I heard a rattling off in the distance coming from outside.

Amory froze, both of us listening intently. The rattling persisted, the sound of metal on metal coming from the street. Stifling an inward groan, I sat up on my elbows, and Amory lifted himself over my body to pull back the dusty curtain and peer through the grimy window.

"Carriers," he breathed. "There's a whole horde of them out there."

Enemy Inside

"But why?"

He swung himself off me and handed me my shirt. "They must have tracked us here hoping for food."

My stomach lurched. *How could we have been so stupid not to cover our tracks in the snow?* Carriers were not the only ones who could follow them here.

I thought about all the carriers the rebels had set free during the riots. Now that Saint Drogo's had been destroyed, the carriers the PMC didn't kill were on the loose. For a fleeting moment, I felt a surge of pity. Being free in Sector X could hardly be better than being a prisoner. They had nowhere to hide, nowhere to seek shelter from the freezing cold. Almost all the old buildings in Sector X had been destroyed. And we had walked right into the only neighborhood that seemed untouched.

Silently, I pulled my shirt over my head, stuffed my feet into my boots, and scrambled to find a pair for Amory in the pile of dirty, mismatched spares.

"They must be starving," I said.

Sure enough, looking out the window, I could see a few carriers overturning trashcans in the street, pawing desperately through the filth for some scrap of rotten food. But there were at least a dozen outside our window: men and women in late stages of the virus. Most were stage five, with the horrible oozing sores around their mouths and withered skeletal frames.

As we watched, a scuffle broke out. It was a pitiful match between two stage five men whose strength was so depleted they could hardly swing at each other. They were grappling over a smashed Styrofoam container of leftover Chinese food. One of the carriers went down, and another joined the fray. The commotion seemed to rouse the others, who spotted the food and rushed the first victor.

"We have to find another way out," I whispered, unable to tear my eyes away from the scene. "There are too many of them."

Just as I said it, another carrier noticed the fire escape ladder. *Why hadn't we pulled it back up?*

He stared at it for a moment and then hoisted himself clumsily up the shaky rungs. The sound of rattling metal seemed to attract the attention of the others, who watched with mild interest as the carrier climbed up to the landing. Then another made a horrible wailing sound and followed.

My heart pounded in my chest. "They're coming up here. Why are they coming up here?"

Amory drew in a sharp breath. His eyes had gone dark. "They know we're here. If they find us, they'll find food."

He strode out of the bedroom and into the kitchen, where the rifle was lying across the table.

"Where are your extra clips?" he asked.

"With my uniform."

"We're going to need them."

I hesitated. "We can't shoot them, Amory."

He sighed. "I'm sorry. I know you don't like it, but —"

"It's not that. If any PMC officers are patrolling, gunshots will lead them straight here."

His eyebrows knitted together. He knew I was right.

"They must have other weapons here."

We split apart, overturning dresser drawers and rifling through the closets. Finding nothing, I moved to the kitchen. I threw open one cabinet after another, rifling through drawers.

"Here!" shouted Amory.

Enemy Inside

He was standing over a chest in the living room. Inside was an assortment of knives, several handguns, and a dozen grenades. Amory handed me a holster, and I quickly fitted several knives into the belt. My stomach contracted, remembering the last time I had stabbed a carrier. Its flesh was soft and rotten. The thought of it made me feel sick.

As I watched, Amory tucked one of the handguns into his holster. I raised an eyebrow.

"Just in case," he muttered.

Weighing the options of death by carriers or death by PMC officers, I thought maybe the latter would be less painful.

I followed Amory to the door of the apartment. Before opening it, he spun around and grabbed me by the tops of my arms. He kissed me forcefully, and my heart pounded.

I pulled away, placing a hand on his chest to hold him back. "Stop. We're going to be fine."

He shrugged, looking distressed. "Just in case. I want that to be the last thing I think about."

Chapter Seven

Throwing open the door, we stuck our heads out into the hallway. It was silent.

We moved wordlessly back toward the door of the empty apartment we had climbed in to. The only sound I could hear was Amory's careful breathing. Standing outside the door, I drew one of my knives.

In one swift motion, Amory kicked the door in and flew backward.

The room was dark, but I could see several shapes hulking in the shadows. The closest carrier — emaciated, balding, and with loose yellowish skin — turned and blundered toward us into the hallway. Amory backed away, looking satisfied. He wanted to control the fight — draw them out one by one rather than fighting them all in the apartment.

As the carrier stepped into the hall, my breath caught in my chest. I couldn't see his features clearly, but I could smell him: the rotten stench of death and decay. He turned and started toward Amory. I didn't hesitate.

While the carrier's back was turned, I jumped up behind him and plunged my knife into his back, aiming for the heart just as Logan had taught me. The knife sank into the flesh too easily. It was rotten — the consistency of ricotta cheese below the surface. My stomach twisted with disgust.

The carrier screamed, his knees buckling, and I yanked

Enemy Inside

out my knife. He fell forward, blood oozing from the festering flesh and staining the carpet.

Another carrier had emerged from the door, howling like a banshee. Her face was almost consumed by raw red oozing sores, and her eyes were yellow and bloodshot. She had gone bald.

She limped toward me, and I backed away. I raised the knife in my hand, but suddenly Amory's hand wrapped around her throat, slicing her jugular with cool efficiency. Blood gurgled wildly from the wound, and he brought her to her knees with another stab to the back. The carrier slumped forward, but he stabbed her again.

"Amory!"

He turned just in time to stop the carrier emerging from the room behind her. Grabbing another knife, Amory skewered him in the gut from both sides. The carrier lumbered forward, and Amory caught him across the face with a vicious slice.

Two more carriers crowded out of the room behind him, and I ran forward. One came behind Amory, but he didn't seem to notice. He was too focused on delivering another gash with his knife down the first carrier's chest.

What was he doing?

I rushed forward just as the carrier behind Amory wrapped an arm around his neck. With as much force as I could muster, I stabbed the carrier in the back. I had intended a clean wound to the heart, but I had missed. The other carrier was getting closer, and I slashed my knife through the air. It jerked out of reach, backing away from Amory.

The carrier still gripping him screamed. Amory bucked forward, trying to shake him off, but he held on too tightly. As they thrashed around, it was difficult to aim another clean jab with the knife. I couldn't tell if I'd hit his heart, but it was enough for the carrier to loosen his grip and stumble. Amory turned and stabbed the carrier in the gut, twisting his knife and shoving him to the ground. Then his lip curled into a snarl, and he aimed a forceful kick at the carrier's head.

That was when I saw it. Amory's eyes had gone cold and dark. His face was twisted in a hateful scowl, every muscle in his body rigid with a focused, murderous rage.

I was so busy watching Amory that I hadn't noticed another enormous carrier push his way out of the apartment. There seemed to be a never-ending supply of them. Before I could react, he grabbed me around the shoulders, squeezing me like a boa constrictor. I choked, partially from a lack of oxygen, and partly due to the putrid stench that filled my nostrils. The carrier smelled like body odor and rotten fruit.

I bucked forward, trying to throw him off balance, but he held fast. I tried to break the hold as Logan had taught me, but I was shaking with panic and exhaustion.

Amory finally finished with the other two. To my immense relief, he turned and flew toward the carrier holding me. The carrier wailed, and I felt warm blood pouring around my shoulder. He had sliced the carrier's jugular. The carrier's hold on me loosened, but he fell forward, bringing me down with him.

The weight of the carrier — the weight of a fully grown man — smashed me into the ground. I was trapped — pinned beneath a writhing, half-dead monster twice my size. I jerked my head, watching Amory, but he did not help me. He stabbed at the carrier on top of me, and the carrier shuddered against me as the knife entered his heart.

"Help!" I cried, but Amory didn't even glance in my direction. I could feel the carrier's warm blood pouring down my sides, and the smell of him was almost enough to knock me out. The carrier shook, gasping and thrashing on top of me. Horror and dread seeped into my stomach like poison. Amory was going to leave me under this dying carrier. He was so heavy. I couldn't get out from under him.

The carrier's death was not as swift as it should have been. I watched with a detached horror as Amory stabbed another carrier and then another. They kept getting closer, growing in number, but he never seemed to tire. Bodies of the dead and dying piled up around him, but he did not stop or glance in my direction.

The expression on his face was one that I had never seen: cold, ruthless, and vacant. He was a killing machine. He never paused in horror or remorse as one of the carrier's tears ran with the bloody slash across her cheek. Her dying cry was so hauntingly human that I felt myself shaking with dry sobs.

The carrier on top of me was still breathing his last gurgling breaths. Warm blood trickled down my neck and the collar of my shirt. Finally, with a painful quiver, he stopped.

The hallway fell quiet. No more carriers emerged from the apartment. All the bloody bodies on the ground were silent.

The only thing I could hear was the sound of Amory's labored panting. Covered in blood and shaking with fatigue, he looked positively insane. His eyes were still cold — sharp and silver like a predator's. I laid my cheek against the filthy carpet, breathing in the stale smoke, mold, and blood. I wanted to die.

A small gasp made me look up. Amory was still standing there, but he looked wild, suddenly afraid.

Covered in blood, his shirt ripped, he jerked his head from side to side, taking in the dead all around. He gasped again, turning to scan for a nonexistent threat. Then he looked lost.

Enemy Inside

"Haven?"

The sound of my own name made me stir.

"Haven!" He was glancing around wildly. He couldn't see me, and he didn't remember where I was. Or he didn't know . . .

I breathed in heavily, trying to summon my voice.

"I'm here," I said. Those two small words took so much energy.

His head jerked around, eyes locking in on me.

"Oh my god!" He rushed forward, reaching me in three strides.

His eyes were no longer insane; they were swimming with confusion, fear, and shame. In one try, Amory heaved the massive carrier's dead body off me. My lungs expanded instantly as the weight disappeared, and I choked in air.

"Oh god!" Amory muttered. He flipped me over as easily as if I were a rag doll. His eyes raked my face and body, checking for injuries. He shook his head in disbelief. "What happened?"

I couldn't speak. I didn't want to say what had happened. He had turned into an exterminator. He had no humanity — no thoughts other than killing.

Amory scooped me into his arms, but I was shaking all over. Without meaning to, I cringed. A hurt look crossed his face, but he pushed it down. I didn't want to admit it, but I was afraid of him.

He got up, holding me against his chest, and walked back to our apartment. Looking worried, Amory sat me down at the table. He looked as though he wanted to say something, but instead, he just backed silently out of the room to go dispose of the carriers.

Enemy Inside

I sat there for a long time, staring at the faded flowery wallpaper. Something was amiss with the coziness of the room and the stench of death that hung over everything. I realized it was me. The carrier's blood and body odor had leeched into my clothes and skin. The dried blood was beginning to flake around my neck and chest. My shirt was stiff with it.

Finally, I got up and went to the bathroom. I peeled off the ruined shirt and pants and stepped into the shower. The hot water pounded against my skin, and I watched the blood mix with the water. I scrubbed my neck and chest raw. After months of bathing in a frigid creek, it should have been amazing. But every time I looked down, all I could see was blood.

I couldn't think of anything except Amory slaughtering those carriers one by one. It wasn't the killing that bothered me; killing them was unavoidable. It was the vacant look in his eyes. He was so . . . *detached*. Whatever happened in Isador, it had changed something fundamental inside him.

As I got out of the shower and dried myself, I half expected the white towel to come away bloody, but all traces of the carrier had been washed away. I found some more mismatched clothing in the closet and padded out into the living room. Amory was still gone. I knew I should go offer to help him dispose of the bodies, but I wasn't ready to face him yet.

Collapsing onto the sagging couch, I watched the early fringes of sunrise peeking around the blackout curtains over the living room window. It was hard to believe that in one night, we had broken Amory out of Isador, run from the PMC, and killed a dozen carriers. My whole body felt as though it had been beaten, and I was tired of fighting.

Some time later, the front door creaked open. Amory stood in the doorway, looking far worse for the wear than I remembered. His arms and face were covered in dried blood, and several bruises were forming on his face. His shoulders sagged, but not from exhaustion alone. Something about the way he carried himself told me he was also burdened with shame and guilt.

Our eyes met across the room, and he sighed heavily, almost a shrug. He looked lost, but I didn't know what to say.

When he finally spoke, his voice was low and broken. "Something's wrong with me."

I didn't speak. I was at a loss for words.

Then Amory turned. His shirt was ripped, and I saw deep bloody marks forming a crescent pattern across his shoulder. A carrier had bitten him.

"Oh my god. When did that happen?"

Amory glanced down to see what I was referring to. He shook his head. "One of them got me pretty good from behind."

"I need to clean that."

He shrugged. "I've been vaccinated. Besides, that one didn't even have the sores yet."

"It can still get infected."

I went into the bathroom and opened the medicine cabinet to find some antiseptic. Amory removed his shirt and stood still while I swabbed the angry red marks. As I cleaned the bite, I took the opportunity to survey his other injuries. A hand-shaped bruise snaked around his neck, and another was blooming on his jaw.

Running my fingers over the back of his neck, I felt a raised bump under the short hair. I touched it. It didn't feel like a random cut from battle. It was a raised square scar just as my CID mark had been, and it was shiny and tender, almost a burn.

I sucked in a huge burst of air, remembering how the surrounding skin had flared up when Amory had come within range of the rover's frequency.

"I think I just found where they inserted your CID."

Amory's hand clamped around the back of his neck.

"Get it out!"

He reached down to his pile of bloodstained clothing where he had dropped his holster and drew out a small knife.

"Cut it out. Please!" he said, shoving the knife into my hand.

"I can't," I whispered. Holding the knife between my fingers, I wanted to. I wanted to cut out his CID and end the pain — end the PMC's hold on his life. "I don't know if I'll be able to find it. You could bleed out and die before I ever get it out."

"No. They just inserted it there so I wouldn't be able to cut it out myself." Amory jerked around, cupping my hand that held the knife. "Please. Do it, Haven. They made me this way. I don't want to be their puppet anymore."

I stood there, weighing the possibilities. I didn't want to tell him that removing the CID wouldn't solve all his problems. We were nowhere near a rover. The way he slaughtered those carriers was likely the result of weeks of brainwashing, not a signal beamed to his CID. On the other hand, if we couldn't get rid of his CID, it was unlikely we would make it out of Sector X undetected. The George Washington Bridge was the only way out, and it was equipped with over a dozen rovers.

"It's now or never," he said. "We have everything we need: antiseptic, gauze, bandages, good lighting . . ."

My hand shook as I brought my eyes up to meet his gaze.

Enemy Inside

His bright gray eyes were burning with hope, pleading with me.

"All right," I sighed. "Tell me how."

Amory cleaned the kitchen table, prepped all the supplies we would need, and tested the sharpness of every available knife we had until he found the best one.

Before sterilizing it, he showed me the proper technique to make an incision. My hand trembled a little, but he pretended not to notice. I knew he did not want to shake my confidence.

"If it's like the last one, they inserted it directly in the center. This one won't be as deep as yours was because they would hit the skull."

I nodded, feeling the bile rise up in my throat.

"Just stick the tweezers in and feel for something small and solid."

I followed him into the bathroom. He was rummaging in the cabinet. "Can you shave the hair that's covering the scar?"

I nodded, and he handed me a disposable razor.

Amory grinned. "I'm not picky, but a smallish incision would be nice."

Running the tap, I splashed some warm water on the back of his head and positioned the razor at the bottom of his hairline. I pulled it down, and pieces of his dark hair fell away. I wondered how I hadn't noticed how short his hair was at the bottom, as though it had just grown over the scar. It looked a little funny, but now I could see the telltale scar where the PMC had inserted his CID. It was no wider than a quarter of an inch across, and it was perfect, mechanical.

Enemy Inside

Amory ran a hand along the back of his neck, jerking his head to try to see his reflection in the mirror. "Those bastards," he breathed.

We returned to the kitchen, and he produced a bottle of clear liquid from over the sink.

"We have real antiseptic," I said, confused when he handed it to me.

"It's for you."

I threw him a dubious look before putting the bottle to my lips. The smell of alcohol stung my nostrils, but I tipped my head back and took a swig. The fire shot down my throat, warming my insides.

Without warning, Amory pulled me against him and brushed my lips with his. The kiss was warm and inviting, but the moment felt all wrong. I couldn't shake the image of him stabbing the carriers with that possessed look in his eyes. I pulled back.

His face was flushed, and his eyes were hungry.

"I need to focus," I said, managing a weak grin.

Lying down on the kitchen table, Amory watched me pull my hair back into a ponytail and wash my hands. I took my time swabbing the back of his neck with rubbing alcohol, waiting for my heart rate to return to normal. My eyes took a final quick inventory of everything I would need, and I picked up the knife.

Hefting the blade in my hand, I drew an imaginary line over his scar exactly where I would make the incision. I only hesitated for a moment. I remembered Amory writhing on the ground in pain, and the decision solidified in my brain.

I bent over the tender skin of Amory's neck and placed the tip of the blade against flesh. In one smooth motion, I pressed down and drew straight across his scar. A perfect

Enemy Inside

line of red blossomed at the incision, but Amory did not flinch or make a sound. I quickly traded the knife for the tweezers, pressing the prongs together as I slipped them between the folds of skin.

Blood pooled over his neck, and I felt my breath catch in my chest. There was no going back. I moved the tweezers, releasing more blood, but I couldn't feel anything. I pushed them deeper, wincing before Amory sucked in a burst of air through his teeth.

My throat constricted. *Where was it?* Trying to make infinitesimal movements, I searched with the tweezers. I heard Amory's great intake of breath again, and my heart rate increased. I *hated* causing him pain.

More blood trickled down his neck, but I forced myself to refocus. Again, I remembered him writhing on the floor and retching in pain. I could end that.

Finally, I felt the tip of the tweezers graze something solid. It was so hard it could have been bone, but it wasn't. Clumsily, I found the other end of the CID and gripped it. Slowly, carefully, I pulled.

Amory yelled in pain, and I almost dropped the CID in panic. I pulled again, but it was stuck. Amory whimpered, trying to stifle his cry, and I blinked back tears that were threatening to drop.

Just get it out! I thought desperately. I pulled again, and Amory screamed. I felt the CID disconnect with something — perhaps a bit of flesh or bone, and I coaxed it out of the incision.

The CID was covered in blood, barely recognizable. I laid it on the table and returned my attention to the blood gushing from Amory's incision. I pressed a towel to the cut and applied pressure. Amory was breathing heavily, and his skin was damp with sweat.

Enemy Inside

"What do I do now?" I whispered.

"Is it out?" he breathed.

"It's out."

"Just keep doing what you're doing. Hopefully it won't need stitches."

My stomach contracted in revulsion at the idea of suturing his skin back together. I held the towel in place as I waited for our breathing to return to normal. The cut wasn't bleeding as profusely as Amory's head wound during the riots, so I felt comfortable cleaning the incision and bandaging it. When I had finished, he sat up and grabbed the bloody CID.

"This one is a lot smaller than yours was," he said. "It's a miracle you even found it."

"We should destroy that."

He nodded but grabbed my hand instead. "Hey." He waited until I looked him in the eye before continuing. "You did a good job. I've never seen someone that calm on their first try."

"I'm not calm," I said, my voice shaking a little.

"It's okay. I'm fine. You did it."

I nodded and sank down into the chair. I realized I still had his blood on my hands, but I didn't get up to wash them. Amory wandered into the kitchen and rummaged in the cabinets. Watching him curiously, I saw him come back into view holding a cast iron skillet and a roll of tape. He taped the CID to the floor, raised the skilled over his head, and brought it down onto the floor with a heavy *thunk* that resonated in the air. He hit it again and sighed with satisfaction.

As he peeled the tape off the floor and showed me the glistening shards of the broken CID, I felt a huge weight lift off my chest. Amory was no longer on the grid. They couldn't control him, and they couldn't track us down from satellite rovers. We weren't safe yet, but we were no longer risking exposure every second.

I washed my hands and followed Amory into one of the bedrooms, watching him as he sank back onto the bed. He winced slightly when his fresh wound made contact with the pillow, but there was an unmistakable look in his eyes. It was as if he was the old Amory once again; he looked strong, in control, and he was burning with that intensity that made my stomach flip. I wasn't scared of him — I wanted him.

Cautiously, I sank down on the bed. I didn't know what I expected — maybe he wouldn't want me to sleep there. Maybe he would think it was too much too soon. But he grinned and put a hand on my hip, rolling me closer until I was right against his shoulder.

It was very strange that, just hours ago, I had not known if he was alive or dead. Now that he was here in front of me, all I wanted to do was touch him.

We lay back against the pillows that smelled like mothballs, and he cradled me in his arms. I rested my head on his chest, listening to his gentle breathing and drinking in the secure warmth of his arm around me. Even though we were in the heart of Sector X, I felt safer than I ever had at the rebel camp.

"Do you know what bothers me most about Isador?" said Amory. "Besides not knowing what they did to me."

I shook my head, feeling him tense under me.

"My dad didn't even *visit* me. I was his test subject — not his son."

"Maybe you weren't *his* test subject. Maybe bringing you to Isador was the only way for him to save you."

Amory shook his head. "It was *his* experiment. He headed

up the whole initiative."

"I just don't understand what they wanted with you."

"To test the new generation of CIDs." He shuddered. "I had a bad reaction to the behavior modification frequency of the old one, but it didn't feel like this."

"How does it work?"

"I heard my dad talking about it once. The rovers activate your CID, and it sends a signal to your brain. The pain when I was trying to escape *felt* real, but it was all just my brain telling me I was in pain."

"But it burned you."

"What?"

"When you were within range of the rover, it looked like it was burning you from the inside."

"They probably had it turned up to the maximum setting. I'm surprised that didn't fry it."

"It would have killed you first."

He sighed angrily. "I hate that you had to see me like that."

"It wasn't your fault . . . it wasn't even you."

"But it *was* me. And it was me who didn't see you with that carrier. I could have killed you."

"No, you couldn't."

For a long moment, Amory didn't answer. I sat up and turned my head to face him in the darkness.

"I still trust you with my life. The PMC can't change that."

He let out a long intake of breath and cupped the back of my head in his hand, bringing my face down to meet his lips.

Enemy Inside

I snuggled deeper into the crook of his arm, not wanting any of the rest of it to be real. Just him. I didn't even have time to marvel at his warmth, the smell of him, or the way my heart was pounding through my chest against his ribcage.

For the first time in a long time, I felt safe. Amory was himself again, and we were together. We had survived the worst.

Chapter Eight

I woke with a start, unable to breathe.

A hand tightened around my mouth. Disoriented, I bit down reflexively, trying to scream, but the sound was muffled by the hand.

Terror — pure terror — clamped down on my chest. I thrashed on the bed, and Amory awoke with a yell. I made a grab for him, but someone seized me roughly by the arm and yanked me up off the bed, nearly dislocating my shoulder. I tried to pull away, but whoever had me was very strong.

Amory.

I wanted to cry out — scream to warn him — but I couldn't make a sound.

Another pair of hands grabbed my other arm, and I lost my footing as two people dragged me out of the room. I twisted around to look for Amory, but I couldn't see anything in the pitch blackness. My feet fumbled to gain traction as they pulled me across the apartment.

The PMC — they were taking me. *I couldn't let them take me.*

I dug in my feet, breaking my face away from the hand clamped over my mouth. I yelled, but the hand clamped down again. My captor crushed me against his chest, dragging me bodily out the front door.

Somewhere behind me, I heard a struggle. I twisted, my

Enemy Inside

captor's fingers pulling painfully against my skin. Through the darkness, I could see three figures lurching from side to side like a drunken caterpillar. One of the three was knocked backward, banging into the doorframe. The other hit the person in the middle, who stumbled.

Amory. I tried to call his name, but I just tasted the skin of the hand around my mouth: sweat and something chemical.

This was it. I only had one chance.

I stopped suddenly, hunkering down and jabbing my elbows into the soft guts of the people on either side of me. My right jab was stronger, and his grip loosened. I kicked wildly, finding purchase with a shin.

Freeing my arm, I swung toward the person on my left. He caught my wrist, and I kicked up my knee as hard as I could. I hit something soft, and his cry of agony told me I had hit the mark. I yanked out of his grip and ran blindly down the hallway.

My bare feet brushed the threadbare carpet, and I tried not to think about all the carrier blood soaked into the floor. At least it was dark. I tried the door on my right, but it was the wrong one. Desperate, I tried the next door, but the first had slowed me down.

The first man who had gone down was just feet behind me. I threw open the door to the decoy apartment, slamming it against his body as he tried to follow me. He grunted but didn't seem badly hurt. I tore through the darkness to the window, heaving it open with one hand.

The cold, sharp wind stung my bare arms, but I threw myself onto the fire escape. The man was right behind me — stumbling, reaching through the window. There was no time for the ladder. I jumped, but his hand caught my ankle. I lost my balance and plummeted sideways toward the ground.

I flailed my limbs, trying to right myself before I hit the ground, but the fall was shorter than I'd thought — shorter and more painful.

The hard, rough concrete cut through the snow, slicing against my exposed skin and scraping down through the flesh. All the wind was knocked out of me.

Get up. Get up! I thought.

Trembling, I tried to stand, but my ankle shook.

A door on the side of the building burst open, banging against the brick. Two enormous PMC officers emerged, dragging Amory between them. He was flailing around, fighting as I'd never seen. His eyes were dark again, his teeth bared in an animalistic snarl as he dug in his feet and jerked his elbow up to connect with an officer's spleen.

It didn't matter. They had him. I crawled forward — desperate to get away — but a boot stomped down painfully on my ankle. I looked up.

The officer who pursued me onto the fire escape was towering over me, a smug look on his face. He had messy blond hair that was a little too long for PMC standards, a hard square jaw, and protruding cheekbones that cut his face into sharp planes. Flinching away, I felt the raw hatred and fear cutting my insides. This was it. After everything we had done, they had ambushed us in our sleep.

I caught Amory's eye. He looked as miserable as I felt. His left eye was beginning to swell, and blood trickled from his nose. At least he had not gone without a fight, either.

A fourth PMC officer emerged from the side door. Hunched over and walking funny, I knew instantly that he was the officer I kicked in the hallway. I felt a cold hand grip my upper arm, and any satisfaction I felt drained away.

The blond officer pulled me roughly to my feet. I stumbled to one side, but he held fast to my arm. My left ankle would not support my full weight. A strange look crossed the officer's face, but he dragged me through the snow toward Amory to stand under the streetlight.

Another one of Amory's officers grabbed my arm, and the blond officer stepped back to look at us, as if admiring his work. I realized we must look like a motley crew. Amory's nose was still dripping blood, bruises blooming on his face. I had scrapes and cuts running all up and down my arms from my fall, and I was shivering barefoot in the snow.

"Yeah, that's definitely them," said the blond man. "Amory Elwood and . . . *accomplice.*" He formed the last word around his lips with a smirk, as if he knew how much it irritated me to be pegged as somehow less important — Amory's sidekick. It was stupid, and I should have been glad that they had not uncovered my real identity, but somehow the officer's smugness dug into me more than our present danger.

"Why don't you run her CID?" said the officer I had kicked. He had red hair and a slurred British accent.

The blond man smirked, grabbing my arm for effect. "She's a defector, you idiot. They both are."

I yanked my arm away, glaring up at him.

"Why don' you tag 'er? I bet she'd be real forthcomin' — "

"We're under direct orders," barked the blond man. "Besides," he grinned, "she knows a thing or two about that already. We'd probably have to give her enough to kill her just to get what we want."

He eyed my arm tattooed with HALLO burns, and I wanted to pull away.

Taking a step toward me, he jerked me forward until I was right up close, causing a surge of pain to shoot up my right side. Amory lunged next to me, but the officer holding him grabbed both his arms. The blond officer slapped a piece of hard plastic over my wrist and yanked the other in place next to it. I looked down. It was a one-piece restraint, like handcuffs.

"Let Elwood deal with her."

"Whah?" said the redhead with marked indignation. "Why 'im?"

"They breached security at Isador. He's curious."

My heart sank as the man holding me gripped my arm and dragged me toward a parked PMC cruiser. Pain shot up my leg in protest, and my eyes watered. He tossed me in the backseat, and the other men followed with Amory. He wore plastic restraints, too. Our eyes met as he struggled against the men holding him, and I could tell he was not really trying anymore. If I was captured, he would not run and leave me.

The car door slammed, and the blond man climbed in the front seat with one of the enormous officers who had taken Amory down. The other officers piled into another cruiser, the redhead shooting me a murderous look. I was glad he wasn't one of our drivers.

Pulling away from the safe house, a sick feeling of dread rose up in my chest.

What would they do to us now that Amory had already escaped once? And what would they do once they found out his CID had been removed?

Either his bandage had ripped off during the struggle, or he'd pulled it off himself, but I could still see the coagulated blood around my shaky incision on the back of his neck.

We pulled through an empty intersection, and, as if on cue, Amory doubled over with a yell.

Brilliant, I thought. He wanted them to think he still had his CID.

Enemy Inside

Twisting around in his seat, the enormous officer smacked him hard across the face.

"Stop!" I yelled. "It's your fault he's like this!"

"It's the new CID," the blond man muttered. His hazel eyes flashed in the rearview mirror. Although he couldn't have been older than twenty-five, they were etched with lines of fatigue.

The enormous officer shifted in his seat as Amory let out another cry, and his fat fingers flexed around the nightstick at his hip. Anger twisted my gut, but I focused on arranging my face to look pained instead. Amory was doing a good job; his face was contorted with agony, his knuckles white as they gripped the edge of the seat.

"Where are you taking us?" I asked. "It gets worse the farther we get from Isador."

No one answered.

As we passed between rows of destroyed buildings, I began to feel a slight prickle on the back of my neck. Something wasn't right. All the functioning bases were farther back the way we came. There was nowhere they could take us on this side of the city. Unless . . .

"Are you taking us out of Sector X?"

The blond man's eyes flickered. "We're under direct orders to take you to Elwood. He has expressed . . . *interest* in the two of you since his son's escape."

My heart seized. If they tortured the information out of me, they would know *who* had initiated Amory's escape. Godfrey would be in danger, his cover blown.

"Where is Elwood? All the bases on this side of the city were destroyed in the riots."

"We're in the rebuilding stage now," said the officer through gritted teeth.

Enemy Inside

A chill shot down my spine. *What did that mean?*

"What about all the carriers? What will you do with them?"

The blond man opened his mouth to answer, but the enormous officer in the passenger seat jerked his head. The skin around the collar of his uniform wobbled. "Don't talk to the prisoners. These ones are slippery."

The blond man fell silent, staring out at the road.

I tried not to listen to Amory's moans of pain. Even though I knew they were just for show, they were hard to hear.

Rising up over the wreckage, the George Washington Bridge came into view through the darkness. It was strange to find myself *not* wanting to cross it when that had been the only thing on my mind for the last twenty-four hours. If we left Sector X, Godfrey would have no way to find us.

"You can't pass under all those rovers!" I said in a panicked voice. "The signal will be too strong. You'll kill him."

The blond man shrugged. "It's the only way in or out of this city."

I glanced at Amory, and I read my own grim satisfaction in his face. Godfrey had been wrong about there being other ways out of Sector X. I couldn't help but think that was an enormous vulnerability for the PMC. Looking up at the gleaming steel buttresses, the bridge looked strong and solid, but I remembered the withered remains of the beautiful silver bridge the rebels had blown up. That bridge had been newer, stronger — built with the best materials dirty PMC money could buy. But anything could be destroyed.

As we neared the rover, Amory cried out louder. He gripped the sides of his head so forcefully it looked as if he might split his skull in two. I could see the shiny bug eyes of

Enemy Inside

the rovers, and my stomach twisted.

The blond man tapped his ear, and I could see a small white device protruding. "Officer Cassidy and Officer Tate transporting prisoners. One defector — unidentified — and Amory Elwood. Over."

There was a sharp beep and then the soft sound of static. Someone was speaking on the other end.

"I have direct orders, ma'am. You can see the paperwork yourself when we cross. Over."

We passed under the line of rovers, and I could see one turn red as it settled on me. Amory cried out, the sound reverberating in the small space.

"Can you shut him up?" asked the enormous officer in annoyance.

"Don't want to rough him up any more than he already is. But if you want to be the one to tell Elwood we killed his son, that's on you."

The man shifted uncomfortably.

I felt the rumble of the bridge as we crossed, and even though I knew our chances of being rescued by Godfrey and the others were destroyed, I couldn't help but feel relief. Once we were out of Sector X, there would be fewer rovers and fewer officers. If we could kill the two transporting us, we might have a shot at making it back to the rebel camp.

The cruiser slowed to a stop, and the blond man's eyes flickered to the backseat again. He seemed nervous.

Through the darkness, I could see a figure in white approaching the vehicle. He rolled down the window, and the officer came into view. I recognized her instantly as the woman who had been stationed there when we first entered the city.

"Good evening, officers," she said in her fake pleasant

voice.

"Officer." He nodded. "How are you doing this fine evening?" The blond man flashed a bright smile, and my stomach lurched. It made me sick when evil people were so friendly and cunning.

"I'm doing well, thank you." She glanced in the backseat at the two of us.

Turning toward the window, I tried to hide my face in the shadows, but her eyes settled on me. Her lip curled into an angry line, and I knew she remembered me in my PMC uniform. She knew we'd tricked her. Fear laced my insides, and I hoped Godfrey and the others were already out of the city and did not try to return.

"Be careful with her," she said in an icy voice. "She is probably more dangerous than the other one."

The blond man smirked. "Oh, I've noticed."

"I need to see your paperwork on these two. It's the new protocol."

"Of course." The man handed over a slip of white paper, and a silvery insignia at the top caught my eye.

"Officer Cassidy, this is unprecedented. I've never —"

He cut her off. "We're in a bit of a hurry. Elwood is very anxious to see this one." He jerked a thumb back to Amory, who was hunched over in pain. "You understand."

"Elwood?" The woman looked suspicious. "That one," she pointed at me, "entered the city dressed as an officer under false pretenses concerning Captain Elwood last night. You'll have to leave her in custody in Sector X."

"Fine," said the bigger officer. "You can have the bitch. She's been nothing but a pain in the ass."

"Elwood wants them both," said the one called Cassidy.

Enemy Inside

"This order is only for Amory Elwood."

"And any accomplices. She was the only one with him." He leaned out the window in a way that reminded me of Godfrey. "She's a defector, so it's not like there's a paper trail . . . digital impression, or whatever you call it."

The woman pursed her lips. "Fine. You can go on through."

He nodded appreciatively. "Thank you, ma'am." The slight twang on the last syllable made me cringe.

We drove on through, and I watched in the mirror as the ruins of Sector X disappeared behind us. The highway was empty, and Amory's groans had turned to pitiful whimpers. The officers did not speak, and I began to formulate a plan. Once we stopped or slowed down, I would choke Tate with my restraints, and Amory could grab his gun to shoot Cassidy. There was no way to communicate this to him, but Amory was quick on his feet.

Suddenly, the blond officer jerked the wheel, and we pulled off the highway onto a gravel road like the one we had taken with Godfrey. I couldn't see anything through the pitch blackness, but I could hear the gravel crunch under the tires. It didn't make sense.

"You lost already? You just stay on ninety-five until —"

In one motion, Cassidy turned and pointed a gun at the other officer's temple.

For a moment, everyone sat motionless. Then I heard the mechanical whirring noise as Cassidy rolled down the windows, not taking his gun off his partner.

Tate was watching Cassidy out of the corner of his eye, not daring to move. He was panting slightly, his open hands hovering over his thighs as if he didn't know what to do with them.

Enemy Inside

Cassidy fired, and I understood why he'd rolled the windows down. His mouth was set in a hard line, and his eyes were dark and empty. Ears ringing from the gunshot, I looked over to see a trail of blood splattered across the leather interior on the passenger side.

Nobody moved.

Cassidy sighed. "For future reference, that CID frequency would have been lost the second we crossed over out of Sector X."

I glanced at Amory, who looked horrified.

He knew.

"I had to expedite this part before he got suspicious." The officer twisted around to face me. "Joke's on you. Now we just have farther to walk."

"Why did you shoot him?" I asked, trying to block out the ringing in my ears. Everything was upside down.

"He was the real deal — a fat, useless yes-man with the PMC's cock in his mouth."

"And you are?" Amory's voice was scratchy, as if he hadn't spoken in days.

The man nodded. "I'm like you." He laughed. "Well, technically, I'm like Godfrey." Pulling up the arm of his jacket, he flashed his perfect square scar.

Chapter Nine

"You're a rebel."

He nodded. "Jared Cassidy. Thanks for not kicking me in the balls."

I didn't smile. "Why did you bring the PMC to the safe house?"

"Godfrey promised he'd get you out of the city, didn't he? It was the only way."

He threw open the driver's door and came around to let us out on Amory's side.

"Why?"

"Well, after your little escape incident, they knew Godfrey and the other two had been in on it."

"Did they make it out?"

He nodded. "They're fine."

Jared bent to unfasten my restraints, and Amory flew up behind him, locking his own restraints around his neck.

Jared gasped and struggled against him, but Amory was just as tall and just as strong. He pulled back against Jared's throat, and I could see the hard plastic cutting into his windpipe.

For a moment, that empty look I'd seen while he was fighting the carriers was back. Fear welled up inside me. Between his swollen black eye and the blood coating the side

Enemy Inside

of his face, Amory looked terrifying.

"Amory!"

"He's lying!" Amory snarled. "He could just be leading the PMC to the rebels."

"He shot an officer!"

"The PMC has done worse."

As crazy as he sounded, he was right.

"What the *hell* is wrong with you?" Jared spat. "I've been dedicated to the cause for a year. I risk my life to rescue your rogue defector asses, and this is how you thank me?"

"How can we trust you?"

"I was there!" he yelled. "The night in the bunker when you showed up. I was there when you threw Mariah to the dogs!" Jared's face was contorted with rage, his blond hair mussed as he shook with anger in Amory's grip.

My stomach clenched when I remembered the look on Mariah's face as the rebels marched her out into the snow to die. She was infected, and they showed no mercy, but it was my fault she was dead . . . or out there all alone.

Jared struggled, watching me process this information. "Just so you know, there are plenty of rebels who were all for leaving you two in Sector X to die. People don't trust you or your friends . . . not after the stunt you pulled to rescue *him*. That mission put the entire camp at risk."

"Rulon would have let him die."

"That's his right!" Jared twisted against Amory, and I was impressed at his ability to argue with someone choking him from behind. "He's the leader. It's his call. He has his reasons."

I staggered closer to him, ignoring the throbbing pain in my ankle. "That's not good enough for me. When you blindly follow somebody without thinking for yourself, you give up all your freedom. That's how the PMC took power. It wasn't hard. People want someone to tell them what to do because it takes away their responsibility."

Jared struggled against Amory's hold, anger in his eyes. "I'm going to pretend you didn't say that. That kind of talk is grounds for discharge. That kind of talk puts the entire resistance in jeopardy."

I thought about something Ida had said to me once: *The only thing necessary for the triumph of evil is for good men to do nothing.*

"I'm not going to blindly follow Rulon and pretend his methods aren't their own special brand of terror," I said.

"Listen to yourself . . . biting the hand that feeds you. It's not like you have another choice!"

I felt a flash of anger and stuck out my arm. The burns on my forearm were just visible in the darkness. When I spoke, my voice shook. "All I know is that the only people who have tortured me were the ones supposedly fighting for my freedom."

We stood there for several seconds, glaring at each other. I realized that my bare feet were frozen in the snow. We would not make it very far without better clothes.

"If you're cold, there are extra clothes in the trunk," Jared muttered.

I moved toward the cruiser to open the back hatch and almost fell over. I'd forgotten how unsteady my ankle was. Between the cold and my own surge of adrenalin, the pain had been temporarily numbed.

"You'll have to carry her," he said to Amory.

Amory let out a long, angry burst of air and pulled his arms back from around Jared's neck. He shoved him forward — hard — and Jared fell into the snow.

"You're *welcome,*" Jared snarled from the ground.

I glared at him as I shrugged on a heavy, oversized coat. He had risked his life to save us, it was true, but it was because he was blindly acting under orders. What was worse, I could see every bit of Rulon's arrogance and self-righteousness etched in his smirk.

Thankfully, he had thought to bring heavy socks and boots, and I could feel the burn of sensation returning to my toes as I shoved them in. The clothes were ill fitting, but they were warm.

"So is there a reason you raided the safe house in the middle of the night?"

"Well, I knew you wouldn't go without a fight, and I didn't want to get shot. I figured the element of surprise was my best option."

When we were dressed, Amory retrieved the dead officer's handgun from the vehicle and tucked it into the waistband of his pants. He moved toward me, and I took an automatic step back — still skittish from our PMC manhandling. He looked slightly hurt, but his expression cleared almost instantly.

"You won't be able to walk there on that broken ankle."

"I don't think it's broken," I lied. I turned to Jared. "You're an idiot. I could have been killed falling from that fire escape."

"You jumped."

"I would have landed right if it weren't for you."

"The plan would be totally screwed up if you escaped."

"Now just my ankle is totally screwed up," I mumbled under my breath.

Enemy Inside

I allowed Amory to hoist me off my feet. The horrible, vacant look was gone, and he was warm and gentle. I put an arm around his neck, more to be closer than for stability.

"Start walking," he barked to Jared.

We trudged through the snow, the wind biting against our raw, frozen faces. In case we were being followed, we carved a wide, curved path through the snow. Luckily, the new snow would cover our tracks when the PMC came looking. I didn't know where we were. The gravel road Jared pulled off on wasn't the one that led to the PMC off-site storage area.

I knew it was a long way off, but it seemed much farther through the snow. Amory never let on that he was tired, but I felt terrible not being able to walk myself. After an hour, I suggested we stop to rest, but Jared shook his head. I didn't argue; it was safest to keep moving in case the PMC was following us.

"Do you want me to carry her for a bit?" Jared asked. "She must be getting heavy — no offense."

Amory glared at him but didn't say a word. I knew his arms would fall off before he admitted he was tired. We walked on, and the air seemed to grow colder. We were definitely getting closer. The trees were denser here, and we seemed to be moving up an incline. I thought of Greyson and Logan and hoped Jared had been telling the truth when he said they were all right.

The thought sent a wave of guilt down my spine; Rulon could not have been kind when they returned from an unauthorized mission with his stolen maps and the PMC on their heels. Would it be more difficult for the rebels to steal supplies from the city now that Godfrey and his fake identities had been compromised?

Now that we were out of the oppressive grip of Sector X, I could not deny that the mission to rescue Amory had been foolhardy and selfish. My judgment had been clouded by a

Enemy Inside

horrible feeling of helplessness I felt from doing nothing in the rebel camp and by the constant fear looming over us in the city. Now that Amory was safe and we were out, the whole thing seemed very reckless, but I knew I would do it all over again to save him.

I peered through the trees, and my heart jumped. Even in the dim light of the early morning, I could just make out the cleared slope of the hill near where the lookouts were stationed.

"Stop," I whispered.

Amory paused, panting slightly from the effort of holding me.

Jared didn't stop. He kept walking toward the hill, seemingly unaware of the sniper who was likely concealed in the trees.

"Stop right there!" yelled a voice.

I looked up, and I could make out movement in the shadows. Without being able to see, I knew the watchman had a rifle trained on Jared.

"It's me. Jared."

"Who are the other two?" The voice sounded less intimidating now, uncertain.

"Two of ours rescued from one of the safe houses."

There was a loud rustling, and I could see someone descending the tree with a rifle strapped on his back. It reminded me of Logan, and my heart ached to see her.

He jumped down, and his face fell when he saw me.

"Oh. You're back."

I recognized his voice from the night we escaped. It was Kinsley. He had a soft, boyish face dotted with freckles and sandy brown hair. By the looks of his lanky frame, he had recently grown about five inches. He couldn't be older than seventeen. I felt a new stab of guilt when I thought about how much trouble he must have been in for abandoning his post and letting us escape.

"I'll bring you guys in so they don't shoot you," he muttered.

He gripped his gun and nudged us forward with it. I doubted very much that Kinsley would shoot us in the back as we marched up to camp, but he looked very young and nervous.

We didn't make it that far.

Halfway up the hill, I could see two dark figures sprinting toward us. I stiffened in Amory's arms, and I felt every muscle in his body tighten simultaneously. He set me on my feet, hand reaching behind him for the gun he had stowed there.

As the figures drew nearer, I recognized that flash of brilliant blond hair.

I sighed with relief, and my heart surged with affection as I saw their faces.

Greyson careened into me — almost knocking me clean off my feet — and Logan threw herself into Amory's arms.

"Oh my god!" she screamed into his shoulder. "I didn't think we would ever see you two again!"

"Thanks for the vote of confidence," Amory muttered, fighting for air in Logan's stranglehold.

Greyson pulled back, and I stumbled. His eyebrows knitted together in concern.

"Hurt my ankle."

"I was worried about you," he said. His tone was accusatory, as though it were my fault. I smiled. Greyson

Enemy Inside

always got angry when he had too many emotions to process.

"I was worried about *you*. I didn't know if you would get out of the city in time."

"We almost didn't," he said, grinning. "You're not the best at avoiding rovers in high-pressure situations."

I punched his arm.

Logan broke away from Amory and threw herself onto me. "I'm so sorry we left you there," she murmured into my coat.

"It's okay," I said, gasping a little for air as she squeezed me.

She pulled away, looking at me funny.

"Really."

Logan raised an eyebrow. "Or am I *not* sorry I left you there . . . with Amory . . . all alone?"

I glanced around to see that no one was listening to us and bit back a smile.

Logan grinned. "That's my girl!"

"Let's go," said Jared.

I looked up. He was standing a few yards ahead, wearing a grim expression. "I need to report back to Godfrey."

Logan's smile faded. "You should probably prepare yourself," she said. "Rulon wasn't happy. And some of the other rebels . . . they still think you're a traitor."

I swallowed, feeling the renewed guilt that Logan, Greyson, and Godfrey had returned to camp to face the consequences of my decision. "Did he . . . do anything to you guys?"

Logan shook her head. "He tried. He wanted to. But I

Enemy Inside

think Godfrey is about done with his bullshit." She looked angry. "It's not just us. Everyone is starting to notice that the resistance isn't doing anything. The riots didn't weaken the PMC as much as they planned."

"Let's go!" snapped Jared.

Amory's face was dark, but he put an arm around my waist and hoisted most of my weight off my right leg. With Logan and Greyson flanking my other side, we continued up the hill through the snow with Kinsley trailing behind us.

As we reached the familiar horseshoe-shaped alcove of trees, I could see the glow of a campfire burning low in the early morning light. Birds were starting to sing, but the camp was eerily quiet. Everyone was still asleep.

"I'll wake Godfrey," Jared muttered.

Looking uneasy, Kinsley pushed past us and shuffled behind him down the first block of tents.

Amory was looking around in wonder. "How many rebels are there?"

"Only a couple hundred left in this camp," said Greyson. "But there were nearly five hundred before the riots."

"This camp?"

Greyson nodded. "There are others. Although this one is probably the largest in the country."

"Except out west," Logan corrected.

Greyson shrugged, but I could see something flicker in his eyes. I looked at him and then glanced away quickly. I felt a painful tug when I thought back to all the plans we had made when we first decided to flee the city. We were going to head west with my parents, and Greyson was going to find a way to bring his mother and sister back from the New Northern Territory. We seemed so far from that reality now.

A sharp, booming profanity shattered the peace of the early morning. I stiffened, and Amory released me. Logan threw me a nervous glance, and the four of us reflexively shifted out into a straight line.

I heard heavy footfalls through the snow, and Rulon appeared around the corner of the block of tents. He was wearing his huge fur coat with thermal long johns tucked into his boots. He looked larger and more intimidating than I remembered. Kinsley trailed behind him looking terrified, and I felt sorry for the boy. He had probably left his family to fight the PMC, and instead of fighting, he was serving and reporting directly to Rulon every day.

I saw Rulon run an agitated hand over his bald, dark head. Gold rings gleamed on his fingers, and his eyes were cold.

"Well, well. Look who's back," he snarled as soon as he was within earshot.

Out of the corner of my eye, I could see the rustle of a tent flap, and I knew some of the rebels had awoken.

"It's the PMC traitor and the disobedient upstart who thinks she knows better than my entire army." His lip was curled into an angry smirk. He was looking at me now. "Not only did you go AWOL and drag three others with you, but you used the movement's resources to do it."

I took a deep breath, trying to stand up straight on my shaky ankle.

"Now, what am I supposed to do with that, soldier? The PMC would have you permanently deactivated for this sort of thing." His voice was low and lethal now. "Am I supposed to welcome you back into our ranks after you disobeyed direct orders? I explicitly told you —"

"The mission was a success," I said.

A look of fury clouded over Rulon's face. "A *success*? You

got four of our legitimate PMC officer IDs flagged, lost one of our cruisers, and put our last Sector X safe house out of commission. You call that a success?"

"We saved him."

"You saved a known PMC spy and brought him back into our ranks!"

"He's not a spy!" I said, hatred boiling over in my chest. "He was their prisoner! They performed horrible experiments on him and *tortured* him for three weeks."

I turned to Amory and grabbed his arm, shoving his sleeve up above the elbow to reveal the row of burns. "Look what they did!"

Amory jerked his arm away, looking ashamed. He didn't meet my gaze.

"I guess that's nothing to you," I said quietly, although I knew the onlookers who had gathered could hear.

Rulon sneered at Amory as if he were something stuck to the bottom of his shoe. "They implanted him with another CID. They'll have every satellite rover in the state out scanning for him."

"It's gone! I removed it myself."

Rulon took another step forward. He towered over me by at least a foot. "You think you're something special, don't you?" His voice was almost a whisper, but it sent a wave of fear through me. "You think you're exempt from the rules. You think you're a hero." His eyebrows shot up. "You're nothing. You're just a spoiled little bitch who ran away from home and decided to join the revolution because it seemed *fun* to you."

"Hey!" Amory shifted in front of me, shoving Rulon roughly in the chest. His eyes were dark and full of warning, and they sent a chill down the back of my neck. "I'm the

Enemy Inside

reason she disobeyed you. Your problem's with me."

Rulon laughed coldly. "No. No, it's not. It's not people like you I'm worried about. Spies are easy to dispose of because they're easy to sniff out. I don't have to *try* to turn this whole camp against you. Nobody trusts a PMC brat. It's people like you." He turned to me. "You're way more dangerous than one PMC spy. Your kind are a disease. You infect the ranks with dissent. You think you're smart, but you're not. You're dangerously stupid. It's people like you who get good soldiers killed, and I won't have it in my camp."

I looked up into his cold eyes. "Are you going to torture me again? Is that how you solve problems here?"

He smiled, and his bright teeth were blindingly white against his dark skin. "Not today."

"You done yelling?"

I looked around Rulon's hulking frame to see Godfrey. He was fully dressed as if he hadn't gone to sleep, and his eyes were gleaming with a challenge. Behind him was Jared, still in his PMC whites and eyeing Godfrey warily.

Rulon stepped back and let out a low breath of disgust. He stalked away, and Kinsley followed in his wake looking panicked.

Glancing around, I could see rebels all down the block poking their heads out of their tents. They looked interested, almost amused. Amory eyed them all angrily, and Logan looked exhausted.

It was Godfrey who spoke first, addressing Amory. "Come on. You can bunk with Greyson and the kid."

Amory looked up, and I didn't want to be separated from him. I didn't trust Rulon, and all of this was foreign to him.

Logan seemed to read my mind. "Greyson, why don't you

go, too? Help find him some clothes and blankets."

Greyson nodded and followed Godfrey and Amory. I felt a little better, but still slightly apprehensive.

"He can handle himself," said Logan. "I seem to remember him teaching you how to shoot a gun."

I grinned. "You taught me that."

She laughed. "But it took a little of Amory's special touch." She ran her hands over her arms in a jokingly suggestive way. "Come on. You look like hell."

Allowing Logan to support some of my weight, I limped over to the medical tent where Doctor Shriver slept, wishing I did not have to see her. She'd examined me for any signs of infection upon my arrival, and it had not been a pleasant experience.

Caroline Shriver was a woman in her early thirties with short, black hair that had a slightly purple tinge. It stuck out all over the place like a lion's mane and framed her enormous glasses in a mad scientist sort of way. She had been a paramedic before the Collapse and had a way with grim facial expressions and morbid comments that made you feel certain you were going to die. Treating rebels with missing limbs and shrapnel embedded in their flesh after the riots had done nothing to tame her tendency toward the macabre.

"Hey!" Logan called through the canvas. "You up, Shriver?"

There was a bit of rustling inside, and Shriver pulled back the tent flap and stuck her head out. She had dark circles under her eyes and wore an oversized jacket over a navy jumpsuit. Her hair looked more unruly than usual, as if she had just woken up.

"How could I *not* be? What happened? It sounded like a trip to the principal's office from in here."

Enemy Inside

I shrugged off her obvious curiosity, not wanting to talk about it. "My ankle's messed up."

She sighed. "All right. Come on."

Logan and I ducked into the tent, and I collapsed onto Shriver's rickety exam table. There were four cots lining the right wall of the tent. All of them were empty except for the one at the end, which was occupied by one of the few seriously injured rebels who had made it out of the city. He lay perfectly still with his arms, legs, and face all bound with gauze, which made me think he was recovering from bad burns.

Shriver lived here, too, but her living area was separated by a thin canvas curtain that ran down the left side of the tent.

She rolled up my pant leg and squeezed.

"Does that hurt?"

"Yeah."

"Does *that* hurt?"

"Yes!"

"Can you move it?"

"Yeah."

She scrutinized my swelling ankle with her glasses pushed down to the end of her nose. "It's just a sprain. Should be fine in a couple weeks."

Shriver wrapped my ankle with a length of fabric, eyeing the ripped knee of my pants and the scrapes running all along the right side of my body.

"We need to treat those cuts," she said. "I don't want to deal with any infection next week."

I nodded and let her clean all the scrapes I had sustained

when I fell from the fire escape. When she was finished, Shriver thrust a crutch at me and dismissed us with a gruff nod.

Moving was much easier with the crutch, and although I was unsteady in the snow, it felt good not to be dependent on Logan or Amory to move around. We went back to our tent, and I fell over onto my sleeping bag. Thankfully, Logan had thought to bring all my things back after they escaped Sector X. As soon as we were alone, Logan sat down to grill me.

"What *happened* in there?"

By "in there," I knew she was referring to Sector X and everything that had happened to Amory and me after we had separated. I told her about the old tunnel that was closed off and how we had run to the safe house to avoid the PMC. When I got to the part about the carriers, I paused, unsure how much I should tell her. It felt like a betrayal to Amory to tell Logan about how he seemed like a different person when he was fighting them, but in truth, I was worried about him and the effects of his brainwashing sessions at Isador.

"It was like he just . . . turned off his emotions," I said. "He didn't even see me there. He was a *machine*."

Logan looked slightly alarmed but cracked a nervous grin. "Let's hope he's just a carrier-killing machine, huh?"

"Do you think that's what they were training him for in there?"

"I don't know."

I shivered. "You didn't see those videos they were showing. And the problem is that stuff is in his brain. I don't know if removing his CID —"

"You really removed his CID?" Logan's eyes widened. "I thought you made that up!"

Enemy Inside

"They inserted it in the back of his head. It was like they wanted it closer to his brain."

"Or somewhere he couldn't remove it himself," she reminded me.

I nodded, feeling strange that Logan was taking the role of the voice of reason.

Finally, she asked the question I had been dreading most. "Is he different now?"

I shook my head. But even as I did, I knew it was a lie.

"I don't know," I said. "He's —"

I faltered, listening intently. Outside, I could hear people yelling. Logan sprang to her feet and flew out of the tent. Struggling to stand, I pulled myself up with the tent supports and limped out into the snow. Several tents down, I could see two figures sprawled in the snow fighting, one on top of the other.

People were emerging wrapped in their sleeping bags, rubbing their eyes and looking less amused by the second interruption.

As I hobbled closer on my crutch, I saw Amory on his knees pummeling another man I did not recognize. His eyes were cold, his muscles taut with exertion and rage. I watched in horror as blood spattered the fresh snow on the ground, and Amory brought back his fist again, knuckles red and cracked. He wasn't the Amory I knew. That Amory was gone.

Chapter Ten

It was like watching a movie.

This couldn't be happening.

But it was.

Amory was pummeling a man into the snow. I could hear the man's soft grunts of pain as Amory's fists connected with his flesh.

He had that look in his eyes again, and I felt the familiar ripple of fear in my chest.

"Amory!" I yelled.

He did not look up.

Ignoring the stares of the onlookers, I limped over toward them and was alarmed to see blood spattered like paint across Amory's face.

"Amory. Stop!"

I drew closer, and he still did not seem to see me. Again he brought his knuckles down to collide with the man's jaw.

I passed Logan, and she grabbed my arm. Her face was ashen. I shook her off and hobbled through the snow. Holding on to my crutch, I bent down and pulled Amory roughly around by the shoulder.

He turned abruptly and, before I could react, shoved me backward into the snow. Amory didn't stop pounding the man. Shock and anger coursed through me like venom, and I

Enemy Inside

aimed a hard kick at his shoulder with my uninjured leg.

"Amory!" I growled.

He turned, panting with exertion. His face was still screwed up in anger, and he was even bloodier than before. Snow was starting to fall. He froze.

His eyes cleared first. They focused on me and immediately wrinkled in pain and regret.

"Oh god," he murmured.

He struggled to disentangle himself from the man he was fighting. Silently, he crouched down to pick me up out of the snow. I cringed away, glaring at him. Even though I knew his outburst was the result of whatever the PMC had done to him, I couldn't stop the anger and distrust pouring off me.

I realized everyone was staring at us.

The man on the ground pulled himself into a sitting position, looking much worse for the wear.

"What the hell was that?" I whispered to Amory.

He opened his mouth to speak but wouldn't look me in the eye.

"He started it," Greyson panted. I hadn't even noticed him standing off to the side, holding back one of the man's friends. He stepped around the beat-up man on the ground, looking down at him with disgust.

"He came at Amory . . . said he was going to drag him and you back to the PMC himself." Greyson muttered. "He started shoving him, and Amory *snapped*."

"I just lost it," muttered Amory, rubbing the back of his neck.

I tried to meet his gaze, but he was avoiding it expertly. He looked ashamed.

Enemy Inside

"You need to see Shriver," I said.

His wounds looked bad.

Reluctantly, he followed me past the mob of angry onlookers back toward the med tent. Me — the traitor — and Amory the psycho. What a pair we made. It was slow going, and I cursed Jared for making me sprain my ankle. I just wanted to get away from all these people as quickly as possible.

When we reached the tent, I didn't even call for Shriver first. I ducked inside with Amory trailing several feet behind me. Shriver wasn't there, but I knew she couldn't be far. In the rebel camp, news of the fight would spread within minutes, and she would be back to tend to the wounded.

When he saw we were alone, Amory finally looked at me. His expression was pained.

Before I could say anything, he drew me into him and took both my hands in his.

"Haven, I'm so sorry. I didn't even see you. I had tunnel vision or something."

I tore my eyes away. It was too much.

"It's just like with the carriers. It was like . . . my instincts took over. I just wanted to end that guy. I was *disconnected*."

"I shouldn't have gotten between you two in that fight," I said. "I know that was stupid." I looked down at my hands and saw they were shaking. "But if you *ever* touch me like that again . . . we're done, you and me."

He nodded. "You have to help me, Haven." His voice broke. He shuddered, as if struggling to form the words. "Something is seriously wrong with me. There's this . . . *monster* in my body trying to get out. All the bad stuff is just too much sometimes."

We fell silent for a moment, and I focused on the warmth

of his hands on me. It was hard to believe they were the same hands that had shoved me aside moments ago.

"I would never hurt you," he said. "I know that seems like a stretch, after what's happened today . . . but that's not just me making an empty promise." He took a deep breath, and his face glowed red. "I've noticed . . . this *feeling* that I get only takes over when I'm afraid. Not normal fear . . . I don't think there's been a day when I *haven't* been afraid since the Collapse. I mean that cold fear that grabs you and leaves you paralyzed. That's when I lose control."

As he spoke, he turned my hand over in his palm, studying the soft skin between my thumb and index finger rather than looking me in the eyes. "The night before when all those carriers came . . . I thought they were going to kill us. I mean, honestly, I didn't think we'd make it. That's the fear that got me. That's when I lost it."

Finally Amory looked up at me. His bright gray eyes stood out sharply against the dark bruised flesh around it.

"It's all right," I whispered. "You don't have to be afraid. I'm here."

He opened his mouth wordlessly, but I pulled his face down to mine and brushed my lips against his.

Just as I felt the warmth of his kiss, I heard the crunch of footsteps outside the tent, and we sprang apart.

Shriver was standing in the opening, looking harried. "You again."

"Yeah . . . sorry. We came here hoping you could treat Amory's wounds."

She let out an irritated stream of air from between pursed lips and rolled her eyes. "Fine. But if you get in another fistfight, I'm going to start charging you."

Impatience pouring off her, Shriver snapped on a fresh

pair of latex gloves and grabbed a bottle of antiseptic. Moving methodically from head to torso, she quickly disinfected Amory's wounds and bandaged the deep ones. When she swabbed a deep cut on his arm, he tilted his head away in a grimace. She grabbed his chin, twisting his head around none to gently to examine the site where I had removed the CID.

"You do this hack job yourself?" she asked him.

That stung.

"No. I couldn't reach it. Haven did it."

Shriver sighed in exasperation. "This should really have stitches. And rolling around on the ground when you have a fresh wound like this isn't smart. I need to open it up to clean it properly."

"Haven had it bandaged," said Amory. "But I ripped it off when the PMC showed up."

Shriver didn't say anything, and I took her silence to mean she didn't care what the reason was.

"Are you a doctor?" asked Amory, not unkindly.

"I was a paramedic," she said.

Amory grinned. "At school, the kids who trained as paramedics knew everything. They'd already been in the trenches, you know?"

"Med school?" she asked.

He grunted in assent, wincing as Shriver opened up his wound. "Never had the chance to finish."

When she next spoke, her voice was kinder than I'd ever heard it. "Well, if something awful goes down and we have a whole mess of wounded people, I could use your help. Nobody else around here knows what's what."

She cleaned and sutured the wound quickly, slapping a

Enemy Inside

new bandage over her work with a glare at me. "You stay away from here. You can't make a clean incision to save your life."

"I was using a kitchen knife!" I said, feeling defensive.

Amory grinned. "She did a really good job. She didn't pass out or anything. Lots of people pass out the first time."

I looked away, feeling my cheeks grow warm at the look he was giving me. He thanked Shriver and helped me out of the tent. We turned to go back to my tent, but Logan was already coming toward me with a serious look on her face.

"What's going on?" I asked.

She looked at Amory. "Rulon's called an all-hands meeting."

My heart sank. I could think of only one reason for Rulon to call a meeting. He wanted to discuss Amory, possibly me and Amory. *Was he planning to kick us out of the camp? Have us killed?*

When we reached the enormous bonfire, people were already milling about the mess line, waiting to get their breakfast. Even after our long hike through the night, I didn't feel hungry. Greyson motioned us over to a log where he sat near the back, and we joined him.

"Do you think we should be sitting here?" Logan muttered to him, staring straight ahead. "We could get some stuff together and be on the move before they realize —"

Greyson sighed. He looked tired. "How far do you think we'd get before either the rebels or the PMC caught up to us?"

Logan looked wounded. "We're smarter than they are. We could do it."

"Where would we go?" I asked.

"If it's me they want, I'll leave," said Amory.

We all turned to look at him. His face was set in a hard line, but I could see the fear flickering behind his eyes.

"No," I said. "If it's you they want, we'll all make a run for it."

Logan nodded, and to my relief, so did Greyson. I felt a twinge of guilt. A little over a month ago, Greyson had just wanted to go west and find a way to bring his family over. After he was captured, he wanted to fight for the rebels. I had dragged him into our problems, and because of that, they would never trust him as they trusted their other soldiers.

The people sitting around us fell silent, and I looked up to see Rulon approaching from the tent block. He was fully dressed now, and he looked hardened and intimidating.

He stepped into the center of the group with the fire blazing behind him. "Comrades." His voice boomed out across the crowd. "I regret to inform you that I have just received intelligence that our position has been compromised."

An anxious murmur rippled through the crowd. Logan met my gaze, and I read the fear there. If Rulon was telling the truth, there was a good chance he was going to assign the blame to Amory and me.

"Apparently, one of the guards at the bridge became suspicious on our latest extraction mission and sent out a satellite rover. Fortunately, it identified Jared and two other undocumented illegals a good five miles away from camp, so our exact location is unknown.

"We should prepare immediately to fortify our ranks and take out the officers they send to investigate. I will lead a small group of soldiers out to their target location. Hopefully we can contain the situation. Any soldier who wishes to fight

Enemy Inside

should meet back here in ten minutes ready to go."

Rulon nodded once and strode back to his tent. The crowd erupted immediately.

"How do they know that?" Amory whispered.

"They've been listening in on the PMC forever," said Logan. "The camp is so close to Sector X they can pick up the dispatch radio frequency on a regular scanner."

Greyson snorted. "That's pretty stupid of the PMC."

"They think this area is secure," said Logan. "That's why they treat this threat so seriously."

"Well, I'm going," said Greyson.

"What?" I turned to him.

"I'm going down there to fight them." His expression was set. "This is what I signed up for."

"It's not what *I* signed up for!" My voice was higher than usual, and I could feel the panic rising in my throat. "I didn't come all the way out here so you could get yourself killed."

Greyson met my gaze, and I recognized that look of determination on his face. That was the look he got when his mind was made up and he was not open to negotiation. "Things changed for me when I was locked up. I have to serve a purpose. Dying in a fight is better than sitting around here, waiting to be killed. When you're afraid, they own you. I'm sick of it."

"Well, I can't go with you!" I said, gesturing to my ankle.

Greyson met my gaze the same way he had done when we were teenagers having one of our telepathic conversations. "I wouldn't want you to."

I stared at him, letting it sink in.

"I'm going, too," said Amory.

"No, you're not!" Logan and I said in unison.

I shot Greyson a deadly look. Not only was he going to put his own life in danger to play the hero, but he was dragging Amory with him.

"Why would you let him go, but not me?" Amory asked Logan.

"He's too stubborn. I don't want either one of you to go."

Amory turned to me. "I need to go."

I shook my head. "Not after what just happened." I lowered my voice. "You can't control yourself in a fight, and none of the rebels trust you."

"That's exactly why I *should* go."

I could see that his decision was made. There was no point arguing.

He and Greyson ran off to their tents to dress and find weapons, and I sank down on a log by the fire and put my head in my hands.

"I hate this."

"Me too," Logan sighed.

Her weary expression caught me off guard. It was sometimes so easy to forget that she had once been an officer. She must be used to watching her friends go off to fight, not knowing if she would see them again. I didn't ask, but I was sure it never got any easier.

A few minutes later, Amory and Greyson reappeared wearing bulletproof vests and carrying two of the most terrifying rifles I'd seen in the rebels' stash. Greyson was doing a poor job hiding his excitement. Amory looked grim.

I got up to hug Greyson first. "Please don't let anything happen to him," I murmured into his coat. "And if anything happens to you —"

"Relax." He pulled away and squeezed my arm once. "I'll make sure none of the rebels shoot Amory before we get to the PMC."

Logan hugged Greyson awkwardly, and I moved to Amory. He looked so tough in his battle gear. The scruff that had grown on his face from two days without shaving only added to his rugged appearance, and I reminded myself that he would have become a field physician for the PMC if he hadn't fled to the farm.

"You know why I have to do this."

I shook my head. "You don't have to prove anything to anyone. This is only temporary."

Lowering his voice, Amory took a step closer to me. "We don't know how long this rebellion is going to last. As long as the PMC is still in power, we are going to need allies."

"It doesn't have to be them," I said, eyeing the rebels milling around waiting to leave.

"Let's go, men!" Rulon yelled.

I felt a sting of irritation. A dozen or so women were also dressed for battle, but they didn't seem to bat an eye at Rulon's address.

Before I could say or do anything else, Amory grabbed me by my coat and pulled me up to kiss him. My feet left the ground for a moment, and his warm lips pressed against mine. The scruff was new, and it burned against my chin in a pleasant way. I tried to memorize every part of him: his smell, the feel of him against me, and those gray eyes I loved so much.

Just as I let my hands settle on his strong chest, someone near us cleared his throat. Amory pulled away, looking dazed, and his face glowed with heat.

Enemy Inside

Greyson raised an eyebrow at me and cocked his head approvingly. My face felt hot.

Without another word, Amory flew in for one last quick kiss, and then he was gone.

He and Greyson followed the others through the trees toward the hill, and Greyson turned one last time to wave before they disappeared out of sight.

"Wow," said Logan. "That was intense."

She was grinning in a way that made me feel embarrassed.

"I mean, I always expected Amory would be really intense, but *man*." She fanned herself with her hand.

I opened my mouth to retort but closed it immediately. I had nothing to tease Logan about. The only guy I'd ever seen her with was Max, and I couldn't sully the few memories she had with him by making a joke.

She seemed to be thinking along the same lines, because her eyes looked suddenly misty.

"Oh . . . I'm sorry," I said. I sank down on the log next to her, feeling like a terrible person. *Why had I let Amory kiss me in front of her and rub it in her face like that?* Max's death was still so fresh.

Melting against my side, Logan let her head fall onto my shoulder. I knew she was crying, although she did not make a sound.

I understood how she felt, even though I hadn't wept for my parents much in the last few weeks. Grief was not a wound; it was emptiness.

"I'm sorry," I repeated to no one in particular.

"It's fine," said Logan. "I'm so glad for you two. And Amory . . . he deserves to be happy. He's had a really shitty life."

Enemy Inside

"What do you mean?" I had always suspected things were bad for Amory to leave his dad and come to Ida's, but I never asked him about his life before the farm. Everyone there had left for a reason, and I made it a point never to ask.

"I only knew the rumors. Captain Elwood was old PMC, like Godfrey. He was a legend — evil. Everyone knew the stories. I don't think he started experimenting on Amory until he got older, but he used to hit him and his mom. One day, she finally had enough. I guess she left him. But that's not even the worst of it."

Logan swallowed, looking sick. "They found her car in a lake . . . with her in it. The papers said she killed herself, but it never made sense. And with her gone, I think things got a lot worse for Amory."

I sat back, my mind reeling with this information. It made sense why Amory used to hate killing carriers as much as I did. He had grown up around so much violence that it probably disgusted him. That was all different now.

I ate breakfast without really tasting any of it. The food was cold as usual, but I knew I should eat.

Exhausted and defeated, I went back to the tent and collapsed onto my sleeping bag to take a nap. It was strange sleeping during the day with all the commotion going on around me. I knew the camp was shorthanded now that half our forces had gone off to fight, but I desperately needed to rest.

I tried not to think of Amory out there marching toward the PMC without breakfast, without sleep, and without any real allies other than Greyson.

I had just nodded off when I heard the screams.

Chapter Eleven

I awoke with a start. High-pitched screams pierced the air and rang out across the camp. I heard shouts, followed by gunshots.

We were under attack.

Tripping and fumbling to extricate myself from my sleeping bag on my bad ankle, I looked around wildly for my weapons. The rifle I had taken into Sector X was long gone. All that was left was Logan's second rifle she had stolen from the rebels and the knives from my rucksack. I stuffed two knives into my holster, grabbed Logan's rifle, and struggled into a standing position.

How could I fight with my crutch? It was absurd. I couldn't even fire a gun leaning on it. Head still spinning with sleep, I limped out into the snow without it.

Crouching in the shadows behind the block of tents, I looked for the telltale whites of PMC officers moving through the camp, but we weren't being attacked by the PMC.

The camp was crawling with carriers. I hadn't seen so many since the riot outside Saint Drogo's. This was an enormous horde of them that had grown and grown as one pack merged with another. There had to be more than a hundred. Judging by how spread out they were, they had ambushed the camp from the woods.

I watched one carrier grab an old rebel woman by the hair

Enemy Inside

and drag her through the snow. Another rebel leapt on his back, but the carrier just shook him off, finally catapulting the woman against the table outside the mess tent.

As I stood there, frozen, I realized something was wrong. These were not the slow, weak carriers I'd seen in the riots. They were too fast.

Some early-stage carriers could take on a human with nearly as much strength as they had before infection, but these carriers were so far along that it was difficult to tell if they were male or female. They had all lost their hair except for a sick, downy fluff coating their scalps, and they were wrinkled and emaciated. Their mouths were raw and chapped, and when they screamed, their unnerving bloodshot, jaundiced eyes bulged from their sockets. Even their clothes were destroyed, hanging in filthy rags from their bony shoulders.

Stunned, I looked around for Logan, but she was nowhere to be found. Many of the rebels who had been taken by surprise when the carriers stormed into camp were locked in combat, using anything they could find to fend off their attackers. Some kneeled behind the tents, guns poised, but very few people were firing shots for fear of hitting other humans. I wanted to shout that shooting the carriers was our only chance — that these carriers weren't like the others — but those who were still at camp were not trained fighters. Many were injured, weak, or timid.

I raised my rifle and fired at a carrier who had broken off from the group in search of a new victim. The familiar kickback stung my shoulder, but my aim was true. Scanning the perimeter of the camp, I took out two more carriers in range who had broken away from the fighting rebels.

A few yards away, another carrier fell. I could see the blood spurting from the back of his head — a perfect shot. I glanced around for Logan but didn't see her.

Enemy Inside

I wanted to yell at the rebels fighting the carriers with sticks and pans and bats. It was too risky to shoot into the fray with so many people, and we were losing.

Hands shaking slightly, I took aim for a knot of carriers who had cornered two older women near the woods. I aimed conservatively toward the carriers and missed. Adjusting my aim, I took a deep breath to fire, and something huge collided with me from the side, knocking me off my unsteady leg.

A sharp pain rippled up from my lower back, and the weight of my attacker crushed my chest.

I couldn't move. I couldn't breathe.

I didn't have to look to know it was a carrier. The stinking rot of his flesh filled my nostrils and curdled my insides. I choked, feeling the fear surging inside my chest. There was no one to help me — no one to pull him off.

Flailing wildly, I struck him hard on the head with the butt of my rifle. He groaned but did not back off. I couldn't shake him. He was the size of a fully grown man and just as strong. He was staring down at me with those horrible eyes, and I could see the skin peeling off the corner of his mouth. He was going to rip into the soft flesh of my neck and dismember me.

Without thinking, I reached up and shoved my thumbs into his eye sockets, fighting the urge to vomit as I felt the wet, round softness against my fingertips and heard the carrier's scream of pain.

He fell off me, and I took the chance to hit him with my gun again and struggle to my feet. He was writhing on the ground in pain, clutching his eyes. When he turned, I stomped on the back of his neck as I'd seen Logan do once and heard the sickening crunch.

He stopped moving.

My throat contracted, and I bent over automatically and vomited into the snow. It was too much.

This time, I heard the carrier crunching through the snow behind me. The sick rattle of his dying breaths made the hair on the back of my neck stand up.

I whipped around, my injured ankle throbbing in protest, aimed, and fired. He was so close I could feel the mist of blood on my face, but he was still coming at me. I backed away, tripping over the carrier I had killed, and fell back onto my elbows.

Another two carriers were ambling over, and I struggled to stand as the one I had shot slowed to a stop. He was too close to shoot again, so I hit him as hard as I could on the side of his head.

I turned to the other two carriers. It was hard to tell from their deteriorating faces and fluffy bald heads, but their features looked eerily similar; these two were twins. I raised my rifle, but my hands were shaking too badly for a clean shot.

Instead, I flung it over my shoulder and felt for the knife at my belt. One of the twins flew at me so quickly that I wasn't entirely prepared. Her bony fingers wrapped around my throat, pushing down hard on my windpipe. I froze, my brain fighting the sudden lack of oxygen. I whipped the knife through the air — grazing her shoulder — but she didn't even seem to notice.

Choking for air, I let myself collapse back onto the ground. She fell forward with me, and I took the opportunity to drive the knife into her back with as much force as I could muster.

It hadn't been a clean shot to the heart, but she screamed in pain. It was an eerie, tearing sound of sinew in her throat that made my stomach turn. I shoved her off and tried to sit up, but her sister flung herself onto me. Out of breath, I fell

Enemy Inside

back again and dropped my knife. Swinging wildly at the side of her head, I watched her sister twitch slowly out of the corner of my eye. The other twin holding me down had a mad look in her eyes. She drew her shoulders back like a snake preparing to strike its prey. I groped behind me for the knife.

Nothing.

My hands shook as they pushed into her rotten flesh, holding her off me. I was exhausted, but she was about my size. I could win this fight. Glowering down at me with her bloodshot blue eyes and wild, drooling mouth, she continued to struggle. She chomped her teeth together, and they made a horrible clicking sound. I shut my eyes — wishing I could shut my ears — and suddenly she stopped.

The twin looked around as if she had lost her train of thought, and I saw the blood blooming on the front of her shirt like a boutonniere.

She let out a horrible shriek, as though she knew she was dying, and I took her distraction as an opportunity to shove her off me and get to my feet. I looked around wildly for the sniper. It had to be Logan, but she was nowhere to be seen. I grabbed my knife and the rifle that had fallen off my shoulder and looked around. There were so many carriers. Some rebels were still fighting, but many were injured or helping those who were get to safety. Without Logan or Greyson or Amory fighting by my side, I felt completely alone.

Undeterred, I threw myself into the fray and picked off one of the carriers who had cornered a woman by the med tent. Once his comrade fell, the other carrier turned and lumbered toward me. As soon as his back was turned, the woman drove her knife into his neck through the carrier's jugular. I winced as blood spurted from the wound. I hadn't used that method to kill a carrier, and since watching Amory

Enemy Inside

do it in Sector X, I didn't think I ever would.

Just as I was about to stab the fat, pale female carrier hovered over a man on the ground, I saw another carrier running toward me. I turned, but it was too late. It collided with my ribcage, and I fell to the ground, smacking my head against something hard hidden under the snow. The stink of death was everywhere.

The carrier holding me down was not as far along as the others. There were no sores around his mouth, and he still had some of his thin, mousy brown hair. Fresh blood coated his mouth like a vampire, and his yellowed eyes had a murderous gleam I'd never seen before. It wasn't the look of pain and desperation I saw in most carriers' expressions; this carrier had been a man who liked to inflict pain before he was infected.

I wielded my knife, drawing back my arm to stab him through the chest, but he snatched my wrist and held it down. This carrier still had his sharp human reflexes. I bucked and squirmed, trying to get him off me, but he was too heavy. I swung my non-dominant fist toward his head, but he grabbed that wrist, twisting it painfully to the side. This carrier was definitely too strong, even at this stage in the virus's progression.

Fear pounded in my chest. I couldn't fight him off. He was going to kill me — bite into my neck and tear out the tendons and rip me limb from limb.

He lurched forward. I twisted to the side, and I felt his sharp teeth connect with my shoulder. I cried out. The bite stung — more than any normal cut should — and I imagined the virus ripping through my veins, poisoning my bloodstream. I was vaccinated, but I felt sick and disgusted as he drew his mouth away for a second strike.

This time, he connected with the tender flesh between my neck and collarbone. His teeth ground together, tearing the skin. The pain emanated from the wound down through my chest, and I screamed in pain.

He was enjoying this. He was going to rip the flesh from my body slowly. I twisted away, sickened by the feel of my own blood soaking the front of my shirt.

A shot rang out, but it did not connect with my carrier. The pain throbbing from my wounds was making my vision go fuzzy, and I fought the urge to pass out. The carrier's eyes gleamed yellow, like two headlights at the end of a long tunnel. Blackness rippled in my line of sight, and I could have sworn I saw the carrier smirk in satisfaction.

I heard more shots and the screams of dying carriers, but mine was still alive. I wanted to yell for someone to shoot him, but I couldn't find my voice. It was as if he had ripped out my vocal chords when he tore into my neck.

Then an arm wrapped around his throat from behind, jerking his chin upward. A knife sliced across his throat, and someone shoved him off me. I saw a guy with short black hair and caramel-colored skin appear over me. His expression looked grim as he took in my wounds.

I closed my eyes. The loud noises all around me were giving me a headache. I suspected I had hit my head hard when I fell to the ground, and now that the adrenaline was burning off, I could feel the throbbing on the back of my skull.

"I dunno . . . this one's got some nasty bites," said the man standing over me.

"Well? Are you just going to leave her there?"

The second voice was a woman's. It sounded strangely familiar, calling back from a distant place in my brain.

I heard the crunch of snow near my head, and when the woman spoke again, her voice was triumphant.

Enemy Inside

"Get her to medical right away. This one's going to live. She's been vaccinated."

I opened my eyes, squinting up for my savior. A curtain of silvery hair shone in the sunlight, and a pair of huge rectangular glasses stared down at me.

"Ida!" I tried to sit up, but everything hurt.

The man who'd wanted to pronounce me dead held me under the shoulders and helped raise me into a seated position. I looked around.

The death all around was astounding. Carriers lay bleeding every few feet in the snow, and plenty of rebels were dead or wounded, too. Those I recognized who weren't badly hurt were huddled in groups, crying or tending to the wounded. Over a dozen new people in black were picking their way over the dead bodies, searching for survivors.

"How did you —"

"Plenty of time to talk later, dear," said Ida. "Right now, you need to get those bites taken care of."

"Where's Logan?"

Ida's puzzled expression hit me hard, like a wave of icy water. If everything was fine, she would be climbing out of her sniper perch to find me.

I allowed the man to help me stand and limped off into the tree where I thought she was hiding. I squinted up into the branches but did not see the glimmer of her golden blond hair.

I looked all around the ground. Nothing.

I stumbled through the snow over dead people and carriers, calling her name. I tried not to look too hard at the faces of the dead; I couldn't bear to see anyone I knew.

Then I saw a puddle of golden waves spilled out over the

ground. I fell, tripping and running on my sprained ankle toward her. There she was near the edge of the woods, her blood clashing brilliantly with the snow.

"No!" I whimpered. I fell to my knees and placed a shaky hand on her shoulder.

Logan's eyes were closed, and she had horrible gashes running from her neck to her shoulder. It looked as if a whole chunk of flesh near her jugular had been ripped away, and precious blood was seeping from the wound onto the ground.

I felt the tears overflowing in my eyes, and I pressed my ear to her chest. Unbelievably, I could hear the faint beat of her heart.

"Help!" I cried. "Over here! She's alive! Help!"

Crying uncontrollably, I placed my hand over the wound, trying to assuage the flow of blood.

Why was no one coming?

I put my hands under her shoulders and tried to heave her up, but my arms were shaking too badly with shock and fatigue to drag her myself. I fell down to my knees, ignoring the cold wetness of the snow.

I waited for what seemed like a very long time.

My head felt fuzzy. Someone pulled me off Logan and scooped me up out of the snow. I wanted to fight them, whoever was taking me away, but I was too weak to lift my head. I didn't want to let Logan out of my sight for fear that someone would pronounce her dead, but my brain was sluggish, and my lips were chapped and raw.

I couldn't form the words. I just let them carry me away.

Chapter Twelve

Slowly, painstakingly, I regained consciousness.

I was lying on something scratchy. There was a sharp sting of antiseptic in the air, and the soft glow of lantern light flickered behind my eyelids.

Opening my eyes, the light beige interior of the medical tent came into focus. I was lying on one of the cots, and I was right about the scratchy brown canvas sheets. There were many more cots crowded in here now than I remembered, all of them occupied.

Shriver's partition had been drawn back to fit in more beds, and I could see the remnants of her life crowded into a corner. There was a fuzzy purple robe, a teetering stack of books, and a small trunk she was using as a nightstand. Perched on the trunk was a goofy hand-painted frame with a picture of a scruffy bearded man with a Dalmatian.

"You're awake," said Shriver herself.

I looked around. She was hovered over a man covered in bandages. By the looks of it, half his face had been torn off, and he had a deep gash in his abdomen.

"You're lucky," she said. "You're in much better shape than most of this lot. Just some blood loss and probably a mild concussion."

Logan. I twisted my head around desperately, trying to find her, and felt a sharp pain in the base of my neck.

Enemy Inside

"Easy!" snapped Shriver.

I felt my neck, where a large bandage was covering the chunk of flesh the carrier had ripped out.

"Where's Logan?" I asked.

Her eyes flitted toward the partition, which was drawn around the bed just across from my cot. A dark cloud settled over her face. "She's lost a lot of blood."

"Will she . . ." I struggled to form the words. "Will she be all right?"

"It's lucky she was vaccinated, but she's in shock. And we don't have any blood put away for this sort of thing."

"Give her my blood!"

"You aren't in any shape to lose more."

"Will that fix her?" I could feel the tears in my throat again, and I swallowed hard to clear the mucus.

"If the transfusion is successful and she doesn't contract an infection . . . then yes, she may live."

I didn't like her emphasis on the word "may."

"Can I see her?"

Shriver regarded me for a moment and then seemed to decide I was strong enough to handle it. She drew back the partition.

Lying under a mound of blankets bandaged up to her chin was Logan. Shriver had cleaned all the blood off her face, and her hair was pushed neatly to one side of the pillow. She looked like a broken doll: deathly pale and still.

The flap of the med tent rustled, and Ida stepped inside. I hadn't noticed before, but she was dressed as a rebel. She still wore one of her billowy skirts with the burlap patches that looked like pieces of carpet sewn together, but she had a utility vest on over it, a baggy coat, and a holster of weapons around her waist.

"Haven! So good to see you're awake."

"How did you —"

"We were in the area on a mission listening to the PMC frequency. They reported a horde of carriers headed this way, and I already knew half your camp was fighting the PMC soldiers sent out to scout for rebels."

My heart raced. I didn't want to think about Amory and Greyson out there fighting the PMC.

Ida looked down at Logan, wearing the same concerned expression as Shriver.

"How is she?"

"She needs a blood transfusion," said Shriver.

Ida held out her arm. "Take mine. I'm O negative."

Shriver seemed to brighten at this. "Are you sure? It will be painful."

Ida nodded. "Anything I can do to help."

Shriver pulled another cot up next to Logan's, and Ida lay down. With her long, silvery hair spilling over the side, it was almost creepy; she could have been a much older version of Logan. Shriver donned a new pair of gloves and bent to swab Ida's arm with alcohol.

"I'm going to apply a local anesthetic. A direct transfusion will be fastest. I have to cut into your arm to expose the artery. You'll have a permanent scar."

"I already have one." With her sleeve rolled up, I could see she already had a jagged X-shaped scar where her CID had been cut out that looked a lot like Amory's.

"You defected?" I asked in awe.

Enemy Inside

She nodded. "It was the only way. And now that the farm is gone —" Her voice hitched, and I could hear the pain there.

I couldn't imagine what it must have been like for her to hand over her farm to the PMC.

I couldn't see exactly what Shriver was doing. She was hovered over Ida on the cot. I knew it had to be painful, but Ida didn't make a sound. When Shriver moved over to Logan to cut into her arm, I could see there was a plastic tube that would run from Ida's artery to Logan's vein, transferring the blood.

"Field transfusions are less than ideal," Shriver murmured. "It's difficult to know exactly how much blood is going to the patient."

"I think what you're doing here is phenomenal," Ida replied.

Shriver beamed.

"You may have your hands full in a while," she added.

My heart contracted. I knew she was referring to all the rebels who had gone out to fight the PMC.

"We'll have to convert another tent," said Shriver in a strained voice. By the look of her, I could tell she was exhausted. The rebels desperately needed another doctor.

"I'm more worried about all the dead afflicted," said Ida. "How many of you have been vaccinated?"

Shriver's eyes darkened, and I knew the answer. Almost all the rebels were undocumented, meaning almost none of them had received the vaccine that protected against the virus. It took a long time for the meaning of that to sink in, and when it did, I felt the panic rising up in my throat.

"Greyson shouldn't come here!" I said. "He hasn't been vaccinated."

"You rescued Greyson after all?" Ida looked proud. "That's wonderful." Her eyes flitted to the ground, as if she didn't dare ask more for fear of shattering this happy revelation. She turned her head toward me. She had to know. "And the others?"

My heart sank. I did not want to be the one to tell her whom we had lost. "Not all of them," I said. My voice shook. I couldn't look at her. "Amory is with us. Roman ran off to join the PMC, and Max —"

It was too much. I couldn't say it.

"Max is dead," I choked. "The PMC killed him during the riots. He sacrificed himself so the rest of us could escape."

Ida's face fell, and for the first time since I'd known her, she looked old. Her eyes darted around the tent without really focusing on anything, glistening with tears. "He was practically my own son," she whispered. "I . . . I can't believe he's gone. But I guess . . . I guess I should have known. He never would have left Logan's side for a minute."

She smiled a watery, motherly smile at no one in particular, and I had a vision of Max going ahead of Logan to check for danger at the drug store — even though Logan was the one with combat training.

My own eyes stung, and I looked away. I tried not to think about Max. The guilt was too much, and there was no one I could talk to about him. It seemed selfish to bring it up with Logan or Amory; I knew their pain had to be greater than mine. Whatever state she was in, I hoped Logan wasn't listening.

"Will she be all right now?" I asked, refocusing on Logan.

Shriver's mouth was a hard line. "I don't know. She may need more blood than Ida can safely give."

"Can we find another donor?"

"She's B negative. She can only receive blood from someone who's O negative or B negative." Shriver's voice became a low whisper. "It's not likely."

The tears were coming now. There was nothing I could do to stop them. I couldn't lose Logan. She'd become one of my best friends.

The tent flap rustled again, and two of Ida's men rushed in carrying another woman. She was whimpering like a wounded dog and bleeding profusely from her abdomen. They laid her down on a cot I couldn't see and drew the curtains around her. Shriver shuffled back to examine her, looking grim. Staring at the ceiling of the tent, I tried to block out the sounds the woman was making. I felt helpless.

Several minutes later, the crying stopped. It was silent for a long time. Then Shriver emerged from behind the partition, and the two men carried the woman back out again with a brown sheet draped over her body.

I shivered. A tent full of those fighting to live had no place for the dead.

I drifted in and out of consciousness, and when I finally became alert again, Shriver had disconnected Ida from Logan. Ida looked fine, but Logan was still too pale.

I turned to Ida, who was sitting at Logan's side with a radio in her lap. It was just static, but I knew she was listening in on the PMC frequency for any news about the rebels who had gone off to fight.

When I opened my mouth to speak, my voice was scratchy. "Is she —" I coughed, and Ida got up to bring me a cup of water.

"Shh. Just rest, Haven. Doctor Shriver is doing everything she can."

"I can give my blood!"

She shook her head. "You can't. You're A positive."

I sighed, wondering if she was just telling me that so I would let it drop. "When the others get back, you have to keep Greyson from coming to camp. I don't want him to catch the virus."

"He will be fine. The virus has a long incubation period. We will know who is infected long before they are contagious." Ida's tone was tired. I understood. She too had watched people she loved die.

"It's not safe here!" I tried to sit up, but pain shot up my neck when I tried to lift my head. I could practically feel my wound ripping open again. "With all the dead carriers? And what if more come?"

"We're hoping to have all the bodies gone tonight. That way, the dead won't be able to infect anyone else, and they won't draw more of the afflicted here."

"Are they burying them?"

"I'm afraid not. There's a large ravine not far from here. We just don't have the manpower to dig that many graves."

I swallowed. For a moment, I was glad I was confined to bed. I didn't want to leave the tent and see all the dead carriers and rebels lying in the snow.

The sun was going down, and I heard the ring of the dinner bell. It seemed strange to me, but even after the disastrous invasion, life went on as usual.

Ida left to get me some food and returned with a steaming bowl of chili and crackers. She helped me prop myself up into a half-seated position so I could eat. The chili was PMC rationed and didn't seem to contain any beef, and I was grateful. Something about a ravine full of dead bodies when meat was so scarce introduced a morbid thought that made my stomach turn.

After I'd eaten my fill, I fell into a fitful sleep. I tried not to listen to the endless static of Ida's radio as I lay shivering on my cot. Several more injured rebels were brought in, and Shriver kept returning to Logan's bedside to pile more blankets on her. The wind rattled the tent poles and whistled in through the cracks in the canvas. It was freezing. When she left the tent to draw fresh water, I could see it was snowing again. Huge, wet flakes were blowing about, and I worried about all the rebels who were out fighting in the elements.

Some time in the night, I heard a screech on the radio and a garbled man's voice. We listened intently, but between the static from the storm and the howl of the wind, it was impossible to discern what he was saying.

Ida got up from her vigil at Logan's bedside and drew her hood up to block the freezing wind. I wanted to run and scream in frustration. What was happening with the rebels? Where were Amory and Greyson?

I waited, but Ida did not return. I lay there listening to the wind, unable to move. Shriver had disappeared to set up another medical tent. As it was, ours was overflowing. It reeked of blood and antiseptic and sick people.

After what felt like hours, I heard a shout in the distance. I tried to sit up again, but my injuries stung in protest. There were more shouts coming from outside, but carried on the wind, they sounded very far away.

I heard footsteps in the snow, and the tent flap was whipped back. Amory stepped into the tent. He was covered in blood and dirt and sweat, but under all the grime, his face was pale white. His eyes locked on mine. In two strides, he crossed to my bed and threw himself down on top of me.

"I didn't know. I'm sorry. I-I would have come sooner." His fingers raked my face as he examined my wounds. "Are you okay?"

"I'm fine," I said in a scratchy voice. "But Logan . . ."

Amory turned, and his face fell when he saw her lying there. The color still had not returned to her face, and she looked so small buried under the mound of blankets. As he sank down on the cot next to her, the tent flap rustled again.

Standing in the entrance with a huge cut running down the side of his face was Greyson.

"Hey." His eyes darted from me to Logan. He pushed his hands into his pockets, looking like a lost little boy.

"I was worried about you," I said.

He let out a burst of air and flopped awkwardly onto the edge of my cot, throwing an arm around my shoulder and pulling me in to him. "I'll take the PMC any day over a horde of carriers, but I wish we'd been here. I'm sorry."

I smiled a little, letting myself relax slightly now that I knew they were both all right. Then I noticed his eyes darting to Logan. She still had not moved.

Finally, when he could delay the question no longer, Amory cleared his throat. "What's wrong with her?" His voice sounded helpless.

"She's lost too much blood," I said. "Shriver gave her a transfusion, but it wasn't enough. Logan's B negative, and that's a really rare blood type."

"B negative?" repeated Greyson.

"Yeah."

"I'm B negative. Give her my blood."

It was too good to be true. I squeezed Greyson around the waist. "Really?"

"Yeah, of course."

Enemy Inside

Before I could say anything, Shriver rustled in looking harried. I shot Greyson a look I hoped communicated my gratitude and relief.

"No. No. No. There are too many of you in here. You need to clear out."

"Shriver!" I tried to sit up to get her attention, but she already had her hand at the neck of another sleeping patient, checking his pulse. "Shriver, Greyson is B negative."

She let out a long burst of air. When she turned, I could see the puffy gray shadows sagging under her eyes. "I don't have time to do another transfusion right now. I've got a whole mess of wounded people in the other tent who need patching up."

"I can get started on them," said Amory.

Shriver looked reluctant, but I could tell she was giving in. "You know, even with the right amount of blood, there's still only about a fifty-fifty chance she'll make it. Her wounds are very serious."

"Please," I said, cutting her off.

She sighed heavily. "All right. Kid, are you sure you're B negative?"

"I give blood all the time."

Shriver turned to Amory. "Get in there and start triaging the returning soldiers. I'll be in as soon as I can."

Greyson sat on the cot next to Logan's, but Shriver forced him down into a reclined position.

"I have to cut into your arm."

He nodded, but I could see a twinge of panic in his eyes. Greyson hated hospitals, and "giving blood all the time" was a generous lie he told about the two times he had passed out at blood drives on campus. I couldn't believe he was doing

Enemy Inside

this for Logan — for me.

This time, I could watch as Shriver cut into his forearm to expose his artery. My stomach turned as she fiddled with the tube that would connect his bloodstream to Logan's and cut into Logan's other arm to expose her good vein. Suddenly I understood what she meant when she said field transfusions were less than ideal. They were much more invasive for both the donor and recipient, and they were much more personal.

Once Logan began receiving Greyson's blood, Shriver stayed for several minutes, watching for any adverse reactions.

Logan did not change.

Finally, she turned and left to go help Amory tend to the wounded, and Greyson and I were left alone with Logan.

We sat in silence for several minutes, me listening to his ragged breathing. It was the sound I only heard him make in times of extreme fear or at the end of a hard sprint.

"Thanks," I said.

"For what?"

"For giving her blood. If anything happened to her . . ."

"I know," he said quietly. "But she's not just your friend now." He cleared his throat, and when he spoke next, his voice was higher than normal. "I like her, too."

"She likes you."

Greyson's head twitched toward me, but he snapped his eyes back to the ceiling. "No, I mean . . . I like her a lot, Haven."

The full meaning of his words hit me, and I felt a smile pulling at the corners of my mouth. It felt oddly foreign. These sunny moments were too few and far between lately.

"I know it's stupid," Greyson continued. "I mean, I know

she was in love with your friend who died."

"Max." His name sounded fragile as it left my lips. He was already fading away.

"I've seen that look she gets . . . when she's thinking about him."

"It's been really hard on her. It's been hard on all of us."

"I know. She'll never want me."

"Of course she will."

"I can't compete with a dead guy," he said bitterly.

"Greyson!"

"I know. I'm sorry. It's just . . . he'll always be better in her mind. When people die, you build them up so much. You forget how to love someone real."

"You don't know that. Just give her some time."

"I *know*! I'm not an asshole. I shouldn't even think of her that way, but she's just . . ." he trailed off, and I understood. Logan was incredible, and it made me happy to think of my two best friends in the world together.

"I wish you'd met her before this happened," I said, fighting a yawn. "When Logan turned on the charm . . . you wouldn't have stood a chance."

He let out a soft laugh and then fell silent.

"What if she dies while I'm connected to her?" he asked after several minutes. "What if my blood kills her?"

"Haven —" The scratchy voice from underneath the pile of blankets was so faint, I thought I had imagined it.

We both stared at Logan's face. For a second, she looked as though she were still unconscious, but then she grimaced with her eyes still closed and spoke again. "Haven, get this morbid asshole away from me. I am not going to die."

Greyson's face lit up, and I felt a cold weight lift off my chest.

"It's working!" he whispered in awe.

"Of course it's working," she said indignantly.

Greyson and I stared at each other, smiling too hard to respond.

Finally, Logan opened her eyes and looked around the tent. Her eyes settled on Greyson for the first time and narrowed as her fuzzy brain worked to connect the dots.

"You shouldn't be here," she said. "This place was crawling with carriers. You'll get infected."

He shook his head. "When I heard you two were hurt . . ."

"Where's Amory?"

"He's helping Shriver with the wounded soldiers."

Logan looked relieved. "What *happened* out there?"

I stared at her, completely stunned. Thirty seconds after waking up, she had already asked the question that had been pushed completely out of my mind upon seeing Greyson and Amory whole and healthy.

"We drove them off," said Greyson. "For now. I expect they've just crawled off to call in reinforcements."

"Do they know where the camp is?"

He shook his head. "They don't know the lay of the land well. They'll have satellite rovers out, and if those get within a mile and pick up humans . . . Rulon's amping up all the signal jammers."

"But they'll find us eventually."

"Most likely," said Greyson matter-of-factly. "We need to rally so we can have enough people ready to fight when they do show up."

Logan and I exchanged looks.

"We've lost so many people," I said.

"Who? Anyone we know?"

I felt a twinge of guilt. "I don't know. I haven't left this tent."

Greyson lowered his gaze. "How many were there?"

"Over a hundred. It was a massacre. If Ida and her people hadn't shown up . . ."

"Ida?" Logan tried to sit up but winced in pain. Still reclined, Greyson reached over and gently pushed her back down.

"She was listening in to the PMC frequency. She showed up when she heard that the carriers were on the move. It's the biggest horde ever recorded. Even the PMC was panicked."

"But who's she with?"

I shrugged. "They looked like rebels to me."

Logan looked doubtful and lowered her voice. "That doesn't make sense. Why would Ida be running with rebels? She never has before, and she doesn't approve of their methods."

"Maybe she didn't have anywhere else to go."

Logan shook her head. "Do you know how many illegals Ida has helped since the Collapse? She has friends all over the country. She would've had her pick of safe houses." Her eyes widened. "If Ida's with the rebels, something is definitely wrong."

Greyson snorted. "Gee, you think? This place just got mauled by a hundred carriers, and the PMC is closing in on the largest rebel camp in the country. I think we're past all that."

Right on cue, Ida breezed in the tent, holding a tray with three steaming bowls of stew, a pitcher of water, and half a loaf of bread. Her eyes flitted to Logan automatically and then did a double take.

"Oh my Lord!" Her face lit up. "You're awake!"

Since I was the only one in a half-upright position, Ida shoved the tray into my lap and collapsed on the side of Logan's bed.

"Oh, sweetheart! I was so worried!" She bent and kissed her forehead, reflexively wiping the area for lipstick with her thumb even though she wasn't wearing any.

Logan smiled and looked over at Greyson sprawled on the cot next to her with his blood still flowing.

"Greyson, I presume?"

He nodded warily, unsure what to say, and Ida chuckled in delight and pulled him into her bosom.

"Ooh, so good to finally meet you! I'm so happy you're safe! It was all Haven could think about, saving you."

Greyson made a muffled noise of assent, face still buried in Ida's fleshy shoulder.

She thrust him away, positively beaming, with one hand still squeezing his arm. "I'll get Shriver and have her unhook you two. She's running Amory ragged over there."

Ida disappeared, and a very irritable Shriver appeared. "I'd nearly forgotten about you," she muttered to herself.

Greyson threw me a panicked look and winced as Shriver bent to fiddle with his arm. He tried to hide his pained expression from Logan, but I could see how ashen he had gone. Watching Shriver remove the tube, even I had to

Enemy Inside

suppress a gag.

"You owe this young man your life," Shriver murmured to Logan as she bandaged Greyson. "If he hadn't shown up, I don't think you would have made it."

"I know," said Logan with a weak smile.

Greyson grinned and sat up abruptly, reaching over to grab a bowl of the hot stew. But the moment he moved, he looked as though he regretted it. "Whoa."

"Well, slow down!" Shriver snapped, rolling her eyes and shuffling over to her corner of the med tent. "Have some sugar." She shoved a package of Oreos into Greyson's lap. "You've given a lot of blood. You're going to be woozy."

"I haven't eaten all day," Greyson muttered defensively, crunching on an Oreo from his inclined position while Shriver patched up Logan's arm.

"How many PMC officers were there?" I asked.

"Dunno. Probably fewer men than we had, but they were better trained. And they kept sending in reinforcements. If we're lucky, they'll think that was all of us."

"Not many of us left," snapped Shriver.

"How many were killed?"

"I don't know. I've lost eighteen injured so far. Nothing I could do for them." Her syllables were sharp and clipped, but I could detect the grief and helplessness there, too.

When she was finished, she helped Logan sit up and went to check on the man covered in bandages. I handed her a bowl of stew and watched her spoon it out tentatively.

"How do you feel?" I asked.

"Like a carrier took a bite out of me."

I finally voiced a thought that had been plaguing me since

Enemy Inside

the attack. "There's something different about these carriers, don't you think?"

Greyson sat up slowly. "What do you mean?"

"They're stronger — faster. They even seem smarter. Do you remember the ones from Saint Drogo's in the riots?" I asked.

Greyson set down the package of cookies and reached for a bowl of stew. "I mean, yeah, but most of those were stage four, and they were locked up for such a long time."

"Maybe. But the carrier who almost killed me . . . he still had that human look in his eyes. It was like he knew what he was doing. And the other ones I fought . . . they were way too strong."

Logan chewed on a hard piece of bread crust thoughtfully. "Maybe the virus is mutating. That happens."

"If it is, then we have a much bigger problem. How do we know the vaccine will work if it's mutated?"

"We don't know if it works at all," Greyson snapped. "The PMC has fed us so many lies."

"But I've never gotten the virus, and I've come in contact with plenty of carriers."

He shrugged, and I felt a cold vise clamp around my chest. We had to get Greyson out of here before he contracted the virus — if he hadn't already.

The tent flap opened, letting in a gust of cold wind and a flurry of snow. Amory stepped inside, looking weary. He sank down on the edge of my bed, and I handed my bowl with the last bit of stew to him.

"Well, hello to you, too," said Logan.

Amory jumped, nearly spilling the stew all over his pants. A grin broke across his face. "Good to see you're alive."

Examining Amory's bruised and bloodied face, I noticed several wounds that weren't there before.

"Did you get in a fistfight with the PMC?"

He looked sheepish. "No."

"These weren't there before," I said, tracing the most pronounced bruise.

He shrugged, avoiding eye contact.

"This sucks," he said, ladling out a lump of pinkish chicken from the bowl.

"Don't change the subject."

He sighed, eyes darting guiltily to the side. "I may have gotten into it with Jared."

"Seriously?"

"That's not like you," said Logan.

I threw her a dirty look. Chastising Amory for aggression that he couldn't control wasn't what he needed right now.

"How come?"

He shrugged, and I thought maybe it was best to let it drop. "What's going on out there?" I asked.

"Regrouping, I think. Trying to see how many able-bodied people we have left who can fight off the PMC."

We fell silent, listening to the wind howling outside. At least the PMC would be unlikely to launch an attack in this weather. Its officers weren't accustomed to fighting the elements the way the rebels were.

Suddenly, nearby voices cut through the wind. I recognized one as Ida's immediately. We all fell silent, listening intently.

"Be reasonable. You have much bigger problems to worry about. None of these people have been vaccinated. An outbreak at a time like

Enemy Inside

this would cripple —"

"My camp is not your concern."

The second voice belonged to Rulon.

"I'm just saying it would be best to be on the move as soon as possible. It's not the PMC or the afflicted you need to worry about."

"What are you saying?"

"I'm saying the PMC is taking its orders from someone you might not have thought of."

"Who then?"

"Aryus Edric."

Chapter Thirteen

The four of us sat there, listening intently to Ida and Rulon arguing.

"That's ridiculous," Rulon scoffed. "Why would Aryus —"

"Why?" asked Ida. "He's the one who stands to benefit from all of this."

"The Private Military Company is its own entity gone rogue."

"Who's giving the orders, then? I know you blew up every general they had in the riots."

"So they've appointed a new general."

"The riots didn't even faze the PMC. Why do you think that is? It's just the military branch of a much larger entity."

"World Corp International owns the PMC?" Rulon let out a harsh, guttural laugh.

"Is that so hard to believe? They distribute the food, they made the largest campaign donations for years before the Collapse, and their scientist developed the vaccine. Every breakthrough agricultural, pharmaceutical, and tech product in the last decade has come from World Corp International."

"What would World Corp stand to gain? The country is overrun. Everyone has migrated north."

"Well, for one thing, people paid for the vaccine. And

Enemy Inside

now they're building a new life in the north. I can think of a few ways World Corp could profit from that. Have any of us actually seen what it's like up there?"

Rulon was silent for several seconds. Finally he spoke again, but with much less resolve. "That doesn't change our strategy. If we continue to push back against the PMC, we will begin to make a dent. Another riot like the ones in Sector X would devastate their ranks. I won't discuss this again."

"Then let's discuss relocation. This place is contaminated. Almost all the survivors are unvaccinated. There's going to be an outbreak, and when it happens, we'll all be sitting ducks for the PMC. How long do you think it will take them to find this camp? A day? A week?"

"You've got some nerve," snarled Rulon. "You barge into my camp and start delivering orders when you've been cowering on your farm for the last year."

I tensed, anger flaring inside me.

"I'm not giving orders," said Ida. "I'm just sharing what I know . . . and sharing my concern. Your ranks took a hard hit today, and I'm willing to join forces. But I will not put my people in danger by sitting around waiting to be found or for those dead people to befoul the water supply when the snow melts."

"Leave, then," Rulon said in a deadly whisper. "Take a few days to regroup. Then get out of my camp."

Rulon's footsteps faded away, and I glanced across the tent to Logan and Greyson, who looked serious.

"Ida's right," I whispered. "We need to leave."

Amory nodded. "Rulon's stubborn. He would get us all killed before agreeing to retreat."

"When do we leave?"

Enemy Inside

"As soon as Logan is well enough to move, I say."

"Do you think it's possible?" Logan whispered. "Do you think World Corp International is really behind all this?"

"I don't know. How much do they control?"

"Everything," said Greyson. "I went to a bunch of protests against them before the Collapse. They've been involved in every major corporate disaster of the last few years. They built those oil pipelines that exploded. They had to recall Deleseltric because it caused cancer. They manufacture almost every tech product you can buy. They're the largest food distributor in the country. They've been linked to everything from E. coli outbreaks to mad cow disease to predatory crops."

We all fell silent as the weight of the information sank in. It wasn't clear to me *why* they would own the PMC — I just knew it seemed very likely, given everything else they controlled.

Amory and Greyson went off to wash away the blood and grime from battle, and Logan and I were left alone in the medical tent, listening to the sounds of ragged breathing coming from the beds nearest us.

"What about all of them?" I whispered. "They might all die."

Logan shrugged. "Some of them would rather die than leave Rulon. I haven't seen anything like it since the PMC. He's got these people completely brainwashed."

"Where will we go?"

"Anywhere. As far away from Sector X as we can get."

"I always thought it was smart . . . hiding under the PMC's nose, stealing food from Sector X. But now it seems like a terrible place to be."

Logan sighed. "They're still dependent on the system that

failed them in the first place. It's putting food in our mouths every day."

"What do you think they do with prisoners now? Chaddock, Waul, Saint Drogo's . . . they were all destroyed in the riots."

"I think they kill anyone who disagrees with them. Who's to stop them? Not the U.S. government."

It was an uneasy thought. Whoever was giving the PMC its orders, that entity was now completely in control. There was no question of that anymore.

Soon, the sound of Logan's breathing became slow and even, and I knew she had fallen asleep. I felt a pang of worry. Her injuries had taken a toll. How long would it take her to recover from such a massive blood loss? How long before we could be on the move?

The tent flap opened, and Ida blew in with a gust of wind.

"How is she doing?" she whispered.

"We're coming with you," I said. "Please, let us come with you."

Ida nodded. "As soon as she's well. And the sooner the better, really. I have overstayed my welcome here."

"And the others?"

"Leaving with anyone will devastate Rulon's ranks, but I think it's only right to offer everyone a choice. I'm not sure anyone will want to come." She laid a warm, motherly hand on the top of my foot, which was covered in blankets. "It's dangerous to let anyone else make your choices for you, Haven. Never forget that. Following blindly leaves you blind."

She left, and Amory returned carrying a rifle. His hair was damp, and he was pale and shivering, but he looked clean and much less worse for the wear.

Enemy Inside

"Greyson's sleeping. I think the fighting wore him out."

As he set his rifle on the floor and sank down next to me, I felt my heart speed up. "You should go back, too," I said.

He looked hurt.

"You should rest," I added. "You've had a long day."

"I can't rest when they're out there. I'm not leaving you in here unprotected. Ida was right. How long do you think it will take for them to find this place now that they've gotten so close?"

"They won't try again — not in this storm."

"Maybe not."

Lying back against my pillow, he threaded his fingers through mine. His knuckles were bruised with lots of small cuts across the tops, but his warm fingers were gentle. I became very aware of every part of our bodies that were touching, and I tried to slow my breathing.

"Is this okay?" Amory asked. He turned his face to me, and I could see the seriousness coming through his expression of longing. "I'll go if you want me to. I don't expect you to trust me after what happened this morning . . . and with Jared. You don't have to be scared, but you don't have to trust me, either."

"I do trust you."

"If it makes you feel any better, I think I'm getting it under control."

I threw him a dubious look.

He laughed. "No, really. This morning, the rage took over, and I felt . . . blind. When Jared started running his mouth out there, I hit him because I just felt like he deserved it."

"What was he saying?"

"You don't want to hear it."

"Tell me."

"It was stuff about you . . . locker room talk." He grimaced. "I don't want to repeat it."

I smirked. "Were you *jealous?*"

Amory looked bemused and then flustered. "Of course I was jealous! I don't want you to be with him. I want you to be with me."

My heart swelled. I looked up at him. "I am with you."

Amory grinned and brushed the hair off my face. I looked up at him, trying to memorize the warm, soft look in his eyes. These days, he so seldom let his guard down that this side of Amory was rare to see.

He pulled me closer, and I laid my head against his chest, drifting off into the first peaceful sleep I'd had at camp.

The next morning, when I finally emerged from the tent, the entire camp was blanketed in snow. It covered the patches of blood, and all the dead had been dragged away to the mass grave. I wondered who had been responsible for moving the bodies — carrying them the half mile to the ravine. Probably the few rebels who had been vaccinated. That sent a ripple of guilt down my spine.

Those who had survived and were not confined to the medical tent milled around in silence. Though the snow concealed the evidence of death, it hung very present over by the mess tent. A couple people were crying silently around the blazing fire, huddled together on a log. I realized I didn't even know who had died in the battle or at the hands of the carriers.

But all these people weren't only grieving for their friends who had died. Most of them were facing the strong possibility that they would become infected and die a slow, awful death as a carrier. What was worse, they wouldn't even know if they were infected for days.

Moving through the mess line in silence, I took my bowl and glanced absently at the rough chalkboard denoting everyone's duties for the week. I needed a job to do.

I was startled when I realized it was the same schedule as last week; none of the dead rebels' names had been removed.

Amory took a bowl for Logan, and I sank down on a log near the fire. I looked down at my breakfast, and my stomach turned. It was a bowl of slop: a mixture of runny gravy, potatoes, corn, and specs of sausage. It made sense. In happy times, the food always seemed to reflect the good fortune of the camp. In bad times, the food was terrible.

I looked around for Greyson, but he wasn't even in the mess line yet. Even though I knew he couldn't contract the virus from the rebels who were infected, I felt a sense of urgency to get him away from the area. Death hung like a dark cloud over the entire camp, and I was determined to escape with everyone I loved.

Once I finished, I limped back to the med tent to see if Shriver needed help with anything. My body was battered and broken, but I was still more able-bodied than a lot of the rebels.

As I rounded the corner of the tent block, I heard a terrible retching sound. The snow was sullied with the spilled bowl of morning slop, and its contents were running together with another sickly substance.

Amory was bent double around the side of the tent. He jumped when he saw me out of the corner of his eye, wiping his mouth with the back of his hand and going red in the face.

"You should see Shriver," I said, instantly worried. Under ordinary circumstances, the flu wouldn't have been an issue,

Enemy Inside

but roughing it in the wilderness, a simple illness could get out of hand and take a person's life.

"I'm fine," he said hoarsely.

"You're sick." My eyes raked his pale complexion and his shaky, clammy hands.

"I'm not. I'm . . . I think I'm going through withdrawal."

"Withdrawal from what?"

"The drug they had me on in Isador. I don't know what it was . . . something that messed with my brain . . . made me more receptive to the sessions." He said the last word quietly, eyes flickering downward, as though the memories still sent a wave of terror through him.

"How long has this been going on?"

He shrugged. "Since we left Sector X."

"And you didn't tell me?"

"I didn't want to worry you. Besides, with the effects wearing off, I'm feeling more like myself again. The fighting is more or less under control now."

I raised an eyebrow at his hedged language but didn't push it. I was happy to be getting closer to the old Amory again, even if the process was making him lose his breakfast.

Once he had recovered, I began fetching food for the injured who were well enough to eat and helped Amory bandage the simpler wounds. Shriver kept me busy running for more bandages, tools, food, and kerosene oil, but the number of injured rebels just seemed to be growing.

All the while, I kept one eye on Logan. She still wasn't well enough to get out of bed, and she slept for most of the day. Greyson hardly left her side, except to bring her food. Hovering over her, it was as if he thought he could personally ensure his blood would help her recover.

Enemy Inside

By dinnertime, I'd had enough of the stench of alcohol and blood. I limped out to the fire where the rest of the camp was gathered. The mood had not lifted at all. Warming my hands with my bowl of stew, I looked around for somewhere to sit. Amory and Greyson weren't there, and every other cluster of people sat in a cloud of despair. Death hung all around them, and sitting down would have felt like an intrusion on their very personal grief.

Finally, I saw Kinsley sitting off on a log by himself. Hunched over his stew, he looked very small, and I was reminded once again how young he was.

"Hey," I said.

His large ears perked up when he saw me. "Hey!"

"Can I sit?"

"Yeah."

I sat down awkwardly, watching him watch me out of the corner of his eye.

"Is your friend doing okay?"

"Logan? Yeah, I think she's going to be all right."

"Good. I like her." His face flushed a little, and I grinned.

"Yeah, I think it would take more than one carrier to get the best of Logan. She's pretty tough."

"And your other friends? They made it back, so that's good..."

I felt a pang of insensitivity. Everyone I loved had survived, but I was in the minority.

"What about you?" I asked quietly. "Did you lose anyone?"

He shrugged. "I don't really have anyone to lose. I'm just kind of hanging out."

Hanging out. That was a strange way to describe what we were doing. Then again, all of us were just "hanging out," hoping we didn't get killed. Somehow, not having anyone to lose seemed sadder. I tried to change the subject.

"Hey. What do you think of Rulon?" I asked. I tried to sound casual, but the question was loaded. As young as he was, Kinsley worked more closely with Rulon than anyone else.

"He's all right."

I nodded, wondering how far I should push him. "Ever hear anything interesting? I know you help him with a lot of stuff."

He shrugged again. I wondered if I had shrugged so much when I was a teenager. "It's mostly just PMC movements. We track them and try to listen in on their frequency, but a lot of their intel is in code. Sometimes I work on breaking it."

"You break their codes?"

"I've broken some of them. My dad had this old book on cryptography. I read it over and over again when I was a kid."

"That's cool."

"It's not that hard."

We sat in silence for several minutes, but it didn't feel awkward. I liked Kinsley, and I wished he wasn't Rulon's errand boy. He was a good kid, and I had the bad feeling that Rulon was leading the rebels into disaster. He wouldn't even listen to Ida, which made me think he was scared — scared of the PMC's power and scared of what we didn't know.

The next day, Logan was still confined to her bed on Shriver's orders, but she was sitting up and talking animatedly to Greyson. By the look of the warmth returning to her cheeks, we would be able to travel soon.

I had Shriver reset my ankle. It was healing, but I needed to be able to walk on it properly — run if I had to. She tsked when she saw how much it had swollen after the carrier fight, but she put it in a brace anyway. It fit into my boot and eased the pain I felt when it bore weight.

I wasn't the only one who was anxious to leave. When Greyson wasn't at Logan's bedside, I caught him throwing wary glances at all the rebels milling around. I knew he was thinking the same thing I was: In a few days' time, the camp would have some hard decisions to make.

Amory shuffled on and off guard duty, sleeping intermittently in his tent for a few hours at a time. With so few uninjured men left, he was pulling double duty and helping Shriver between shifts.

That lack of sleep combined with his withdrawal symptoms and the fact that he, Greyson, and Kinsley shared a tent with Jared had put him on edge. According to Greyson, the mood in the tent had not improved since Amory started the fight with Jared. Now, whenever the four of them were in there at the same time, there was just a strained, awkward silence.

Kinsley was the only one who seemed to be taking the carrier attack and imminent PMC invasion in stride. He had more responsibilities than ever, especially as Rulon's lackey, and he seemed to mature overnight into a much older boy. He relieved the older men of guard duties without being asked, brought food to some of the other rebels who were grieving in their tents, and took it upon himself to restore the awkward harmony that had existed between our group and Jared.

One night, after Logan had begun to regain her health, there was an odd rustle at the flap of the med tent. Most of

Enemy Inside

the rebels who remained under Shriver's care bore more serious injuries, so they had been moved to the auxiliary tent to be cared for en masse. The four of us nearly had Logan's tent to ourselves, and we all looked up in surprise when Jared stuck his head in the tent.

It was strange seeing him without his PMC whites on. He was wearing black cargo pants and boots like everyone else and a half-zip black sweater. His messy blond hair stood out starkly against all the black.

Jared cleared his throat uncomfortably. "Hi. Good to see you're looking better," he said with a nod in Logan's direction.

Logan's mouth twitched, and I could tell she was suppressing a laugh. "Thanks. I'm almost . . . good as new."

"Right. Well, that's good." Jared's eyes wandered around to us. He gave a general nod of acknowledgment and then ducked out without another word.

"He's got some nerve," said Amory under his breath.

"I think it's nice," said Logan.

"Why?" snapped Greyson.

I looked over in surprise. Greyson had never expressed dislike for Jared since he had extracted Amory and me from Sector X. He was sitting on the floor against Logan's cot — her own personal watchdog.

"I mean —" he stammered. "After fighting with Amory and all . . ."

"Amory started it," I pointed out.

"You wouldn't say that if you heard what he said about you," Greyson muttered.

I let the topic drop. I didn't want to know what Jared had said about me because it was awkward enough being around him and knowing he'd said anything at all. Plus, seeing Amory bristle at the very sight of him made me even more anxious to leave camp.

Four nights after the attack, Ida found me at dinner. I could tell it was her approaching by the way her skirts swished through the snow. She sighed and sat down on the log next to me, holding two cups of hot tea. It was a motherly gesture, but I knew something serious was on her mind.

"It's time for us to leave," she said. By her tone, I could tell the decision weighed on her heavily.

For the first time since I'd known Ida, she was really showing her age. She had deep crevices around her mouth that ran together and split off to form shallower tributaries. The eyes behind those huge glasses were deep set and tired. Her long hair now looked less platinum blond and more white and raggedy — like Father Time's beard.

"I know."

"You don't seem very upset."

I smiled bitterly. "I shouldn't even be here now. Rulon hates me. He thinks I'm a traitor."

"If he really thought you were a traitor, you'd be dead. You just make him nervous."

"So do you."

"No. He thinks I'm a crazy old woman who spent too many years 'cowering on my farm.' And maybe I am, but I've moved on. You don't get to be *my* age without a little self-preservational instinct."

"He still won't listen to you?"

She shook her head. "He's leading these people without any real strategy or direction. When he was with Mariah, he was *too* reckless. She pushed him — goaded him — into doing things against his better judgment."

"Like bombing the base."

Ida nodded gravely. "If I had known what they were up to, I never would have sent you with them." She hung her head, and I knew she was thinking of Max. "Now with Mariah gone, he's paralyzed. He doesn't know what to do. He was never cut out to lead all these people. She was. Rulon just brought the charisma . . . the people skills. Mariah was the one with a brain for strategy."

"She manipulated him."

"Of course she manipulated him. Behind every great leader is the real brains of the operation, Haven. Remember that."

We sat in silence for several minutes, blowing on the hot tea.

"When did it get like this, Haven? It's something I never thought I would do." She continued, not expecting me to chime in. "Turning my back on people who need my help. But I'm not wanted here. And frankly, I won't let my people risk their lives under Rulon's leadership any longer."

"How did you end up with the rebels?"

She sighed, looking tired. "What else am I supposed to do? The PMC confiscated my farm. They took my deed and handed me my migration papers. That farm has been in my family for over a hundred years, and they took it in a second. It was only a matter of time, I suppose. We're a dying breed, we 'independent resistors.' Most of my old friends have gone deep underground. My husband died years ago, and we never had any children. I don't have any other family."

"You never thought about going west?"

She shook her head. "I don't have any interest in fleeing. Not when the country is falling apart. Joining the resistance . . . at least I can be of use."

I felt a twinge of guilt. I didn't have Ida's heroism.

Greyson and I had planned on going west, but that dream seemed so distant now. "Is your camp like Rulon's?" I asked.

"Not quite, no. You'll get to see it for yourself. It's a camp run by one of my oldest friends. He doesn't inspire loyalty by using intimidation and torture. We do our bit . . . collecting intel that will help us weaken the PMC." Ida was staring off into the fire. "There's a war coming, Haven. All it takes is for people to realize what's happened. It's right there in front of them, but nobody wants to believe it. When they see the PMC for what it really is, the American people will be at war with World Corp International."

"How are you the only person who's figured this out?"

Halfway into a sip of tea, Ida wrinkled her nose. "I'm sure I'm not. But most people don't believe one corporation could ever be strong enough to hold us hostage like this. And the PMC was contracted out by the federal government. The people think their elected leaders orchestrated this, which in their view means it must be the best thing for us."

"But the government is in hiding."

"No one really wants to believe that."

Something Ida said earlier surfaced in my mind. "Have you been up north?"

"No. But I don't imagine it's going so well. If we don't go to war against World Corp, we'll be at war with the Canadians."

I sat back, letting her statement sink in. Somehow, it was hard to imagine a war so close to home.

"When do we leave?"

"Tomorrow. Before first light. I think Logan is strong enough to travel. We need to be gone before any of the people here start showing symptoms. There's going to be a panic, and I don't want to be caught in the middle of it."

I nodded. "We'll be ready."

Chapter Fourteen

It wasn't difficult to pack up the few belongings I had accrued since leaving Columbia. A few knives, extra socks, the FN SCAR Logan had stolen for me, and a copy of *Animal Farm* from Shriver were scattered around our tent. The rest of my belongings were already packed away. I felt a pang of sadness that I didn't even have a photo of my parents like Greyson's to remember them by. It was as though the PMC had erased my family entirely.

Logan breezed through the back tent flap holding a bundle of clothes and a smug grin.

"It pays to flirt with the supply tent guys," she said, tossing a pile of clothes on top of my sleeping bag.

Apart from being a little thinner and slightly pale from her ordeal, Logan seemed to be herself again, which had its advantages.

Examining her haul, I was glad to see she had found a heavy winter jacket for each of us, several pairs of heavy wool socks, and what looked like ski pants. These were hot commodities we couldn't even get when we were on relatively good terms with the rebels. And now that we were defying Rulon and leaving their ranks, there was no way they would let us take anything like this.

"I can't believe you raided the supply tent without stealing any extra ammunition," I chided. "It's not like you."

Logan looked at me as if I were crazy. Pulling aside her

sleeping bag, she tugged at the zipper of the thin pallet underneath. She yanked out a long, flattened bag, and the foot of the pallet deflated considerably.

"Please. You know me better than that. I swiped these the day we got back from Sector X. And I swapped out Greyson's HK416 for another SCAR. I doubt he even noticed."

"You're a genius," I said. "We should get some stuff for them to wear."

She scoffed. "My flirting is much less effective when I say I'm taking clothes for my two male travel companions."

I raised an eyebrow. "They're going to need them."

While Logan returned to the front entrance of the supply tent, I peeked through the crack in the canvas from the back. Her high-pitched giggle was the signal — a sound I never heard her make in regular conversation. I ducked in silently and crept to the men's clothing side.

There were bins and bins of shirts, pants, socks, coats, boots, and long underwear. The pants were loosely organized by size, but I realized I had no idea what size either of them wore. I grabbed several different pairs, hoping whatever didn't fit one might fit the other, two winter jackets, and as many pairs of heavy socks as I could carry.

Logan was saying something about hockey players versus wrestlers on a scale of relative hotness, and I rolled my eyes in her direction to signal that I had found what we needed. She giggled, and I made my exit. We met back at our tent, Logan looking disgusted with herself.

"It's really not even fair," she said. "They're like middle-school boys. Too few women rebelling, if you ask me."

I snorted. "You should start a movement. Equality — more women for the male rebels to flirt with."

Enemy Inside

Stomping through the snow to the back entrance of the boys' tent, we heard two people arguing: Jared and Amory.

Logan poked her head in through the tent flap. "Hey, shut the fuck up. We can hear you guys all down the block."

She squeezed inside, and I followed reluctantly, elbowing around Amory and standing at his side. Jared was seething by the front entrance, his shoulders raised in a defensive posture, and Greyson was sitting on his sleeping bag, looking frustrated.

"What's going on?" Logan asked in a falsely cheery voice.

"Just found out you and your friends are traitors," said Jared. "Your old friend Ida is causing a huge riff."

"Ida came to Rulon first," I said.

"Sure she did," Jared muttered.

"She *did*. I heard her. But Rulon's stubborn. He won't listen!"

Jared cracked a snide grin. "Yeah, I heard about her crazy World Corp International theory."

"No, we need to move because this camp is going to collapse when the virus sets in," said Amory. "The PMC is closing in. We can't just stay here and wait for them to find us when we're most vulnerable."

Jared shook his head, eyes still burning with fury. "Isn't that nice?" He pointed from me to Amory to Logan. "You . . . and you . . . and you have all been vaccinated. A handful of the few people guaranteed not to become infected are leaving."

"Everyone has the option of coming with us," I said. "Right now, everyone else has the same chance of becoming infected."

"And what do you plan to do once they start showing

symptoms?" he shouted. "Throw them out in the cold?"

Being reminded of Mariah felt like a slap. Even though I had not been the one to throw her out of the bunker to die, revealing her secret to the rebels had doomed her instantly.

"What I did wasn't right," I said. "But I would do it all over again. She threatened my friends."

"Can you blame her? She was just doing what any of us would have done. She was protecting the cause." He laughed coldly, looking up over our heads. "That's the problem with you people. All you care about is each other!"

"They're all I have left."

"She was all *I* had left!" Jared yelled. "She was my sister!"

It hit me like a ton of bricks. I didn't know what to say.

Staring at my shoes, his last word hung on the air between us in the crowded tent. I opened my mouth to say something — anything — but he backed out into the snow with a huff.

Logan let out an audible sigh and found my hand. She squeezed it once, and I felt the warmth travel up my arm in a comforting way. "Everyone is someone's sister," she whispered, "or brother or friend. But that doesn't mean we do anything differently."

Hearing Logan of all people say that broke my heart. *How could she still have so much resolve after losing Max?* After everything that had happened, I felt as if I were losing mine.

I knew she was right. I couldn't think about who might be affected every time I killed a carrier or shot at a PMC officer. As terrible as it was, given the choice between saving an unknown person's loved one and saving one of mine, I'd choose Amory, Logan, and Greyson every time.

"I should apologize," I said.

Enemy Inside

"Who's that going to help? You or him?"

I gave her a funny look.

Logan sighed. "Sometimes it's easier if you have someone to hate."

We gave the boys the supplies we had stolen and returned to our tent to catch a few hours of sleep. We changed into our warmest clothes, and I decided to sleep in my gear. The coat was a little baggy, but it was warm and had lots of pockets for knives and extra ammunition. It felt as though I had barely closed my eyes when Logan was shaking my shoulder to wake me again.

It was still pitch black as we rolled up our sleeping bags and traipsed out into the snow toward the meeting place at the top of the hill.

The bonfire in the center of camp was burning low, and no one was out talking late tonight. After the carrier attack, a chilling fear had settled over the camp. I imagined no one wanted to be out alone.

The only other light came through the cracks of the medical tent. On impulse, I crossed over and stuck my head inside. Most of the beds were still occupied, and Shriver was sitting on a stool, cleaning her instruments.

"How are you feeling?" she asked without looking up.

"Great."

An awkward silence hung in the air, and I didn't know what to say.

"Are you leaving now?" she asked.

Her question took me by surprise. I nodded.

"Safe travels, then." She reached over and tossed me a lightweight canvas bag. "Make sure your friends change their bandages regularly. Infection kills."

I smiled. "Come with us."

She looked up at me through those enormous glasses. "My place is here. There are going to be a lot of sick people very soon."

"Aren't you worried you'll catch the virus?"

"I've been vaccinated," she sighed. "Wish I could say the same for this lot."

My insides squirmed uncomfortably. I realized I knew very little about the woman who had taken care of me and my friends without asking anything in return. I didn't even know she had been documented, and now seemed like a strange time to ask about her story. I nodded. "Well, thanks . . . for everything."

"Just doing my job."

I took one last look around the crowded tent where she worked in silence caring for sick people, glanced at that picture of the man with the Dalmatian, and ducked back out of the tent.

"What was that about?" asked Logan.

"Just seeing if she wanted to come with us."

Logan gave me a strange look.

"Don't you ever think about the people who get left behind?"

She shook her head. "You can't think that way. It's too much for any one person to deal with."

We continued toward the hill, and I tried to forget about all the rebels sleeping in their tents who might wake up in a few days and realize they were just months away from a terrible death.

Up ahead, I could see a cluster of dark figures waiting. As we drew closer, I recognized several of the people who had come with Ida and some of Rulon's rebels. She had gone from tent to tent in the night, inviting anyone who wished to leave.

"What about provisions?" I asked the man standing next to me. He was the one who had found me after the carrier attack.

"It's taken care of," he said.

I heard a murmur of voices coming from the direction of the tents, and three figures materialized in the darkness. I recognized the outline of Amory's broad shoulders and slim torso and Greyson's brisk, effortless gate, but the third person stormed behind them with a purposeful, angry stride.

A glint of blond hair caught my eye, and my heart sank.

It was Jared.

"What's he doing here?" Logan muttered to Greyson.

"He wanted to come."

Logan gave him a threatening look, and I saw her instinctively reach for one of the knives in her holster. "He better not make trouble for us."

Greyson grinned.

We waited for several minutes, and Ida finally arrived. She was dressed in heavy pants and boots with tufts of fur sticking out near her kneecaps, and she wore a furry hat with flaps that came down over her ears. Trailing behind her and looking nervous was Kinsley.

"He wanted to come and you were going to leave him behind?" I asked Amory.

He shrugged. "He's Rulon's errand boy. I never see him."

"Is this everyone?" asked Ida.

I exchanged looks with the people standing nearest me. No one said anything. Most of the people from Rulon's camp avoided each other's gaze. I knew they must feel like deserters.

Enemy Inside

"Hold up a minute," called a deep voice.

I looked back toward camp to see a bulkier figure loping toward us through the snow. A feeling of dread settled in my chest. If Rulon had caught us leaving, there would be trouble.

Then the outline of a shaggy beard began to take shape, and Godfrey came striding toward us. He was wearing a heavy coat with the furry hood pulled up around his leathery face. For a moment, I thought he might be coming to make trouble, but he had a rucksack slung over one shoulder and an AK-47 in his other hand. He looked terrifying.

"Room for one more?" he grunted.

Amory shot me a grin.

"Of course, Leo," said Ida.

Logan snorted, but Ida just beamed.

"Well?" he said. "Let's get the show on the road."

As we trudged down the hill, I noticed that each of the rebels Ida had come with carried rifles, but she did not. The back of my neck prickled as we passed the tree where the lookout was usually posted before remembering that Kinsley was with us. No one called out for us to stop, and I felt slightly unnerved that no one was watching for approaching carriers or PMC.

I caught up to Ida, who was stomping cheerfully through the deep snow.

"Where are we going?" I asked.

"We have two vehicles stowed a mile away with enough fuel to get us to our camp. We can regroup from there."

"Regroup?"

She nodded. "We'll decide as a group what our next steps should be. Rulon's camp *was* the largest rebel force in the east. Now that he has given in to his fear, we may need to take a larger role in the rebellion."

"What's going to happen if some of these people become infected?" I asked.

Ida sighed. "I don't know. Let's take it one thing at a time."

I thought back to the time I'd spent on the farm with the rest of the illegals Ida had taken in. At the time, she had a policy of not hosting carriers, and I hoped her stance on that had not changed. There was a fine line between helping those in need and suicide.

I fell back to walk with Logan, Greyson, and Amory. Greyson had a worried look in his eyes, and I followed his gaze to Logan. She looked paler than she had back in our tent and was breathing heavily. Although the walk through the deep snow was strenuous, I knew something was wrong.

"Are you okay?" I asked in a low voice.

She nodded, but I could see the exhaustion in her eyes. Even after her transfusion, the injuries she sustained in the carrier attack had weakened her significantly.

To distract her, I nodded toward Jared, who was walking far ahead by himself. "Why do you think he decided to come?" I muttered to Greyson.

He exhaled. "Rulon cut out his CID when he got back from Sector X. It was too risky now that they were onto us."

"And that's why he decided to leave?"

He shrugged. "Being a mole was part of his identity. Besides, I think he hoped that one day he would be able to go north."

"Why didn't he?"

Greyson grimaced, and I could tell he didn't want to say.

"Why?"

"Mariah."

I felt another pang of guilt.

"There's nothing left for him now that he can't go into Sector X. I think he just wants to have a purpose again."

"What I don't understand is why he came to rescue us if he knew I was the one who outed her."

"It's his job, Haven. Besides, he's loyal to Godfrey. Rulon didn't care if you two lived or died in Sector X. It was Godfrey who sent him in to get you."

As the camp disappeared behind us in the thicket of trees, I felt a surprising weight lift off my shoulders. I realized I had never felt comfortable in Rulon's camp. The two times I had been tortured under his direct orders were seared into my brain, and it was disconcerting to live under the protection of someone who didn't really have your best interests in mind. I still didn't trust Jared's motives for coming along with us, but I felt much safer with Ida and the people she surrounded herself with.

We followed Ida through the woods in pitch blackness, tripping here and there on exposed tree roots and snagging branches. Unsteady on my ankle, I tripped more than usual. The moon was just a sliver in the sky, and the only thing I could discern was the bright snow and the sound of Ida's footsteps up ahead. It was so dark I didn't see the two huge trucks until they were a few feet away.

They looked a lot like the truck we had traveled to Sector X in before the riots, except these had open beds with tarps over the top that sagged under the weight of half a foot of snow. The tires were enormous and came up to my hip. I knew they would have no trouble plowing through the deep snow.

Ida tossed Godfrey a set of keys, and I followed Greyson and Amory toward the nearest truck. A dozen rebels had already piled in, slipping on the frozen puddles inside from water that had dripped down through the canvas. Greyson helped Logan in first, who collapsed onto the bed and laid her head against the side of the truck. Even in the darkness, I could tell she wasn't right.

Amory squeezed in next to me, and I felt the warmth of him through my coat. I leaned against him and felt myself relax. Soon we would be at Ida's camp, and Logan would be able to rest.

The truck rumbled, and I was suddenly very aware of how crowded it was in the back. I counted fifteen people, most of whom were Ida's rebels. The few who had come from Rulon's camp looked around nervously. Kinsley was on Greyson's other side, and I was struck once again by how young he looked.

"How old are you, Kinsley?" I asked.

"Seventeen," he muttered.

Greyson shot him a disbelieving look, and his ears went red.

"I'll be sixteen in December."

"Where are your parents?"

He shrugged. "They're gone. The PMC was recruiting, but I . . . I defected."

Logan's eyes widened. "How did you end up with Rulon?"

The side of his mouth twitched. "I sorta ran into him in the woods."

"You were captured?"

He nodded. "He said I could stay if I cut out my CID. I didn't have anywhere else to go."

She shook her head. I realized the rest of us had been very lucky to find Ida's farm when we did.

The truck groaned as it plowed through the deep snow,

and the bed rocked from side to side whenever we reached a patch of hard-packed snow that wouldn't give. It was slowgoing through the woods and freezing in the back of the truck. One of the rebels from Ida's camp passed around bottled water, and we all gulped it quickly.

Logan was the only one who sipped reluctantly. She looked queasy.

"You have to drink," I murmured. "You need fluids."

She nodded, but I couldn't help thinking that there was something seriously wrong. Even her bright blond hair seemed to have lost its luster; it hung in limp, sweaty strings around her face.

I knew Ida's camp couldn't be very far from Rulon's, but the entire journey was longer due to the truck's sluggish pace through the snow. No one was saying much, but the steady clouds of breath made the group look as though they were immersed in animated conversation.

The heat of our bodies packed in the small space began to melt the snow piled on top of the truck, and drops of cold water leaked through the canvas on top of our heads, trickled down the backs of our necks, and collected on the already wet floor. It soaked through our snow pants and refroze, leaving our clothes stiff and cold. Compared to our days-long journey to Sector X with Rulon's crew, this trip was miserable.

After several long hours, the truck puttered to a stop. I heard the cab door slam and footsteps crunching through the snow.

Ida's excited face framed in her ridiculous fur hat appeared, and she opened the truck bed.

"Home sweet home!"

Chapter Fifteen

A few people smiled half-heartedly at Ida's excitement, but most of us shimmied out of the truck without a word, blinking in the early morning light.

I rubbed my hands together, trying to restore some feeling, and Greyson stretched like a cat. I had to laugh. In the month and a half since we first left Columbia, he seemed to have gone through a late growth spurt. Without our long runs, he had bulked up a bit, and he seemed not to know what to do with himself.

I looked around for the camp but saw only trees.

"Where is it?" asked Logan.

"It's just over yonder," said Ida. "Not far at all."

I groaned inwardly and followed her through the snow.

This walk seemed even longer than our march away from the rebel camp. My pack had grown heavier since our last walk, and my clothes were soaked through and refrozen stiff in places. I could feel my lips turning blue and ached for the warmth of a fire or a hot shower.

I told myself that wherever we were going, it had to be better than Rulon's camp. But my weary body would not let my mind settle. We were runaways, and now our lives were nothing more than running from one temporary home to another. We would never be able to rest.

Through the trees, I heard a heavy *thunk* that sent my

heart into overdrive.

I stopped dead, ears piqued for another sound.

"It's all right," said Ida. "He's one of us."

Following her cautiously with my fingers humming on my rifle, I jumped when I saw a tall figure appear through the trees. He was an old man dressed in a heavy plaid coat, swinging an axe down on a piece of wood balanced on a tree stump.

"Mr. Murphy!"

"Ida," he said, turning and setting the axe down against the tree. His face was half-concealed by a wild gray beard and a furry hood. It had the ruddy glow of someone who had spent a lifetime outdoors. "You've picked up some strays," he observed.

"These are the folks from Rulon's camp — survivors from the carrier attack."

The man's wiry white eyebrows shot up and disappeared behind his hood, but he didn't look alarmed. "These the only survivors?"

Ida shook her head. "They were ready to leave Rulon's ranks."

He made an irritated tsking sound. "Rulon's a damn fool. All piss and vinegar and no brains."

"He's been . . . reluctant to believe the reality of the situation."

"Well, y'all are welcome here. Name's Eli Murphy."

"Haven Allis," I said, extending a hand. He shook it enthusiastically, nearly yanking my arm out of its socket.

"It's good to meet you, sweetheart. I'm so sorry to hear about your parents."

"You knew my parents?"

"I knew your daddy. Good man."

He released my hand, and I stared at the ground in shock. If I needed any further confirmation that my father had been a rebel, I had it now.

Murphy turned to Amory and Greyson to offer his hand but paused when he came to Logan. His brows knitted together.

"Ida! Ida, this one's sick. What's your name, sweetheart?"

"Logan."

"Have you been vaccinated?" he asked.

She nodded, looking alarmed.

He examined her carefully. "You should be all right in a few days. Your body's just fighting off the virus." Murphy turned to Ida. "I'd keep her away from the rest of this lot that hasn't been vaccinated. She could be contagious."

I was surprised at his relaxed attitude.

"I'll stay away from everyone in your camp," said Logan.

"Oh, no need, sweetheart," said Murphy. "We're all defectors!" He pulled up his sleeve to reveal a long, jagged scar even larger than Amory's running up his weathered brown skin. "Cut it out myself fleeing from Ottawa." He whistled. "I'm a survivor, and I figured I'd be better left to my own devices."

"You were up north?" I asked in awe.

"Sure was. I was one of the first to migrate. I saw this country going to hell in a handbasket. Then I got up there and realized they were all fucking commies."

I must not have shown the reaction he was hoping for, because he waved a dismissive hand and turned to lead us

Enemy Inside

through the trees.

At first, all I could see was the back of a small cabin tucked in a stand of fir trees, but then the clearing opened up, and the entire camp came into view.

It was smaller than Rulon's camp, but much nicer and more permanent. Instead of tents, twenty or so log cabins were dispersed among the trees. There was one large cabin that stood out near the center with an intricately carved entryway and a flagpole out front. The American flag flapped in the wind, and I felt a surge of hope.

This camp was not mired in despair. The people here looked hearty, tough, and busy at work feeding the campfire, carrying baskets of food to the large center cabin, and hauling gallons of water.

The rebels who came with Ida looked relieved and broke off from the group, yelling hello to people meandering through the snow and getting their backs slapped and hands shaken in greeting.

"Did you build all this?" I asked.

"Nah. It used to be a weekend getaway spot — a 'nature excursion' for big-city yuppies looking to escape the rat race. We were lucky to find this place. No electricity and no running water when it's this cold, but there's a nice lake for fishing and plenty of game in the area. Really stupid deer, actually. They're a little too used to humans . . . almost takes the fun out of it."

He gestured to the largest cabin. "That over there is the mess hall. Morning mess is served after the hunt, noon mess is at noon, and evening mess is served at sundown. You'll hear the bell.

"Each camper's duties will be posted outside the mess hall. Work is from dawn 'til dusk, and when you're not working, you're training. Now which of you are good with a rifle?"

Logan raised her hand, along with a few others.

Murphy nodded. "You'll be in the hunting party. What we don't eat, we trade for food at the Exchange. No sucking at the PMC's teat here. Rulon's lucky those bastards haven't poisoned his corn flakes yet."

Greyson snorted in appreciation.

"We've only got a few rules here. Don't leave food out. We're in bear country. Drag animal carcasses far out away from camp, too. Don't steal from the supply cabin — Mrs. Miller gets real agitated when supplies turn up missing. Don't venture out alone, especially without a weapon. Don't trust anyone you meet in the woods. Bring 'em straight to me. Shoot any carriers on sight, and don't throw trash down the pisser. Any questions?"

We all shook our heads, and Murphy led us out to show us to our new sleeping quarters.

"Two empty beds in cabin twelve for the ladies," he directed. "You'll be bunking with Maggie, Dolores, and Camille."

Logan and I broke off from the group. Up close, you could tell that these cabins had been built to house tourists and were designed to withstand the elements. The wood had a shiny finish, and there were bears and leaves carved into the posts that wrapped around the small porch. We stomped the snow off our boots and pushed open the creaky door.

Dim morning light filtered in through the windows, illuminating six beds facing each other from opposite walls. Three were covered in a double layer of heavy quilts. Slippers, drying socks, sweatshirts, and a few books were scattered around the cabin in the orbit of the occupied beds.

We left our boots on the mat by the door. Logan collapsed onto one of the empty beds and put her head in her hands. At first I thought she was just tired, but then I heard a muffled sob escape between her fingers.

"What is it?" I asked, sinking down on the bed beside hers.

She shook her golden head but continued to cry. I stared, utterly lost, until she turned her blotchy face up to look at me.

"He's really gone, isn't he?"

My heart contracted. She was talking about Max.

I moved over to her bed and squeezed her around the shoulders. Her body was giving off an alarming amount of heat.

"I k-kept thinking one day he might just stumble into camp. I thought maybe he survived somehow and that he would find us. Now that we've left . . . there's not even a chance I could see him again."

"I'm sorry," I whispered.

Her teary voice broke into a higher octave. "What if he comes back and we're not there?"

"Logan. He's gone." It sounded as though I was pleading with her, but I could feel the tears welling up in my own eyes. "He's gone. We all saw him."

My tears burned hot where they pooled in my eyes, and I couldn't contain them anymore. The memory of Max in his ridiculous apron was too fresh. He was so happy and pleasant and funny. And he loved Logan. It wasn't fair. Of all of us, Max deserved death the least.

Grief wasn't what I expected. You didn't feel all the sadness and anguish at once. It crept up on you when you were least prepared for it.

My tears dried up before Logan's. The door creaked

open, and Greyson poked his head inside. He froze when he saw Logan crying and looked panicked, wishing he hadn't come. I blinked furiously to hide the fact that I'd been crying, too. Greyson had never known how to deal with this sort of thing.

"I'll just —"

"Can you get us some bedding?" I whispered. "She needs to rest. She's burning up."

He nodded, grateful for an excuse to leave, and disappeared.

After several minutes, Logan's sobs seemed to dissipate. Greyson reappeared in the doorway carrying a pile of quilts and sheets, but he was not alone. Behind him stood an old Native American woman dressed in a heavy coat that fell to her knees. She was carrying a large woven basket. Slightly withered with leathery copper skin, she had to be nearly eighty, but her eyes were bright and her gait was quick and effortless.

She padded across the room on tiny feet in furry boots and placed her hands on either side of Logan's face.

"Don't cry, child," she said in a voice like a bell. "You're going to live."

Greyson helped me make Logan's bed. These quilts looked the same as the ones on the other beds. The fabric was soft and worn, but the tiny stitches along the seams were strong.

Outside, I heard the clang of a bell signaling morning mess.

"Run along," said the woman without looking up. "She's in good hands."

Hesitantly, Greyson and I backed out of the cabin. Logan was already half-asleep in her new bed. Her face glistened with perspiration, but she looked calm.

"What was that about?" Greyson asked as soon as we were out of earshot.

"She was just upset about Max." I hoped he hadn't noticed my tear-streaked face. I hated crying in front of Greyson.

"Oh," he said. He sounded dejected.

I looked at him funny, but his disappointed expression cleared instantly.

"I'm worried about her," I said.

"Why is the virus affecting her like this but not you? You got bitten, too."

I shook my head. "I guess her immune system wasn't strong enough to fight it off completely. She lost a lot of blood. That's why it's come on so quickly."

"But she'll be okay, right?"

"I hope so."

We followed the steady flow of people trickling into the mess hall. They were all dressed like Murphy in heavy fur coats, and they had his rugged look. Most of them were older than those at Rulon's camp. The majority were over forty, and some looked as old as seventy. The men's faces were hidden behind heavy beards, and the women were stronger and stockier than the rebel women, with silvery gray hair and leathery skin.

Inside, the mess hall looked just like a hunting lodge. The rafters were visible in the high vaulted ceiling, and the lanterns were situated in deer antler candelabra on the walls. Several trophies were also mounted around the room. I identified a black bear, a few deer, and even an elk. Everyone had crowded inside around the long wooden tables that stretched from one end of the hall to the other.

Enemy Inside

Amory appeared at my elbow, and we followed the line around the back of the hall to where the cook was serving food. She gave us each a plate of biscuits and gravy and a cup of weak coffee. We found a table and joined the others who were bent over their food, eating with enthusiasm.

The biscuits were hot and fresh, and the gravy had a taste I didn't recognize.

"It's venison gravy," Amory whispered.

I gagged reflexively but took another tentative bite. It was good. Whoever had made the gravy clearly knew what they were doing.

I heard a *thud* like a gavel, and I looked up to see Murphy standing at his table. Every head turned up to look at him, and the chatter subsided.

"Good morning, friends," he said. "I wanted to let you know that the scouting mission was a success. As you may have noticed, we've brought in some new folks. They are our guests from Rulon's camp, and they will be staying here as long as they would like. Please make them feel welcome — and put them to work!"

He laughed a hard, old-man laugh, and several people around the hall joined in.

"On another note, I've received some disturbing news. We've come to understand that the PMC is being run by World Corp International. They're more powerful than we initially realized, but we may have intelligence as to the whereabouts of their leader, Aryus Edric. Our next step will be to terminate Edric and weaken the corporation. Please stand by for details." He paused slightly. "That is all."

A wave of chatter rippled through the crowd. No one was eating anymore.

"*Aryus Edric? I can't believe that old nutcase is behind all this.*"

"World Corp controls everything. It makes sense."

"I'd love to take him out. Let me at him."

"If we dismantle their supply line, the PMC goes down."

Amory shifted uncomfortably beside me, and I knew why. No one here knew who he was, and he was just waiting for someone to ask his name and link him to his father. I squeezed his hand under the table, and he returned it just as forcefully.

Before we had finished our meal, Murphy appeared at the head of our table. I noticed that all the other rebels from Rulon's camp seemed to have gathered around us.

"Let's go, you lot. Work is starting, and we need all hands on deck here."

We followed him back out into the snow. He turned to us, did a quick head count, and cleared his throat.

"All right. We need somebody to apprentice under Seneca in medical. It's mostly basic first aid, patching up cuts and the like."

I looked expectantly at Amory, who was staring at his boots with determination. Finally, a wiry older man raised his hand.

Murphy continued. "We could also use a few more folks on rotation for carrier watch, especially evening guard. I know it's not the most appealing job, but there's the added perk of sleeping through the day."

Nobody said anything.

"I'll do it," said Amory, raising his arm.

"Wonderful. Can you shoot?"

"Yes, sir."

"Perfect. Report to me before evening mess."

Enemy Inside

I elbowed Amory in the ribs and gave him a look. I didn't like the idea of him out there guarding the camp against carriers, especially with his uncontrollable rage.

"I'll go too," said Kinsley.

"Can you shoot?"

"Yessir."

"How old are you, son?"

"Sixteen."

Murphy nodded gruffly. "That's good enough for me, even if it's not good enough for the great state of New York. I'll be needing someone else to go on the hunt — preferably someone who's a good shot. I don't want to be wasting ammunition."

Jared's hand shot up, and Murphy gave a gruff nod. "We'll take you to Miller and get you outfitted for tomorrow. The rest of you . . . I need someone else to help with supplies — inventory and going along to the Exchange to barter for goods we need."

My hand shot up. Ever since Ida first mentioned the Exchange, I'd always wanted to go.

Murphy looked taken aback. "All right. It's at your own risk. You'll be traveling with large amounts of contraband. Think you're up for it?"

I nodded.

Amory bristled beside me, but I felt a surge of grim satisfaction.

I barely heard Murphy giving out the other assignments, but I knew the rest were fairly tame. Greyson took a job with camp operations, which surprised me. His duties would include maintaining the fires and doing simple repairs around camp.

We all scattered to go to our jobs, but Amory grabbed my elbow. He looked agitated.

"Why did you take that job?" he asked. I could hear the anger in his voice. "After everything we've been through, you want to go back out there and risk your life?"

"I didn't know it would be dangerous."

"Of course it's going to be dangerous!"

"What about you? Why didn't you take the first aid job?"

"I just didn't want to."

"You'd rather kill carriers instead? This isn't like you."

Amory raked an impatient hand through his hair. "I know!" He sighed in frustration, eyes burning. "I just want to. I feel like . . ." He trailed off, looking as though he felt foolish finishing the statement. "I feel like it's what I'm supposed to do."

I stared at him. "You think killing carriers is your purpose in life?" I felt the fear rising up in my chest. It alarmed me that his time imprisoned at Isador had changed something so fundamental about his personality.

"You hated killing them on the farm." I lowered my voice and held both his hands in mine. "What about being a doctor? I thought that was your purpose."

"Even that was a lie. I was in training to be a PMC physician. I was enrolled at the Academy." He looked disgusted with himself. "They're not the kind of doctors that heal people, Haven."

I stared at him, sensing I had not heard the worst of it.

He sighed. "They specialize in behavior modification and CID insertions. They're the type of people who tortured me in Isador."

Chapter Sixteen

The next day, our new roommates were gone before sunrise.

When the early morning light fell across my pillow, I poked my nose out from under the covers and felt the chill in the air. Reluctantly, I swung my legs over the side of the bed and into my boots.

My eyelids felt heavy. It had been a restless night. I couldn't stop thinking about Amory and his newfound passion for slaughtering carriers. And I was thinking about what he had trained for at the Academy.

Logan was still curled up in a ball under a layer of quilts, her hair fanned out over her pillow. Sinking down carefully on the edge of her bed, I brought my hand to her forehead. Before it even touched her skin, I could feel the heat coming off her. When I touched her with the back of my palm, she was boiling. A thin layer of perspiration coated her usually perfect skin, and her face had lost its rosy hue.

She stirred, twisting around in her covers uncomfortably, and opened her bleary eyes. "Haven?"

My mouth hung open, a cold vise choking off my airways.

"Haven, what is it?"

Her bright green eyes stared up at me unfocused, and around the edges, I could see a yellowish tinge spreading out around the iris.

Enemy Inside

"Oh my god. Logan!"

"What?"

Not wanting to tell her, not wanting to confirm my own suspicions, I pulled off the covers and yanked the neck of her sweatshirt down. She still wore the neat gauze bandage Shriver had put in place over her carrier wound. Gently, I peeled back the tape to reveal an ugly, gaping gash. Though Shriver had disinfected it religiously and given Logan antibiotics, it was festering around the edges.

Hands shaking, I dropped her bandage and pulled away.

It wasn't possible. Logan was vaccinated. Murphy had said the sickness was just her body fighting the virus, but I knew the signs of early infection. I took a deep breath.

"Logan . . . the carrier who bit you . . . What did he look like?"

"I don't know. He was, uh . . ." She closed her eyes as she remembered, her lip trembling. "Bald . . . miserable . . . rotting like a walking corpse. And his mouth . . . it was oozing with puss and blood from the sores." She covered her eyes with her hands, pressing into her temple.

My stomach dropped. "He was stage five. You're sure?"

She shook her head once, and I could tell she was crying. "I don't know. He looked like it."

Her shoulders started to shake as she succumbed to tears, remembering the attack. I smoothed her hair back, not knowing what to do.

I swallowed. "Logan . . . I don't think your body's fighting off the virus."

She nodded. "I haven't felt right. Ever since I woke up from the attack, I've felt really weak. At first I thought it was just my body recovering from the transfusion, but . . . I think I'm infected."

I didn't say anything. I didn't want it to be true. Then Logan said something I didn't expect.

"You have to kill me, Haven. When the time comes . . . I don't want to hurt anyone. I don't want to be a monster."

"What? No." I shook my head, but even as I did so, I could imagine no other likely scenario.

"You have to. Soon I'll be contagious. I'll lose my mind, and I'll kill people."

"Not for a while. We still have time."

Logan let out a muffled, watery sob.

"I don't understand," I muttered. "You were vaccinated."

"Roman used to say the PMC could have been lying about the vaccine."

"But Amory was bitten back at the safe house, and nothing happened to him."

"Haven." Logan pulled the covers away and looked at me seriously. "You can't tell them yet. They'll make us leave camp. Just give me a few days. I-I'm —" Her voice broke. "I'm not ready to die yet."

I nodded, willing myself not to cry. I wanted to grab Logan and hug her as hard as I could, but I forced myself to keep her at arm's length. I couldn't get emotional — couldn't break down. I had to make a plan.

If Logan was infected, we had weeks, maybe a few months before she would have to be put down. It just depended on how quickly the virus spread. I tried to remember how long my mother had been herself after infection, but my memory of that time was fuzzy.

Then another thought occurred to me: We needed to warn the others. Everyone at Murphy's camp thought they were safe because they had received the vaccine, which made them vulnerable. I couldn't delay the truth for long.

"Can I get you anything?" I asked.

Logan shook her head.

"I'll tell the others you still aren't feeling well. We should have a couple days before anyone gets too suspicious."

Her eyes were puffy and watery. The yellowish hue mixed with the pale pallor of her skin had a startling effect. "Thanks."

I closed the cabin door behind me and almost smacked right into Greyson, who was sauntering up the steps to check on Logan. His easy grin and the bounce in his step made my stomach ache.

"Hey," I said uneasily.

"Hey yourself. How's Logan?"

"Oh, you know . . . she's still got the chills. In and out. She's sleeping again."

"Right." The way he said it, looking at me out of the corner of his eye, I could tell he knew something was off.

"You want to get some breakfast?"

"I already ate." Greyson paused, still eyeing me suspiciously. "But I'll go sit with you. I'm just going to go in and check on her real quick."

"She's sleeping," I repeated too quickly.

Greyson glanced around to make sure we weren't being watched and took a step toward me. "Haven, what's going on?"

I sighed. There was no point trying to hide anything from Greyson. He always knew when I was lying. Grabbing his arm, I pulled him away from our cabin and into the trees until we were out of sight.

Enemy Inside

We stopped, Greyson staring at me expectantly.

"Logan's infected."

He backed away, blinking in confusion. "What? No. Is this a joke?"

I gave him a serious look, bracing myself for his reaction.

"No. She's vaccinated. Murphy said her fever was just her body fighting off the virus. She was weakened by all the blood loss from the attack . . ."

I shook my head slowly.

"Haven . . ."

"My mom was infected. I knew something was wrong with Mariah before anyone else did. I recognize the signs. It's all in the eyes, and hers have already turned."

He stared at me, flabbergasted. "What?"

"Her body isn't fighting it off."

Greyson shook his head, struggling to process the information. "But that means . . . the vaccine doesn't work."

"I haven't quite figured that out yet."

"Haven! We have to tell Murphy! All these people . . . they think they're safe with the vaccine. If nobody is really immune, they can still get infected."

"We don't know that. When Amory and I got trapped in Sector X, the safe house was attacked by a horde of carriers. Amory got bitten, but he didn't turn. Aren't you curious why Logan is infected and he's not?"

"Yeah, of course. But we need to tell him what's going on."

"We can't."

"Haven, we *have* to!" Suddenly he looked seven feet tall — angry and intimidating. "You can't keep this from them!

It isn't just about us anymore. People's lives are at stake!"

"Just give me a few days."

"To do *what?*" he snapped. "You know better than anyone how this ends."

Cold helplessness shot through my chest, and I took a step back, shuddering at the finality in his voice. "I can't kill her."

He swallowed, looking helpless and devastated. "Do you see another way?" His voice broke on the last word, and I felt hot tears burning in my throat.

For a long moment, we just stared at each other. My heart was breaking, and Greyson was wound so tight I thought he might be close to tears, too. His warm brown eyes had turned to stone, and he was breathing heavily.

"I'm not going to give up on her," I whispered.

"Me neither, but — Jesus, Haven!" He turned away from me, yanking a fistful of his hair in frustration. "How long do we have?"

"A few weeks . . . maybe a couple months. It just depends on how quickly the virus progresses."

He raked a hand over his face. "I can't believe this."

"I know."

Then he turned, aiming a hard kick at the nearest tree and swearing loudly. "God!" he yelled. "It isn't *right!* Why did this have to happen? It's like we walk out of one shitty situation right into another. Everything we do just makes things worse!"

I watched him, a little terrified by his outburst.

"I'm sorry."

Greyson shook his head, and I took this to mean he

didn't blame me. He just needed a minute away from everyone else to vent.

He stood still, shoulders heaving as he panted, trying to recover. Finally he looked at me, and I knew it had passed. He was himself again.

"Don't worry," he said quietly. "I won't say a word to Murphy."

I softened a bit, taking a step toward him and pulling him into a hug. "I know you won't."

He seemed to deflate in my arms. I squeezed him once and pulled back, not trusting myself to keep a level head with Greyson and Logan breaking down. "I should go," I said. "I'm late for supply duty."

He nodded. "What should I tell Amory?"

"Nothing yet," I said, feeling a stab of guilt as the words left my mouth. "I need to think."

Schlepping back to camp toward the supply cabin, I felt an even heavier weight on my chest than before I'd told Greyson. Tentatively pushing open the cabin door, I was immediately engulfed by a collapsing pile of linens.

The room was larger than the cabin I shared with Logan and the other women, but every available inch was crowded with supplies: stacks of clothing, pyramids of canned goods, buckets of ammunition, guns and knives hanging on hooks around the room, hatchets, toilet paper, pots and pans, flour, sugar, coffee. There was a pillar of wooden crates that had not been unpacked to my left, and the dim lighting made it difficult to see a path through the stuff.

"You're late," said a voice from the abyss.

"I'm sorry."

A diminutive woman with army fatigues ballooning over tall combat boots emerged from behind a wall of canned corn carrying a clipboard. Her hair was pulled back into a tight French braid at the back of her head, and harsh square glasses rested on the bridge of her nose.

"In case you can't tell, we're drowning here," she snapped. "There's a supply run scheduled for today, and I have no room to put anything! I have canned corn coming out my ass but not enough ammo or first aid supplies."

My heart thudded painfully in my chest at her mention of a supply run, and I instantly wished I had not gotten on her bad side so quickly.

She shoved the clipboard into my hands, and my vision immediately clouded as I squinted down at the minuscule rows of numbers. In tiny, cramped handwriting was the description of an item, followed by a number for each week to show how many had been used or lost.

"You won't get to everything this week," she said. "Pay special attention to our commodity items: flour, coffee, sugar, toilet paper, antiseptic. We check the weapons and ammunition daily. If anything goes missing, it's on your head. If someone needs something, you write down what they took. All the food goes through the mess hall. This isn't a vending machine. Always bolt the door when you leave to keep out bears."

The door creaked open, and Ida stepped inside. "It's almost time to go. Are you ready, Mrs. Miller?"

Miller squinted up at me over her bifocals, and a gleam of satisfaction twinkled in her muddy brown eyes. "Take the new girl. I have things to do." Then she wrinkled her nose despite her obvious delight. "Hell, I'd like to go on an adventure now and again, but I'm stuck here trying to keep this place afloat."

Yanking the clipboard out of my hands, she pulled a folded slip of paper out of her pocket. "Here's my list. Don't short me on ammunition. We're running low."

Enemy Inside

"I'll do what I can," said Ida.

Miller turned back to her work, and I followed Ida through the maze of clothes and food outside. She looked uncharacteristically grim. "Go get your weapon. It's time to go."

The tone of her voice scared me, but I was glad to escape Miller and the cramped supply cabin. She reminded me a bit of Shriver, but without Shriver's obvious care for the people she tended.

I was burning to tell Ida about Logan because *she* would know what to do, but the thought of getting back on the road to visit the Exchange pushed the virus out of my mind.

Back in the cabin, I grabbed my SCAR, two knives, and extra magazines. I wasn't sure if the real danger would be the PMC or carriers, but I thought it best to be prepared for both. When I emerged, I was surprised to see Ida waiting with a gun slung over her shoulder. During my time on the farm, I'd never seen her wield a weapon.

The truck we had taken into camp was already idling on the edge of the narrow dirt road, and two of the hunters were loading packages of venison into the back.

"This week's location requires us to get on the main road," she explained. "The stretch we'll use doesn't have any rovers, but we still need to be on high alert. Trucks like these are a dead giveaway. Whatever happens, we can't lead the PMC back to camp."

Ida turned to one of the hunters, a scraggly man in his late forties with several days' worth of scruff on his chin. "How much will that get me?"

He appraised the pile of deer meat, scratching his stubble. "It's a good haul. I wouldn't take any less than four hundred rounds."

When the last package was loaded, Ida thanked the men

Enemy Inside

and climbed up into the cab of the truck. I followed, nervously taking in the men's weary expressions. Even they seemed to think we might not return.

With her long skirt, Ida looked comical in the driver's seat, but she deftly put the truck in gear and pulled out of camp.

The narrow dirt road quickly opened out to a wider gravel drive, which must have been the entrance to camp when the place was a tourist spot. The snow along the road was punctuated with rustic-looking signs with cheery messages carved into the wood: "Have a safe trip!" and "Visit us again!"

The ride smoothed out as we turned onto a smaller county road, which wound around sharp curves and made me feel a little carsick. Finally we reached the highway, and Ida squinted in both directions. The road was empty. There was no going back now.

Chapter Seventeen

As we drove, I noticed that Ida's eyes kept darting nervously to the rearview mirror. We were silent for several minutes, and I kept expecting to see an overpass with rovers looming in the distance or the flash of blue PMC lights on the horizon.

Soon, however, when we hadn't seen another vehicle for miles, Ida appeared to relax. Without the imminent threat of danger, the sick feeling in my stomach returned. I needed Ida's advice, and she deserved to know about Logan.

"I have to tell you something," I said.

Ida turned her head toward me, looking vaguely surprised.

"But you can't tell anyone . . . especially Murphy. Not yet."

"I won't make that promise, Haven. Not if it's something he needs to know. We are guests at Murphy's camp. He's responsible for all those people."

"You can't. Please. Just not for a few days."

She looked conflicted but sighed. "Go on, then. Your secrets are safe with me."

I took a deep breath. "Logan is infected."

The words hung in the cab between us.

"That's impossible."

"She is. I don't know how, but all the signs are there."

Ida's mouth was hanging open slightly. She was staring out into the empty road, looking completely lost.

"I'm sorry. I know you love Logan."

"Couldn't love her more if she were my own blood. How did this happen?"

I didn't answer. I knew she wasn't talking about Logan becoming infected.

"We need to let Murphy know," she said abruptly. "All his people think they are safe."

"Won't he make us kill Logan?"

Ida shook her head. "Murphy's not a cruel man. But Logan will need to be put down eventually."

Taken aback by her matter-of-fact tone, I stared out at the road, contemplating life without Logan.

"What stage was the . . . carrier who bit her?" Ida said the word "carrier" with some hesitation. I knew she didn't like using a word that implied they were anything other than human.

"Stage five."

She nodded. "There's been speculation that those are the ones that spread the virus. The data we have isn't very good since the outbreak happened so suddenly, but most of the recent cases I've seen have been from someone getting bitten by a carrier with the sores."

"Maybe it's bloodborne."

Ida shook her head. "It doesn't explain the first outbreaks. How did all those people come in contact with infected blood?"

"There were two major outbreaks, right? One in the

winter and one in the summer, meaning they had to come in contact with the virus sometime in late fall and spring. What happened to all those people?"

Ida was deep in thought. "The first outbreak was much worse. Almost everyone was infected between last October and November, and there were a lot of elderly people who became sick."

"Maybe the vaccine only works if your immune system is capable of fighting the virus," I said, thinking of Logan lying on that cot looking like a corpse.

We fell silent, both frustrated by how close we were to the truth. Ida resumed her frantic scan of the road, and a moment later, we decelerated.

Searching the right side of the highway, Ida changed lanes and slowed almost to a stop as she turned down a tiny road tucked into the trees I had nearly missed. The tires groaned as we drove through the hard-packed snow. No one had plowed the road here.

We passed several private gravel roads, and I felt a twinge of sadness imagining all those empty houses. My dad had wanted to move out to a place like this. He loved the country, but he tolerated the suburbs mostly for my mom. She loved the neighborhood barbecues and the green lawns, but my dad had always been more of a lone wolf. Now he would never get his dream home in the woods.

Through the trees, I could just make out a dilapidated white building. It blended in with the snow, but as we rounded the corner, a squat steeple came into view. The half-collapsed sign sticking out of the snow read "Salvation Baptist Church," and the windows looked dark. Several other vehicles were parked along the road and in the gravel drive. Ida stopped the truck.

"Got that list?"

I withdrew the folded piece of paper Miller had given me, and Ida squinted through her glasses to read the tiny, cramped handwriting from the clipboard.

"She must be dreaming," Ida muttered. "She wants four hundred rounds of ammunition plus two gallons of antiseptic, gauze, forty rolls of toilet paper, and thirty gallons of gasoline."

"How much is meat worth?"

"A lot. The only thing worth more is ammunition and fuel, but that's gotten more and more expensive every time I've come here. We're not importing oil anymore, and all the factories, refineries, and oil rigs are now PMC controlled. There's a finite supply."

As Ida muttered some mental calculations to herself, I studied the old church warily through my foggy window. If I hadn't seen the other cars, I would have thought the church was empty. There were no people milling around outside, and the windows looked dark.

"Leave your gun," Ida said, putting her own on the floorboard behind the seat. "These people are a little . . . on edge."

I tucked my own gun away with some hesitation. I didn't like walking into the unknown without it. Following her through the snow, I began to feel the excitement and nerves humming in my chest.

"Shouldn't we get the venison?" I whispered.

She shook her head once. "It's not a good idea to show your hand. These aren't the Murphys or even the Rulons of the world. Most of these people are preppers."

"Preppers?"

"Survivalists. They're the ones who saw this coming. They made it big after the Collapse because they'd already

Enemy Inside

stockpiled enough food and weapons to last for years. But you can't trust them. They're only looking out for themselves and their families. They're not afraid to kill anyone who gets in their way."

I swallowed, feeling the knife hidden under my coat.

"Keep a sharp eye."

As we drew closer to the church, I heard the murmur of voices inside. Ida pushed open the door, and several dozen pairs of eyes snapped in our direction. They were scattered between the pews, vendors using the benches to display their wares as traders prowled up and down the aisles. I couldn't tell which group looked more unsavory. The vendors all had a smug, rugged look about them, and most of the people looking to make a trade were thin with pinched, tired faces.

A few vendors nodded at Ida, but she returned their greetings with a tight, closed-mouth smile so unlike her usual warm, toothy grin. I had never seen her more ill at ease.

To my left, a shout erupted. I turned in time to see a vendor with a scraggly beard spit on the shoes of a man in a tattered winter coat. The trader shoved the man across the pew, and the vendor pulled out a handgun and pointed it at his temple. I froze, preparing to hit the deck, but no one else seemed to notice. The trader whimpered and backed away, clutching a tin of motor oil he had tried to barter.

"Don't stare," Ida murmured to me.

I snapped my eyes away from the vendor but continued to drink in my surroundings. Most of the vendors were selling an odd hodgepodge of items: clothes, tools, weapons, ammunition, car parts, kitchen utensils, canned food, coffee, eggs, vegetables, breakfast cereal, soap, makeup, farm equipment, and even live chickens.

Ida walked straight to the back and stopped in front of a man in his mid thirties with a thick red beard and a leather vest. Tattoos snaked up his folded bare arms, and his skin was smeared with grease. He smirked when he saw us approaching.

"Well, look who the cat dragged in," he said with an appreciative twang in his voice. Something about the way he said it made my skin crawl.

Unlike the others, he didn't have a bunch of random items spread out in his pew. Instead, there was an array of disassembled guns spread out on a greasy towel and neatly stacked boxes of ammunition.

"What can I do you for?"

"Hello, Rick."

"It's been too long."

"I've been on the move. And there's been some trouble."

"Sorry to hear that."

Rick's voice was pleasant enough, but something about him still made me uneasy.

"Who's this?" he asked, looking me up and down.

"This is Haven."

I smiled, not wanting to.

Rick cracked a grin and extended a greasy hand. "Well, Haven, it sure is nice to meet you."

The way he said it made me slightly uncomfortable, and Ida stepped smoothly between us.

"How are you set for meat this winter?"

He shrugged. "We're doing all right. Can't complain."

"You must be spread pretty thin . . . trying to do all the hunting while protecting your family. I heard that area was hit really hard by carriers this summer."

Enemy Inside

"We manage," he said. There was a note of defensiveness in his voice.

"How many pounds of venison would twenty rounds cost me?"

"Venison?" He chuckled. "Damn, I was hoping you'd decided to slaughter one of them fine cows of yours."

She smiled, and again I noticed it did not meet her eyes.

"Twenty rounds will cost you ten pounds of venison."

"How about five pounds?"

"Sorry, Ida. I want to help you out, but venison just isn't worth that. Now if you had beef . . ." He smacked his lips. "But it's getting harder and harder to find ammunition."

She nodded. "All right."

"How many boxes can I put you down for?"

"Fifteen."

"That's three hundred rounds." He laughed. "What am I supposed to do with a hundred and fifty pounds of deer meat?"

"Freeze it."

He studied her for a moment, and there was an odd gleam in his eye. "All right. But only because I like you. The wife's gonna be pissed that she has to cook venison for the next three months."

"We'll be right back," said Ida. "We have a few more trades to make. Then we can exchange payment."

He nodded and winked at me.

I followed Ida back down the aisle, keeping Rick in my line of sight for several feet. Something about him wasn't right.

To my surprise, Ida's voice sounded worried when she

spoke next. "We need to make the next trade and get out of here. I trust Rick, but I don't like people knowing what we've got."

We made the rounds to a few other vendors Ida knew, trading pounds of meat for the goods on Miller's list. For the smaller trades, she sent me out to the truck to get the meat. The hunters had wrapped it in brown paper with the number of pounds of cut meat written in grease pencil.

Once we had gathered all the first aid supplies, the food we needed, and gasoline for the truck, Ida nodded to Rick to follow us outside to make the trade. I opened the truck bed and piled the packages of meat into a wooden crate. I hopped down into the snow and stared at him loping toward us.

Something was wrong.

He wasn't carrying a crate of ammunition; instead, he cradled his rifle lazily in the crook of his arm.

"Well, we'd like to be on our way," said Ida. I knew she was thinking the same thing I was.

"That's what I'm counting on," said Rick. There was an odd note to his voice. "Why don't you unload all that meat there and be on your way."

"Where's my ammunition?"

Rick sighed. "That's your problem, Ida. You're always too eager, and you make these massive buys." He laughed. "That's dangerous."

"I do business with you because you're an honest man." Her voice was strong, but I could detect anger beneath the surface.

Rick rocked back on his heels, smiling like a crazy man and looking around. "I used to think so. But times are hard, Ida. I can't let you just walk away with three hundred rounds.

Enemy Inside

It's all I got. I have my family to think about."

"So you were planning on robbing us blind?"

"That's the general idea."

"After all the years we've known each other."

"Well, I —"

Rick stopped abruptly, cut off by the wail of sirens in the distance. We all looked down the gravel drive, panicked, and he was the first to refocus.

"Unload that meat. Now!" he yelled.

I shook my head, but Ida was still looking around for the direction of the sirens. We stood there with Rick's gun trained on me, and I slowly got down from the truck and motioned as if I was going to unload the venison.

But just then, there was a flash of blue light through the trees, and I saw the white PMC cruiser rumbling down the road on the other side of the church. Rick wiped the sweat from his brow and then started backing away toward a pickup truck parked several yards behind us. He fumbled with his keys and started the engine. He peeled out of the gravel on the side of the road and spun around to face the other direction. With a rumble and a spray of gravel, he was gone.

"Get in the truck," said Ida.

"The other people," I muttered. "The ammo!"

"It's not worth it."

But I was already running toward the church. I burst in the back door and ran down the aisle. "The PMC is here!" I yelled.

The vendors' eyes widened. It was mass chaos. People grabbed whatever they could carry and ran, shoving each other aside and crowding through the back door. Rick's guns were still laid out across the pew, and there was a crate full of ammunition lying on the ground. I grabbed it and sprinted back the way I had come just as the front doors of the church burst open.

"Freeze!" yelled the officers. They fired, and I heard the groans of several vendors being shot as they scrambled to pack up their wares.

I didn't turn around. I didn't stop. I flew through the snow and jumped into the passenger side of the truck. Ida peeled out of the gravel drive, and we rumbled down the road. She didn't say anything, but I could feel the anger coming off her.

The sound of more sirens pierced my eardrums. I looked around desperately but didn't see any other cruisers. Then I looked in the mirror.

Trailing behind us through the snow was a white SUV, its bright blue lights unmistakable.

We pulled onto the highway, and I felt the truck shudder slightly as Ida accelerated. There was a shadow of panic in her eyes. I followed her gaze to the dashboard, where the needle on the fuel gauge was hovered over E. We hadn't refilled yet, and we wouldn't have enough gas to make it back to camp.

Our only chance was to lose the cruiser, but it was right on our tail.

"I could shoot out their tires," I said.

Ida shook her head once. "Their tires are reinforced. Even if you made the shot, it would only waste ammunition."

Seeing the huge crate filled with boxes of rounds out of the corner of my eye, I understood her true meaning: It would only waste energy. And as soon as we started shooting, they would open fire as well.

Then I felt it: the lurch of the truck as the engine gobbled up the last fumes of gas. The truck slowed abruptly, forcing

Enemy Inside

the cruiser to swerve around us to avoid collision. The SUV spun out, coming to a halt in front of us as we stopped. Two officers in full riot gear jumped out, pointing their guns in our direction.

"Drop your weapons!" yelled the officer. "Drop your weapons, and exit the vehicle slowly."

My gun was cocked on my lap. Without thinking, I threw open the passenger door and fired.

Miraculously, one of the officers staggered, and I ducked behind the door just as the other returned fire.

"Get down!" I yelled to Ida, and I heard the officer I'd shot collapse onto the pavement.

I crawled back into the truck under the dashboard with Ida, waiting and breathing heavily. My heart was pounding so loudly I couldn't think.

Another shot punctuated the heavy quiet.

My mind was racing. Now that I had shot an officer, we wouldn't be taken prisoner. We would be killed on the spot.

Just as I was weighing the risk of shooting again, another shot made contact with the truck — closer this time.

"You hear that?" Ida whispered.

"*Yeah.*"

"No. All three shots came from the same gun. It's just one officer shooting."

The collapsed officer wasn't returning fire. Maybe I had killed him.

"If we both jump out," breathed Ida, "he can't shoot us both without getting shot himself. One of us can get away."

I nodded. "Okay."

"One. Two. Three."

Ida and I jumped out of the truck simultaneously, and I whipped my gun around to point it at the lone PMC officer standing in front of the truck. The other officer lay on the ground completely still, blood seeping from a wound in his chest.

The officer already had his gun pointed at Ida. If I missed, Ida would be killed.

"Drop your weapons," yelled the officer. The voice was muffled by the heavy helmet, but it was definitely a female's. I immediately thought of Logan.

It's not her, I told myself. I tried to clear my head, unsure what to do. I could shoot and kill the officer, and Ida would live, or I could miss the officer, and Ida could die. Or I could surrender, and we would both be killed.

There was only one option I could live with. I took aim and fired.

It all happened so quickly that I had no time to change the plan. In the second it took me to decide, the officer had turned her gun on me and pivoted her body. My shot grazed her hand and ricocheted off the rifle. She cried out, dropping her gun.

I flew forward, tackling her to the ground and kicking her weapon back toward our truck. Her head hit the pavement, knocking her helmet askew.

I recovered first, straddling her body and pointing my gun at her head.

Then two catlike hazel eyes looked up at me with loathing.

I leaned away from her, feeling sick.

No. My eyes had to be playing tricks on me.

But then she spoke, and her horrible voice was one I instantly recognized.

"Didn't think you had it in you," Mariah snarled.

Chapter Eighteen

I stared down at Mariah, utterly transfixed. It was definitely her, but she didn't look the same.

The last time I saw her, she was frighteningly thin with pale, sallow skin and a sickly look about her. Her cat eyes had been feverish and hungry with the look of early-stage infection.

Since then, her stringy bleached-blond hair had faded to a more natural brown, and her sharp features were no longer pinched with sickness. Her face was fuller, healthier, and her eyes were hateful and alert.

"What happened to you?" I asked.

She smirked. "Surprised to see me?"

"Mariah?" Ida came up from behind me. "Is that you?"

My heart sank. Ida didn't know what had happened in Sector X. She only knew that the rebels had thrown Mariah out during the riots — not that I'd exposed her as a carrier. Until now, I hadn't known if Mariah had been captured as a carrier, killed as a rebel, or if she simply froze to death in the snow.

"Funny," Mariah sneered. "You don't seem quite as surprised."

I glared down at her. "How are you alive . . . and still human?"

"Wouldn't you like to know?"

I wanted to shoot her right then. All the hate and loathing I felt for Mariah before came flooding back, but she knew something we didn't. She should be worse by now — nearly a fully fledged carrier — but instead she looked better.

I glanced back at Ida, whose gun was still trained on Mariah. Mariah's rifle was far out of reach, but I bent down and grabbed the handcuffs strapped to her white PMC utility belt for good measure.

"Hands," I demanded.

She held out her wrists, glaring up at me, and I snapped on the handcuffs.

"Haven," Ida murmured. "What are you planning to do with her? We can't take a PMC officer back to camp with us."

I knew she was right, but I couldn't kill Mariah until I had the answers I needed. If she could survive, maybe Logan could survive, too.

"We have to."

Mariah smirked, as if she could read my mind. She was smart. She knew that information was her ticket to staying alive.

"I won't do it, Haven. Taking her puts us all in jeopardy."

"Please," I said, lowering my voice to a whisper. "You know why we have to."

She stared at me for a long moment. "This isn't us, Haven. We don't take hostages."

I locked eyes with Ida, not wanting to plead with her in front of Mariah. If Mariah knew *why* we needed the information, she would never give it willingly.

Finally I said, "Think of what this could mean . . . for

everyone."

Ida gave me a look of unwilling agreement. "We have to be smart about it."

"Why would I help you?" spat Mariah. "You're just going to kill me once you get what you need."

"Maybe we will . . . maybe we won't," I muttered, clambering off Mariah and training my gun on her. "Right now, cooperating seems like your best option."

I turned to Ida. "We have to get out of here. The other officers won't be far behind."

Ida nodded and began fueling the truck with the gasoline we had traded for. It wasn't very much, but it was enough to get us back to camp.

"Get up."

With a hateful glare, Mariah struggled to her feet. I removed her utility belt, searching the leather pouch for the handcuff keys. I pocketed them and pushed Mariah toward our truck, bending to grab the dead officer's rifle.

I tried not to look at the man's face. I couldn't think about him now.

We squeezed back into the truck with Mariah in the front seat between us, and I blindfolded her with one of Ida's kerchiefs. Ida was quiet, but I could feel her anxiety.

"What are you planning to do with her, Haven?" she asked finally. "We could be leading the PMC right back to camp. They'll be sending out satellite rovers to look for her soon." Ida nodded at Mariah's arm.

I yanked up her sleeve, but I couldn't see the telltale scar where her CID would be.

"Where's your CID?"

"It's in there."

Enemy Inside

"But you trained with the PMC before you joined the rebellion. You had a CID the whole time?"

"I was deactivated. My scar was so faint no one ever questioned that I was undocumented."

My head was spinning.

How had I not put it together before? Logan had told me Mariah was PMC, yet I hadn't thought about what that meant. If she had been a PMC officer before the rebellion, she'd been vaccinated. I should have known the vaccine didn't always work.

I knew I had to keep Mariah alive to learn how to save Logan, but there was something else — rotten guilt eating away at my insides. With Jared waiting for us back at camp, I couldn't kill Mariah. I would never be able to look him in the eye again now that I knew she was alive. The first time I had sentenced her to death, it had happened so quickly I could tell myself it was unavoidable. But now I was the judge, the jury, and the executioner.

"Leave us in the woods," I said to Ida. "Park a few miles from camp at least and then send Amory out to us. He can cut out her CID."

"Like hell!" snapped Mariah. "I'm not letting that kid do some hack surgery on me!"

"Shut up!" I yelled. "You'll let us do what we have to do if you ever want to see your brother again."

"What the hell have you done with my brother?"

"Nothing. He's fine. He's at our camp." I considered for a moment and then came to a decision. "If you cooperate — let us remove your CID and tell us what we need to know — we'll let you live."

"I'm not going back to those people who would have let me die in Sector X."

"We're not with them anymore."

"Jared left Rulon?"

I nodded.

She let out a burst of air. "That kid was the *only* reason we were with him in the first place. Rulon was an idiot and a tyrant."

Thinking back to what I had seen Mariah and Rulon doing in that house on the road, it struck me as an odd thing to say.

At the time, I'd thought Mariah was manipulating Rulon, but maybe she was just looking out for her and her brother's interests. Maybe she was just trying to survive. Knowing she had someone else she was protecting gave me new appreciation for Mariah's cunning and deceit. I knew better than anyone how your loved ones could make you do crazy things. After all, I had just shot a man. I was in no position to be pointing fingers.

Ida pulled down a road I didn't recognize. She was leading us toward camp from another way. Crunching through the thick blanket of snow at such a slow pace, my mind slowed too, and I was forced to come to terms with what I was about to do.

I was asking Amory to remove Mariah's CID against her will out in the middle of the woods. It was a risky undertaking even with ideal conditions, but I realized I didn't care. I could live with killing Mariah; I *couldn't* be the one to put Logan down thinking there was something I might have done to save her.

Pulling off the road into the thick tangle of trees, I had the fleeting worry that the truck would get stuck. This path wasn't well worn like the other trail through the woods, and thick branches kept snapping off in the undercarriage.

Finally we came to a stop.

Ida reached behind the back seat and fished out a bulky men's coat with a furry collar.

"Put this on her," she said. "It's freezing out there, and that uniform doesn't look very warm."

I could vouch for that. I draped the coat over Mariah, buttoned it over her crossed, handcuffed arms, and tried to ignore her murderous glare as I pulled off the blindfold.

"Do we have any rope?" I asked.

"You're going to tie her up?" There was something about Ida's motherly tone that made me feel terrible about it.

"Just while I build a fire. I'm not about to let her run off."

Ida sighed and got out to look in the back of the truck. She emerged with a small duffle of supplies and turned to me.

"I'll send Amory, but if you three aren't back at camp in four hours, I'm sending out a search party. You don't want to be out here on your own come nightfall."

I nodded.

Ida shot me one more disapproving look and climbed back into the truck.

Mariah slid out and staggered off through the snow. We entered a small clearing sheltered by three large pines, and she sat down against a tree. I moved in to tie her up.

"You come any closer, and I'll claw your eyes out," she snarled.

"Either you can let me tie you up, or we can sit here in the cold without a fire. Your choice."

She glared at me, and I took that as assent. I tied her more tightly than I had originally intended; something about being alone in the woods with Mariah — a trained PMC officer like Logan — made me very nervous. I had the feeling she was only cooperating to lull me into a false sense of security, waiting for the opportune moment to attack. Logan would have never let herself be taken so easily.

I didn't wander far looking for dry wood to build a fire, and I ended up with a pile much smaller than I would have liked. As I started it, I kept myself facing Mariah, watching her out of the corner of my eye. Even handcuffed and tied to a tree, I didn't trust her for a second.

Once the fire was crackling, I busied myself with inventorying the supplies Ida had given us: a few bottles of water, a small first aid kit, some deer jerky, and four hard bricks of what looked like homemade granola bars. My stomach growled, and I hoped Amory would hurry. I wasn't sure how far we were from camp, but that wasn't what worried me. Being alone with Mariah meant no talking, and in the silence, I was forced to sit with my guilt.

"So which one of your little friends is infected?" she asked finally.

I didn't say anything. I didn't want to give her any information she could use to manipulate me.

"Is it your boyfriend Amory?"

I didn't say anything.

"It's not your friend from prison, is it?" Mariah stopped for a moment. "It's Logan!" She let out a short, cold laugh. "Of *course* it is. She always thinks she can win a fight. Even in basic, she always took on husky girls twice her size . . . got more banged up than she needed to. But she always won. That made her cocky."

Mariah stopped and sneered at me. "What makes you think I'm going to tell you anything?"

"I don't know," I said. It was the truth.

She laughed. "You really don't know, do you? You have

nothing to bargain with! Once you take me back to your camp —"

"I said I'd let you live if you cooperated. I didn't say how," I snapped. Now I knew she was trying to get a rise out of me. "Just know that if she dies, you die." I shuffled over until I was standing right above her. "If you say nothing and she turns full carrier, I'll make you wish you were dead."

Mariah smirked. "You've changed."

"I didn't have a choice."

I collapsed on the other side of the fire, keeping my rifle trained in her direction. We sat in silence for a long time, and I began to worry about Amory. *What if something happened to him on the way here? What if he got lost or ran into a pack of carriers?*

No. Amory could handle himself.

Scooting closer to the fire, I tried to thaw my frozen hands. I knew Mariah must be freezing, judging by her proximity to the fire, but I wouldn't risk untying her. Training with Logan was enough to tell me that I was no match for Mariah.

"So what happened to you?" I asked. Now that we were just sitting there, I realized I had a thousand questions burning in the back of my mind.

Mariah glared at me through the flames. "Before or after the rebels threw me out to die in Sector X?"

I shrugged. "After, I guess." The guilt was thick in my voice.

"You hoped I was gone," she said. "You wanted me to die, didn't you?"

"You tried to get me and my friends killed, but you knew we weren't a threat."

"I knew you were cowards. I don't have time for

cowards. Cowards get you killed."

"You were blowing up a building full of people!"

"Oh, and you tried so hard to save them all, did you?" she asked, her eyes gleaming with malice.

I fell silent, hating her and trying to stifle the memory of those horrible moments before the blast.

She was right. Amory and I had run.

"That's what I thought." She nodded and slumped back against the tree, sneering and looking satisfied. "We're the same, you and me."

"How's that?"

"We're both out to save ourselves. Our survival instincts are . . . spectacular."

Anger flared in the pit of my stomach. "That's not true."

"No?"

"I look out for my friends. You only look out for yourself." Even as I said it, I knew it wasn't true. Now that I knew about Jared, it made me think we *were* alike, but for a different reason.

She laughed — a hard, cruel laugh. "Stop *lying* to yourself! You're not saving them out of *love*. You're saving them because you're terrified of being alone."

I stared at her. In that moment, I wanted to kill her. I wanted her to suffer.

Instead, I forced myself to refocus on the ultimate objective: saving Logan. I needed the truth.

"How did you rejoin the PMC after the rebels threw you out?"

Mariah rolled her eyes. "I wandered around for a bit, looking for someplace to get warm. I stumbled across these two dead officers lying there on the sidewalk. I took one of their uniforms — just for warmth. I also took one of their rifles. Basic survival. I didn't really know where to go.

"Somehow, I wandered into a big pack of them. One of them yelled at me for breaking rank, and I realized I could do it.

"They'd lost so many men that order was breaking down. I knew it would be easy just to slip back in. It didn't matter that I was deactivated. There were too many carriers and rebels running around, triggering all the rovers. I helped them shoot down a bunch of rebels at the bridge, and then I marched right back to base with them."

"They must have realized you were deactivated eventually."

She nodded. "It took them about five seconds after I entered their last standing base to figure it out. But they needed bodies to throw at the problem, so they gave me amnesty. When they realized I was infected, they sent me to World Corp International."

"Why? Why not kill you or just lock you up?"

Mariah smiled to herself, not really looking at me. "I was an anomaly — the first case of the virus they'd seen in someone who was vaccinated."

"And they cured you?"

She swallowed in disgust, as if pushing down a terrible memory. "It was horrible. The cure is . . . sloppy. Think chemotherapy. It works . . . if it doesn't kill you first."

"Still. They have a cure, but they tell the public they don't know how to cure it or what caused the outbreak."

"If you don't know what caused the outbreak, you're a fucking idiot," snapped Mariah.

"World Corp?"

She nodded.

"How?"

"I don't know. But the joke's on them. The virus mutated. I was infected with a new strain they hadn't seen before. The vaccine didn't prevent it, and once you're infected, it's a much slower decline.

"I was sick for weeks before I realized. I was angry all the time. I wanted to kill people, but my brain was on overdrive. It was like I was still myself, only not quite. All I thought about was surviving, which is how I ended up with Rulon's crew."

I thought back to the carriers who had grabbed me in the woods and tied me to a tree. They had been further along than Mariah, but they still had enough sense to tie me up. They wanted to use me to help them survive. I imagined myself as the carriers' hostage, stealing food from grocery stores and bringing it back to their camp. It showed a high level of thinking on their part that made me shiver.

If Mariah was telling the truth, then everything that had happened since the Collapse had been part of World Corp's plan — except the mutation. It was too horrible to consider. It was too much to process.

"The only thing I don't get," I said, "is why you never led the PMC to Rulon's camp. You could have betrayed all the rebels who turned against you."

"Including my brother."

I shrugged. "You could have gotten him amnesty in exchange for what you knew. But you didn't."

Mariah sneered, but it was a poor cover for her misery. "Insurance. If they ever decided I was disposable, I needed that as leverage. Why should I trust the PMC? They'd thrown me out once already for Logan's crime. Fool me once, shame on you. But nobody fools me twice."

I stared at her, and for just a second, I felt sorry for Mariah. There really was no one she trusted. I didn't blame her. Both the PMC and the rebels had thrown her away for something that wasn't even her fault.

From far away, I heard the crunch of footfalls in the snow. I jerked my head around and jumped to my feet.

There was a lone figure running toward us through the snow. As he drew closer, I recognized Amory's long stride. I'd almost forgotten why we were there.

He was panting, and he carried a small backpack. Looking from me to Mariah, I saw his eyes widen, as though seeing her confirmed what he hoped wasn't true.

"Where did you find her?" he panted once he was within earshot.

"The Exchange was raided. She followed us."

Amory's eyebrows shot up. "That's never happened before. There must be a traitor on the inside."

There was something off about the way Amory was speaking. His voice was cold, and he wasn't looking at me directly.

"Are you all right?" he asked.

"Yeah. You?"

"I've been better," he muttered.

"Hey!" I grabbed his arm and pulled him behind a tree, out of the range of Mariah's smug expression. "What is it?"

Now I could see his face. It was distorted in an uncharacteristic look of anger.

"When were you planning on telling me that Logan was infected?"

My heart sank. He should have been the first person I

told. He and Logan had been friends long before I had met them, and I shouldn't have let him be blindsided by the news.

"I'm sorry. I just found out this morning."

"You had time to tell Greyson." His voice was accusatory, and I remembered that Amory was still not himself.

"I'm sorry. He came by, and I didn't —" I broke off, looking at my feet. "I didn't know what to do."

"You could have told *me*! I had to find out from Ida while she was telling me that you'd taken a PMC officer hostage."

"Mariah's alive, Amory. She was infected, and now she's not. What the hell would you have done?"

"I would have thought it through!"

"There was no time!" I yelled.

My raised voice seemed to startle him, bringing him back to reality. In an instant, he was himself again, and I felt my anger dissipating as quickly as it had come.

"Are you sure about this?" he asked in a low voice. "It's dangerous under the best circumstances. Out here, it's . . ."

"I'm sure."

"And what do you plan to do with her once the CID is gone? She isn't going to stop being a PMC officer just because we take her off the grid. The others won't want her kept alive."

"We have to."

We stared at each other, locked in a stalemate, but Amory read the desperation in my eyes. He didn't say anything, but I knew he would do it.

Sometime that day, I knew I had crossed a line, even if it

was hard to tell where.

I had shot a man. I'd taken a hostage. And now I was bringing a fox back to the nest. We had no other option.

Chapter Nineteen

Amory stepped around the tree to survey Mariah. She was glaring up at him like a cornered animal, but he seemed undeterred.

"You'll need to uncuff her," he said. "But keep her tied up."

I squatted down in front of Mariah and dug the key out of my back pocket. As soon as the handcuffs clicked open, she thrashed out with her arms, swatting at me with her nails.

Ducking out of her reach, I stumbled backward.

Amory and I exchanged a look, and he bent down to examine the site of her CID insertion. She swung out her other arm to strike him, but Amory seized it in his grip. That cold look was back in his eyes, and I remembered that he too had basic PMC training. Mariah stopped struggling for a moment — just long enough for Amory to plunge a syringe I hadn't seen into her arm.

Mariah swiped at him again with her free hand, but she'd already given up. Amory pulled back, and she yanked her other arm out of his grip.

"What did you give her?"

"A sedative. I can't work on her when she's like this."

"Wish I'd had one of those," I muttered, remembering my own painful extraction.

"Yeah, well, the defectors' medical supplies are much better stocked than Ida's cupboard at the farm."

We waited in silence for the drugs to kick in, but Mariah already seemed more docile just knowing she had lost the fight. When Amory reached for her arm the next time, she glared at him but did not lash out. She was slumped down against the tree and pliant enough for Amory to spread her arm palm up on a clean towel he had lain in the snow. He gently swabbed her arm and withdrew his scalpel.

"This will hurt, but I've done it twice before," he murmured. His voice was cool and professional. "The less you move, the less painful it will be."

Mariah didn't make a sound.

As I watched, I felt a stab of ugliness. I knew it was wrong to forcibly remove her CID, but we didn't have another choice. If Mariah had been any other officer, we would have shot her. Forcing her to defect and bringing her to the rebel camp was hardly a fair chance at a new life, but it was the most we could do. And if I was completely honest with myself, I would have condemned her to much worse if it meant saving Logan.

Amory made a small incision as he had done for me and used his forceps to pull apart the folds of skin. I hadn't watched this part of my own procedure, and it was much more gruesome than I'd originally thought. Blood pooled up over the site of Amory's incision, running down her arm and over the towel.

Glancing at Mariah, I saw she wasn't watching either. Her face was screwed up, but whether it was from pain or anger, I could not tell.

Amory sucked in a breath of air through his teeth. "Shit."

"What is it?" I asked.

"I nicked her artery."

Enemy Inside

My chest constricted, as though cold chains were snaked around my rib cage, crushing my heart and lungs.

"She's losing a lot of blood."

Mariah's face had relaxed from the sedative, and she was staring bleary-eyed at Amory.

"What can I do?" I asked.

Amory shook his head once, but I couldn't see his face. His shoulders were taught as he bent over her arm, and I could see by his elbows that he was working quickly.

He paused to wipe his brow with his sleeve. "If I don't find it soon, I'll have to stop."

"You'll find it," I said quietly.

He sighed and continued to work. I didn't dare step over to look at Mariah. I didn't want to see the blood — didn't want to consider that if she died, I would be responsible.

After another long minute, Amory froze. "It's done."

He began swabbing away the blood, and I caught a glimpse of the soaked towel. My stomach turned as he began stitching up Mariah's arm. Over his shoulder, I could see her looking at him with an expression of defeat.

Watching Amory work, I felt a swell of affection at his care and precision. To Amory, it didn't matter if Mariah was one of us or an officer who wanted us dead. He did the job with the same concern for his patient.

"So that's it, then?" I said to break the heavy silence. "No CID."

"Oh, I got it," said Amory, turning to look over his shoulder. His face was serious, but I could see the pride in his eyes.

He finished bandaging Mariah and bent over to retrieve something from a Petri dish with his forceps. When he held

Enemy Inside

it up to the light, I saw the glint of gold around the edges. He held it out to me, and I took it carefully between my fingers.

Amory turned to Mariah. "I'll be checking to make sure the cut is healing all right. Should be a fairly clean scar."

Her eyes lingered with pointed distain on the jagged scar on Amory's own forearm.

"I did a much better job on Haven," he said, following her gaze.

As Amory began gathering up his supplies, I wandered off into the trees until I found two sizable rocks. Clearing away a patch of snow at the base of a tree, I carefully placed the CID on the flattest of the two and held the other rock over my head. In one clumsy motion, I brought the rock down and smashed the chip, nearly crushing my fingertips in the process. When I lifted the rock, the CID was glimmering in five separate pieces of gold and white.

"We better get moving," Amory called. "It's going to be dark soon."

He had already re-cuffed and blindfolded Mariah, and I felt another stab of guilt. I swallowed it down, remembering that she was our ticket to curing Logan.

It was a slow march back to camp. Night was coming quickly, and the icy wind was kicking up, cutting through our clothes and making it almost impossible to breathe. I had a grip on Mariah's good arm, and she stumbled between us through the deep snow. Between the sedative and the blindfold, she was having a hard time avoiding the concealed tree roots and underbrush, and I was having a hard time keeping us both upright.

When Amory spoke after nearly an hour of silence, he startled me with the obvious question I had been dreading.

"What are we going to do with her?"

"We need to hide her until we can get the information we need," I said, avoiding his gaze. "No one can know about Logan."

"I don't know how we're going to keep something like this a secret." I could hear the grating frustration in his voice. "We'll have a couple days at most before someone figures out Logan isn't getting better. That's if we can keep Murphy and the others from finding out about *her*." He nodded toward Mariah.

We fell back into silence, and my feet began to drag with exhaustion and dread.

Amory led us around the perimeter of camp. We were close enough to discern the outline of cabins through the trees, but I couldn't hear any voices. Now that it was nearly dark, most people were already packed into the mess hall for supper.

I pointed to one of the empty cabins that sat farther back in the woods. "We can keep her there for now," I murmured.

Checking first to see if the coast was clear, Amory motioned for me to follow with Mariah. He reached up and felt over the doorframe for the spare key and fitted it into the lock. The door swung open, and a heavy whiff of mustiness and rodent excrement hit my nostrils.

I guided Mariah over the threshold, and she doubled over in a sneeze. I lit the lone kerosene lamp hanging near the entrance and surveyed the room. This cabin served as a permanent storage area for spare bunks and odd supplies, but the disorganized crates and rusted bed frames stacked haphazardly around the room told me it wasn't part of Miller's domain.

Amory dragged one of the mattresses over to the defunct

radiator, and I clipped one end of Mariah's handcuffs to the part of the fixture that was bolted to the wall. When I removed the blindfold, she was glaring up at me, still wheezing from the dust. I could tell that the effects of the sedative were wearing off.

"What makes you think I'm going to tell you anything?" Mariah growled. Her eyes were red and blotchy, making her look even more frightening.

"I think you'll want to get out of here eventually," I said, searching the nearest crate for some blankets to make her more comfortable.

"You can't keep me tied up forever."

She was right. Even in the few hours we'd had her, this hostage business was really starting to wear on me.

I sighed. "We'll go get you some food . . . let you think about it."

Feeling like a terrible person, I gagged her and checked her restraints. Amory followed me out of the cabin, locking it behind him.

Grateful to be rid of Mariah, I sank down on the bottom step and put my head in my hands. "What are we going to do?"

"We?"

I looked up. Amory was staring down at me with anger and detachment.

"You brought back a PMC officer from the Exchange — an ex-rebel — and called me out to the woods to perform an extraction. You didn't think I had a right to know about Logan, but you dragged me into this mess anyway."

"She had us, Amory. I was going to kill her, but then I saw who she was. She hadn't turned. That's never happened before."

"It was a bad idea bringing her here."

"I didn't have a choice!"

"Yeah, well neither did I!" he yelled. "I would never perform a CID extraction out in the middle of the woods like that. It's too dangerous. But you forced my hand. And now I'm helping you lie to all the people who are feeding us and giving us shelter when it's incredibly dangerous for everyone. Having *her* here . . . not telling them that their vaccinations don't keep them safe . . . It isn't right."

I drew back. Amory had never yelled at me like this before, and it looked as though he regretted it as soon as the words left his mouth.

"It's *Logan*."

He sighed, running a hand through his hair and sinking down onto the step next to me. "I know."

I stared off into the darkness, not wanting to look at him.

"I'm sorry I got you involved," I said, trying to keep my voice steady. I was on the verge of tears, but I didn't want Amory's sympathy. I didn't deserve it.

"No. I'm sorry," he said.

"I know it was stupid bringing her here. But she's our only chance."

"I would have done the same thing," he murmured, his forehead wrinkled in frustration. "Hell, I'm impressed you and Ida got back alive."

I grinned, but my victory was hollow.

"I was just mad you didn't tell me about Logan."

"I know. I'm sorry," I said, hanging my head in shame.

"How do we get her to talk? She won't want to help Logan. I don't think she ever forgave her for getting her kicked out of the PMC. And she hates the rebels after what happened in Sector X."

Tentatively, I voiced the solution I'd been dreading. "Maybe . . . maybe we promise her a place at camp."

Amory snapped his head around. "What? No way."

"What else do we have to bargain with?"

"Why would she agree to that?"

"Jared. He's her brother. And she can't go back to the PMC. She can't join the rebels. Where else is she going to go?"

But Amory was already shaking his head.

"What other option do we have?"

"Mariah only cares about Mariah. She'll play along just as long as it's convenient for her."

"So what?" I cried.

"Do we really want her around? I know I won't sleep well knowing she could give us up to the PMC any day."

"We just have to offer something she wants," I said, lowering my voice so there was no chance of Mariah overhearing. "Survival. In return, she leads us to World Corp International to steal the cure for Logan. After that . . . I don't care what we do."

Amory sighed. "I don't like this. Once we involve Jared, all bets are off. He could run and tell everyone about Logan."

"Not if he wants to keep his sister alive. He has just as much to lose."

Amory let his head fall between his fingers, breathing loudly against his palm, and I could tell by his agitation that he was giving in. I didn't know what we would do about

Enemy Inside

Mariah after we'd found the cure. Amory was right — we couldn't keep her around. But for now, playing her was the only way to get what we wanted.

We walked over to the mess hall looking for Jared, but he was nowhere to be found. The hall was busy, but there were more empty seats than usual. I spotted Ida from the line talking to Murphy, but judging by Murphy's easy expression, she hadn't told him everything about our supply run. She looked visibly relieved to see Amory and me, and I nodded once to indicate everything was fine.

Discreetly swiping two of anything I could stuff in my pockets, Amory and I situated ourselves at one of the long tables nearest the door so we would be able to avoid chitchat with the other defectors and make a quick exit as soon as we found Jared. I kept my eyes fixed on the door of the mess hall, waiting for him.

Finally, the doors swung open and a group of hunters walked in. They were a motley crew. Their boots were caked with mud, their long, wild hair tangled from the wind, cheeks red from the cold. Trailing at the back of the group, her hair plastered to her sweaty face, was Logan. My pulse quickened in alarm to see her out of our cabin socializing with the others, but they didn't seem to notice anything strange about her. Only the yellowing in her eyes, the feverish glint of her skin, and the slight droop in her shoulders showed she was not herself.

She was chatting animatedly to Jared, looking as happy as I'd ever seen her since Max's death. Jared looked comically sullen in comparison.

They shuffled through the mess line, and I waved them over. Jared looked stony and then suspicious, but he followed Logan over to our table.

"How was the hunt?" I asked, my voice a little too high to sound casual.

Enemy Inside

Jared grunted, digging into his meatloaf to avoid speaking.

"It was awesome," gushed Logan.

"Do you really think you're . . . up for it?" I asked pointedly.

Her smile didn't quite meet her eyes, but she waved a hand dismissively as my gaze settled on the blood splattered across her white thermal shirt. "I couldn't stick around while they were field dressing it, but I'll work up to it."

I grinned despite myself. Logan, the least squeamish girl I'd ever met, couldn't stand the sight of blood. I tried not to think about the fact that she might not *ever* get to field dress a deer.

She pushed her food around her plate, looking a little pale, but bowed her head to deflect any more of my questions.

"So we could use your guys' help," I said, hoping the slight waver in my voice wouldn't give me away. "I'm supposed to clean out one of the cabins in the back for overflow supplies for Miller, and . . . there's this bat we can't get out of there."

Logan raised an eyebrow. "So leave it in there until tomorrow. That way you'll have an excuse to ditch her in the morning."

"I think it will be easier at night."

She chewed her food, staring at me with that sharp look that told me she didn't miss a thing. "All right."

As we finished our meatloaf and got up to leave, I stuffed my roll in my coat pocket with the extra baked potato I'd stolen and led them out into the snow.

Walking back toward the cabin, I felt the anxiety twisting my gut into knots. We really hadn't thought this through very well, and there was no way to know how they might react.

I stomped up the steps outside the cabin and turned, feeling nervous. Logan looked expectant; Jared looked bored.

"There's something you should know," I said, looking to Amory for help.

He didn't say anything, so I continued. "I lied about the bat."

Logan looked caught between irritation and intrigue. "What's going on, Haven?"

"I need your help." I squeezed my eyes shut for a moment, realizing that no matter how I revealed Mariah, it would be cruel and insensitive to Jared. "Something went wrong at the Exchange. The PMC showed up, and two of them followed us to the highway."

"What?" snapped Jared. "Why didn't Ida say anything?"

"I'm sure she'll talk to Murphy. She probably doesn't want to start a panic."

"Start a panic? We need to move! If the PMC followed —"

I shook my head. "I shot one of them, but the other one . . ." I looked into Jared's eyes, trying to gauge his reaction. "I don't know how it's possible, but I couldn't kill her once I saw who she was."

Watching Jared, I saw his expression go from cold and confused to furious. "Who? You couldn't kill who?"

"Amory removed her CID in the woods a few miles from camp, but —"

Jared pushed past me roughly, fumbling with the lock on the door. Amory handed him the key, and he bolted inside.

Stepping over the threshold behind him, I watched his

gaze snap to Mariah. He stopped in the middle of the room, his shoulders hunched comically, prepared to strike.

Mariah straightened up from her slumped position against the wall, and for the first time since I'd known her, I saw something ignite behind her cold cat eyes. Then it was gone.

"What the hell is this?" Logan spluttered.

"She's infected," said Jared.

"No, she's not."

Logan gave me a sad look. "That's impossible."

"Check her eyes."

She crossed the room in three strides to where Mariah sat, grabbed Mariah's chin, and cocked it upward to catch the dim light of the lantern. She examined her for nearly a whole minute before releasing her — none too gently — finally satisfied.

But it was Mariah who looked smug, even tied to a radiator. Logan yanked down her gag, nearly dislocating Mariah's jaw in the process.

"Who cured you?"

Mariah sneered. "How does it feel to be dying?"

Logan's eyes narrowed into slits, yanking the gag back up between Mariah's teeth and grabbing a fistful of her hair.

"Logan —"

Mariah made a noise like a low growl, and Logan pulled back her head to expose her throat, as if wondering if she could rip out Mariah's jugular with her bare hands.

I glanced nervously at Jared, expecting a reaction.

Finally he spoke, his voice low and cracking. "Why did you bring her here?"

He turned, and I saw that his eyes looked red, the corners

of his mouth uncharacteristically downturned. "Isn't it enough I had to watch them throw her out to die once?"

"She's not infected," I repeated.

"So what?" The way he said it sounded hopeless and broken. "It's not like she'll be allowed to live here. They'll kill her when they find out."

"We removed her CID," I said. "It doesn't have to happen that way."

"Haven," said Logan in a quiet voice. "What were you thinking?"

"I was thinking that she's the first person we've ever seen who's cured," I said, my voice shaking. "We can't just let her go without knowing where she got it. If there's a chance we could save you —"

"What?" snapped Jared. He turned to stare at Logan. "Are you telling me she's infected?" A look of disgust flashed across his face, followed by fear and anger.

"You can't tell anyone," I said in a low, deadly voice. "We just need time."

"Time for what?"

"To find the cure."

"Are you fucking crazy?" yelled Jared. "You're putting us all at risk!"

"No," I said. "Logan's not even contagious yet."

"She will be! Then she'll be ripping us open in our sleep."

I glanced at Logan, feeling horrible. But her face was calm. She was in problem-solving mode.

"Haven, maybe she just . . . got better?" Logan's voice was softer now, pacifying. "We don't know that she found a cure."

"No! World Corp studied her. They cured her."

"World Corp International?" Jared looked irate. "Not this again!"

"Ida thinks they're behind it all — that they own the PMC. And after what Mariah told me . . ."

"Don't you think she's just telling you what you want to hear so you'll let her live?"

"No! We never even said anything about World Corp."

"What's your plan?" Jared asked. He hunkered down next to his sister, studying her. "How do we keep her from running off and giving the PMC our location and keep the others from killing her?"

"I was hoping you could help with that."

Jared didn't answer. He just sat there for a long time, staring down at his sister as if making a decision that had weighed on him for years.

Finally, he reached over to loosen the gag on Mariah's mouth again. It fell down around her neck, and her mouth cracked into a smirk.

"Hello, little brother. It's been a long time."

Chapter Twenty

We left Jared with Mariah, knowing there was no use worrying that he would set her free or tell the others. From the look on his face, I could tell he was conflicted. He was shocked to see his sister alive but torn by the risk she posed to the rest of the group. Maybe I had expected him to treat her differently, but spending a lifetime in Mariah's dark shadow must have meant he knew better than anyone how dangerous and manipulative she could be.

Amory left. Tonight he was due on carrier watch with Kinsley, though it seemed silly when the real threat was already in camp.

I knew I had to tell Greyson, but I didn't have the energy.

Most of the campers had already returned to their cabins for the night, so Logan and I sat down by the dying embers of the fire, waiting for Greyson to make his rounds.

"Haven, I can't stay here," Logan said finally.

My stomach clenched with dread, but even as she said the words, I knew she was right.

"It's only a matter of time before someone finds out. It's already in my eyes. I can't hide it much longer."

"When should we leave?"

"We?"

Enemy Inside

I looked at her, puzzled, and then the realization dawned on me. She wasn't talking about leaving camp to find the cure as a group. She was planning on leaving by herself — going off alone to die.

"No!" I stammered. "No. You're not leaving us."

"I have to. Haven, I'm going to be contagious soon. I won't take the chance of infecting any of you."

"Ida and I think it's bloodborne. None of the other rebels who fought the carriers and lived became infected."

"You don't know that."

"I was bitten, and *I'm* not infected."

"I'm not willing to risk it on a guess."

"Mariah said the virus mutated. That means that the vaccine doesn't protect against any carriers with the new strain. Think about it. Most reported cases of infection were transmitted by carriers with the open sores because it passes from person to person through the bloodstream. And Mariah was with us the whole time on the way to Sector X. None of us are infected."

"How did she get it?"

"I don't know yet."

"And what about the thousands of people who were infected before the outbreak? It doesn't make sense! I think people would have remembered being bitten."

"Maybe sharing needles . . . blood transfusions . . . I don't know."

"Millions of people would have to be heroin addicts or blood donors, Haven."

She was right. That was the piece that didn't fit.

"What about your mom? When would she have come in

contact with the virus?"

Logan didn't need to ask. I'd already been racking my brain trying to remember what she had been doing that spring that could have brought her in contact with contaminated blood. I sighed. "It doesn't matter. If you leave, we're all leaving. We're going to World Corp International to get the cure."

"We need Jared to come with us."

"Why do you want to bring him?"

"He's the only way to guarantee she won't lead us into a trap and drop us right on the PMC's doorstep."

I nodded. "When do we leave?"

"As soon as possible. No point waiting until I get worse. I don't want to be a burden."

I looked at her. She was staring into the fire, face still flushed from the hunt. If it weren't for her eyes, I wouldn't have been able to guess that she was infected.

"We need to tell Greyson about Mariah."

"I'll do it," she said.

"Are you sure?"

Logan nodded, looking tired. "I'll meet you back at the cabin."

As she walked off, a horrible image flashed through my mind: Logan as a carrier, sickly and emaciated, her long blond hair gone. Logan gasping for air through infected lungs, not remembering who I was. I wondered if I would fight her like any other carrier — kill her to save Amory or Greyson.

I pushed the image out of my mind. I couldn't think that way. We still had time, and our shot at finding the cure hung on Mariah.

Enemy Inside

The wind kicked up, cutting through my jacket and sending a shiver through my entire body. The naked trees caught the breeze, creaking and swaying. Realizing I was all alone in the center of camp, I got up and headed back to the cabin.

It was already dark inside when I pushed open the door, and I could see the lumpy outlines of Maggie, Dolores, and Camille already curled up in their bunks. I sank down on the bed and pulled off my boots, taking care not to disturb the other women.

Lying back onto the sheets that smelled like cedar and pulling the soft quilt over my head, a sudden wave of sadness washed over me. Soon we would have to leave the comfort of the defectors' camp, and I had a feeling we wouldn't be coming back. Nothing post-Collapse seemed to stay the same once you left it.

Then I heard a gunshot.

Camille jerked awake with a tiny yelp, and I sat bolt upright. I twisted on the bed to peer out the dusty window, but I couldn't see anything through the darkness. I heard another shot and then another.

Springing up, I shoved my feet into my boots and ran out into the snow, ears piqued to discern the direction of the shots. Moving through the shadows toward the sound, I almost collided with Greyson and Logan. Greyson was trying to situate his gun and pull on a coat at the same time. Logan looked eerily pale, but her coat was fastened, and she was calmly loading her rifle.

Another shot fired in tandem with a second.

"Carriers," she muttered.

"Amory," I choked. "Kinsley."

"They'll be fine," said Greyson. "Get your rifle, and we'll go help them."

Enemy Inside

My mind felt jumbled. *Why hadn't I grabbed my gun?*

I tripped back up the cabin steps and whirled around in my room, looking for anything else I might need and ignoring Maggie's and Dolores's panicked questions.

I grabbed my rifle and the knife sitting on the window ledge beside my bed, stuffing two boxes of ammunition in my pockets on my way out. When I emerged, Greyson and Logan were already edging along the line of trees, weapons poised. More gunshots punctuated the darkness, and it was easy to follow them. I heard a shout ring through the bare, frosted trees, but it was too low and far away to tell if it could be Amory.

Up ahead, I heard the sound of footfalls. Someone was crashing through the underbrush. I raised my rifle, squinting through the shadows. Finally, I could discern the bulky outline of someone running toward us. He moved too quickly to be a carrier, but I did not lower my weapon.

He was nearly on top of us before I could make out a face. It was Kinsley.

"What's happening?" Logan hissed.

"Carriers," he gasped. "A whole horde of them. Too many. I have to warn the others."

"Amory?" I choked.

"He's holding them off."

I heard more gunshots.

Without another word, we were running again in the direction of Amory's shots. We came to a stand of tall spruce trees, and the shots became deafening.

At first I couldn't see him, but then I noticed something moving in the trees. My eyes caught the outline of Amory reloading his gun.

Enemy Inside

It was impossible to see clearly in the low light, but as my eyes adjusted, I could just make out a dozen hulking shapes lurching in the shadows.

"Oh my god," Logan breathed.

There were so many carriers — more than I could count. All of them wore ragged scraps of clothing that hung off their coat hanger–thin frames. Some were missing shoes, their toes blackened from frostbite. As soon as I finished counting one group of them, more seemed to materialize out of the fog. We began shooting with Amory, taking them out one by one. But for each carrier we shot, two more seemed to take its place.

"We need to fan out," yelled Greyson. "They could try to go around us."

He and Logan moved in opposite directions, and I stood shoulder to shoulder with Amory. The largest groups seemed to be headed straight for us, and I knew he had to be running low on ammunition. I raised my rifle and aimed for the closest ones on my side.

As he fumbled for more rounds, I saw his ashen face and the strain in his eyes. His hands shook a little as he reloaded.

"What is it?" I asked.

"Nothing," he said, brushing me off as he raised his rifle.

But I could tell something was wrong.

"You're fighting it, aren't you?" I yelled as I took aim on another encroaching carrier.

He didn't answer, but I knew the urges born from Amory's conditioning at Isador were fighting for dominance. He was struggling to remain in control — to stay himself.

After several minutes, when the carriers didn't seem to be diminishing in number, I had the fleeting thought that we might have a better shot if he just allowed himself to lose his

Enemy Inside

tenuous grip on control. But once he gave in to that part of him, there was no way to predict how he might react. He could shoot Greyson or Logan. He could shoot me.

As Amory ran out of ammunition, I split the spare magazines and the boxes of rounds from my coat pocket, but we still weren't making a dent in the enormous horde. If anything, they seemed to be coming at us more quickly.

Where were Kinsley and the rest of the hunters from camp? I thought desperately.

Then I heard a shout behind us. I jerked my head over my shoulder just long enough to see Murphy running in our direction. His coat was flapping, showing the bright red long johns he wore underneath. Even after shooting with Amory and losing ground as quickly as we lost ammunition, it was the look on his face that told me we were truly fighting a losing battle.

"Pack it in," gasped Murphy.

"We can't," grunted Amory as he reloaded. A bead of perspiration was trickling down his brow, and he brushed it off impatiently as he took aim.

"There's too many of 'em," said Murphy. "Pack it in, and run back to camp."

Amory ignored him.

"Now!" he barked. In that moment, Murphy looked terrifying. His face, brown and rough as tree bark, was superimposed against the stormy night sky. He looked like Zeus. I suddenly understood why all these people trusted him to protect their camp.

Amory's face was screwed up, conflicted. The carriers nearest us were lurching forward at an alarming rate, slowed somewhat by their fallen comrades sticking out of the snow.

"Amory," I breathed. They were getting closer.

Finally he sighed, and we turned to run back to camp.

"Greyson! Logan!"

They both snapped their heads around, and I could read the defeat on their faces. They saw us running and followed.

Stumbling through the snow, I barely registered the twisted thorns and underbrush catching on my boots or the small branches that smacked me across my face as I ran. I didn't stop to glance over my shoulder, but I could feel Amory jerking his head back to look.

As the trees began to clear, I could see the chaos that had descended upon the camp. Several of the hunters and watchmen stood with their rifles trained in our direction, and everyone back at the cabins was running in and out with bags and crates overflowing with supplies.

"What's happening?"

"We're getting overrun," said Murphy. "I got Kinsley up there with a birds-eye view, and it ain't lookin' good." He gestured to one of the tallest trees near the perimeter of the woods, and I could see Kinsley roosting up in the highest branches with a pair of binoculars.

"Where will we go?"

Murphy ran an agitated hand over his beard. "We'll try to regroup. There are other camps north of here, but this horde's moving fast from that direction. I'll be surprised if there's anything left."

He was right. The swarm was moving fast, but I couldn't wrap my mind around the idea that a single group of carriers could wipe out an entire camp. These were not the carrier problems we had faced on the farm — this was a siege.

Suddenly, Kinsley lurched forward, almost tumbling from his perch as he strained for a better look.

"PMC!" he yelled. "PMC approaching from the north!"

Enemy Inside

My stomach clenched.

"That's the direction the carriers are coming from," said Logan.

My brain struggled to piece the two together, but then Murphy sighed, removing his hat and rubbing the top of his head. "Holy mother of god. They're driving them toward us. They've *weaponized* the carriers."

I heard the rumble of a truck engine and turned to see a small convoy barreling into camp from the road entrance. I recognized the supply trucks we had taken to get here, but there were several smaller trucks and even an old pickup.

Murphy tossed Amory a pair of keys. "You've got two minutes to get your friends and get the hell out of here. There's a walkie-talkie in the front seat. As soon as you shake the PMC, tune to channel seven. The nearest safe house is thirty miles west of here if you get into trouble. We can't all go there, but you four have your whole lives ahead of you. Don't do anything stupid."

A gunshot drowned out his words. I saw a carrier who was lumbering out of the woods fall, and Amory grabbed my arm. Letting him pull me away, it took several paces before I realized he was leading us to the trucks.

"Stop! We have to get Mariah."

"We can't. This solves all our problems. We don't have to kill her, but she can't lead them to us. She's already done that." His voice was clipped and angry.

"We still need her," I growled, jerking out of his grip and sprinting back toward the cabins. Logan came with me, breaking off to grab our things.

I was so focused on getting to Mariah that I didn't notice the figure leap out from behind a tree in my peripheral vision. I turned too late, and we collided. The brute force of the impact knocked me into the snow. My rifle went flying, and I jerked sideways to free myself from the tangle of limbs, but the man had his arm around my neck.

"Give me the fucking key," Jared growled. "You can't leave her here."

"I — wasn't — going to."

"Liar." He tightened his grip around my throat, choking me in the crook of his elbow.

Struggling for air, I tried to squirm out of his grip, but he was too strong. I jerked my elbow back to collide with his face. He grunted, shifting on top of me, and I jerked my knee up. Missing my original target, I felt my knee connect with his abdomen, and he coughed. In one clumsy motion, I shoved him off me and struggled to my feet, pounding up the cabin steps. Throwing my shoulder against the door and inside, I could see Mariah sitting bolt upright against the radiator, looking more scared than I'd ever seen her. Jared was hot on my heels.

Crossing the room, I collapsed onto my knees and fumbled with the keys. My hands were shaking too badly to fit the tiny silver key into the hole, and Jared shoved me aside to do it himself. He pulled her free and tossed her a coat he'd slung over one of the metal bunk frames. It covered her PMC jacket, but she still wore the telltale white pants. It didn't matter; everyone was too distracted to notice her as we ran out of the cabin.

Greyson and Logan were already waiting outside the girls' cabin, rucksacks over their shoulders — Logan with two loaded rifles in her hands. The red Ford Ranger screeched toward us through the snow with Amory in the driver's seat. We tossed the bags into the back with the spare containers of gas, and I shoved Mariah into the backseat to be sandwiched between Greyson and Logan. I didn't trust her back there with Jared for a minute.

"She's not going with you."

"Yes, she is," I growled.

Jared opened his mouth to protest, but Logan had her gun trained on him from the backseat.

I jumped into the front with Amory. "You coming or not?"

Jared shot me a murderous expression and then climbed in on the other side of me. It was a tight squeeze.

Amory toggled the clutch, and we plowed through the snow. By now, several carriers had emerged from the woods. The hunters had abandoned their posts, and I could see the flash of PMC officers clad in white emerging behind them.

It was an odd sight. Some carried rifles with what looked like bayonets on the ends; others toted stun guns that they were using to drive rogue carriers forward.

"Shit," Amory muttered. "They've seen us. We need to ditch this truck as soon as possible. It's too easily recognized."

By now, the other defectors' vehicles were long gone. We wound through the trees down the snow-covered gravel road.

"Where should we go?" I asked, directing the question to Logan. "Where do you think they're coming from?"

"No idea. Those officers could have been sent from anywhere."

We crunched through the snow in silence for several minutes. Finally, I asked the question I knew no one wanted to hear.

"Where is World Corp based?"

No answer.

I could see Mariah in the rearview mirror, sandwiched between Greyson and Logan. She wore an oddly blank expression.

"There's no reason for you not to tell us," I said. "Nobody has to know you used to be PMC. You can join up with us, and we'll just . . ." I trailed off, partially because I had no real plan of what we would "just" do, and partially because I realized I was also speaking for Greyson, Logan, Amory, and Jared. I didn't care what Jared thought, but I knew it wasn't fair to tether Mariah's fate to the rest of theirs.

Mariah didn't answer. She wasn't even looking at me anymore. She was staring out the window, seemingly oblivious to what I was saying.

"Don't you want to stay with Jared? It's not as if you can go back to the PMC anyway. And now you don't have to. If you help us —"

"Stop," Amory snapped. "Just stop. She's not going to help us, and we're not going on some wild goose chase for a cure that might not even exist."

I looked at him, feeling the anger and hurt churning in my stomach. After everything we had been through, Amory had always been on my side. Even when my rescue of Greyson from Sector X amounted to a suicide mission, he was always willing to follow.

What had changed? Was I being selfish and reckless, or had he simply stopped believing in me?

I fell silent, the hurt and humiliation pooling in the pit of my stomach. I could sense Greyson's sympathetic stare burning a hole in the back of my neck, and with my thigh pressed up against Jared's, I could practically feel the smugness radiating from him.

"So. It's finally happened," Mariah crooned.

I snapped my head around to look at her, and she wore a wicked smile I longed to smack off her face.

Enemy Inside

"The golden boy has finally stopped swallowing your bullshit. Nobody wants to listen to you, and you're all —"

The sharp smack like a whip cut off Mariah's voice. Logan was so fast I didn't realize what was happening until I saw her blond hair fly around like a cape. A moment later, Mariah was lying in Greyson's lap — an angry red patch glowing on her cheek — with Logan's hands gripping her throat.

"You fucking bitch," Logan whispered. "We could have let you *die* in there." Logan laughed one sharp, scary laugh. "Believe me! *Nothing* would have made me happier than to see a horde of carriers rip you apart.

"If you don't help us find the cure, I'm sure I'll have a chance to do it myself. When I've turned, you'll be my — first — victim." She punctuated the last few words by shaking Mariah by the throat.

In that moment, Mariah looked much smaller than Logan. She gagged and choked, and an alarmed Greyson had flattened himself against the other side of the cab. Jared twisted around, swatted once at Logan, and then unbuckled and tried to climb over the seat.

Amory jerked the wheel once, and the truck slid across the snowy road, nearly colliding with a tree and sending Jared flying into the window. I smacked into his left shoulder — hard — and Greyson flew into Logan. Losing her grip slightly, she stayed hovered over Mariah, but she seemed to have lost the murderous gleam in her eyes.

"Calm the fuck down!" Amory yelled. "Logan, cut the drama. We have bigger problems right now. We need to get off the road or ditch this car."

"Where are we going?" Logan screamed in Mariah's face, her huge green eyes bulging.

"Head north," Mariah gasped. "You have to cross the

border to get to headquarters."

The cab fell silent.

"Across the border?" repeated Greyson after a long pause. "Well, that's just great. How are we supposed to get across?"

"That's why it wasn't even worth it to tell you," croaked Mariah. She had freed herself from Logan's clutches and was massaging her throat. "You'll never get three defectors and one carrier across the border."

As she punctuated the word "carrier," I threw a sympathetic look at Logan, but she was still relishing Mariah's reaction.

Watching her watch Mariah, I could tell that lashing out was only masking the helplessness she felt. Her eyes looked yellow and bloodshot around the edges, and there was a distinct sheen of fever on her brow.

"We have to try," I said.

Amory turned his head toward me. "It's a suicide mission."

"I know. You don't have to go with me. No one does. I can take Logan and try to get us across. It's a long shot, but we don't have any other options right now."

"I'm coming with you," said Greyson. "Going into Sector X to save me was crazy, but you did it anyway."

Logan seemed to soften slightly at this, but she turned icy when her eyes met Amory's in the rearview mirror. "I'm not sure when you turned into such a coward."

A pang of rage flashed across his face, and I saw his grip tighten on the steering wheel. "You have to *think*, Logan. I know strategy seems to come as an afterthought around here, but it's going to get us all killed."

"You don't have to go," I said, quietly enough so only he could hear. "You're right. I can't ask you to do this."

Amory groaned, pulling his hand down over his face. We had reached the highway.

For several seconds, all I could hear was the loud hum of the truck idling. Then Amory let out an exasperated breath and pulled onto the road headed north.

Chapter Twenty-One

We drove on for several minutes before we were forced to pull off at an exit to avoid a rover.

We had reached a cluster of abandoned gas stations and restaurants — a good place for a pit stop on the highway. Amory turned on the ramp and pulled into the snow-covered parking lot of an abandoned fast food restaurant with a sun-faded kids' slide in the courtyard.

"How are we on supplies?" he asked.

"I had some in my pack ready to go," said Logan. "There's four bottles of water, a few granola bars, deer jerky, and some almonds."

"I've got instant oatmeal and two cans of beans," said Greyson.

They looked expectantly at Amory and Jared. Jared continued staring out the window, and Amory jerked his head once. "I got nothing."

"I didn't stash any food," I said. "But there's about five boxes of rounds in the bottom of my pack."

Logan grinned. "You stole from the supply cabin?"

"Technically, Ida and I stole from one of the vendors at the Exchange who was trying to steal from us, and we ended up with way more than we would have paid for. I figured that would be much harder to get than food, and we're always running away at a moment's notice . . ."

"All right," said Amory. "We still need to get more food. I don't want to risk this kind of exposure again — not while the PMC is looking for us. Greyson, you stay and guard Mariah. Jared can go over to that store and try to find food. Haven and I will try to find another car we can take."

"What am I supposed to do?" Logan snapped. "I'm not an invalid."

"You can go with Jared. But if there's any sign of trouble, get out of there."

I didn't like the idea of splitting up and leaving Logan with Jared, but watching her holster her knives and sling a rifle over her shoulder, I knew she could more than handle herself.

I helped Greyson tie up Mariah and left knowing he was the best person to guard her. Of all of us, he was the most levelheaded and the least likely to kill her on impulse if provoked.

"Meet back here in thirty minutes," said Amory. "And look alive."

Grudgingly, Jared followed Logan across the parking lot toward the mega store on the other side of the road, and Amory and I headed toward a cluster of connected parking lots behind the restaurant. I felt in my pocket for my spare magazine, trying to ignore the nervous twitch on the back of my neck.

The strip was eerily quiet. Most of the parking lots were completely empty, and the shelves inside the gas station were white and bare.

The only car I could see was an abandoned Corolla parked near the employee entrance. Amory inspected it with a furrowed brow. One of the windows was missing, the frame covered by a sheet of opaque plastic and discolored packing tape that rippled in the breeze. The front hood was slightly rumpled, and all the hubcaps were gone.

Once he cajoled the hood up, he hunched over to look inside and let out a long, exasperated breath. "This won't work."

"You think?"

"Well, we might have to settle. Beggars can't be choosers, but this looks like it just died here."

"It's also way too small for six people."

"Our options are fairly limited," he said through gritted teeth. I was taken aback by his tone.

"What's wrong with you?"

"What's wrong with *me*?" He rolled his head around. "Are you kidding?"

I gave him a blank look, which only seemed to enrage him more.

"You told me that after we rescued Greyson, we were going west. You didn't say we would be teaming up with more rebels and then marching to our deaths up north."

"I didn't know! And in case you forgot, I had to join the rebels to save *you*! What was I supposed to do? And with Logan —"

"Logan wouldn't be infected if we had just left the camp. This only happened because we stuck around with Rulon's sinking ship."

"You could have said something. And we were in no shape to go anywhere. Why are you blaming all this on me?"

"Because you're a leader!" he yelled. "And you don't see it. You just think you make decisions for yourself and people follow you because it's the right thing, but that's *not* how it is.

"Me and Logan and Greyson . . . and even Kinsley would

follow you anywhere, and it's not because you make the best decisions. It's because people want to believe in you. You have to take that more seriously."

The tension stung harshly in the air between us.

"I thought you guys followed me because we were friends."

Amory raked an angry hand through his hair. "Yeah, but Logan and I are friends. Max and I were friends. But you know how many times we've shot down one another's stupid plans because they were too dangerous? They stick with you because they know you'll go alone, and they think you're smart enough to do the right thing."

"Stop," I said, trying to hide the waver in my voice. "This is your conditioning talking. You wouldn't be saying this if —"

"If what? If I hadn't gone along with your plan to break Greyson out of prison? If I hadn't been captured?"

His words felt like a punch to the stomach.

"And what about you?" My voice shook, and I could feel my lip trembling as I turned on him. "If I'm so awful at making decisions, what's your excuse?"

"I go along with it because I'm in love with you!" he yelled.

His words were out there, and I didn't know what to do. His angry expression told me it was not a romantic declaration, but I felt it could not go unacknowledged.

"Amory..."

"It's not smart," he said. When he looked at me sideways, his eyes were dark. "Everything was fine before you came along. We were safe."

I blinked back the tears that threatened to spill over.

Basically, he was saying his life would have been much better if I had never come to the farm.

"But then you showed up and . . . you breathed life into us again. You gave us something to fight for, and that's . . . dangerous."

"I'm sorry I dragged you into this."

"I'm not," he said. "It would be easier if I were. Besides, I let myself get dragged in." He took a step toward me, and I could see the frustration in his eyes. His anger, unleashed by the PMC simulations, was fighting with something else and fading quickly.

"I just get so angry now . . . in a way I never did before . . . and it *scares* me." He sighed. "I'm sorry."

"It's all right," I whispered. "I'm not going anywhere."

That was all he needed. Wordlessly, Amory closed the gap between us, reached up to cup the back of my neck under my hair, and planted a kiss on my forehead. "Come on. We have to find a better car."

We scoured the parking lots along our side of the road. Most of them were rusted-out junkers that had died there when their owners attempted the journey north. During the migration, hitchhikers had run rampant along the highway. Some were harmless ordinary people trying to get a ride, and some were murderers, rapists, and carjackers trying to take advantage of people's implicit trust in troubled times.

Finally, as we took the corner around the back of a mini-mart, I saw it: a white twelve-passenger van with the words "God Deliver Us to the Great White North" running in streaked car paint across the elongated side window.

Amory whooped loudly, and we ran across the parking lot. Each of the doors had "North Glen United Church of Christ" emblazoned in blue paint with a thin cross. Yanking open the door, I slid in the passenger seat and admired the spaciousness. There was a cross knitted in rainbow yarn hanging from the rearview mirror, and the keys were dangling in the ignition as though they were waiting for us.

Amory hopped in beside me and turned the key. Nothing happened.

"No gas. Must be why they left it here."

"Praise the Lord," I muttered.

We got out and walked around to the pumps. The first one had a crumpled, sun-faded paper sign that flapped in the breeze. "Sorry, no gas" was barely discernible in the smeared, dripping writing.

"They're all out of gas," called Amory from across the parking lot. "We should see if there's anything else here we can use before we head back to the others. We can siphon from the truck and fill it with the two tanks in the back."

Crunching through the snow around the pump, I took in the overflowing trashcans and the faded signs propped in the dark windows: "NO GAS — DON'T ASK." Amory pushed against the front door, and I was surprised when it swung open.

Behind the counter, the empty cash register drawer was hanging open. The coolers, which were dark, had been looted of all the soda, beer, water, and energy drinks. The racks for candy and snacks were nearly empty, as was the convenience section near the back. Somehow, the greasy, burnt stench of hotdogs from the rotating display still stung my nostrils.

The only food that was left on the shelves was gum and a few dusty cans of Spam. In the convenience aisle, there were pens, an emergency sewing kit, dental floss, bandages, shoe polish, and a few boxes of tampons. I grabbed the tampons and the bandages and shoved them in a plastic bag with the Spam.

As I inspected the aisles for any salvageable food, Amory nicked a key hanging behind the counter and unlocked the door to inspect the back room.

He emerged a moment later lugging a jug of water in each hand and wearing a huge grin.

"Idiots. The looters forgot to check the back. There's food in there, too. We should get the others to gas up the van and pull it around."

I deposited my haul on the counter and followed Amory back to where Greyson and Mariah were sulking in the truck.

"Hey! Let's go. We found a van," said Amory. He was clearly very proud of himself. "Where are Logan and Jared?"

Greyson shook his head. "They should have been back by now. How long does it take to get a few groceries?"

"Maybe they had trouble breaking in," I said, the nerves creeping into my voice. It was five minutes past the half-hour mark, and I didn't like that they were late.

"We'll be right down the road," said Amory. "They'll see us."

Climbing into the truck, I could feel the tension emanating from the back seat. Amory coaxed the engine to life, and we rolled through the snow and parked next to the van.

"What the hell is that?" Mariah asked with a sneer.

"Salvation," said Amory with a smirk. "We need a long tube to siphon the gas out of the truck." He turned to me. "See if you can detach one of the hoses from the soda machine."

I nodded and went back into the store, pushing open the door to the back room to get a look at the hoses. Amory was right — the haul here was much better than the picked-over remains on the shelves. There were big boxes full of chips, nuts, jerky, and other snacks, and even two pallets of canned soup and tuna.

I found one of the hoses Amory was talking about and tugged it free from the machine. As I emerged from the back room, I could hear voices outside.

Peering out through the grimy window, I could see Amory arguing with Jared next to a cart full of groceries. Amory's face was contorted in a yell, the planes of his face more prominent than before, and Jared's slick blond waves were disheveled, as though he'd been arguing animatedly.

Logan was nowhere in sight.

"Where is she?" I yelled.

Jared shifted his weight from one foot to the other, avoiding my gaze. "Look, she went fucking crazy. I had to leave her."

"The fever's set in! She's not in her right mind!"

"Yeah, I know that, all right? I know it's not what you want to hear, but she's a fucking liability. We can't just drag her around with us anymore. She's gonna get us killed."

I took two strides toward him, my rage boiling over. In that moment, I could have killed him. I didn't care if he took pleasure in hurting me, made crude jokes about me behind my back to get a rise out of Amory, or hated me for throwing Mariah under the bus. That was his deal — his way of asserting power and getting back at me for wronging him. But now he had put Logan in danger.

Before I was aware of what I was doing, I had Jared by the collar. "The only person who's going to get killed is you!" I hissed, shoving him into the van. "If *anything* happens to her, I swear to god . . . I will end your life."

I pushed him again for good measure and turned back toward the grocery store.

Amory reached out and caught my wrist. "You shouldn't go by yourself."

"I'm fine," I growled. I must have been shooting daggers out of my eyes, because Amory took a step back, looking wounded.

I shrugged off the guilt. If he was going to accuse me of dragging people into my reckless decisions, he couldn't be offended when I didn't want his help. Backing away, I stepped off the curb into the road.

It was unnerving seeing six lanes of traffic completely empty and covered in a blanket of unmarked snow. It was especially deep near the gutter, and my leg sank in too far, twisting my still-tender ankle painfully. As the snow and slush filled my boots, I became increasingly anxious to get on the road and far away from this creepy pit stop.

The automatic doors remained stubbornly closed as I approached. The store was dark except for a few emergency lights illuminating the aisles. One of the sliding doors was propped open with an overturned trashcan, as if Logan and Jared had wedged it in to squeeze through.

Stepping inside, it was strange to see the wispy cloud of my own breath in the dark store. The stand of ads had tipped over, papering the damp floor in weekly specials, and carts were strewn around haphazardly.

"Logan?" I called. I hoped she was close. The deeper into the store I walked, the darker it got.

Triggering the motion sensors, the emergency lights flickered on as I walked through the produce section. Nearly all the bins were empty — save for a few lone rotten pieces of fruit — but that had probably happened before mandatory migration was over. The shelves in the snack foods aisle were completely bare, as were most of the canned goods. I called out for Logan as I went, my voice getting progressively quieter as I entered the belly of the superstore.

Enemy Inside

The only aisle that looked relatively untouched was the cleaning products aisle. No one had much use for air fresheners or floor cleaner when they were abandoning their homes and moving north.

Making my way around the back, I wound around every aisle. Most of the electronics had been looted, and the clothes were depleted, too.

Logan wasn't in the sporting goods or the camping sections — two aisles I thought she might be scavenging in hopes of finding a fishing rod, a pocket knife, or extra ammunition. Then I remembered Logan's penchant for toiletries and made a beeline for the beauty section.

I heard a soft whimper.

It was an odd sound — halfway between a sob and a pant. I quickened my pace, footsteps scuffing on the dirty tile, and flew around the corner of the pharmaceutical aisle.

Logan was slumped on the floor against the shelves, fumbling with a bottle of Tylenol, trying to get the plastic seal off. She didn't see me right away, and she wore a far-off look on her glistening face.

"Logan."

She turned her head slowly, as if barely seeing me. "Haven," she mumbled, not making direct eye contact. "Help me."

"What's wrong?"

"My head's burning up." She popped the top off the bottle, and it slipped from her hands like a bar of soap, sending the capsules skittering across the floor.

I bent to retrieve the bottle.

"I'm really glad this never happened to them," she murmured, her eyes swimming with tears.

"Who?"

"Mom, Dad, Sebastian . . . at least you know it was quick."

I handed Logan two capsules, and her hand shook slightly as she popped them in her mouth and dry swallowed.

"What do you mean?"

Logan had told me about her parents. She had stayed to train with the PMC so they could afford to go north.

"My family. They're dead."

"How do you know?"

"What do you think the PMC does to an officer's family when that officer is a defector?"

My heart sank. She was probably right.

"Haven, what's wrong with me?"

I sighed. "It's the fever."

Shaking her head, Logan pulled her knees up to her chest. Her eyes were bright, almost insane looking, and her face had a faint grayish tinge to it.

Then I heard it: a low, shaky intake of breath behind me and the pop of mucus in infected lungs. I dropped the bottle and spun around.

Ambling toward us from the front of the store was a carrier. My hands tingled, empty, and I realized I'd left my gun back at the van.

I grabbed Logan by her arms, pulling her up into a standing position, and dragged her over to the next aisle. Moving awkwardly supporting half of Logan's weight, I began shuffling us toward the doors.

I heard the sound again, this time coming from my left. There was another one, further along than the first, saliva oozing over the bloody sores around his lips. His head was bald and covered in scratchy dry patches, and his clothes hung about him in shreds.

For the first time since I'd known Logan, she was regarding the carrier with fear, as though seeing her own future. I pushed her down past the pharmacy window and around the corner. We stopped dead when we reached the front.

Shuffling around, noses tingling with the smell of their next kill, stood over twenty carriers. Some of them were balding and decrepit, slower than the others. But some looked only a few weeks along. They looked human — hungry and sick, but just as strong and fast as me.

We backed away around the perimeter of the store.

"Is there another way out?" I hissed.

"There has to be," whispered Logan, stumbling slightly in my grip.

We backtracked to the lawn and garden section, and I saw the closed doors to the nursery that led outside.

Fumbling with the door, my sweaty hands slipped over the smooth metal and glass. To my surprise, Logan yanked it open without much trouble, and we ran out into the nursery.

Pallets of soil and fertilizer were hidden under the dusting of snow, and I tripped over a lone pallet, flying face-first into the snow and skinning my knee. We made it to the gate, which towered high over our heads. I shook the chain links, and a heavy padlock rattled against the bars.

"No!"

I pushed it forward as hard as I could, but the fence swung open only a few inches — not wide enough for either of us to squeeze through. Grabbing Logan's arm, I dragged her back through the snow toward the door. We skidded

Enemy Inside

inside, our wet boots squeaking and slipping on the tile.

Moving along the perimeter and searching for a fire exit, I could hear the groans of carriers echoing in the big empty space. My heart leaped when I found the double doors. I pushed, and the door cracked open, sounding the fire alarm. A cold burst of air whipped in through the opening, and I pushed harder.

My stomach clenched when I saw it: a chain and a padlock holding the door handles together from the outside — no doubt to discourage looting during mandatory migration. We were out of options.

I pulled Logan into the sporting goods section and down the row where they kept the guns locked behind a glass cabinet. Feeling broken glass underfoot, I looked up. Someone had already raided the cabinet, and all the guns, bows, and knives were gone.

"There has to be something," I muttered wildly, scanning the shelves.

In the next aisle, a wooden baseball bat caught my eye. I snatched it up and yanked Logan back in the direction of the front entrance. Her eyes had glazed over again, and she was tripping and faltering more than before.

Some of the carriers had wandered off toward the decimated produce section, but there were still at least a dozen crowded around the sliding doors.

Ducking behind a drinks cooler in front of the checkout, I picked out the smallest ones I thought I could take out easily. They were too close together, and I would have very little time with one before I would need to move on to the next.

The sliding doors rattled, and another squeezed himself in and looked around for the source of the food. It was now or never. We had to try before even *more* came.

Enemy Inside

I grabbed Logan by the shoulders, pulling her back to earth to refocus. Logan, the best carrier slayer I'd ever known, could do this in her sleep.

"Stay right on me," I said. "And whatever happens, get across the street to the gas station and find the others."

She nodded. The vacant expression was gone, and I thought I saw that old gleam in her eyes that she always had just before the kill.

I moved into a crouched position, sneaking around the checkout station. "Now!"

Breaking into a run, we sprinted straight for the door. Several carriers turned their heads, shuffling toward us. One faster, newly infected one stepped into my path, and I whipped the baseball bat up at his jaw as hard as I could. It made a sickening *thunk,* and he staggered backward.

With a groan, another carrier turned on us. She was hunched over to one side, wearing a broken heel and a torn black dress. Her thinning hair hung in dirty cobwebs over her shoulder, not quite concealing a long gash across her forehead. I got into batting position and let it fly against the side of her head. She fell to the floor, blood gushing from her skull, and my shoulder burned from exertion.

I turned over my shoulder, and Logan was several paces back, cornered by two surly teenage carriers in baggy pants and beaters, their chests shrunken to ribs under their shirts. Logan didn't have a weapon.

I brought the baseball bat down like a hammer on the first carrier and swung it left to connect with the other's neck. They both stumbled out of the way but were still kicking. I grabbed Logan's wrist, pulling her forward.

In the time it had taken to retrieve her, several more carriers had impeded the small amount of progress I'd made and were blocking the entrance. Shoulders aching and hands sweating, I swung out wildly. Barely watching where I was swinging, I connected with heads, chests, elbows — anything to get them out of the way. Occasionally I would hear a sick *thud* that told me I had made a major impact, and the carrier would fall to the ground at my feet, wailing in pain.

I slipped on something, reaching back for Logan to steady myself. I felt the vomit burn my throat as I realized it was blood and flesh from a carrier's split skull.

Just feet away from the door, I swatted at one more carrier who had her leg stuck on the other side of the trashcan wedged in the door. I hit her over the head and used the bat to push her out of our way. She collapsed in a heap on the other side.

Pulling Logan by the wrist, we emerged into the strangely bright parking lot. A few straggling carriers were lumbering over by the cart carousel, but it was nothing we couldn't manage.

I heard a hard, dry sob escape from Logan as I yanked her along through the snow. I didn't look back. I was barely holding it together as it was, and seeing her face would only unravel me.

As we ran through the snow lifting our feet like deer, I didn't feel the slush soaking into my pant leg. I didn't feel my burning shoulders or the sweaty, feverish skin of Logan's arm. My vision had narrowed, as though I were looking down a tunnel with a bright light at the end instead of running in broad daylight across the street. The gas station came into view, and I gasped in relief.

Chapter Twenty-Two

We rounded the corner, and the three figures between the van and the truck turned in our direction. Their mouths fell open, and I realized I was still clutching the baseball bat, which was covered in a sticky residue of blood, human hair, and bits of flesh.

"We have to go," I gasped. "Carriers. There's a horde of them in the store. I don't know where they're coming from."

Amory took three cautious steps toward me and coaxed the baseball bat out of my hand. His eyes didn't leave mine as he tossed it into the snow and pulled me toward the truck.

"Jared, finish loading that shit," he called, still not tearing his eyes away from me.

I realized I was shaking, sweaty, and clammy like Logan.

"Are you okay?" Amory asked. "You didn't get bit?"

I shook my head, focusing on the van, unwilling to turn to see the look on Logan's face. Jared was heaving the jugs of water into the cargo area, and Greyson was loading supplies from the grocery cart into the back seats, watching me with concern.

Amory guided me to the van, and I turned to find Logan. She seemed to have recovered. At least she didn't have that glazed look on her face anymore. Silently, we all climbed into the van. I grabbed one of the water bottles rolling around the floor at my feet and handed it back to her. She looked as though she could use it. She gulped gratefully, and I gripped my knees to steady my shaking hands.

Amory got into the driver's seat, watching me carefully, but I didn't look at him. I didn't know what to say. I didn't want to talk about the slaughter at the store, and some of the shock was wearing off. Now, instead of pure emptiness, I felt anger and hatred lapping at my insides. *How could Jared have left Logan there?*

If I had not been there, she might have died, or she might have joined the horde of carriers. I wondered at what point an infected person began to view them as her own kind. *Probably at the same point they started trying to kill their human loved ones*, I thought grimly.

Amory turned the key in the ignition, and the van hummed to life. Out of the corner of my eye, I could see that the back rows were completely full of food and supplies, and Greyson was sitting near the back, watching Jared and Mariah closely.

"Where do we go?" Amory asked in a hoarse voice. "North?"

"Where is World Corp?" I asked, twisting in my seat to look at Mariah. As she regarded me with her lazy, bored expression, I felt my rage boil over. "Where *is* it?" I screamed again.

Nothing.

Taking in her greasy hair, those unremorseful eyes, and the way she sat with her hips thrust forward in defiance, I felt myself cross over a line again. My rage became white-hot, burning insanity. Then calmness washed over me like death, and I pointed across the street.

"Go back to the store," I said to Amory.

"I thought it was overrun."

Enemy Inside

"I just need to do something real quick."

Looking at me with a bewildered expression, Amory turned the van and plowed across the street and over the median. In the rearview mirror, I could see Greyson's confusion, but Logan was watching me warily.

Amory stopped in front of the store, eyeing the door with the slumped, dead carrier nervously. "You can't go back in there. Haven —"

But I was already halfway out of the van. I grabbed his handgun from between us on the floor and stalked around the front of the vehicle. The five of them watched me silently, and I could still see a few carriers wandering around the cart carousels, sniffing the abandoned shopping baskets for lingering food residue.

I clicked the safety off Amory's gun as I walked and checked the chamber. Without warning, I swung open Mariah's door and grabbed her by the throat. Even tied up, I would never have gotten the jump on Logan. But Mariah was cocky, unafraid, and less skilled. Her arrogance was a liability.

Jared lurched toward me, but I pushed the gun into Mariah's temple. He froze.

Digging my fingernails into her windpipe, I pulled her toward me until she was tripping out of the van.

Grabbing her by the hair, I nudged her toward the sliding door propped open by the trashcan. She let out a sound that was halfway between a whimper and a growl.

I could already hear the sounds of carriers thrashing around inside, upturning candy racks at the checkout and pushing each other out of the way to get their hands on any remaining food.

In one swift kick, I dislodged the trashcan holding the door open and shoved Mariah down to the ground half

Enemy Inside

inside the store, planting my knee in the small of her back. The door slid back into place, sandwiching her there.

"Maybe I can't shoot you," I growled. "But I bet you'll lead us to World Corp if you're infected again."

Carriers nearest the door had noticed Mariah lying half inside the store like bait.

"Here's hoping we snag a stage five carrier on the first try."

"No!" she whimpered.

"Haven!" Amory yelled. "What the hell are you doing?"

I barely heard him. All I could feel was my burning rage against Mariah.

"I'm done playing games with you!" I yelled, watching the carriers amble toward us out of the corner of my eye. "This is her life! I won't let her turn, but I don't give a *fuck* about you!"

Back at the van, I heard the sounds of a struggle, as though Amory and Greyson were restraining Jared.

Mariah whimpered, tears filling her eyes, but she looked more resolute than ever. She tried to laugh her cold laugh, but it came out more like a gurgle. She was struggling now, watching in horror as the carriers inched in our direction. The slobber was dripping down the oozing sores on their chapped mouths, and their eyes were unfocused, delirious with hunger. I squeezed the door shut on her abdomen and she yelled, struggling to free herself.

"Just tell me!" I screamed. "What do you have to lose? Tell me!"

"Take 416 north to the Queensway! It's the Infinity Building! You can't miss it. Let me out!" she screamed through her tears. "Let me out!"

I snapped back to life.

The disgust at what I'd done came first, followed by the urgency to free Mariah. I pushed the door aside and pulled her to her feet. She yanked herself out of my grip and stumbled to the van. I pushed her inside, slammed the door, and climbed into the front seat.

Amory floored it, and we spun out in the snow toward the road.

"You catch that?" I asked Amory from the passenger seat.

He didn't answer, which led me to think he had heard *everything* that had happened out in front of the store, not just Mariah's directions to World Corp International. Nobody else said a word.

I knew I should have felt ashamed by what I had done, but overwhelmingly I felt the immense relief that we now had directions to the place where Logan could be cured. What scared me the most was the slight shaky feeling that told me I had gone over the edge. All the killing and fighting and running — it had affected me. I was a much different person than I had been on the farm. Maybe when you had so little left to lose, you clung desperately to preserving the only things that mattered.

I sneaked a look in the mirror at the four in the back. Logan was checked out, her feverish, sweaty face pressed against the window as she fell in and out of sleep. Mariah's face was blank, her cuffed hands folded demurely in her lap. Jared was white with rage, kept at bay only by the gun Greyson had pointed surreptitiously at his back. Greyson was the only one who looked normal, a subtle look of approval in the arch of his brow as I made eye contact in the mirror. He had known me long enough to doubt I would have ever let Mariah get bitten.

I tore my eyes away. The person whose silence bothered

me most was Amory's. I couldn't even bring myself to look at him.

I tried to dismiss my concern. He was the one who had uncontrollable fits of rage where he would kill anything in his path. Of course, he had been brainwashed by the PMC, and he was successfully working against his impulses. What excuse did I have?

I told myself I'd only done what I did to save Logan, but really, there was a small part of me that was desperate to exert some control over our lives. I'd been in reaction mode since I'd left Columbia, and I was tired of it.

I was sick of running — sick of barely surviving.

Merging onto the highway, I redirected my thoughts to how we would manage to cross the northern border. Even if we managed to steal some dummy CIDs, mandatory migration was over. If the PMC accepted our fake identities, we would likely be imprisoned for failing to comply with the law.

"We have to cross as PMC," I said to the silent car. "We can't go as civilians. They'll be suspicious."

"We don't have CIDs," said Logan. "Or uniforms."

"We have two uniforms," I said, gesturing at Mariah and Jared. I didn't know whether Jared had packed the uniform he used to go on runs for Rulon, but I suspected he had. When you were a rebel, you carried everything you owned in the world with you.

"That helps us *how?*"

"They can pose as officers, and we can be their prisoners."

"That's brilliant."

"One problem," said Amory, startling me when he spoke. "We still don't have any CIDs. Unless you want to find two officers to kill."

His words stung, and my cheeks burned with shame. It was no use telling him I hadn't planned on letting the carriers get Mariah. I had no idea what I would have done.

The silence festered in the van for the next several hours, and I began checking behind us every few minutes for any sign that we were being followed by the PMC. We were making slow progress. Whenever we saw a rover up ahead at an overpass, we had to take the nearest exit or drive around it. Sometimes we ended up backtracking or had to drive several miles off course. If we were being followed, it would be obvious what we were doing.

As the darkness settled, I started to notice the gnawing hunger in my belly. I heard a growl escape from Greyson's stomach behind me, too, but I knew no one wanted to suggest that we stop to make camp for the night.

Finally, without a word, Amory took an exit. I wasn't sure where he was going. The only signs were for an RV campground off the highway. He followed the signs, and we turned onto a smaller road that wound into the trees.

The camp was deserted, and the snow-covered trees and picnic tables gave me a strange sense of security. I'd gone on lots of trips with my family to campgrounds just like it. As a kid, I'd hated it. There was no TV, and I was bored sitting around in the woods for days with just my family. Now I would give anything to go on one of those trips again.

Nobody spoke as we parked in a secluded pocket of trees. Greyson jumped out and began hunting for firewood. Amory started rooting around in the back for our dinner, which was difficult in the darkness. We hadn't taken inventory of our supplies, and nobody really knew what we had yet.

I helped Greyson start the fire and began cooking a few cans of chili in the Dutch oven Jared had found at the store.

Amory was still rummaging around in the back rows, busying himself to avoid me. Logan was huddled up by the fire, wrapped in a blanket. Her face was pale, and her hair was hanging in stringy, sweaty waves around her face.

Finally, there was nothing left for anyone to distract themselves with. We were all hungry, so we slumped around the fire on the picnic table benches and ate the chili. It was too salty and a little gamey, but I began to feel slightly better as it warmed my belly and filled me up. As everyone ate, the tension began to dissipate slightly. Jared was still sulky but seemed satisfied when I handed him the keys to uncuff Mariah. There was no point keeping her tied up now; we had what we needed, and there was nowhere for her to go.

"Where are we going to get the CIDs?" Greyson asked.

"I don't know."

Jared sighed. "I have some extras. They actually trick the rovers. The rover you pass under reads the CID, but it bounces the location data from another rover at random, so they never know where you are."

"That's perfect."

"How far do you think we are from the border?" asked Greyson.

Jared shrugged. "Only a few miles."

I nodded. Tomorrow was the day. Judging by the look of Logan, I knew we were running out of time. Somehow I doubted that the PMC's miracle cure would work on someone once they had fully turned.

We passed around water bottles and cooked some more of the food Amory had been able to find in the dark. Once everyone had eaten their fill, they piled back in the van to get out of the wind.

I still felt nervous about sleeping only feet away from

Jared and Mariah, so I stayed out by the fire. I didn't feel tired. I was wide-awake, thinking about what might happen the next day.

Amory got up to join the others in the van but stopped. Hearing his slow shuffles behind me, I turned to look at him.

He was staring at me with such intensity that I didn't know whether I would yell at him or kiss him. I settled for hostility.

"You have to trust me," I growled. "I don't need you fighting against me, too. I don't always make the right decisions, but I'm trying to. And I can't believe you wouldn't have done the same thing." I lowered my voice so it was barely more than a whisper. "You can't tell me that if it was one of us or Mariah, you would let her live. Don't *blame* me for making a choice. Someone had to do something."

Amory didn't say anything. He just collapsed next to me and sighed, our shoulders touching. It was hard to discern his expression in the dancing firelight.

"You're right. It's exactly what I would have done if it were you. And god knows you watched me do pretty horrible things. But I . . ." He trailed off for a moment, staring into the fire. "I never wanted all this to change you. I didn't want it to change me, either."

"But it *has*."

"I know. But one day, this is all going to be over. Maybe not soon, but someday. And if we're still alive, we're going to have to live with all the things we've done."

He looked at me, and I could see the love and concern reflected in his eyes. "I never want you to hate yourself the way I hate myself when I think of what the PMC made me do. I was their pawn, and they turned me into a monster."

"You're not a monster."

Enemy Inside

"Not anymore," he corrected. "I'm trying really hard not to be."

I sighed and leaned into him, savoring his warmth and allowing the peace from the day's victory to overtake my guilt. Just that connection — the feel of Amory's strong shoulder pressing into mine — made me feel more in control.

Amory seemed surprised at my closeness, as though he expected me to be angry at him for the way he looked after I had threatened Mariah or for the way his temper had been boiling since escaping Isador. I wasn't. I was tired of being angry. He softened against me.

"I'm still on your side," he whispered. "I'm always on your side."

I wanted to reach up and kiss him, but it wasn't the right time. I knew he was still struggling with his anger — a residual effect from the conditioning — and we were still struggling to restore what we'd had on the farm. That easy trust that had existed between us was gone. It was possible Amory would always have to fight against his violent impulses, and I was different, too. But I was determined to stick with him because he was the bravest person I knew, and he'd fought for me when no one else had.

After a while, Amory helped me to my feet, and we climbed back into the van to curl up in the uncomfortable cloth seats. It was cold, and the armrest dug into my back, but I was so exhausted that I fell asleep almost instantly.

The next morning, I woke with a start. I half expected Mariah to be hovered over me with a knife at my throat, but I could hear the others milling around the campfire outside, stoking the disintegrated logs and making breakfast.

I could see my breath inside the freezing van, and the

windows were mostly frosted over. Cracking the door, a rush of frigid air slipped up the sleeve of my coat.

Greyson had a pot of oatmeal going on the fire while Amory struggled with a packet of instant coffee. Even though it was expensive after the Collapse, coffee had been one of his vices on the farm.

"How much gas do we have?" asked Jared. He did not look up from the boxes of ammunition spread out on the tarp in front of him. He was taking inventory of what we had left and divvying up the rounds.

"Not enough," said Amory. "We might make it into the city, but we need a full tank if we want a shot at getting away."

"There's more ammunition in my bag," I said to Jared.

Logan shot me a look from where she was huddled by the fire, but I ignored her. Since he had told us about the CIDs, I felt I should make some gesture of goodwill. I still didn't trust him, but we would have to cooperate since we were posing as his prisoners. The thought made my gut twist uncomfortably, but after all his time undercover as a PMC officer, he was our best shot at getting across the border.

Jared nodded at me once. "Good news is we have plenty of rounds and food, but we should try to scrounge some gas before we go any farther. I'll take a look around and see if there are any cars left out here we can siphon from."

"I'll go with you," said Mariah.

An alarm bell went off somewhere in my brain, but I tuned it out.

"Are we just going to let them go off together?" Amory asked once they were out of earshot.

"What are they going to do?"

"Make a plan to kill us? Trade us to the PMC at the

border?"

"We have to try to trust them," I said.

"No, we don't!"

I didn't say anything. Whatever Jared and Mariah were up to didn't interest me. I was too worried about Logan. She was slumped over the picnic table, scooping up her oatmeal and letting it slide back into her bowl. She had dark circles under her eyes as though she hadn't slept, and her skin had a pale, yellowish-gray tinge.

"So how do we plan on finding the cure at World Corp International?" asked Greyson. "Are we just going to storm in and demand they cure Logan?"

"No," said Amory. "We need to know what we're going into."

Instantly, I felt myself fall into planning mode. I'd spent so much time reacting and making impulsive decisions that going back to my nature of meticulous planning felt like greeting an old friend.

"We need to get Mariah to tell us how we're getting inside: How many guards are there? What's the building's security like?"

"How do we know these CIDs won't give us away by pinging the wrong rover?" asked Greyson.

Amory's eyebrows knitted together. "We don't."

"They will," croaked Logan.

We all turned to stare at her.

"The CIDs Jared has . . . they'll only trick the long-range rovers . . . the ones designed for overpasses and major intersections. The close-range rovers — like the ones at Isador — those are designed for one data entry at a time. They don't 'miss' a CID like the ones on the highway."

"So what do we do?"

Logan grinned. "We have to trick a human into letting us in."

But Amory was already shaking his head. "No. No way. It's too dangerous."

"Not if we go in the main entrance," said Mariah from behind me.

I jumped. "What do you mean?"

"The Infinity Building isn't some high-security military facility. It's open to the public for tours and school field trips."

"So is the White House," said Amory through gritted teeth.

"We go in the front entrance and con our way up to the restricted access floors. The visitors' entrance isn't guarded by officers. There's a receptionist."

Amory and I exchanged a look. Something was off. It didn't seem as though World Corp International would be so careless with its most carefully guarded secret.

"Is this the place where they cured you?" I asked.

"There's a private lab on one of the restricted floors. Any studies there are strictly off the books — nothing like a PMC test facility. They can't risk something like this getting out, can they?"

With no choice other than to trust Mariah's word, we packed up the van and followed Jared's directions to an old pickup truck they had found parked behind the ranger's station.

As he and Amory started siphoning out the gas, I felt the nerves beginning to thrum in my chest. My anxiety over what we were about to attempt was mixed with the sweet possibility of relief. After today, it would be over — one way or another.

Chapter Twenty-Three

Once we had enough gas, we piled back into the van and drove toward the border. We followed signs for the nearest precinct in the hope of procuring a PMC vehicle. Hiding the van off the road about a mile away, Jared changed into his officer's uniform and set off for the station on foot.

This first part of the plan was key. If he could convince the station he had experienced car trouble in pursuit of a suspected illegal, they might give him a cruiser. If they didn't believe him, or if they demanded to scan Jared's CID, we didn't know what we would do.

With the rebels causing so much trouble with their bootlegged CIDs, some checkpoint officers had begun demanding to see the site of the incision. Anyone with a scar from home removal or no CID scar to begin with was immediately taken into custody.

At first, I wasn't sure why Jared willingly volunteered for such a dangerous task, but then I realized it either had to be him or Mariah. After our stunt at Isador, it was likely that Amory, Greyson, and I all had our pictures in the PMC database of most wanted illegals. We were too easily recognized.

As we waited, I ran through the plan Amory and I had discussed. Jared, Greyson, Mariah, and I would be the ones infiltrating the building. Jared and Mariah would pose as PMC officers; Greyson and I would be two apprehended

Enemy Inside

illegals. We would pretend to use the wrong entrance — the visitors' door, which wasn't guarded. If Mariah and Jared could convince them that we were wanted for questioning, it was possible we would be allowed up to the restricted floors. According to Mariah, the lab where the cure was stored was on the top floor of the building. Once we had the cure, we would pull the fire alarm and escape in the confusion. Amory would be driving the getaway car.

I didn't like bringing Greyson into danger, but Amory insisted that two of us would be better. If we ran into trouble with the PMC, it would be four against one. If Mariah and Jared betrayed us, it would at least be a fair fight. Amory had wanted to accompany me himself, but after his time in Isador, I didn't think it was a good idea. He probably had a "kill on sight" status in the system.

Suddenly I heard the screech of a siren up ahead. We all froze, unsure if we should run. It couldn't be Jared. That was just too easy.

A huge white SUV rolled into view. Sure enough, I saw the glint of his blond hair reflect through the windshield. He was smirking so deviously I was sure he would give us away.

Greyson laughed. "He got the paddy wagon."

Just as we planned, we all jumped out of the van and grabbed as much as we could carry, sticking to the essentials. I heaved a case of bottled water into the trunk of the cruiser and jumped in the middle row of seats. Logan, moving more slowly than usual, focused on loading all our rifles and ammunition carefully into the trunk.

There was a cage partition separating the front row from the back, and I couldn't help shiver as I crawled in behind bars. Jared and Mariah got in the front, Mariah already looking smug in her white uniform. It was a little dirty and wrinkled from several days without washing, but she was still in her element.

Enemy Inside

Logan curled up in the very back row to hide the fact that she was clearly in the first stage of the virus. The siren screeched, and we rolled back onto the highway. Jared had one hand draped lazily over the steering wheel, and Mariah didn't even bother to conceal her smirk.

"Try anything funny, and I'll blow your brains out," muttered Logan, although her threat didn't carry much weight when she was curled up in the fetal position on the seat.

"Don't worry," said Amory. "They won't." There was a hard edge to his reassuring tone, and when he moved his arm, I caught a glimpse of the handgun he had pointed at Jared from under his coat.

I wasn't the only one who had noticed it. Jared was sitting stiffly upright in his seat, now gripping the steering wheel with white knuckles at ten and two.

"So, did you have any trouble getting the cruiser?" I asked, trying to break the tension.

"Uh . . . no. There was only one guy manning the whole station. Older guy, second string by the looks of it. Told him I was in pursuit of a group of illegals and my partner was waiting with my cruiser. That way our story will match up if he radios ahead to the border."

The longer we drove, the more otherworldly it seemed that we were about to attempt what was supposed to be impossible: crossing the border as illegals.

At first, the signs along the road seemed innocuous enough — basic messages urging drivers to be ready for identification and informing them that their data was checked for their safety but kept confidential. The closer we came to the border crossing, the more threatening the signage became.

Transporting undocumented illegals is a CRIME. Violators will be punished.

No CID, No Entry. No Exceptions.

C1~~XX~~ — Not in my city!

"C1~~XX~~?" I asked.

"That's what they're calling the virus now," said Mariah.

"Do you really think illegals get this far and think they can get across?" asked Amory.

"I mean . . . that's what we're doing."

"Hey! Shut up and put these on," said Jared. He tossed back a bundle of zip ties, and I caught them. I took two and passed the bundle to Amory, my breath catching in my chest as I fastened them in loose loops. They reminded me too much of my first encounter with carriers when I'd been tied to a tree, convinced I was going to die. If I looked closely, I could still make out the scars from where their bonds had cut into my wrists.

Amory looped his very generously — loose enough that he could still keep his gun trained on Jared from under his coat.

Up ahead, I could just make out the checkpoint. It looked like an ordinary tollbooth, except the barricade had dozens of rovers mounted under the overpass — all of them trained in our direction. My palms felt sweaty, so I focused on taking deep breaths. I told myself a little anxiety would not raise a red flag for the officers — after all, I was supposed to be a fugitive — but I couldn't help worrying that my shallow breathing would give us away.

We moved forward at a crawl in the long line of vehicles — all of them PMC cargo trucks. Officers in white were inspecting the cargo, questioning the drivers, and consulting the CID data flashing across their smartlenses.

"Do you think it's suspicious that we have the guns and

supplies in the trunk?" I whispered, not turning my head in case we were being watched through the security cameras.

"Too late now," breathed Jared. "Lucky all those guns were stolen from the PMC."

My heart pounded against my ribcage. I couldn't do this. If we failed, it would be my plan that had gotten us in this mess.

But it was too late.

We continued to inch forward in the line until there was only one truck in front of us. Logan slumped against the window so that her golden hair fanned in front of her face. If the officers noticed she was infected, we were done. They would never let us pass.

One of the officers approached our vehicle. It was a smug-looking man with greasy black hair and just the right amount of stubble that made me think he grew his facial hair that way on purpose. He had a smartlens perched on the bridge of his nose, the glare obscuring half his expression.

"Morning, officers," he drawled, his eyes hovering too long on Mariah. He sneered.

"Morning," said Jared automatically. His expression was perfect: slightly tired, bored, but trying to be friendly. No wonder he'd worked undercover as an officer.

"What have we got here? Undocumented illegals?"

Jared sighed. "Defectors."

The man nodded. "That's good. You can't bring any undocumented people in for any reason. Not even prisoners."

I watched Jared in the side mirror. He swallowed. "Yep. They're all defectors. Caught 'em on the run headed west."

The greasy man chuckled. "That's a pretty common story.

They're not, uh, rebels, are they?"

"Not from what I could tell. Picked up just the four of them. Half-starved, too, by the looks of it."

"Why are you bringing them in?"

"World Corp is collecting test subjects that match their ages."

The man stopped suddenly, shining his flashlight into the back seat. My heart stopped as it settled on Logan.

She turned her face ever so slightly toward him, and I caught the glint of yellow in her eyes as the flashlight beam illuminated her face.

"Hang on a sec," said the man.

My heart was pounding so loudly, I was sure the officer could hear it.

He'd seen Logan's eyes. He knew.

He appraised her for a long moment. "You sure caught yourself a hot little piece."

I breathed out, releasing the edge of the seat I'd been white-knuckling.

The man smacked his lips. "I sure hope you got to have a little fun first." He sneered through the window at Logan and me. "This one ain't bad, either."

I looked away, feeling my face burn with anger. Logan put her head down, trying to hide her flared nostrils and murderous eyes.

"Sure did," Jared said with a hard laugh, not missing a beat.

I glanced at Amory sitting next to me. His hands were curled into fists, and the zip ties were making deep divots in his skin as he focused on restraining himself.

"All right. Open up the trunk. Gotta check for contraband."

I exhaled the breath I'd been holding as the officer moved around to open the trunk of the cruiser. I heard his boots scuffing on the asphalt, and then I felt a rush of cold air as he opened the tailgate.

For a long minute, there was nothing but the nearly inaudible sound of his smartlens computing. Then I heard his boots again as he approached the front of the vehicle.

"Any reason you have six unregistered weapons back here?"

He knew. I couldn't breathe. We were finished.

Jared made a guilty clicking sound with his mouth. "Yeah, I'm sorry about that. I know it's against regulation, but our precinct was overrun about a week ago. We grabbed what we could and ran for it."

The greasy man's eyes glazed over, and I knew he was checking something on his smartlens. "Says here you two are from different precincts." He gestured between Jared and Mariah.

"Right. When I said 'we,' I meant my partner. He was killed raiding a rebel camp. I picked up this lady at the debriefing. She'd lost somebody, too, so we figured we'd team up and look for illegals."

The man glanced away from the stream of information flashing across his lens and regarded Jared. Then, as if seeing nothing wrong with this explanation, he nodded. "Well, I'll need to confiscate two of those weapons. No more than two rifles per officer at any time. That's regulation. But I'm not going to write you up for it . . . extraordinary circumstances and all."

"I understand."

Enemy Inside

Logan was fuming silently behind me, and I begged her silently not to speak. We couldn't have one of her outbursts blow our cover. Losing two guns was unfortunate, but at least we still had the hidden handgun.

"Man, you sure got a lot of food back here," the man mumbled from the back of the truck.

"Well, we've been on the road for a week. Not a lot of places to stop."

"Is it that bad?" The officer reappeared. "*Phew* am I glad I was stationed at the border. Those poor sons of bitches in Sector X were overrun. *Overrun*. Were you there for that?"

"Nope. We were part of the cleanup crew, though. Absolute mess."

The officer nodded. "Well, I'll let you go on through. But you take them straight to World Corp, you hear?"

Jared grinned. "Will do."

The man waved us through, and Jared accelerated a little faster than he should have, blowing past the other officers watching idly from the checkpoint. The rovers swiveled like crazy trying to latch on to our CIDs, but we were through.

Amory aimed a hard kick at the back of his seat, and Logan leaned over behind her to reach for a gun.

"Hey!" Jared yelled. "Just playing along."

"He did what he had to do," I said, watching Amory. "And he was good."

"Thank you! Jesus Christ. You know what I'm risking for you people?"

"I bet you were right at home with these assholes," Amory growled.

Jared shot him an angry look in the rearview mirror. "They make me just as sick as you. Don't act like you wouldn't have done the same exact thing to get us through."

Amory slumped back, still fuming.

"Besides, it was a close call with those guns. Why didn't any of us think to hide them? Now we're down two SCARS."

"There were quite a few close calls," muttered Mariah. "I can't believe he bought that story about your partner."

"I can't believe he didn't see her eyes," I said.

"Yeah, me neither."

"No more screwups," snapped Mariah.

"Did that seem strange to anyone else?" asked Greyson. "It seemed a little too easy to me."

Jared shrugged, and we continued toward the city. We passed under more rovers, which made me nervous. Even though we had cleared the checkpoint at the border, I worried our vehicle was being monitored closely since the officers knew it was full of illegals.

Mariah directed Jared to take the first exit off the highway, and I began to see buildings on the skyline. The first thing I noticed upon entering the city was how many rovers there were. Not only were they mounted at nearly every intersection, but they were also above the entrances to most buildings. Officers in crisp white uniforms paced the sidewalks, and we watched a couple dressed in white scrubs shuffle by quickly. They didn't speak to one another but walked purposefully with their heads down.

Then we saw a white stone building rising up in the distance. It took up the entire city block, and a crowd of people dressed in white coveralls was spilling out. There was an inlet on the side of the building projecting motivational messages down its facade: *Forward for progress . . . Order and compliance are the foundation for our future . . . World Corp*

International: perfect science for an ideal world.

"Where are they all going?" I asked.

"To the factories," said Mariah. "When they migrated north and came to the refugee commune, they could either work for the factories, the farms, or the PMC. The people with some education go to the labs."

"And they all live here?"

"Not here, necessarily, but there are lots of communes like this one. Some are nicer than others."

"Who pays for all this?"

"They do. Their wages just cover room and board."

As we passed the commune, I watched the tired-looking men and women in their coveralls trudging toward the factory.

"Why would anyone agree to live here?" I asked.

"It's safer — patriotic. Canada is fighting back."

"And everyone up here is fine with the PMC?" asked Greyson.

"They don't have to be. Everything is owned by World Corp International."

Soon the meticulously trimmed bushes and trees flanking the sidewalks around the commune disappeared, and dingy-looking buildings covered in graffiti rose up out of the concrete. Fast food containers spilling from overturned trashcans blew across the street like tumbleweed.

The people here weren't dressed in crisp white coveralls. One woman lingered on the corner dressed in a baggy gray sweater with a damp cigarette sagging between her lips. She had a small dirty boy wrapped around her ankles and carried a crumpled plastic shopping bag. She stared at us as we passed, and I felt a shiver.

Enemy Inside

It was too quiet on the street. Up ahead, a silvery beacon appeared over the filth — a building towering over all the rest, reflecting the sunlight back into our eyes.

"Welcome to the headquarters of World Corp International," said Mariah.

We continued to stare at the behemoth building. It was impossible not to.

More imposing than its sheer size was the conspicuous lack of windows and the foreboding shadow it cast over the buildings in its wake. The Infinity Building appeared to be one continuous sheet of titanium that sloped on the side, hollow in the center to form a cylindrical space within the outer shell.

"It's a stretched Möbius strip," said Mariah. "You can only really tell from the aerial view, though."

We all stared.

"Pull into that parking garage across the street," she instructed.

Jared turned down a side street running perpendicular to the building and entered the dark underground garage. Sparse beams of light flickered through the slits in the concrete as we drove down the steep slope. I imagined we were driving under the street that ran in front of the building. We passed the main parking area until we reached the bottom level. It was empty save for half a dozen World Corp vans and two PMC cruisers identical to ours.

Jared parked between the other two cruisers and got out. Logan glared at him through the car window as she struggled to tear off the plastic zip ties.

"You and Amory are staying here," I said.

Logan's face twisted in indignation. "No way."

"You aren't well enough to fight if something goes

wrong. Besides, they'll know in a second that you're infected."

"Exactly," said Mariah. "She has to go. She's our 'test subject.'"

Logan arched a brow in satisfaction. Even with the virus coursing through her veins, she couldn't resist the action.

"No," I said. "It's too dangerous."

"We don't have a choice."

"They could kill her on sight."

"If we're caught getting the cure, she's as good as dead anyway. She should take it immediately in case we don't make it out. Better to be a human prisoner than a free dying carrier."

My stomach clenched, every fiber of my being screaming in protest. It didn't make sense for Mariah to suddenly pretend to care what became of Logan, but her motives didn't matter. She was right. Logan had to come.

Before I could answer, Amory grabbed my elbow and pulled me out to the other side of the cruiser, out of earshot of Mariah and Jared.

"You two aren't going in alone with them. They could turn you over to World Corp. You and Logan . . . it wouldn't be a fair fight right now."

"I know that. But Mariah's right. Logan's our way in, and if we're captured on the way out . . . at least she will have taken the cure."

"If you're captured on the way out, you'll probably be killed! This isn't an option. I'm coming with you."

I shook my head. "You know you can't. It's too dangerous. If they recognize you as the one who escaped —"

"Then we'll send Greyson in."

"No. You both should stay here. If anything goes wrong, there's two of you."

Amory sighed, furrowing his brow. "I don't like this."

"Neither do I. But we don't have another choice."

"If they take you . . ."

"That's not going to happen."

Amory's mouth was a hard line, and his eyes were crinkled in fear. "If you aren't out in an hour, I'm coming in."

I locked eyes with him, shaking my head once. "You have to be smart about this. Don't do anything you wouldn't normally do just because it's me and Logan in there."

"But it *is* you and Logan."

"Still. Don't forget you and Greyson have a bigger part to play in all this." I made a serious face. "If anything happens to him, I'm holding you personally responsible."

That did it. He sighed in frustration and looked at me as though trying to memorize my face.

I met his gaze, but I didn't know what to say. I didn't want to pour out my heart with Jared and Mariah five feet away, so instead, I wrapped my arms around his waist and buried my face in his shirt. He squeezed me with uncharacteristic force and planted a kiss on top of my head.

"Please be careful," he whispered into my hair.

My chest filled with warmth at the tenderness in his voice, and I gripped him tighter.

"Are you ready to go or what?" Mariah asked. Her voice was dripping with boredom and irritation.

Reluctantly, I pulled out of Amory's arms and turned to

face her. "Let's go."

Logan appeared at my shoulder. I could tell she was trying to look like her old self — confident, lethal, ready for a fight — but her face was too pale, pinched in fatigue, and her shoulders slumped a little.

My skin crawled as I folded my hands behind my back and allowed Jared to loosely fasten another set of zip ties on me. I didn't like the feeling of the plastic cutting into my skin, but I knew I could wriggle out of them if I needed to. Mariah had Logan's upper arm in her bony grip, and her sneer told me she was enjoying it. Jared had his big hand resting loosely on my shoulder, as though he was afraid to touch me with Amory watching so closely.

Before Mariah and Jared could push us forward, Greyson elbowed in and wrapped an arm around my neck. I breathed in deeply to soak up the comforting, familiar smell of him. He was much taller than I remembered. Greyson pretended to hoist me off my feet in an intense hug — just enough to pull me out of Jared's grip.

"You don't have to do this," he breathed into my neck.

"Yeah, I do."

"I'll go with you."

"No. Stay with Amory. If anything goes wrong —"

"I know. Don't trust Mariah for a second, though. She's planning something — I can just feel it."

He released me quickly and moved to Logan, folding her carefully and with mild awkwardness into his arms.

"Be safe, okay?"

She nodded, flashing him a cocky grin that made her look stronger.

"Jesus," muttered Mariah, rolling her eyes and shoving

Logan forward.

Jared cleared his throat and pushed me to follow Mariah and Logan toward the elevator.

Mariah stabbed the "up" button, and the rover over the sliding door swiveled in to focus on us. The light turned red, and a security camera focused in on me. Jared made eye contact with the person on the other side of the camera, as if to say all was well and they had us under control — two criminals ripe for World Corp's experiments.

Like any parking garage elevator, this one had sticky black tracks of dirt on the floor, grimy walls, and old gum wrappers collecting in the metal crevices. It gave no indication that we were headed up into the bowels of World Corp International headquarters until a robotic female voice sounded.

Welcome to the Infinity Building, headquarters of World Corp International. To ensure the safety of all personnel, please be prepared to surrender any weapons upon arrival.

A tinny bell sounded as the circle over the door was illuminated, signaling we had arrived at the ground level of the building. The doors swung open, revealing a large foyer. The floor and walls were pure white marble. We shuffled through the glass doors into an enormous round atrium fitted inside the outer shell of the building. Its gleaming brushed titanium walls gave off a cold, industrial feel, and rovers hidden over the threshold swiveled toward us and blinked red.

In the center of the floor stood a white circular desk. A woman wearing a white pants suit and a smartlens sat in the center on a swivel stool. Her gray hair was pulled back into a neat bun, stretching the loose, wrinkled skin around her eyes back into her hairline. The desk in front of her was empty except for a tablet computer, on which she was swiping frantically as her eye flickered over the stream of information flashing across her lens.

"You have the wrong entrance," she said in clipped, bored syllables.

"Actually, we're here to deliver two test subjects," said Jared. "Rather . . . time-sensitive research. Sure you understand . . ."

"Security!" she barked, not making eye contact with us. "I'm sorry, but this is the *visitors'* entrance. You simply can't march in here with prisoners."

A red banner flashed across her lens, and she scoffed in irritation. She tapped the edge of the glass, and the projection faded.

"Fine. How can I help you?" she asked Jared, finally making eye contact and forcing a harsh smile.

"As I said, we have two test subjects. Top floor."

The woman wrinkled her nose. "Let me see." She swiped her finger over the tablet in front of her, clicking her nails impatiently on the desk. "No, I'm sorry," she said, distraction creeping in the edge of her voice. "There's been some sort of mix-up. We're not expecting any test subjects until next week."

Mariah gripped the side of the desk with her bony hand and whispered through clenched teeth. "Perhaps you've misunderstood. This was a personal request from Aryus."

I glanced at her in surprise, and the woman looked up. She arched a brow and tried to settle her sneer into a polite expression. "That's not what I have here."

"I'm sure you can appreciate the delicacy of the situation," hissed Mariah, in a voice that was anything but delicate. "It's absolutely need to know. Maybe Aryus's assistant didn't see the need to clear it with you."

The woman smiled again, but this time she did not bother

Enemy Inside

to hide her contempt. "I think *you* must be mistaken. Everything here goes through me. There isn't a single arrival to which I'm not privy."

"Call up to Aryus's girl *now*," snapped Mariah.

The woman's cold eyes focused in on her for the first time.

"Tell her Mariah is back. I wish we could give more details, but as I said . . . it's classified. As in, *above your pay grade*."

The woman didn't take her eyes off Mariah but tapped the edge of her lens. Her eyes flitted back and forth once, and I could see the reverse video image of another woman dressed the same way.

"Kale, I have two officers down here with a pair of illegal test subjects. They claim Aryus ordered them, and I said they were mistaken. Do you know if Aryus is expecting a woman named Mariah?"

I could not hear what Kale said on the other end, but she disappeared from view for a moment and returned looking harried. "Send them up."

"I don't understand —"

"Send them up, Marge."

Marge swallowed with displeasure and tapped her lens, refocusing on us. "You're free to go up."

My breath caught in my chest as Mariah shoved Logan forward across the atrium to a set of three elevators with white doors. Jared pulled me along in his strong grip, and the doors closed automatically behind us. I looked for the panel of buttons, but the elevator walls were completely smooth. There were no buttons at all, but a rover fitted into the ceiling above us settled on Jared, giving me a very carsick ache in my throat.

"Where are we *going*?" I whispered, the urgency creeping in.

Nobody spoke.

"Where are we going?" I repeated more desperately.

"She controls the elevators," said Mariah.

Jared jerked his head around. "What?"

"The woman at the desk. She controls where all the elevators go. She's sending us up to Aryus Edric."

Chapter Twenty-Four

The elevator shot up through the titanium shell, and I felt sick. The acceleration was just fast enough to make you feel as though you were losing your stomach. We stood in silence for a moment as the realization set in.

Mariah had gone rogue. We were not prepared to face Aryus or whatever else might be waiting for us.

"Mariah!" Jared snapped finally, his eyes darting to the rover uncomfortably. "Are you insane? What's going to happen when we get up there and he realizes we're a bunch of defectors?"

"There's nothing to do about it now." Mariah was staring blankly ahead, which filled me with a sense of dread.

"We have to get off. We have to get off before it gets to his floor."

"Why?" she asked in a lazy voice. "This is what you wanted. All of them . . . out of our hair. Gone."

"What?" he spluttered.

"It's what you wanted."

He shook his head, looking disgusted. "Not like this."

"What about the cure?" Logan's voice was low and deadly, and the dark purplish shadows under her eyes made her look demonic.

Enemy Inside

Mariah gave a demure smile. It clashed wildly with her cold eyes and stringy, greasy hair. "I'm sure you'll get your cure. Aryus loves healing the infected. It's like he wields the hand of God himself."

My stomach clenched in anger and fear, the bile burning in my throat.

The elevator stopped suddenly, and we lurched forward. Bound by the zip ties, I couldn't throw out a hand to stop myself from flying against the wall, and my shoulder banged into it.

I heard the harsh, metallic *ping*, and the doors slid open to reveal a steeply curved hallway. The walls were titanium as well, and several panels were inlaid with rippling sheets of industrial steel shaped into abstract designs. Water cascaded over the top panels and trickled into the next. Down and around the wall they wound like stacked building blocks, filling the narrow space with the tranquil sound of a trickling spring.

We followed the hallway until it ended in front of a white door with no handle. Behind us, a panel in the wall opened, a stainless steel tray sliding out. A robotic voice sounded.

Please deposit your weapons.

Mariah laid her gun down without hesitation, but Jared clung to his. He locked eyes with his sister, doubt and betrayal etched all over his face.

"This is crazy," he said. "We won't make it out of there alive."

"You don't have a choice," said Mariah. "You see that?" She pointed up. Above the door was an apparatus that looked like a rover, but it had an extra lens. "They're watching you right now."

He swallowed and laid his gun on the cold metal tray, looking at his sister with anger and distrust. "You better have a plan."

No sooner had the tray with their guns disappeared back into the wall than the white door swung open of its own accord. Mariah pushed me roughly inside, and I stopped just past the door. We were standing in a wide-open room much like the atrium on the first floor that took up the entire inner shell. The only difference was the brightness of the place. The entire ceiling was made of glass — a building-sized skylight. Right now, it shimmered with artificial frost that seemed to dim the amount of light shining into the open space. The brushed metal walls were paneled in white.

I glanced around, half expecting someone to shoot me on sight. We had been duped by Mariah; that much was clear. But Mariah's recklessness was her weakness. If we were lucky, maybe there was some way Logan and I could escape.

Our footsteps echoed on the marble floor as we stepped inside, the back of my neck prickling uncomfortably. Modern-looking chaise lounges in the shape of half-moons were spaced evenly around the room on a fleecy white rug. In the middle was an artificial-looking green space with a live bonsai tree planted in the very center of the sphere. I followed the sound of trickling water around the room until I reached a marble fountain that rose up through the floor, forming a large circle. Water rushed up the wrong direction into the wall.

"Reverse osmosis," called a voice.

I jumped, looking around for its source.

"Isn't it fascinating?"

I turned my head. A diminutive man was standing across the room near a door I hadn't noticed. His short hair and goatee were so gray they were nearly white, and he was wearing white cropped pants and a velour turtleneck. He was startlingly tan.

"Ah! Mariah," he said, stretching out his arms and padding barefoot across the rug. "So good to see you again."

As he reached us, I could see that his tanned, aged skin was much too taut and smooth, as though it had been buffed.

"I'm so sorry. I'm being rude." He beamed, revealing immensely white teeth. "Mariah is my greatest work of art."

"You cured her," I said.

"Well, yes!" he exclaimed, positively delighted.

"I've brought you two new subjects," said Mariah. "One recently infected, and one who is perfectly healthy despite prolonged exposure to different strains of the virus. Perhaps you can see —"

"Can you cure her?" I asked, throwing caution to the wind and stepping up beside Mariah.

Aryus laughed musically, as if I had told a wonderful joke. "If only it were that simple. If I cured everyone, that would rather defeat the purpose, wouldn't it?"

I stared.

"Humanity needed a reset, Haven."

"How did you —"

He waved his hand. "I know a lot of things. For instance, I know you defected immediately after your friend Greyson was arrested. Now you represent a flaw in the system. You should have become infected or been caught. Darwinism may have favored the selfish survivalist, but we live in the modern age. We are . . . *refining* the perfection of nature. We are culling the human race."

"I know World Corp released the virus intentionally."

"Very good," he said with a smile. "So clever. Well, we didn't have a choice, I'm afraid. Think of all the major outbreaks of the last millennium: the bubonic plague, Spanish influenza, HIV . . . We haven't had a deadly outbreak on this scale in more than fifty years! Humans have gotten too smart. We have . . . *outfoxed* mother nature. That's why we had to be just a little bit smarter."

"The virus has killed millions of people!"

"Yes, exactly! Haven't you been paying attention? This planet cannot support its current load — not the way we farm or transport ourselves. We were destroying it anyway. We wouldn't have lasted another hundred years, the way we were going."

I stared at him, aghast.

"Do you know *why* we ordered the mandatory migration? Do you know *how* we selected those we would save on our own little ark?"

I didn't answer.

"People who respect the law. People who can function in a progressive society."

"Progressive?" spat Logan. "You've wiped out a quarter of the population."

"Only in the United States. It was . . . a risky choice for a test group; I'll give you that. Nowhere are people more defiant than in America."

Logan lurched forward, but Mariah held her back. "You won't get away with this."

"Look around you. We already have. The American people are resilient. They have rebuilt here — expanded the empire. Your children's children will be reading about the acquisition of the New Northern Territory in their history books. It's our Louisiana Purchase."

"You took it by force."

He smiled. "It's the American way. We will find a way to live peacefully with the displaced Canadians eventually. It's all part of the colonization process."

"What about the rest of the country?" I asked. "What will you do once all the remaining illegals are infected?"

"We will humanely euthanize the ones that remain, and then we will rebuild. We have accomplished astounding feats in genetically engineered agriculture. We have *oranges* that can grow all year round in Minnesota now. We truly can feed the world."

"And what about the people here now?"

"They are already changing. The way they work, the way they live, the way they consume . . . We aim to cultivate a society where every person serves a purpose, and every person is working for the greater good of the populace."

"That's already been tried."

"Ahh, yes. But the key here is that they had a *choice*."

"They didn't have a *choice!*" shrieked Logan.

"Sure they did. You had a choice. You chose wrong. But at least now we know. Now we know you can't be allowed back into the fold. The defectors are the ones who cause trouble, because the defectors have been to the other side and declared the grass is *not* greener. The 'free' are not freer; the first worlders are not more prosperous. The defectors are the people who bring societies down."

"So what now, then?" I asked. "Why did you tell us all that? Are you just going to have us killed?"

Aryus smiled in a tight line, all pleasantness gone. "Oh, no. I am a merciful man not in the habit of taunting my prey. Don't worry. You will serve a greater purpose."

He walked over to the wall and pressed against one of the panels. A drawer opened automatically, and he withdrew a large, flat case. He opened it and pulled out a syringe filled with clear liquid. As he walked toward Logan, I had a flash of panic. It had to be poison or a sedative.

"Give me your arm."

Logan jerked away, but Mariah still held her in a clawlike grip. "What is that?"

"It's what you came here for."

"Liar," hissed Logan from behind her disheveled curtain of hair.

"I assure you. It will work," chuckled Aryus. The sound made my skin crawl.

"Has it been tested?" I asked.

"She would be the first. The formula I used on Mariah was much more aggressive. It had to be. But it came with a number of . . . *adverse* side effects. This was a new form of the virus." He turned to me. "Funny how nature works, isn't it?"

Logan glared at him, unmoving. But Aryus would not be deterred. Obediently, Mariah cut away Logan's zip ties, and, with surprising strength for a man of his size, Aryus grabbed Logan by the arm and twisted it around to eye level.

I wanted to scream — to stop him from injecting Logan — but couldn't bring myself to speak. That formula could be deadly, but one way or another, we were not meant to walk out of here alive. And without the cure, Logan would certainly die.

I watched the liquid disappear into her veins and did not immediately notice Aryus's eyes on me.

"You may be of use to me, as well."

I snapped my head to him, my hands curling into fists automatically.

Enemy Inside

"You are somewhat unusual. You have had prolonged exposure to the virus but have never become infected, even after being bitten." He gestured to the scarred bite on my neck.

"I've never had blood-to-blood contact with a carrier. That's how it spreads, right?"

Aryus's eyes danced. "You *are* clever."

"Sometimes people get bitten, but they don't become infected," I continued, wanting to keep talking as long as I could. I just needed more time to form a plan. "It's the carriers that are further along . . . the ones with the sores on their mouths. Those are the infectious bites."

"Very good."

"But how did you introduce the virus in the first place? How did you get it into people's bloodstreams?"

Aryus was watching me with a look of morbid fascination. "You haven't worked that out yet?"

I thought of Mariah and my mother — the only two people I knew who had become infected without being bitten. It couldn't have been from a blood bank. My mom didn't donate blood and had never received a transfusion. The last time she had been to the doctor was —

"The flu shots!" I said. "That's how you did it. That's why there were so many older people who became infected the first time."

"Yes, yes. Very good!" Aryus clapped his hands together once. "But you're forgetting something. There were two outbreaks."

I considered Mariah — remembered her wheezing in the old storage cabin. "Did you infect the supply of allergy shots, too?"

"You're very smart, Haven."

"Allergy shots?" snapped Mariah, stepping in front of me and looking at Aryus in disbelief. "But I was vaccinated. If it was a controlled outbreak —"

"We made a slight error in judgment on the second release. We had run out of the original strain, so we pulled the virus from a few living carriers. By then the virus had mutated, and we were unknowingly advancing an outbreak we couldn't control."

Aryus smiled. "You were my first positive case." His voice was quivering with excitement. "You had survived with the virus for such a long time . . . you were the first to fight it." He turned to me, as if letting me in on a very funny joke. "It's fascinating."

"That's despicable," I breathed. "Those people were all innocent. You'll spend the rest of your life in prison for this."

"What prison?" he laughed. "One of *my* prisons? The prisons with the PMC Xs on them? The prisons bought and paid for by World Corp International?"

"You'll never get away with this . . . this . . . scale of killing."

"My dear, people have been getting away with it for millennia."

"No," said Mariah in a low and deadly voice. "I don't believe it was an accident. You *introduced* that strain knowing it could beat your vaccine!"

I felt a swell of satisfaction. Mariah had betrayed us, and she had thrown in her luck with the wrong person.

Aryus gave a sad smile. "Too many vaccinated people were defecting. They were out of control."

"So how do you want to use me?" I interrupted. I was sick of listening to the psychotic ramblings of a mad scientist.

"I want to see if you have built up any immunity with your prolonged exposure to the virus."

"You're going to infect me."

"Then I will cure you. You have my word."

"And then what?"

"And then . . . we will find a way for you to be of use."

A chill shot down the back of my neck. I was going to be one of his experiments. He was going to lock me up like Amory, probably for the rest of my life. "Please. Please just kill me . . . when you're done with the test."

Aryus looked at me for a long moment, and his tight face drooped ever so slightly. "What a waste that would be."

I looked at Logan, trying to gauge how the cure was taking hold. She looked nauseated, but whether that was the virus or a side effect of the cure, I could not tell.

"How long will it be until she is recovered?" I asked. "Will you let her go then?"

"Patience, my dear. We need to run some more tests. For now, why don't you make yourselves comfortable while Mariah and I chat?"

Aryus touched a small white button on the wall and spoke into an intercom I could not see. "Security."

"W-what about Jared?" stammered Mariah. "He's my brother."

But Jared was staring at her with a mixture of shock and loathing.

"My boy!" said Aryus. "Can I recruit you for my military company?"

"Go to hell," breathed Jared, his face contorted with rage.

Mariah looked stricken.

The door to Aryus's office slid open, and three PMC officers stood crowded in the narrow hallway.

"What are you going to do with him?" Mariah asked, her voice shaking.

The guards filed in, pushing her aside. She looked the way she had when the rebels had marched her into the snow the night of the riots.

"Sir? The spare?" asked an older guard with a shaved head.

But Aryus was already pacing around his bonsai tree in the center of the room, holding a tiny pair of sheers to one of the branches. "Kill him."

I felt strong arms grip me under my shoulders and yank me out of the room. I twisted to look at my guard, but he would not make eye contact. He was much taller with sallow skin and a thick neck like a football player.

"Logan!"

I tried to slow down so we would not be separated from Logan and her guard, but mine was too strong.

Then the man holding Logan turned his head, and I recognized him. He looked beefier, but his buzz cut was exactly the same — as was his stony, aggressive expression.

It was Roman.

The officers frog-marched us in single file down the rounded corridor to the elevator. We crowded in the tiny space, and I stood shoulder to shoulder with Roman. He still wasn't looking at me, but the vein in the side of his neck was pulsing quickly. If he had an ounce of sympathy left for us, we might be able to take our guards.

Logan was too busy struggling against Roman to notice

Enemy Inside

who he was. Her face was ashen and sweaty. Maybe I imagined it, but she looked worse than before. Glancing over my guard's broad shoulder, I tried to make eye contact with Jared. His eyes flitted to mine and then back to the front of the elevator. That was as good of a signal as I could hope for.

We still weren't quite evenly matched, considering Logan's weakened state, but with Roman and the element of surprise, we would have one chance.

My immediate fear was for Jared. He did not have much time left, and we were being taken to different places. Too soon, the elevator slowed to a stop, the circle above the door illuminating.

Lobby, said the robotic woman's voice.

The doors flew open, and we were standing once again in the enormous lobby with the round desk in the middle. The woman was still swiping away on her tablet, blissfully unaware of what was about to happen.

As we shuffled out of the elevator, I took tiny steps and focused on my breathing to fortify my nerves.

When I was ready, I didn't yell. I didn't think. I twisted abruptly in my restraints. My guard, taken by surprise, was holding me with a relaxed grip. I jutted out my right elbow and swung it into his gut with as much force as I could muster. He made a grab for me, but my movement had alerted Jared and Logan.

Jared knocked his head back against his guard's face, and I heard the sickening crunch of a nose breaking. He squirmed free and brought his boot up to connect with the man's groin. I tried to copy him, but my guard wasn't badly hurt. He gripped me around the neck and spun me around into a chokehold, and I saw Logan trying to escape Roman's grip.

Enemy Inside

Roman was much bigger, and he was more alert than the other two guards. He had known I would try something.

I threw all my weight downward, trying to wriggle out of my guard's stranglehold, but his arm was crushing my windpipe. It was no use.

In the second it took for my guard to get me back under his control, I saw Roman lock eyes with Logan. Her face was a mixture of shock and agony. He wasn't prepared for her appearance: pale and withered from the virus already, a shadow of her former self. I watched his hands release her, and she flew out of his grip and staggered toward the door.

Jared's guard fumbled for the gun at his side, his nose gushing blood all over his spotless white uniform. He aimed it at Logan, who was closest, but Roman's gun flew into his hand so quickly I hadn't been prepared for it.

He turned to his right and shot the guard.

The woman at the circular desk screamed, and Roman aimed a shot at her head. Her scream was cut off, echoing around the room before she dropped to the floor.

As my guard fumbled for his gun, I tried to twist out of his grip again, but he was too strong. He and Roman had their guns pointed at each other's heads as Roman backed quickly toward the door after Jared.

Logan turned, watching me struggle.

"Run!" I yelled, but she stopped to come back for me. "Go!" I screamed.

Roman took one look at me and grabbed Logan around the waist. She struggled, but Roman dragged her bodily toward the front door. My guard shifted his aim to Jared, who was passing through the first set of doors.

A shot rang out, but it was Roman's gun.

My guard yelled, and I felt a spatter of warm blood on my

Enemy Inside

face. Roman had hit his hand. The gun skittered across the marble floor as a stream of officers stormed in through a side door.

I wriggled free of the guard's grip and shot toward the front of the lobby, but a second later, I saw a blur of white in my peripheral vision and I was on the ground. My head smacked the marble floor, and I saw stars. Struggling to get to my feet, I could hear shouts echoing off the atrium walls.

"Haven!"

I looked up. Roman and Logan were gone, but Jared was running in my direction. Then another shot rang out, and he yelled, hitting the floor several yards away. Red was spreading from his abdomen over the front of his white uniform. I looked at him, and all I could see was Mariah's face. But it didn't quite look like her. There was sorrow and regret and compassion in his eyes.

I heard another gunshot. Then there was nothing.

Chapter Twenty-Five

Far off in the distance, I could discern a faint beeping sound. I was in line at the grocery store, and the cashier was scanning my items one by one.

Beep. Beep. Beep.

Why was I at the grocery store? I didn't feel well at all. I had no business grocery shopping. I was burning up, my head was pounding, and my mouth was so dry I couldn't even speak.

Was I sick? I didn't remember getting sick.

Peeling my eyelids apart, all I could see was the ugly square upholstered pattern on a white curtain in front of me. It was wrapped all around my bed, and the overhead fluorescent lights were much too bright. I turned my head and felt my range of motion obstructed by something on my face — tubes.

I lifted my hand to my face, but there was a tube coming out of it, as well. There was also a plastic clothespin stuck on my finger. At least it looked like a clothespin.

All over my body, I could feel weird pieces of tape and tubes holding me back. A strange yellow liquid had dried on my arm, and I stifled a gag. Fighting the bleariness, I concentrated on putting the pieces together. I was in a hospital bed, but I couldn't remember why.

The curtain rustled, and a fat woman in white scrubs

Enemy Inside

poked her head around. She was carrying a tablet and looking irritated.

"You're awake," she said, as though I had inconvenienced her by staying unconscious for so long. I noticed that her thinning eyebrows were disappearing into her straight, honey-colored bangs, and she looked tired around the mouth.

"What happened to me?"

The woman ignored me, her fingers gliding over the glowing tablet in her hand and punching the screen to record my vitals.

"Why am I here?" I asked.

She didn't look at me, but her puckered mouth tightened a little more, as if she was purposefully avoiding eye contact.

"Why am I here?" I yelled.

"Take some deep breaths, Haven."

The woman was absorbed in swiping her finger across the screen, checking boxes, punching in numbers, and dismissing notifications. It was infuriating to watch.

"Why won't you tell me what's wrong with me?"

"Nothing is wrong with you. You're just recuperating. As soon as you calm down —"

"I don't *want* to calm down. I want you to tell me why I'm here." My voice was shaky, and I longed to knock that stupid tablet right out of her hand.

"All right," she said in a stern voice. She turned around, set the tablet on the counter, and fiddled in the cabinet. She withdrew a syringe filled with clear liquid.

"What is that?" I snapped. "I don't want any more medicine. I feel weird as it is."

She ignored me and tested the syringe.

"No!" I yelled, louder than I'd intended to. I wanted to be firm, not make her think I needed to be sedated.

"Just try to relax, Haven," she said. I could tell that the voice she was using was an attempt at a kind, reassuring tone, but I could hear the irritation and impatience thrumming at the edges of her syllables.

"I can't relax. Please . . . please don't drug me. I just want to know what's going on. I don't remember —"

But it was too late. She'd already jammed the needle into my arm. Watching her tight, frowning face, I thought I saw a satisfied smirk ghost across her pinched lips.

"What happened to me?" I asked. Now I sounded pitiful and weak. "Please. Just tell me."

"Just lie back and take deep breaths. The doctor will explain everything shortly."

Incensed, I lay back against the cheap, flat pillow and tried not to think about the plastic tubes sticking out everywhere, tethering me to the bed. I tried not to think about the sedative coursing through my veins or my growing suspicions that I was still in the Infinity Building, locked away in the private lab Mariah had talked about.

Mariah. A flicker of recollection ignited in the back of my mind. *Mariah had betrayed us. Jared was dead. Logan and Roman had escaped. I was Aryus's prisoner now.*

Before the drug could work its way through my system, I lifted the hand that was free of needles and felt the sticky piece of tape that was pulling on the hairs near the nape of my neck. Some of the gauze had peeled back during my fit, and I could feel the raised bump of a tender square scar at the base of my skull.

Then everything went dark.

Enjoy this book? *The Last Uprising,* book three in the Defectors Trilogy, is now available on Amazon.

You can also connect with the author at www.tarahbenner.com.

Printed in Great Britain
by Amazon